D0234414

THE MAP

Also by T.S. Learner

Sphinx

THE MAP

T.S. LEARNER

sphere

SPHERE

First published in Great Britain as a paperback original in 2012 by Sphere
Reprinted 2012

Copyright © Tobsha Learner 2012

The moral right of the author has been asserted.

*All characters and events in this publication, other than those
clearly in the public domain, are fictitious and any resemblance
to real persons, living or dead, is purely coincidental.*

All rights reserved.
No part of this publication may be reproduced, stored in a
retrieval system, or transmitted, in any form or by any means, without
the prior permission in writing of the publisher, nor be otherwise circulated
in any form of binding or cover other than that in which it is published
and without a similar condition including this condition being
imposed on the subsequent purchaser.

A CIP catalogue record for this book
is available from the British Library.

ISBN 978-0-7515-4550-0

Typeset in Caslon by M Rules
Printed and bound in Great Britain by
Clays Ltd, St Ives plc

Papers used by Sphere are from well-managed forests
and other responsible sources.

MIX
Paper from
responsible sources
FSC
www.fsc.org   FSC® C104740

Sphere
An imprint of
Little, Brown Book Group
100 Victoria Embankment
London EC4Y 0DY

An Hachette UK Company
www.hachette.co.uk

www.littlebrown.co.uk

For Jeremy

Izena duen guztia omen da.
'All that has a name exists.'

Old Basque proverb

Author's Note

This is a work of fiction written to illuminate, entertain, inspire and intrigue, and should be read as such. Any similarity to a living person or actual institution is entirely coincidental. However, I have endeavoured to depict the history of the Lincoln Brigade and the experiences of both the Basques under Franco and the French and Germans who fought with the International Brigades as realistically and as empathetically as is possible. Again, many thanks to all those who have contributed to the writing of this book.

Prologue

The bitter wind blew flurries of icy flakes around Shimon's ankles. His feet – bare and bleeding from the heavy chains – were frozen beyond pain. If only the rest of me were as blessed, he thought, a wish that was instantly carried up by the erratic snow, whirling high above the jeering crowd running alongside the prison cart. A minute later it was brought crashing down by a rotten apple that hit him squarely in the chest. He fell back onto the sharp wooden stakes that fringed the cart. Painfully, he steadied himself against the jostling of the vehicle. The crowd shouted words that shot into him as sharp as arrows – 'Spy! Traitor! Devil lover!' The young Spaniard closed his eyes against the angry English faces, shutting out the grinning woman holding up her infant grandson to see the spectacle, the screaming hate that roared down the lane.

He knew he was going to die. He'd seen it. He had been given the gift of the eyes of God. The Eyes of God. He had seen his own burning body and yet he'd chosen not to run.

And now his secret hung like an oasis, tantalisingly out of reach, the last hope before death.

'*¡Soy inocente!* I am innocent!' he shouted, but his voice was lost in the laughter and in the clatter of horses' hooves. Suddenly, the cart swung into a small courtyard hidden behind high walls, guards swiftly pulling the gates shut behind the two noblemen escorting it on horseback, preventing the rabble from entering.

Shimon, looking from under his long matted hair and now far beyond fear, wondered whether they planned to execute him in secret, and if so how?

In the centre of the courtyard sat an ornate lacquered sedan chair, two uniformed footmen stood patiently at either side of it. The curtain across the window was drawn, but the chair, varnished in black and gold, was the transport of a nobleman. Recognising the coat of arms adorning the centre of the door panel, Shimon felt his heart begin to pound pitifully against his gaunt ribcage – a desperate hope flooded his tortured body as he was dragged from the cart to the ground and forced to kneel.

The two noblemen dismounted their horses and approached the sedan chair. One pulled the curtain across, while the other bowed low, the feather plume of his hat brushing against the cobbles as the man inside stepped out.

He stood before Shimon, austere in black, except for the royal emblem of the lion and the unicorn embroidered on the breast of his doublet and a plain silver cross a blatant declaration of the pious hanging over the quilted satin. An expression of both suspicion and curiosity was the only flicker of life in his bulbous eyes. Shimon knew this was the king who had drawn and quartered the Spanish sympathiser and heretic Guido Fawkes, but he also knew the monarch was a father in mourning.

'Does the wizard speak?' King James leaned heavily on a cane, his thin legs chicken-like under the pleated breeches, stuffed like the doublet to guard against the knife of the assassin. Pressing a scented posy against his nose to block the foul smell of the filthy prisoner, he swung around to the taller of the noblemen, Henry Howard, the elderly Earl of Northampton. The earl was about to translate the King's words when the prisoner, a Shimon Ruiz de Luna, a Spanish Jew whom the English had suspected of spying, and, to the earl's great frustration, had nothing humble about his demeanour except for the rags they had clad him in, bent forward, the chain around his ankles rattling as he did so.

'Your majesty, I am not wizard, spy nor alchemist, I am a physic,' he croaked, in English, his breath foul from starvation. 'I come as a friend of England, I come to bring you warning of a war. A war that has not yet happened, a war that will set Christian against Christian, brother against brother, and will poison Europe for thirty years or more—'

'Enough! I will not have my time wasted by such nonsense! You are just a commonplace agitator!' the King interrupted.

'Your majesty.' The earl stepped forward, his aged frame placating, his hands seeking to calm. 'The Spaniard has told us of events that had not yet taken place, and then Time proved him correct. I can't tell you how, but the alchemist has the powers of a seer, he is to be taken seriously.'

'A war! A thirty-year war? How am I to prevent this?'

'We found maps upon his person, perhaps they are clues to the future, your majesty. Think how it would serve both yourself and England to have such information, think how such knowledge would play against your enemies.'

King James turned back to the prisoner. After pulling both

his gloves up to stop his skin from being contaminated by contact with the Spaniard, he lifted one of Shimon's filthy hands and, turning it, examined both the palm and fingers. His courtiers, the earl and Justice Humphrey Winch, looked on, knowing they had no choice but to indulge the monarch's self-professed ability as a witch-finder.

'Have you interrogated him as a wizard?' the monarch finally enquired.

'Extensively, your majesty,' Justice Winch replied. 'As the marks and bruises on his body will testify, but over and over again he would not reveal the methods by which he has gained this knowledge of what is to come.'

'And the maps?'

'Strange gardens, caves and mountains, perhaps locations of future battles – none of which appear to be on English soil, your majesty.'

'Then they do not concern us. Execute him as a wizard,' the King declared, before signalling to the guard that he wished to leave.

The earl and Justice Winch exchanged a glance behind the King's back.

'Your majesty, we have been deliberating – it might be more politic to make the charge that of spy,' Winch ventured. 'The people have begun to tire of the burning of witches and wizards. The charge of spy has more gravitas. It would also send another warning to King Philip that we will not be toyed with.'

'And I should listen to the people? I am the King, I have divine right.'

Justice Winch nudged the earl sharply in the ribs. Reluctantly he stepped forward. 'Given the popularity of your dear departed son, the late Henry, Prince of Wales, it would be prudent to do so.'

King James sighed. 'Spy it is.' He glanced back at the prisoner, who stared up at him. 'Pity, he has a certain beauty for a Hebrew,' he observed, before turning away.

Shimon, struggling in his chains, threw himself at the monarch's feet. 'But I have brought you a huge gift, the gift of the future! You must listen! Your majesty!'

King James turned. 'I might consider a pardon if you tell me how you arrived at your magical maps and stories of battles and deaths to come.'

Northampton dropped to his heels and grabbing Shimon's narrow matted head, jerked it up. 'Save yourself, Jew, tell the King the method by which you came by this knowledge and you will live.'

'I cannot. If I did so, everything would become undone!'

'Then why come to these shores and demand an audience with his majesty – if not to spy?'

'To stop a war but not betray Time itself.' The consequences of his odyssey loomed over Shimon, and the blind tenacity with which he had pursued his one hope – to find a man with the power and intelligence to understand and use what he had discovered. He thought King James this man, now he'd lost everything, but there was still the map he had made – carved into landscapes someone in future years, decades, centuries would surely find, then follow.

'What does the prisoner say?' King James did not like this foreign muttering, the hysteria that seemed so unchristian. The earl stood and bowed his head.

'He will not reveal his methods, your majesty.'

'Then he must burn.'

'Burn, your majesty? Spies do not burn,' Justice Winch interjected.

'This one will,' the King announced, before hauling

himself into the sedan chair and pulling the curtain closed. A moment later Shimon was dragged back onto the cart.

Outside, the rabble was waiting and the prison cart trundled out again into the jeering. As it entered the lane Shimon caught sight of a woman standing back from the crowd, her black cloak wrapped around her statuesque figure, the long red hair concealed beneath a cowl. Shocked, he stared over at her. He would have recognised her anywhere, and, for the first time that day, he felt terrified. It was his sister's tutor, an Englishwoman who had betrayed his family to the Inquisition a lifetime ago, and one of the reasons why he had been forced to flee Spain.

'¡*Maldita seas!*' he spoke out. 'I curse you with my death and those of my parents, brother and sister.'

The earl, now back on his stallion and following the cart, noticed the prisoner's sudden agitation. He turned to Justice Winch.

'I still think it a strange execution for a spy.'

Winch, his long face shaped by grievance and avarice in equal parts, spat down onto the cobblestones. Then, concealing a loathing of Catholics – secret or otherwise – he turned back to Northampton, his features now smoothed into neutrality.

'You know how stubborn the King is when it comes to the persecution of occultists. However, by burning him we can be reassured his power as both wizard and spy will be vanquished.'

The earl glanced over at the shivering prisoner. Despite the marks of torture on his hands, feet and face, and despite the shower of rotten fruit and ridicule raining down, the Spaniard had managed to stay upright, his thin frame infused with a dignity Northampton would normally associate with religious martyrs and not foreign heretics. Wizard execution and all other manner of witch-burning were practices the earl only supported in public and then to appease King James, who'd taken a personal interest in such persecution since his days as a Scottish ruler, when he had even written a book on the subject: *Daemonologie*. It had been because of political pressure that the earl, now an elderly statesman of seventy-five, had agreed to represent the King at the execution at all.

'Nevertheless, Justice Winch, 'tis a pity you did not manage to squeeze the location of the Spaniard's great "treasure" out of him during his interrogation. I have it on good authority that the King wanted the treasure himself to present as a gift to King Philip of Spain.'

This time the judge did not bother to address the earl to his face but kept his eyes fixed on the swaying prisoner.

'If there is any great treasure ... Besides, my dear Northampton, can't you see that it's because Ruiz de Luna was able to use his wizardry to block his pain that I failed to procure the information you needed. If his great treasure involves witchcraft, 'tis perhaps better his secret dies with him. When England fights it fights with Christ by its side.'

'Amen to that,' the earl added, just to clarify where his own politics lay.

Before them the narrow lane suddenly opened out into the town's marketplace. Beside the gallows a huge pyre of wood had been constructed with a pole rising up through the middle like a ship's mast. Already the crowd stood waiting, oblivious of the snow gathering upon their heads and shoulders, faces sharp with anticipation.

Leaning forward, out of hearing of the King's guards who rode with them, Northampton snarled into the judge's ear, 'Just remember, Winch, such magic might be mistaken for courage. If there has been treachery afoot here, I promise

you I will find it. And if not me – History. At the end of the
day she will judge both of us and that day, my friend, is not
far for either you or I.'

The guards were already helping the prisoner off the cart
and towards the unlit pyre. Stumbling and near fainting,
Shimon was pushed through the crowd who'd now fallen
silent as if the proximity of death awed them. Some even
reached out and touched him as if to bring them good luck,
their outstretched arms a forest of strange affection, while
others spat and muttered prayers. It was not how Shimon
had imagined. He had seen a greater glory, one in which his
last confession had been heard loudly and defiantly across
the town plaza. He reached the platform. A masked executioner stood by the piled wood, a massive, muscular man,
sinister in demeanour.

As Shimon was led to the stake he tripped. In an instant
the executioner was by his side, helping him up.

'Steady, lad,' he whispered, his gentle voice belying his
threatening presence, as he tied Shimon to the stake.

A hooded priest approached offering him his last rites.
Shimon shook his head. Immediately the crowd began to
murmur in disgust – such a refusal proved the alchemist
guilty. One man cried out, 'Satan worshipper!' Ignoring
them, Shimon looked up into the pewter sky – utterly alien
from the blue heavens of his homeland – and began to
mutter his own prayers, in Hebrew. So intense was the dis-
course with his God, he barely noticed the whoosh of the
igniting stake the executioner now held.

Glancing over at Northampton, the executioner waited
for the signal. The aristocrat nodded solemnly. In a strangely
graceful gesture the burly man bent and lit the pyre. In seconds it was transformed into a flaming sun against the grey of
the city square.

'The eyes of God, the eyes of God,' Shimon said, over and over to himself, the flames now lapping at his feet. He stared out into the captivated crowd, searching for a face, his final solace.

At last he found her, standing at the back, her pregnant form hidden beneath a robe, her Basque features hooded against English eyes. Uxue. Their gaze met, and, though weeping, she smiled. Or was it his imagination? Then she held up a pendant for him to see – he recognised the symbol instantly. His secret was safe. Finally, Shimon surrendered to the searing pain that had begun shredding his feet and legs, before losing consciousness.

The earl crossed himself, thankful that the writhing figure now hung limp. He turned back to the crowd, his gaze searching for the dark young woman he'd seen the spy exchange glances with, but she'd vanished.

Catacombes de Paris, 1953

The man worked swiftly and furtively, the torchlight throwing long dancing shadows across the rows of neatly stacked skulls and bones. He was comfortable with the dead. The dark subterranean cavern, just one chamber in an endless labyrinth, with the faint scurrying of rats and dripping water, did not so much frighten him as throw his instincts on razor-sharp alert. He paused for a moment, resting on his walking cane, in front of the large iron cross set against a wall of tightly compacted bones topped by a row of skulls that seemed to stare back down at him in vacuous bewilderment. The last time he'd stood in this strange place was six years earlier, at the end of a war and the beginning of the most profound loss he'd ever experienced. That night he had come to hide something and now he was here to reclaim it.

He counted the skulls from the wall's edge and found the one he sought. Reaching up he managed to pull it from its tight niche without toppling its ghoulish companions. Holding it in the torch beam, he found the cracked seam and lifted the back of the skull away – hidden inside was a small object folded into a leather cover. He unwrapped it with trembling fingers, finally revealing an ancient chronicle, its vellum yellowed cover cracked like veins, the small brass lock clicked shut, the handwritten Latin dancing like spiders across the front. It lay in his hands heavy like she had lay dying. It was the only thing he had left of her.

'Andere,' he said, softly under his breath, as if to say the name itself might make the woman manifest, the dusty scent of the book taking him back to a war, to Spain, to the poignantly simple ideals of his youth that had made him, for a moment, a hero to a people, and, perhaps more importantly, to himself. Days that had evaporated with the grief and the sun, and afterwards the other Spain and the love he'd lost his soul to and had then later lost, a violent death that had made him run and had kept him running – until now.

Fuck them, they haven't won yet. His reverie was interrupted by a sound in the next catacomb, imperceptible to normal ears, but to his sharp musician's hearing audible enough for him to tense up his body. He froze. A second later there was the squeaking of rats and more scurrying. He relaxed – just night creatures, like myself, he reflected with some affection.

Then, with a sudden and violent thud, the assassin was upon him, the thin wire of a garrotte gouging his neck. Immediately, the musician deliberately fell back against his attacker, toppling the slight figure to the stone floor and managing to slip a thumb under the wire as they fell, buying him the moments he needed to reach for the cane with his other hand. The figure pinned under his large body appeared surprisingly small, but the assassin moved with the expediency of the professional killer, pulling on the wire ruthlessly, twisting and turning to get from under him. The musician, his brain racing with the clarity of an ex-soldier, eased the tip of the cane under the wire in place of his thumb. He then jerked the cane forward with both his hands and all his strength, snapping the garrotte. Swinging around, he wrestled with the assassin who he could now see wore a balaclava. The musician, although ill, was strong and used to combat. In seconds he had his hands around the assassin's throat – it took another minute to finish him.

The assassin fell back lifeless and suspiciously light in the musician's arms. He laid the body out on the freezing flagstones, allowing the silence of the catacombs to close back over them. Crouching over the prostrate figure, he waited listening, half-expecting others to follow. There was nothing; apart from him and the corpse, the catacombs were empty. Reaching down he pulled the balaclava off – black hair shorn close to the skull in army fashion framed the face of a young woman, devoid of make-up, her body slight and flat-chested. Under the jacket hung a pendant, a curious symbol that seemed vaguely familiar. He pulled the chain off the corpse with an indifferent jerk. He would keep it: it might be a clue.

He turned back to the chronicle now lying under the cross. It was undamaged. Deeply relieved, he picked it up. It must be returned to the family, he told himself. He would not live long enough to take it back, but there was one man he knew, someone he had also loved and who owed him his life. This man, more than anyone, would be able to take the heirloom back and perhaps more, perhaps even unlock the stories of the strange maps within it. He glanced at his watch, it was 3 a.m., the hour of the wolf as they used to say in the trenches. He would leave tonight before they try to kill him and steal the chronicle again.

1

'Harder, harder, big boy! I am yours!' The girl, straddling August, screamed in Russian, her long hair a curtain that fell across his face, the small high breasts pushing hungrily between the strands as she pressed herself against him.

'Big boy, *da*!' August yelled back in an effort to lose himself in her pleasure. It was the fourth time they'd made love in seven hours and he'd travelled from very drunk to sober like a speeding car about to crash, the expected hangover now beginning to explode over each eyeball.

'*Da!*' She came, and he followed, an orgasm that accelerated into a pounding headache as she fell back, her slim body arching away from him like a gymnast. It was an interesting perspective, August noted, reminded of an Egon Schiele drawing. The sweep of her thin pale body topped with the thick black bush of her sex was both lyrical and erotic, but then again, he was a sap for beauty. Was this why he had let her spend the whole night? he wondered to himself, as she lifted herself off him, rolling to the other side of the unkempt bed.

Sitting up, August began rolling a cigarette then realised

with a sudden panic he'd forgotten her name. Irina? Yelena? Yolanta? From Leningrad, that much he remembered. Large green eyes, a narrow cat face and an intellectual passion he had found impossibly sexy. They'd met in a jazz bar he frequented, one that was always full of students and European emigrants. Armed with a smouldering anger and a sexuality that crackled through the air, she'd approached him and asked whether he was a saxophone or trumpet aficionado, then demanded he bought her a vodka. Full of idealism and bittersweet anecdotes about occupation, she'd taken him back to his own youth and all he'd lost growing cynical, and that had been motive enough to ask her back to the flat, but he hadn't planned for her to stay the night. He never let them stay the night, not the one-night stands. It was too messy; there were women for one thing, and other women for another, that was how he functioned, had always functioned. Besides, August had a vague feeling he'd made arrangements for that morning, he just couldn't quite remember what they were and the hangover wasn't helping.

'You read my language?'

He turned. She was holding up a copy of *War and Peace* in Russian.

'I speak a little, badly,' he told her in Russian, reluctant already to expose much more of himself.

'Is good,' she replied then sprung up in that restless way some women get just after lovemaking. Stark naked, and in the morning light, he could now see she did indeed have both the body and grace of a dancer. She was also achingly young, younger than he remembered from the night before. She went over to the mantelpiece and picked up a photograph entitled, '1933, Harvard, Boston.'

'This is you with father, yes?'

A shimmeringly young August stared defiantly out of the frame, an aura of privilege and entitlement enveloping him like a faint smudge. Very blond, dressed in his graduation gown and cap, optimism radiating from every pore, he stood beside his father – Senator Winthrop of the Republican Party. The patrician's hand grasped the young August's shoulder – the king with his heir under his command. August lit the roll-up then exhaled a long cool plume of white smoke, the nicotine dampening down his hangover.

'Once upon a time,' he answered, more bitterly than he'd intended.

'Once upon a time? This is not a fairy tale, this is your life, no?'

'I haven't seen him in a long time. We argued.'

'Argued?' She put the photograph back carefully, as if she were placing an offering at an altar.

'About Marx, if you have to know.'

'Ah, like we did last night.' She smiled, and for some strange reason looked less naked for doing so.

'No, not like last night. My father is a fascist.'

'An American fascist, this is not possible.'

'It is possible.'

She shrugged, moving onto the next photograph. 'And this one, this was when you were student?'

He glanced over. It had been taken on the River Cherwell in Oxford – three students punting on a lost sunny day, suspended in memory, himself, Charlie and the girl, hauntingly beautiful. Iris? Chantelle? He vaguely remembered the love-making, tears and a few terse letters but that was all. But who'd been the fourth element, the photographer himself? It was odd August had forgotten but there he was, on the punt sitting between Charlie and the girl, smiling across at this unseen chronicler. *God, I look so much older than in the first photograph, so formed in my determination.* Gone was the air of entitlement, in its place something more vulnerable, more angry. *What did I lose in those years?*

Staring across, he was back there, the gentle splash of the punt as it slipped into the water, the sudden cry from a startled duck flapping its wings wildly as it skimmed across the river, the murmur of Charlie reciting Donne, and colouring all of it the sense that they were blessed, poised on the edge of something vast, eternal and incredibly exciting, perfectly placed to change the world. August's heart beat faster just thinking about it. He could even smell the faint smoke of coal fires drifting up from houses along the bank, the scent of lilac threading the soft air like light. *And there was Charlie, with his longish hair and a goatee in that workman's flat cap he always wore, staring moodily across the water. I miss you, more than life.*

The two men had met in August's first year at Oxford, both reading Classics and Oriental Studies, but Charlie Stanwick had been a scholarship boy, a streak of brilliant rhetoric and lateral thinking, son of a Glaswegian bricklayer and teacher, and determined to transform the world. A dedicated Marxist, he'd persuaded August to join the party and volunteer with him for the International Brigade when the Spanish Civil War broke out. They both left together for Spain in January 1937.

August, now yearning for the quick oblivion of a glass of whisky, turned to the window. Outside the last-gasp spring snow fell in wilful gushes, in a determined chaos that reflected the turmoil in which he felt he had, again, stupidly placed himself.

'Yes, I was a student, at Oxford.'

'So you must be academic, but what is this photograph, of you as soldier?' She held up the last picture of a burned-out and barren olive grove, in which a battalion of battered-looking makeshift soldiers posed. There were eight of them, armed with ancient Soviet rifles, some with knives pushed into their leather belts, all with the red beret pulled low over the brow. Visibly older, August stood in the second row, holding his fist up in the characteristic salute of the Spanish Republican Army. The contrast between the August in the first photograph and this August was extreme. He'd lost that tight cast of hope that defines the jittery years between fifteen and twenty, the years in which all seems possible. There was a new maturity to his face, a bleak realism in his gaze. The wound that would become the scar was now visible on his left cheek. *The Abraham Lincoln Brigade and Hemingway, Jarama Valley, 1937* was scrawled in ink at the bottom of the photograph. The writer, tall and instantly recognisable, stood in the middle of the men, a rifle slung over his shoulder for the sake of authenticity, looking back at the camera acutely aware of posterity's glare.

'Soldier or academic, which is it?' the Russian girl insisted. Irritated, August got up out of the bed. At thirty-eight years of age he had a rangy physique that marked him – no matter what clothes he wore or language he spoke – as definably American, of old blue-blood Bostonian, a heritage he'd done his utmost to escape. He was a striking figure: missing the tip of his signet (shot off at Fatarella by a Spanish fascist), the angularity of his face was softened only by the mouth that was curiously feminine in shape and size, a broken nose and a scar that zigzagged from the corner of the right eye down to his lip. Conflict, both inner and outer, was stamped all over his body, contributing to an air of masculinity that was fatally attractive. He stubbed out the roll-up, then took the photograph out of her hand and put it back on the mantelpiece.

'Listen Yelena—'

'My name is Yolanta.'

'Yolanta, it's getting late and I have work to do ...'

She snaked her body around his, her nipples brushing against his chest, her sex touching his. She was almost as tall as him and the total effect was undeniably and annoyingly arousing.

'You answer my question, then we make love for the very last time and then I go. Deal?' She paused. 'Soldier or academic?'

Now erect, he couldn't help himself. 'Fighter,' he murmured into her tangled fragrant hair as he lifted her up onto his hips. Entering her with a violence that made her gasp, he carried her over to the bed. Lowering her down, he began to pound into her, the quickening of both of them pushing all thought out of his mind, the delicious tightness of her, the soft taut skin enveloping him, taking him away from himself, from all that he'd become ...

'August!' The voice was outraged and chillingly familiar. He stopped mid-penetration, then looked over his shoulder at Cecily, his fiancée, still in her coat and with a bag over her shoulder, standing at the end of the bed, staring at them horrified.

'How could you?' Her voice tiny and strangulated, she seemed paralysed in disbelief.

'What are you doing back from your holiday!' He rolled off the girl, so shocked he found himself taking refuge in banalities. Cecily still hadn't moved. It was as if she couldn't believe the tableau before her.

'I came back early, to surprise you. I thought you'd be pleased.' She reached into her bag and pulled out a package of cigarette boxes. 'I even brought you the cigarettes you like.' She threw them at his head, causing him to duck. 'Lucky Strikes!' Now she moved, running for the front door.

August leaped off the bed.

'Your wife?' the Russian girl ventured from the bed, revelling in languid nudity.

'Just get out! Get out!' August shouted back at her as he rushed to catch Cecily. 'I can explain!' He caught Cecily's arm at the door.

'What have you done? You've broken us, you've broken us into pieces!' Cecily told him, struggling, then burst into tears as the Russian pushed past, still dressing, slamming the door behind her as she left.

'She means nothing, Cecily!' He fought her flailing arms as he pulled her into an embrace. Eventually her sobbing receded into a sullen anger. It was then that she broke away and started pacing the bedsit furiously.

'What I don't understand is why you gave me your keys if you intended to sleep with other women!'

Cecily's voice pounded like nails into his head, his hangover having transformed it into a fragile glass bowl out of which he now found himself peering. Yearning to escape, August glanced towards the window, the events of the evening before seeming to drift across the windowpane as elusive as the fog that cloaked Kensington. He barely noticed a black car pulling away from the other side of the kerb. Suddenly he remembered he was still naked.

He grabbed his dressing gown; with it wrapped around him he felt less vulnerable. A certain self-righteous indignation now swept away the humiliation of being caught in flagrante delicto.

'It wasn't like that, Cecily. She seduced me, if you have to know. Besides, I was drunk, I didn't know what I was doing, what I was risking,' he said.

Cecily stopped pacing. She stood in front of the small gas fire set in the old Georgian hearth. Ominously it spluttered then died. In the kitchenette over the sink the gas meter gave out a click as it switched off. In seconds the room began to cool. In ten minutes it would be freezing, even though it was April. Ignoring the heater, Cecily stared at her lover, angry with herself for desiring him even now, covered by another woman's caresses like invisible tattoos. 'You're drunk a lot lately, and you've stopped writing. It's like you're careering towards disaster and I just can't help you.' Her eyes welled with tears again, making him feel even guiltier and even more filled with self-loathing.

'You can help, you do help, Cecily. Listen, I don't want to lose you.'

'Then why don't you share things with me? Your past? What really happened in Spain, what really happened to Charlie!' She was shouting now and August hated shouting women.

'Stop it, Cecily, you're on dangerous ground.'

'Have you ever thought that you might be unconsciously sabotaging any possible happiness you could have? It's not just the women or the drink, what about the debtors, August? Don't think I don't know about them. You had a job, a well-paid lectureship and you gave it up to pursue your "research", and now you have writer's block . . . '

Close to losing his temper, August closed his eyes then opened them again. To his relief Cecily was still there.

'Look, maybe I am just hell-bent on destroying myself, maybe I'm a lost cause, just another loser addicted to risk—'

'We are not at war now!' Cecily screamed, despite herself. Outside there was the soft thud of snow, as if her voice had dislodged it.

'Do you think I don't know that?' he murmured, one hand twisting into another. Why couldn't he just touch her? Staring at him, Cecily felt her anger dissipate, like a puff of air leaving her body. She didn't want to fight any more.

'Why *did* you ask me to marry you?' Her voice had shrunk to a plea.

August shrugged, there were no words left. The pain over his temple was beginning to throb again and the whisky from the night before had started to rise up in nausea. He tried stretching his face into a smile but his scar ached – phantom trauma.

'I guess I thought I needed saving.' He didn't sound convincing, even to himself.

Cecily pulled the diamond ring off her finger and placed it on the mantelpiece.

'You're married already ...' Her hand flew up towards the rows of books that sat against the walls, piles marked with notes that read 'The poisoning of Germanicus by Piso – the use of poison and witchcraft in Ancient Greece', 'Myths and magical herbs', 'Virgil's Eclogues', 'The Annals of Tacitus', and other titles interspersed with Marx, Descartes and copies of *Life* magazine. '... to your work, your past, your research and that manuscript you will never, ever finish. I was an idiot to think I could change you.' Picking up her hat, she started to walk out.

Incredulous, he stared after her, at the seams of her stockings, the neatly arranged hair, the back of her shoulders as she swung towards the door, not believing she'd actually reach it. He waited for her to turn back to him, only when her hand reached out for the handle did he spring into action, bolting across the thread-worn rug.

'You can't leave, not because of a lousy one-night stand!' He grabbed her arm.

The doorbell interrupted them. Startled, they both stopped struggling then Cecily shook herself free. But it kept ringing, drilling through their argument, through August's blinding hangover.

'You'd better answer it, it's probably the next woman you intend to seduce,' Cecily stated, flatly. The doorbell rang again. It was August's cue – he knew somewhere under his throbbing headache he didn't want to lose her but he was too exhausted, existentially and emotionally, to win her back – not again.

He pushed past her, out into the corridor then pulled the front door open angrily. The freezing wind billowed out his dressing gown and blew against his naked legs, jolting him back into a sharp reality.

There was no one there. He stared out into the fog peppered with late snow. It wasn't quite nine and the morning was still gloomy, the pea-souper thick enough to hide ghosts as August's sixth sense stretched out in the white. Nothing. He turned back to the door, then heard a voice he hadn't heard in years.

'August?' A tall, thin figure clutching a guitar case and a walking cane stepped out of the bushes to the side of the front path.

'Jimmy? Jimmy van Peters?' The battered face was now visible, aged almost beyond recognition, but August recalled the way Jimmy had always held his head, bent slightly to the side as if he were regarding the world at a certain ironic distance, the hang-dog bloodshot blue eyes that revealed none of the prowess he'd show on the battlefield or the cold precision with which he always handled a bayonet. And despite the new fragility to the heavily lined face, August knew those heavy black eyebrows and those eyes; of Irish and Russian heritage, the ex-wharfie and consummate soldier had a distinctive virility still evident in his large but shrunken frame.

'Let me in, Gus, it's fucking cold out here and we're probably being watched,' Jimmy croaked, then, as August watched in amazement, swept past him into the house. After checking the road for any unwanted observers, August followed.

Cecily stared across at the musician: the old leather coat, the mud-encrusted boots and the battered trilby, boasting a ledge of melting snow, pushed down hard onto Jimmy's cauliflower ears, the tattooed scorpion on the top of the hand. Jimmy gawked back, a glint of bald-faced sexual appreciation beetling up under his heavy eyebrows. While August stood by the door, paralysed by the shock of seeing two of his carefully compartmentalised worlds collide once again that morning.

'Gus didn't tell me he had company.' Jimmy's voice was a smoky blast from another era. He held out a gaunt hand large enough to span Cecily's entire waist. She looked down at his grimy palm in open disdain then swung around to August.

'Gus?' she repeated, as if by sounding out the moniker Jimmy had exposed a whole other persona of August's even more alien to the one she knew he kept hidden from her.

'Jimmy van Peters, wonderful to meet you too,' the musician replied, sarcastically. He placed his guitar case against the wall then threw his trilby on the couch to collapse onto August's favourite armchair with his soaking wet coat still on, his gaze falling on the low coffee table upon which a couple of half-empty glasses sat from the night before.

'Jesus, is that whisky?' he asked August. Ignoring him, August swung around to Cecily.

'Jimmy's an old friend from Spain, we were comrades together.' But she was now halfway across the room.

'How nice for you.' She started to turn the door handle. Indifferent to the drama unfurling before him, Jimmy lifted one of the glasses and sniffed it.

'Hallelujah, it is too,' he observed.

'Don't go.' August reached out to touch Cecily but found he couldn't quite bring himself to stop her. They both watched his hand hover then drop back to his side.

'You see, I have to,' she concluded, quietly, then left August staring at the door closing behind her.

Over in the kitchenette above the sink the gas heater gave out another groan. For the second time that morning August found himself unable to move.

'Great legs, pity about the personality,' Jimmy cracked from the couch, whisky glass in hand. August burst back into the moment, his head splitting.

'Jimmy, that's my fiancée.'

'Was your fiancée, right?'

August wrapped the dressing gown tighter then sat opposite Jimmy. He reached for the packet of Lucky Strikes and broke open a box.

'Right. You want one? Cecily just brought them back from Washington. She was on a trip with her father. I thought she was due back tomorrow. Have one, they're like gold around here.'

Jimmy shook his head. 'Would love to, but the lungs have gone.' He broke into a broad grin, revealing a row of badly neglected teeth. 'Gus, I cannot tell you how great it is to see some things never change.'

'You're wrong. Everything has changed and how the hell are you on my doorstep, Jimmy? I haven't seen you since—'

'Paris, just before the occupation. I was prettier then.'

'Prettier? You were gorgeous.' August exhaled, trying to calm his pounding heart.

Jimmy chuckled. 'Yeah, well, the clock turns ... Your fiancée? That really *was* something.'

'One day, Jimmy, one day I'll figure out the difference between love and need.'

'Either way you're screwed, good and proper.' Jimmy held up the used glass. 'Good whisky, little corked but it survived the night, which is more than you did, judging by the look of you.' He pointed to the lipstick smudge along the rim of the glass. It was red, Cecily's lipstick had been pink. 'The other woman, right?'

August didn't bother answering, but that was enough for Jimmy who broke into another chuckle. He filled the glass up from the whisky bottle and toasted August.

'To my comrade – cocksman supremo.'

'I'm not proud of it. Say, are you still playing at that dive in the Latin Quarter?'

'I was, until a month ago. Now the fingers tremble too much to get a note out.'

'That's a real shame, you were one of the best jazz guitarists around.'

Outside there was the sound of a car passing, then the ring of a bicycle bell. Startled, the musician jumped, his face tightening as he went to the window.

'Jimmy?' August asked. He'd never seen him so jittery, not even under fire.

'Ever since I got off the ferry in Dover I've had this feeling.' Fear was pinching his voice. 'I left Paris in the middle of the night, I was sure I lost them.' He pulled off his scarf and threw it onto the chair, revealing the vivid purple bruise around his neck. He caught August staring at it. 'An assassin in the catacombs, some crazy chick, left me with a souvenir.' He reached into his pocket and showed August the pendant. 'The kind of fuck-up voodoo you're familiar with. No one knows I'm in England, no one, right? Except your ex-fiancée.'

'Cecily's trustworthy. Don't worry, you're safe here. No one's interested in me unless it's a jilted girlfriend or a debt collector. Nowadays I'm just an unemployed academic and a philanderer. Amen to that.' August poured himself a whisky.

'You sure there's not a watcher out there?'

'They stand out like dogs' balls: black Wolseley car, raincoat and cheap hat. Oh, and they hate working Sundays.'

Jimmy pulled the curtains shut. 'No one's safe, least of all you and me. Once a Commie, always a Commie, you think government forgets? They keep tags, buddy. The Department is watching me, that's for sure. I'm going to have to move in the next day or so, else ...'

'Else what, Jimmy?'

'Else they are going to kill me.' Jimmy suddenly looked terrible, his skin was greyish and his hands trembled. He moved back to the couch. 'Not that my death matters. I'm dying anyway, Gus, cirrhosis of the liver, I have about six months, five if I finish this glass. But I want those five months.'

'Jesus, I'm sorry to hear that.'

'I figured I had it coming, I mean how many times have I thumbed my nose at *La Muerte*. Life's a debt, my friend – one day he's gonna come around to collect. Good news is there's going to be a hell of lot of *soldados* waiting on the other side. But I guess that's why I'm here.'

He carefully pulled the guitar out of the case, then held it across his knees and, to August's amazement, began unscrewing the front. Once he'd lifted it off a small parcel taped to the inside of the instrument became visible. He pulled the parcel out of the guitar and placed it reverently into August's hands.

'I brought you something I want you to take back to Spain for me.'

It was a book, a very old book. The cover was aged vellum, laced with fine lines, the title in Latin written in delicate flourishes, on one corner a brown-coloured stain that had soaked through, which August immediately recognised as blood, old blood, ancient even. But yet more compelling, the leaves of hand-made parchment pressed between the thick covers seemed to whisper to him as he ran his fingers down the hand-cut edges. They sang of uniqueness, of priceless antiquity.

He paused, his fingers touching the vellum lightly as he struggled to contain a wave of excitement that almost gave him vertigo. He couldn't quite believe his eyes.

Embossed into the centre of the cover was a symbol. August glanced at it, then looked at it more closely. At first he'd assumed it was a version of the German swastika. It certainly was the same shape, and the post-war black market was flooded with valuable artefacts and antiques originally 'appropriated' then stamped by the Nazi regime. But on closer inspection he recognised the symbol from an entirely different era. It was in the shape of the swastika but the four arms seemingly rotating anti-clockwise were formed of petals. A little like the ancient Chinese Yin-Yang symbol, only instead of the universe being divided into two spiritual realms, this was divided into four spiritual realms – at least that's what August remembered reading somewhere.

Last time he'd seen the symbol had been in 1938 in the Pyrenees fleeing Franco's troops. It had been painted defiantly on the side of an old Basque farmhouse: the Lauburu, the symbol of the Basque people, evoking the old pagan worship of both the moon and the mountain Goddess Mari, a magical symbol to protect and bless.

But this depiction was different. In the centre of the symbol was the drawing of an eye. He looked up at Jimmy.

'This is extraordinary.'

'I know and you're exactly the man to take it back to Spain, back to the ancient family it belongs to.'

*

Jimmy held the glass up to the flame, his face rapt, the whisky glowing amber in the light. 'As you know it was chaos during the retreat back in March '38. Like most of us, my name was on a CIA list, and I knew if I wanted to stay fighting Der Führer, I might have to sacrifice a few political ideals to join the main game.'

'You changed your identity?'

'I smuggled myself into France and hung low until 1940. When Germany invaded France I hitched a boat back to the US and enlisted immediately. By the time Pearl Harbor happened, I'd already convinced them that with my trilingual abilities, experience in guerrilla warfare and knowledge of Western Europe, I might prove useful in Wild Bill Donovan's outfit.'

'You got a posting with the Office of Strategic Services?' August had trouble keeping the disbelief out of his voice.

'Like I say, I was good at reinvention and back then they were desperate for intelligent men who could fight and were bilingual, in my case trilingual. Before I knew it I was down in Area F training with the rest of the rookies. Crazy to think I was working for what was to become the CIA, but back then the bastards believed me and I had a great war, the best, August, right up until '45. Then things went bad after liberation day. How's that for irony?' Jimmy pushed his nose into the glass full of whisky and inhaled deeply. 'Christ, it might just be enough to smell the damn thing. Sweeter than a woman's pussy.'

'Pussy won't kill you.'

'Really? I seem to recall it nearly killed you a few times.'

'Wish I could say those days are over,' August deadpanned. Jimmy broke into laughter that ended in a bout of coughing.

'Boy, have I missed you.'

'Then why did you disappear, Jimmy? We thought you were dead.'

'I had to disappear. They'd have killed me if they'd found me.'

August looked up from his glass. The Jimmy he knew had never been given to paranoia.

'Who are they?' he asked, softly.

The musician got up and went to the window, this time pulling the curtains across just enough to see out unnoticed. August watched, recognising the tension in the musician's body, the muscle memory of anticipated violence, his whole frame taut with observation. After a tense moment Jimmy turned back to August.

'You've got to take the book back. I can't go back to Spain, not after all I lost there.' His voice was urgent and low, the desperation uncharacteristic for him, and shocking to August.

'I can't, Jimmy. It's not the danger, it's the memories. It would be like going back into the labyrinth, only this time I wouldn't expect to find my way out.' It was the most honest thing August had said in months, and, to his secret dismay, he knew it. Jimmy studied his face.

'Don't try and kid yourself, Gus, that war still burns inside of you and the only way you're going to save yourself is if you walk right back into those flames and let them consume everything – the dying men you held in your arms, the exploding skies, the screaming women – until it all turns to ashes and then you walk out the other side. I'm dying, I'll never get that chance. I'm giving you a gift. It's up to you whether you take it or not.'

August turned away, unable to bear Jimmy's scrutiny any longer. *Can't you see? I'm not Joe Iron any more, I'm a patchwork puppet made up of fragments of memory – a pretender trying to live a normal life. God help me.* 'Listen,' August finally told him.

'I've stopped fooling myself about changing the world, knowing I might have educated a few people is enough.'

Jimmy stared at him. 'Maybe you're right.' The musician swung around, wildly gesturing at the piles of books lined up against the wall. 'Maybe I should just start believing in all this crap, because I'm telling you there's cold comfort in being a dying atheist.'

'I'm not asking you to believe in God. I just follow belief back to its beginnings, like making a map. A map of why people believe and what they chose to believe in. There's a whole connection that runs up through the pagan rites of southern Europe straight into Dionysian rituals of first-century Greece. Mountain god, Pan, Satan, everything is connected to everything, nothing we do is without reason even if we don't know it.' By the time he was finished August was aware of how his own passion always carried him away, even when he was conscious of the indifference of his audience. Jimmy, picking up August's chagrin, broke into a grin, his battered face puckering up around the smile.

'Hell, you just reminded me of that time at Jarama when we were packing to move the front and you went missing. Found you later down some dried riverbed, clutching a weed like it was gold. Daddy-o, that was crazy.'

'Angel's Trumpet – a hallucinogen used in witches' rites.'

'And that time you skipped off in Córdoba, looking for a library that used to house those Jewish kabbalists, while the rest of us were at the whorehouse? You were like a kid in a candy store, reeling in all that history. The New World hungry for the Old. That's exactly why you're the right guy for this job.' Jimmy moved over to the fireplace and picked up the framed photograph of the group of International Brigadiers. 'I remember this.'

'Remember? You took the photo.'

'Ernest fucking Hemingway, what a phoney. Always kept his distance from the frontline.'

'He was okay.'

'Christ, you all look so green.'

'We *were* young, you were the grand old man at thirty-eight.' August took another swig of whisky. 'And what do you know, I'm that age now.'

'Happens to the best of us.' Holding the photograph up, Jimmy pointed to the young unshaven man standing with his arm loosely thrown over August's shoulder. 'That's Charlie, ain't it?'

August got up and took the photograph from him and placed it carefully back in the exact position that it was in before.

'You know it is,' he said, already battling that old wave of emotion.

'So what really happened at Belchite? Charlie cracked, right?'

'I don't think about it, ever.'

'But you took over command—'

'I said I don't think about it.'

'And you're lying.' For a moment the two men stood close to blows, heads lowered, shoulders hunched up. A lorry passed outside and there was another thud of thawing snow. *What the hell have I become, that I can hit a dying man?* August caught his own clenched fists before they flew in an instinct of their own. In the same instant Jimmy's shoulders rolled forward, popping the tension between them like a balloon. August ducked but Jimmy was merely reaching out to put a hand on his shoulder.

'There are things I can't remember, it's like my brain don't allow me,' August confessed, dropping his gaze.

'If you go back to Spain, Charlie's ghost will be waiting for you to make peace with him. Go back for him.'

August pulled away. 'Somebody had to take charge. I was carrying out orders Charlie couldn't.' The memory rose up like bile, the misery of that dawn, the prisoners – four captured fascist soldiers and their officer, pale and drawn in his tailored uniform, the youngest not even twenty. August asking for the hundredth time whether they would consider capitulating, only to have the leader spit at his feet. His own doubts gathering like fear at the pit of his stomach. Someone's prayer hanging – filigree on the air. Charlie's stricken face as the men waited for his order. Then the ricochet of August's own shouted command high above all that he believed. *Thou shall not kill. Thou shall not.* The report of the firing squad, the thud of bodies hitting the dusty ground, the gun smoke drifting across the square.

'Hey buddy, we've all stepped over the line.' Jimmy's gravelly voice pulled him back into the present. 'That's what marks us, sets us apart from ordinary men.'

'I *am* ordinary.'

'No, no, you're not.' Jimmy reached across and helped himself to one of August's cigarettes then lit up. He threw himself back into the old leather chair then smoking, stared out into the room, memory washing across his face like light.

'At the end of the war, in '45, I found myself in an OSS squad headed up by an operative called Damien Tyson. There were six of us – all officers with extensive clandestine experience in and out of the field. All of us had experience with hand-to-hand combat, guerrilla tactics and liaising with local resistance. But no one except me had fought in Spain. Apart from Tyson, the other five had all seen service in the Pacific theatre – two of them had been on the ground in Papua New Guinea.

'We'd been called together for a black op set up to arm and train the remnants of Basque freedom fighters hiding out in the hills of Pais Vasco. As you know Roosevelt was worried that fascism might rise again in Europe and Franco, being one of the only fascist dictatorships left standing, was suspect. Roosevelt hadn't trusted him, Churchill was ambivalent and Stalin positively hated the guy. So Operation Lizard had been born under the dictate of President god-damn Roosevelt, God bless FDR. He died before we were issued our orders.' Jimmy shifted restlessly in the armchair. 'They came in September and we were in the mountains by October. And Gus, the unit of Basque fighters we had been sent to train up and rearm was headed up by none the less than La Leona herself.'

'The Lioness?' August failed to keep the awe out of his voice.

Jimmy nodded.

August whistled. He'd first heard of La Leona from a Basque soldier he'd befriended during the siege of Bilbao. Famous for both her beauty and her ruthlessness, she was every Republican's – Spanish or foreign – pin-up. He remembered the saying, if you put La Leona, Franco and a bull all in the same room, she would have the bigger balls. For many she became the shimmering Madonna that appeared over the battlefields, the woman you could fight beside during the day, make love to at night and still respect in the morning. Even August, who ridiculed his fellow sol-diers' obsession, had found himself secretly dreaming of the statuesque black-eyed revolutionary who regularly appeared in grainy black-and-white photographs in the *Gaceta de la Republica*. La Leona herself had disappeared after the defeat in 1939, rumoured kidnapped and executed by Franco's men, but she lived on as a myth in the minds of many.

This was the first time August had heard her name since then and now it hung in the room like a small red banner

only just unfurled, as tantalising as news of an old lover one
still secretly loved.

'I thought she was from Galicia?'

'No, her late husband was Gallego but Andere herself
came from a village in Gipuzkoa, impossible to get to by
road, the perfect hideaway. Her real name was Andere Miren
Merikaetxebarria. Tyson, our commander, had been liaising
with the exiled Basque government in Paris, both him and
the US high command had no illusions. They were well
aware of La Leona's reputation and what that alone could
muster in terms of later recruitment should the operation
succeed.

'At the beginning things went fantastically well. La Leona
and her men were eager to learn new combat techniques, to
handle weaponry they'd never had a chance to see before.
We gave them state-of-the-art Ryan FR-1s, Winchester M1
Garands, even a small rocket launcher. It was like Christmas
and Los Sanfermines had arrived all at once. But you should
have seen Andere. I swear she was one of the bravest soldiers I have ever had the honour to meet. We got close, I
mean all of us, out there in that forest, we became like
family. Maybe that was a mistake, but those people, it takes
so long to win their trust that when you have it, it's like some
great profound victory. Your soul falls in love.'

'Believe me, I remember.' August poured another whisky
out, filled with a sudden desire to get drunk, to forget.
Ignoring him, Jimmy continued.

'We'd been there about six weeks when I realised there
was something more between me and Andere than rifle
training. I guess I'd finally met my match.' Jimmy paused,
his voice breaking a little. He stubbed out his cigarette in the
overflowing ashtray. 'Well, better to have met your match
late than not at all. For the first time in my lousy murder-

filled life I felt like a child, all the cynicism fell away and I
stepped out like a friggin' new born angel, me, trembling at
the touch, the very presence of this woman. I've never been
happier, not before, not since. We had four weeks, August.
Those weeks defined my life, I swear.'

'What happened, Jimmy?'

'One night the three of us ended up around the camp
fire, just me, her and Tyson. The others were drunk, already
in their tents. It was nearly the end of the training, we were
just awaiting an order from HQ that would have okayed our
first hit against Franco. Excitement and hope were running
high. It was one of those electric full moons, you know, with
the halo circling round the old man like the promise of eternity, one of those nights when everyone starts spilling their
history like there's no tomorrow ...' Just then August
noticed the way Jimmy glanced at the chronicle and looked
away almost like it pained him to look at it. '... I can't
remember exactly how it came up but I remember Tyson
starting talking about the local beliefs, about their mountain
goddess and the forest spirits. He seemed to know an awful
lot about it, talking about some witch trial that had happened near there, centuries before ...'

'Logroño.'

'That's right. Tyson talked about an old chronicle that
was rumoured to have been written around then, sometime
in the early seventeenth century, retracing some illustrious
mystic's journey, like a map that if followed would lead you
to a great treasure, but the chronicle had disappeared.
Andere had been tight-lipped until then, I knew her to be
religious but dismissive of the deeply superstitious people
around her. But I could feel her getting tenser and tenser, sitting there, listening to all these fairy tales he was spouting.
And I tell you, being in the middle of the forest with that

moon staring down at us, and the occasional wolf howling in the distance, it didn't seem so far-fetched. Then Tyson suddenly starts bragging that he has evidence this chronicle never really existed, that some eighteenth-century French prankster invented it to sell a fake antique, a fake that set up a whole mystery and cult around it, tricking people into fruitless searches for two hundred and fifty years.

'Andere stared at him, I swear I thought she was going to explode or leap across the fire and strangle the guy. But she announces in this serious voice, like she is defending her people's belief, that "*Las crónicas del alquimista* exist". And that's all she said. There was this silence afterwards in which me, the idiot musician, cracked a joke but Andere had turned to stone. Tyson laughed and it was like the whole thing was forgotten. Water closing over an iceberg.

'Only later when we were finally alone and in each other's arms, did Andere confess that her family had been safeguarding this actual book for centuries. I could hardly believe it, but her terror was real and that scared me – I'd never seen fear in her face before. She told me she didn't trust Tyson and made me promise I would take the book and safeguard it with my life if anything happened to her and her men.' Jimmy paused, steadying his trembling hand against the whisky glass. 'A week later the order finally came from US headquarters. Tyson wouldn't let me read the cable – instead he tricked me into making a false supply trip back to France over the Pyrenees. While I was gone, he gave the order to close down Operation Lizard and destroy all evidence ...'

'They executed Andere and her men?' August couldn't keep the shock out of his voice. Jimmy's face was now ashen with the memory, his voice tightening with emotion. 'Ambushed them and shot them firing-squad style. They

didn't stand a chance. They were killed and buried.' He
poured himself another whisky and downed it like a dying
man. 'I'll never forget the date, October the 31st, 1945.
I've carried it with me all these years.' He faltered, near
tears then pulled himself together. 'But what Tyson wasn't
calculating on was me making it back to Irumendi alive. I
was lucky. Terrified, the rest of Andere's family had
escaped the massacre and had hid, waiting for Tyson to
leave. Izarra, Andere's sister, found me before I reached
camp and told me what happened. At first I just wanted to
kill Tyson, but the execution was a direct order from OSS
HQ – my own government! What could I do? Gus, I've
never felt so helpless and so betrayed in my whole life.
There was no way I could avenge her murder. Instead I
took the chronicle back into the forest, back over to France
and into the chaos that was post-war Europe. I became one
of the disappeared.

'Since then, the others involved have all died, all except
the commanding officer himself, Tyson. One guy went mad,
one theoretically killed himself, another died suddenly of
some inexplicable disease and the last was killed in an unbelievable accident – all of them under thirty, all within four
years of the massacre. I've been hiding ever since. I'm telling
you, it's only a matter of time before they shut me up in the
same way. Now I need you to return the chronicle to Andere's
sister.'

'I don't understand, why did the US government change
their minds over supporting the Basques as a means to overthrow Franco?'

'Simple. It was Roosevelt who originally ordered the
black op, then after he died and Truman met Stalin at
Potsdam the whole thinking on post-war Europe changed.
Overnight Stalin and Communism became the new threat.

They wanted to destroy the operation before it got politically embarrassing.'

Jimmy took a sip of the whisky then doubled over, his eyes watering. One skinny arm shot out as he steadied himself.

'Easy.' August helped him down onto the couch, the musician's frame under his hands painfully gaunt.

'What happened, Gus?' Jimmy wheezed, staring up at him with bloodshot eyes. 'You had the strongest moral compass of all of us – when the rest of us were lost we'd always turn to you. Like a damn lighthouse you were, shining in that almighty shitstorm of a civil war.'

'C'mon, Jimmy, it wasn't just the ancient weapons, the slaughter of untrained men, it was the factionalism, all that in-fighting between the Anarchists, the Marxists, the Trotskies, the social democrats and whoever had a drum to beat. The Republican movement cannibalised itself and I lost my youth watching it.'

'Fuck you, I saved your life and you ain't even living it,' Jimmy retorted, softly.

August flinched, he was right.

The musician leaned over and put his hand on August's arm.

'Look, I know what you'll be risking by going back into Franco's Spain. But the chronicle's worth it. It has properties you'd understand better than me.'

'Properties?'

Jimmy looked over at the chronicle. In the lamplight the embossed gold-leafed symbol on the cover seemed to be glowing. 'It's like it's possessed. Oh, I know it has all the history of Andere's death for me, but it's something else, something far older, far more haunting. Eight years and every day the presence of the damn thing in my mind seemed to grow, like it was trying to propel me into action. It's like holding a life and a death in your hands and it's started to scare me. Sometimes I think it might have something to do with the fact that I am dying now. The book's got a soul, a story, and it wants that story told now. I'm telling you, Gus, you're the man to crack it.'

2

The musician lay sleeping on August's couch, his snore a faint drone that washed in and out of the room. He'd asked August to wake him by midday – Jimmy intended to return to Paris that evening, and it was only when August reassured him that he would wake him on the very hour that Jimmy had finally relaxed enough to fall instantly asleep. As August looked down at his aged face, the skin grey in illness, it was easy to see how fine a veil lay between life and death in the musician. 'Sleep well, old friend,' August murmured, after laying an old blanket over him, then walked over to the window. Staring out, he wondered whether the flat was being watched, and the idea unsettled him. He couldn't afford the surveillance, and it was hard not to feel ambivalent about his old comrade's unexpected visit. August lifted another cigarette to his mouth then, searching for his Zippo lighter, slipped a hand into his dressing gown pocket and discovered a piece of paper and a single gold and amber earring. He unfolded the paper – on it were a couple of lines written in Russian and framed by quotation marks, with the name 'Yolanta' scrawled in English beneath. She must have done it last night, when he was sleeping. There was only a smattering of words he recognised from the little Russian he knew – 'blood', 'river', 'my heart' ... it looked like poetry. How Russian to leave a poem after a one-night stand, he thought, wryly wondering if it was worth translating.

On the other side of the room Jimmy stirred in his sleep and turned on his side. August glanced over, thankful when he stayed sleeping, then held the earring up to the light. Suspended in the amber was a tiny insect, its bulbous eyes seeming to stare out at August, the veined filigree of its two tiny wings visible through the smoky gold of the stone. The insect's drowned flight reminded him of how in some profound way his own existence hung suspended, unexamined and unresolved since Spain, since Charlie's death. He'd been so successful in burying the past, losing himself in the daily drama of navigating a life, but now Jimmy's arrival had upended all his meticulous reinvention.

Perturbed, August sat down at the battered campaign desk set under the window and pulled open a drawer to take out a small cardboard box. Inside were a dozen single earrings he'd collected over the past five years, twelve nights of transient intimacy with women he'd made a point of never seeing again. But every one of them had left his bed with the same fragment of history that echoed in all his nightmares – the memory of walking Charlie out into the forest, the terrible small talk that barely veiled August's own bright fear while his revolver burned in his pocket.

August could only remember so far, to the point where they reached the ravine. The rest was too traumatic to recall. But it had made him a murderer, whether or not an army or a set of beliefs or an order had legitimised such an action. August lived with the belief he had killed his friend. This was what he'd never been able to tell Cecily, nor any other woman he'd truly loved. *This is mine – my minotaur trapped in the labyrinth.*

He put the letter in the drawer, then the amber earring into the box, and closed the lid. Turning back to the chronicle, August pulled the old brass lamp over and switched it on. Under the yellowish light the age of the book was clearly apparent. The vellum was etched with minute cracks and under the heat of the light bulb it now started to emit a musky sweet smell, almost like a perfume. August lifted it to his face and sniffed. It was like a woman urging him into a dangerous seduction, impossible to resist, but fatal to surrender. He hesitated, then reached into a drawer and pulled out a pair of cotton gloves he always used when handling old documents. After slipping them on he carefully opened the chronicle. As he surveyed the pages he noticed that the last page was missing, torn out – in a hurry, judging from the appearance of the frayed spine. August glanced back through the chronicle searching for some clue as to whether this had been deliberate sabotage. There was none.

The first page was covered in an urgent floral scroll, of notes beside sketches of herbs. Most of the paragraphs had been written in an archaic Spanish but some were in what August guessed was Euskara, the language of the Basques. A flower had been drawn at the top of the first page. A carnation in blood red, the frills of its petals delicately etched. Under it ran several paragraphs in Spanish. Translating as he read, August understood the book to be a seventeenth-century standard text on the medical and spiritual uses of the herbs of the Iberian Peninsula.

The carnation is often red. Red is the colour of blood, of anger and sometimes found in the threads of the brown robe of the Dominicans.

Too bland.

There was something about the prose that was too banal, too obvious – it was almost allegorical in its simplicity.

August lifted up a magnifying glass that he kept on the desk and examined the paper. It appeared to have an uneven thickness, heavier towards the middle. The surface looked waxy. Around him the temperature in the flat dropped another degree, the edges of the window now misting. Absorbed in study, August noticed nothing. He reached into another drawer and pulled out a sheaf of almost translucent paper, a small roller and an inkpad. He placed one piece of paper over a page of the chronicle, making sure the fine paper overlapped the edge slightly to ensure he didn't damage it. He then inked the roller and, with painstakingly slow strokes – almost caresses – drew the roller over the page, covering the paper. Immediately, tiny ornate handwriting appeared in negative, almost as if a spider, its feet dipped in white, were dancing wildly across the paper, trailing the text behind it.

Running down the left side was a column of paragraphs, and opposite it a picture of a small landscape drawn with almost anatomical detail – it was somewhere between a map and a sketch. He peered closer, both through the magnifying glass and with his naked eye.

Latin. He was sure of it. As a classicist, August found it easy to recognise the letters – even in mirror form. He removed the inked paper, making sure he didn't get any of the ink onto the original chronicle. Then, after placing a blank page over the inked sheet, he took a pressing. Now he had the reverse image of the writing. It stared up at him – no longer an incomprehensible jumble. Translating the first line, August read out loud, his words blooming like exotic flora against the dullness of the heavy wooden panelling and yellowing wallpaper of the studio flat:

This is the chronicle of Shimon Ruiz de Luna – Alchemist and Physic of ancient ways – his account of his search of a great treasure – a great mystical gift that could change the future of mankind itself. 7th of November, in the cursed town of Logroño, in the year of our Lord 1610.

The drawing opposite the writing appeared to be that of a cave, the entrance of which looked like a dark mysterious mouth. Small arrows indicated how it was hidden in a forest clearing in a valley surrounded by mountains. A scrawled Christian cross pointed to a holy shrine beside the cave – no doubt an early medieval attempt to Christianise a sacred site that was both ancient and pagan, August noted, familiar with the appropriation of such sites from his studies. The language was fascinating, drenched in arcane references and symbolism, while the personality of the physic – a Shimon Ruiz de Luna – shone out from the descriptions. He appeared a passionate young man convinced that the chronicle was of great importance. A desperate urgency ran through his prose and August had the distinct impression Ruiz de Luna was someone running as well as discovering, someone in great danger.

As August read, the shadowy outline of the alchemist seemed to form in the dim light of the room. Narrow-shouldered, the gaunt angles of his aquiline face catching the light, the eyes burning into August's back, the ghost leaned forward anxiously, pleading to be heard finally. Sensing the presence, August didn't dare look up, despite his professed atheism. He felt gripped by an urgency directed by some unseen power.

Over the next hour he inked up the first chapter of the chronicle, until he felt he had enough comprehensible pages at least to get a grasp of the book. Tired of the painstaking

process and eager to immerse himself in the actual translation, he clipped the pages together in order so that he had a
mirror of the chronicle itself, then turned back to the first
page. There would be time to translate the rest of the chronicle over the next few days, he consoled himself.

It appeared to be a diary, beginning with Shimon Ruiz de
Luna's own introduction and account of his expulsion from
his hometown of Córdoba. The diarist was prolific, his
thoughts tumbled on to the page, and August skipped forward, rapt. Later on in the chapter the tone seemed to
change as Ruiz de Luna started to record his search for a
secret place, somewhere in the Basque country. This new
urgency of the author began to take over his writing.
Intrigued, August stopped to wonder how the chronicle
related to the family of La Leona, turning the date over and
over in his mind – there was something strangely familiar
about it.

Suddenly, he remembered. He went to a pile of books
stacked in the corner of the room below a bookshelf groaning
with papers and hardbacks. Crouching, he found the reference book he was looking for – one he'd purchased in an old
bookshop in Barcelona in 1938, on one of his rare R & R
breaks from the Abraham Lincoln Brigade. The title of the
book was embossed neatly into the plain cloth cover: *Brujas
y la Inquisición*. He flicked through and found the chapter on
auto de fe. There it was – the *auto de fe* of Logroño took place
on the 7th of November 1610.

*There is an argument that many of the old pagan beliefs of the
Basques could be conveniently interpreted as witchcraft when
seen through a Christian paradigm. Indeed there is a mountain
god – Basajaun – described as a hairy man who lives on the
forested slope of the mountains and sometimes depicted as a*

half-man, half-goat – very much in the style of Pan or Satan himself. There is also Sugaar – a snake god who is the sometime companion to Mari, the supreme female goddess in the Basque pantheon. Mari herself is rumoured to manifest in a ball of fire and is seen shooting through the sky from mountain top to mountain top. In the hysteria of the Inquisition and its propensity for witch-hunting, it was easy for the Spanish to equate Basque pantheism with sorcery – especially as the animosity between the Spanish and the Basque peoples was centuries old, and many of the isolated village communities spoke only Euskara, giving great scope for misunderstanding between them and the Inquisition forces. The auto de fe of Logroño was initiated by the return of a peasant, a Maria de Ximildegi, to her tiny remote mountain village, Zugarramurdi. Whatever motivated the young girl to voluntarily confess she had become a witch, the results were both fatal and disastrous for the tiny community.

The first to be arrested was a twenty-two-year-old Maria de Juretegia and her husband who Ximildegi accused of participating in the sabbath, a kind of mass orgy. Juretegia denied it but Ximildegi's graphic descriptions of sexual congress with a goat, of women smearing their chests with herbal paste and flying to the field where the sabbath took place were so convincing that she was believed. To save herself, Juretegia in turn denounced her aunt and her aunt's eighty-year-old sister – described as the queen witch of the village. At this point the matter would have been resolved if the Inquisition had not been informed. But a year later the Inquisition arrested four supposed witches and a Euskara translator. Many other arrests followed and the confessions (given under torture) were as graphic and extreme as the accuseds' imaginations – sorcery that enabled them to pass through walls and small holes, orgies, cannibalism and extraordinary rituals involving witches' familiars. By the time of the auto de fe in 1610, within Logroño a total of thirty-one witches were accused (only nine had confessed and already thirteen had perished in jail), and the rest who refused to confess would be burned at the stake. But the Inquisition had also condemned a further twenty-two for heresy – six of Judaism, one of Islam, one of Lutheranism, twelve of heretical utterances and two of impersonating agents of the Inquisition.

The crack of an icicle breaking off outside broke August's concentration. He was suddenly acutely aware of being observed. Had Jimmy's paranoia infected him? If it was true the US government wanted to suppress all knowledge of Operation Lizard and the massacre at the village, Jimmy would still be on their radar, but would they have really sent an assassin to kill him – a female one at that? August picked up the pendant Jimmy had thrown onto the coffee table. The design of the strange copper star was familiar. He studied it under the lamplight. It was a six-pointed star that if drawn would not be made of two triangles, but rather one continuous line. Abruptly, it came to August – it was a unicursal hexagram, a design that had occult connections, a curious choice for a CIA assassin, he noted. Either way, weakened by illness, Jimmy was an easy target. Had August been naive in letting him stay? He had his own secrets to hide.

He glanced up towards the window, at the band still visible running below the edge of the pulled blind. Just then something travelled across that band, a flicker of movement. He sprung up and pulled the blind open.

A large raven was perched on the sill outside, its beady eye to one side as it stared into the room. For a moment man and bird confronted each other, then in a whirl of feathers it was gone. August swung back to face Jimmy, still sleeping, one arm now flung across his face, oblivious to the world around him. Was the musician deluded? One thing was for sure, the chronicle he'd kept for all those years would be perceived as being invaluable to the right collector. That alone made it a dangerous artefact. But there was the moral issue of returning it. Jimmy had made a promise to La Leona and he had also saved August's life – after the murder and betrayal of Leona and her men, returning the chronicle was the least he could do. Suddenly, August knew he had to get it back to Spain. With a shiver, he realised that the apartment was freezing. He threw on an old cardigan over his dressing gown and went into the bathroom.

The bathroom, although small, also functioned as a dark-room. August used photography as a way of archiving his visual research – especially his fieldwork. A wide wooden board lay propped across the rickety chipped bath, upon which August stored his developing trays and chemicals. Overhead slung from wall to wall were lengths of cord from which he would peg the drying photographs and wet rolls of negatives. The enlarger – a machine that looked a little like a large microscope and a vertical projector – was tucked up against the side of the toilet. And an infrared light bulb – which when switched on would plunge the room into a sub-terranean dimly lit netherworld – hung down next to the normal light fitting on the ceiling. A stop clock was perched on top of the white tank of the toilet, the position of which had never failed to amuse Cecily.

August caught sight of himself in the cabinet mirror. He looked drawn. 'What do you expect after a collision with the past, four hours sleep and being left,' he told his reflection as he rubbed the two-day stubble on his chin. With a sigh he opened the cabinet, revealing an old bottle of cologne, a row of plastic canisters containing undeveloped film, a packet of

French letters, a badger-hair shaving brush and a round bar
of shaving soap. He filled the sink with the last of the hot
water and began lathering up. The least he could do was
shave. He was interrupted by the sharp ringing of his alarm
clock – it was midday already and time to wake Jimmy.

3

Damien Tyson stared out of the hotel room in the Madrid Ritz hotel that had served as his office for the past few months. A view devoid of people, a panorama of rectangles, horizontals and verticals, of shuttered windows, rooftops and ornate ironwork, it created a mathematical grid, a rhythm in his head he found soothing. It took him away, allowing him to focus all his intelligence into one searing point, as precise as a weapon. The CIA operative had much to think about. First there were the secret negotiations he'd been setting up – the careful courtship and angling of the Spanish generals, even of Generalissimo Franco himself, on behalf of his country. Then there was the security issue. As an agent who'd had extensive experience in the region, he'd been sent to oversee and facilitate secret talks between the US and Spanish military personnel. It was now late April, the US general – yet to be named – was due to arrive in July and Tyson had nearly all the parts in place. There was to be a deal – a military pact – one that would finance Franco's regime and benefit the US for decades to come. The fact that such a deal would be breaking a UN embargo imposed on fascist Spain did not concern Tyson. For him there was no morality, just opportunity and a cold fascination with power – one he'd had his whole life. He glanced down at the page of parchment he held in his hand, a gift from one of the Spanish generals, Cesar Molivio, an old friend who shared a couple of propensities – apart from a love of a certain violence. The parchment was a sixteenth-century letter from a Jewish kabbalist in Cadiz to a Dutch occultist in Leyden – you couldn't accuse the general of lacking taste, whatever you might think of his sadistic tendencies, Tyson observed, amused. Hidden in a paragraph was a sentence that he found himself returning to again and again:

> *In relation to your query about 'Los ojos de Dios', the original document is rumoured to be in possession of an old family in Córdoba, conversos, who guard it like it is a great treasure, which, in the right hands, it would indeed prove to be . . .*

He was interrupted by the sound of the telex machine in the corner whirling into action as it punched out a message. After carefully slipping the parchment back into its folder and locking it in a desk drawer, he walked over to the machine and tore off the telex that had appeared.

> 'Long-standing suspect on list Jimmy van Peters has resurfaced in England, passport number reported in Dover two days ago. Request command. Repeat request command.'

He smiled, marvelling at the synchronicity of two seemingly unlinked events – the letter and now this, an old foe re-emerging. A slow burn began to unfurl at the pit of his stomach, it was like a hunger – a gnawing excitement that

made him feel gloriously sharp, gloriously predatory again.
After tearing the telex into indiscernible pieces, he picked
up the telephone and booked a flight to London.

The engine was dead, so August pushed the heavy Triumph
Trophy down onto the tarmac and began running the motorcycle down the tree-lined street. As it putted into spluttering
life, he swung himself onto the seat and roared off, the cold
air swirling around his goggles and face. Calculating the
amount of petrol he had left, he reasoned he had enough to
get to the library at London University situated at the back
of Russell Square Gardens. He'd seen Jimmy off earlier that
day, in an emotional farewell, with the musician's illness
hanging over them like a cloud. Nevertheless Jimmy had
made August promise to visit him in Paris after returning the
chronicle, saying August could always find him at the jazz
cellar he used to play in the Latin Quarter. But August
sensed neither of them believed they would see each other
again. A verse from a song the International Brigade would
sing about the Battle of Jarama kept sounding out in his
head:

> There's a valley in Spain called Jarama,
> It's a place that we all know so well,
> For 'tis there that we wasted our manhood,
> And most of our old age as well.
> From this valley they tell us we're leaving,
> But don't hasten to bid us adieu . . .

Adieu. Looming out of the fog the lampposts flew past
August like sentries guarding their posts. Sometimes it was
like he was still there, hiding in some mud-filled foxhole
waiting for the mist to lift from a field, waiting for death. *Did*

I ever really come back from Spain? Or is this whole existence some imagined projection taking place in the time it has taken for a fascist bayonet to pierce my heart? Sometimes it was hard for him to believe he survived, to keep a grip on reality. 'The whole world a dream beamed into my mind by a malicious demon' – Descartes' quote was his favourite as a student. Then he'd found it liberating, now he yearned for a simpler mind, a simpler life. *Damn you, Jimmy, what have you begun?*

He passed a bus and wove his way west through Kensington. There were still gaping holes between the buildings, many of which remained boarded up – bombed-out vacant lots, the legacy of the war, playgrounds of ragged-trousered children shouting wildly and pelting each other with snowballs.

August swerved around a cart and horse as a rag and bone man in a battered cap and overcoat atop yelled, 'Any old iron!' optimistically.

Britain was on its knees, reeling from an economy that had failed to redefine itself after the industry of the Second World War, a nation now deep in debt to the United States and a power that had yet to admit its hold on the colonial world was rapidly becoming symbolic – Britannia was floundering on the rocks. Churchill had been re-elected in 1951, swing bands had returned to the concert halls and the Festival of Britain had been opened on South Bank for the last eighteen months, offering some respite to the frugality and grimness of the last decade, but in reality little had changed since the war. Itinerant tribes of the unemployed – the returned soldiers – wandered the city streets. You could still see these men walking in threadbare overcoats, trying to conceal the newspaper in their shoes, looking hopefully at every corner shop notice board, perplexity and disappointment marking their faces – was this the utopia they fought to defend? It was not the world they fantasised returning to, on the ships, in the air, in the trenches, not remotely. Everything was drab, the clothes, the shops, the grocery shelves with their rows of canned rationed food: Spam, sardines, powdered milk, broken only by the occasional locally grown tomato or apple. Only in Mayfair and Piccadilly was it possible to see imported luxury items brightening up store displays, on New Bond Street, like Christmas lights, outrageously overpriced for most. The last time August could remember attending a large party full of brightly dressed people unmarked by anxiety and fear was in the late 1930s upon his return from the Spanish Civil War. Beaten and demoralised from witnessing the ravages of both Franco and Hitler, he'd been flabbergasted by the naivety and optimism of his peers, as well as Chamberlain's vacillating diplomacy. But now, after all the bloodshed and conflict, when everyone had expected a miraculous return to prosperity and hope but instead found themselves facing more rationing, more grim governance, August had secretly begun to yearn for the colour and heat of the old Spain, even the glittering jangle of the New York he remembered as a child, anything to break the relentless monotone of London. Perhaps shadows from the past had begun to claw him back.

August hadn't seen his parents and sister in America since before the war. Then it had been a question of principle, now he wasn't so sure. Was it possible for a man to divorce himself from his childhood completely, from what formed him? He used to think so, but after nine years of reinvention, the construct he'd made of himself – this benign apolitical academic whose only weakness seemed to be hedonism and rare books – had begun to fragment. The monster was pushing through. August felt it more and more – in his nightmares, when he stared into the mirror, in inexplicable emotions and rages that swept through him. Jimmy was right – he had to go back to be freed.

The imposingly tall art deco block of Senate House appeared above the mist, a monolithic white stone building that looked like it belonged more in Washington or some futuristic version of ancient Rome than here. The fact that August conducted his research in the same building that the Ministry of Information had been set up in during the war amused the American. He had given lectures at the London University and had an honorary membership to the library, and it had become his intellectual safe house. Turning the throttle, he raced towards it, hoping the searing wind might blast away the rising sense of loss he felt, despite the intrigue of the manuscript. So he had loved Cecily after all.

The reading section of the University of London library was a long rectangular auditorium filled with benches and desks, lined by dark wooden walls. The space felt older than the building itself, as if the hours of study that had occurred within its four walls had imbued it with an antiquity. The gallery above was lined with full-length windows and book-cases, while the main bulk of the library ran off the reading room in annexes of bookshelves. The large windows allowed a great pool of natural light to cascade gently down onto the leather-topped reading desks, tranquil and still. It was the kind of atmosphere August loved to work in, the hushed silence creating a timelessness in which it was possible to lay hands on a book and become submerged in the era depicted between the pages. It was seductive, and August used the library as a sanctuary.

The American was known to many of the librarians, who were happy to put aside any sixteenth- and seventeenth-century botanical texts for him. His favourite librarian, a

willowy spinster in her middle thirties, who always wore the
same black long-sleeved dress with padded shoulders and a
narrow belt, a single strand of pearls defining her class as
aspiring, sat behind the information desk.

'Mr Winthrop.' She looked up in undisguised pleasure
then smiled, the pink powder on her cheeks cracking in a
fragile prettiness. 'Is it botanical today? We were just
bequeathed an extraordinary collection of prints – some of
very rare herbs indeed.'

'Actually, I was after some information about an individual – turn of the seventeenth century, Kathleen. It's a long
shot, he was a Spaniard. A Shimon Ruiz de Luna. He
describes himself as both physic and alchemist, which is a
conceit, alchemists naturally being of an earlier era.'

'Indeed, let me look under his name first.' She pulled out
a small metal drawer and began sifting through the index
cards.

'Ruiz . . . ?'

'. . . de Luna, as in "of the moon".'

'Aha, found him – a court report of a trial – 2nd of
September, 1612.'

'A court report, an English court report?'

'Indeed, it says here, "Shimon Ruiz de Luna was to be
burned at the stake for espionage". But you should read it
yourself.'

The librarian set him up in his favourite corner of the library,
a small table, quiet and comparatively secluded, then left
him. August switched on the desk lamp and pulled the file
towards him. The sound of the rustling paper made several
readers at nearby tables look over. Within seconds August
made a psychological assessment of his fellow readers, a
trained reflex from his SOE days. There was a couple of stu-

dents, both bearded, obviously folk-music lovers, perhaps
even beatniks, August decided, guessing that their chosen
era of study would most likely be that of the French
Revolution and its fall-out across Europe. He glanced over;
appropriately one of them was reading *Rights of Man* by
Thomas Paine.

Diagonally across from them an attractive redhead was
now eyeing him flirtatiously. August, not wanting to encourage conversation or contact, smiled faintly back. Twenty-one,
undergraduate, father a banker judging by the expensive
imported clothes she was wearing, he mused, perhaps the
eldest child with no male siblings – hence her pursuit of a
career. Although she appeared to be more in the market for a
husband, he suspected. The girl, sensing his scrutiny,
blushed and dropped her gaze. Opposite her, hunched over a
pile of books, sat a man in his late thirties. He wore his hair in
a military cut and there was a gaunt severity to his posture
that August recognised instantly. A mature student, one of
the many returned servicemen, who, having missed out on an
education, had gone back to university – the campuses were
full of them. He had been the only one not to glance up at
August and despite the cheap frayed shirt and slightly stained
tweed jacket, August trusted him instantly.

Reassured that no one had followed him there, August
opened the file. Inside were the photocopied papers of the
original seventeenth-century document – the actual court
report was locked in a safe in the library's archives. He was
glad to see that the handwritten scroll was legible. On the
first page was the simple sentence 'The Court Report of the
Prosecution of Spanish Physic Shimon Ruiz de Luna.'
August's heart quickened at the name, again he had the sensation that the alchemist was leaning over him, silently
urging him on in his investigation.

This is the testimony of Justice Winch, his account of the trial and interrogation of the Spanish Hebrew Physic and self-acclaimed Alchemist Shimon Ruiz de Luna, accused of both wizardry and spying, an accusation that resulted in a guilty verdict and the execution of the same gentleman. Dated January 12th, 1613.

So Shimon Ruiz de Luna did reach England and was executed despite all his precautions in coding his chronicle, August observed, and yet Shimon's prosecutors had failed to find the chronicle – what did it contain that Ruiz de Luna felt was worth dying for? Again, August felt a strange intimacy with this mysterious Spaniard, a curious affinity, but why?

He read on, the account describing how Shimon was arrested at St Martin's-in-the-Fields after apparently trying to bribe a courtier to take a message to King James, a letter asking for a secret meeting with the monarch. This was interpreted as a potential assassination plot after the Spanish ambassador identified Ruiz de Luna as being one of the accused named in the witch trials of Logroño.

Shimon Ruiz de Luna and his Basque Catholic wife – named as the sorceress Uxue of Cabo Ogoño – were the only two who had escaped. Justice Winch's prose was dry, detailed and painfully analytical and August could imagine the frustration of the unfortunate clerk whose sole job must have been to transcribe the judge's pedantic account, the official's objectivity only serving to heighten the horror of Ruiz de Luna's torture.

When it was established the prisoner had some skills in foretelling of the future, I had the torturer follow the wisdom and proven techniques of revealing evidence of Devil worship and sorcery through the referring of such insightful works as the King's own tome – Daemonologie – *and the great Germanic text* The Malleus Maleficarum. *This involved dunking and the placing of hot irons in the areas of the body where marks of the Devil are said to be seen – the armpit, genitals and the soles of the feet … the first iron was applied to the inside of the upper arm, an area known to display flesh marks and other unusual bodily growths that are a sign of the Devil. The prisoner, tied at the time to the wheel, did scream most loudly and yet refused to surrender any further evidence of his satanic practices.*

August froze, his fingers now gripping the side of the table. *No, not now, not here.* His rattling heart quickened his breath and a sickening panic swept through him. He closed his eyes and the face of an older man, with dark eyes and hair, flashed through his mind, the man's patronising smile and apologetic air a brutal contrast to the searing pain August felt: fingers broken over the edge of a metal table, urine and blood pooling around his chair, wires crossing his lacerated torso, the distinctive acrid smell of curing leather, the soft murmur of Spanish, himself hovering high up in the room looking down at a naked man being tortured, then the terrifying realisation that he was that man. The cellar of a leather factory, Madrid, 1937. The memories were all there, under the surface of his waking mind. *I will never escape them. Breathe, breathe yourself back into the moment.*

August focused his gaze on the most ordinary, most prosaically anchoring object he could find – a pencil, sitting on the desk opposite, a blue pencil, its end neatly sharpened, ready for use. *Forget, forget, you are in a library, you are safe.* But his body, ignoring him, began to burn – at the back of his neck, the soles of his feet, his testicles – all the places where the fascists had attached the electrodes. He closed his eyes and tried escaping into a pleasant childhood memory – night fishing in the Massachusetts Bay with his father, under a high yellow moon, the silent rhythmic activity of hauling the nets in, one of their only truces. *I will not be dictated to by the past, I will not.* He took one last shuddering breath, and willed the face of his torturer General Molivio away.

Embarrassed, he glanced across the reading room – no one seemed to have noticed his sudden lapse of concentration, no one except the ex-serviceman who was now staring over at him. August caught his gaze and knew immediately that the man had recognised August's symptoms, the telltale tremors, the clenched hands as if the whole world were unexpectedly lurching. The ex-serviceman paused over his page as if waiting for August to ask for help. August shook his head almost imperceptibly. Tactfully, the ex-serviceman looked back down at his book.

August returned to his reading.

In past interrogation I have found torture to be of remarkable effect and have witnessed countless witches' and wizards' confessions when these techniques are applied. But in the case of Shimon Ruiz de Luna, the accused remained stoic and uncooperative.

The accused displayed remarkable foolishness in that he hath refused to give up the name of the devil he worshipped nor any witch accomplices he might hath had congress with. Instead he was heard to utter one name and one name only over and over. A name I can only assume was of a fellow Hebrew, an Elazar ibn Yehuda. The utterance was almost a chant and indeed the first time the accused uttered this name I hath misheard him and hath thought he said Beelzebub and was summoning Satan himself. This was the cause of some fright and mishap but I hath recovered myself and sent men to find this Elazar or at least some information. They found none and yet upon further ques-

tioning the accused would not give up further information. Unfortunately, he then fell into a fever and was no use to me from then on.

The account then went onto to describe Ruiz de Luna's trial that, to August, sounded like a sham, rustled up quickly to ensure the Spaniard was executed as a spy and not a wizard. Reading between the lines, he assumed this final charge was to send a message to King Philip III of Spain, but there was one footnote August was particularly interested in. It described how King James himself had a secret meeting with the prisoner on the way to the gallows in the hope Ruiz de Luna would surrender up his methodology and tell the monarch how he had come to his accurate predictions of the future. According to Justice Winch's account, the King had insisted there would be no record of the conversation between king and alchemist.

It were on the fourth day of his imprisonment and before my interrogation hath begun that, to my great surprise, King James himself, requested a secret audience with the prisoner. The only witnesses to this audience were the Earl of Northampton and myself. The King, as flabbergasted as ourselves as to how this young Physic had prior knowledge of great battles and events, was determined he hath used sorcery or perhaps some great magical secret that heralded from Biscay, and sought to secure a confession. The prisoner offered up neither, claiming he had come to the King to prevent a great war from occurring in the future. Thereby the King declared the prisoner's first charge to be that of a spy, the second of wizard and that he should burn. He then, grim-faced, departed as empty-handed as he hath arrived ... 'twas maybe just as well, for, I wager, whatever the prisoner was concealing was not a Christian secret.

Again the mention of a great secret. Did the chronicle contain such a thing? If August was to decode it, trace Ruiz de Luna's journey, perhaps even find the very object he appeared to be looking for and tried to warn the English about, such a subject would finally secure August's academic reputation. It was a seductive thought. August turned back to his reading.

After the body was pronounced dead, I ensured that the charred remains be collected to be buried in an unmarked grave away from a churchyard or any other sacred ground, as is the custom of those executed for sorcery. However, as the body was being transported, a highwayman held up the cart. To the astonishment of the coach driver, the highwayman demanded only the remains of the condemned and nothing further. This confounded me greatly and I took it upon myself to question the driver personally. All he could say was that the highwayman was of small stature, masked and hooded, and spoke in a foreign accent, and that he was, however, mightily convincing with a pistol. Therefore I regret

August turned the page. Instead of the final page of the account, there was a blank page with a note attached that read, 'Last page missing from original document – never found.' Like the chronicle, the last page was missing. He gazed down, pondering the fate of the mysterious seventeenth-century physic. He shut the file – if anyone knew anything about Elazar ibn Yehuda and his significance to Shimon's story it would be August's great mentor and old Classics professor. He glanced at his watch. It had been many years since he last saw the professor but he knew if he moved swiftly, he would be able to catch the professor before his customary afternoon stroll in Regent's Park. As soon as August stood up to leave there was the slam of a door somewhere above him in the gallery.

'By Christ, it's good to see you, Winthrop. Unusually cold for this time of year, come in and take your wets off. I've often wondered what happened to my most brilliant protégé.' Professor Julian Copps ushered August into the elegant high-ceilinged reception room of his apartment, part of John Nash's neo-classical Park Crescent, which encircled Regent's Park. August was pleased to see that the apartment had managed to survive the hardships of the war and was still resplendent with an array of art deco and Victorian furnishings. The professor, a tall stooped man in his late seventies, his face peppered with sunspots earned on countless expeditions in the Middle East, walked with a cane, having lost a leg below the knee in an accident as a younger man – an incident that had led to various outrageous undergraduate myths around the event. As the professor led August into a narrow but spacious sitting room that had a line of windows each framing a view of the park, his characteristic limp sent August straight back to the tutorials of his early twenties.

'Just in time for tea, you will take tea, won't you?' Without waiting for an answer, the aged academic pointed with his cane to a small Regency armchair by a marble fireplace. 'The guest chair is there.'

'I went to fight in Spain, remember?' August ventured, cowed slightly by the professor's authoritarian manner. He took off his leather jacket, hung it over the back of the chair then sunk down in the seat, noting regretfully that he was now lower than Copps, who, after ringing a servant's bell, had taken a higher chair opposite. *I have become the stuttering rookie again, in awe of his intellect.*

'Well, naturally Spain was a good cause, but talk about a brilliant career suffocated in the cradle. Because that's what you did, Winthrop, you committed academic suicide before you'd even given yourself a chance. And after all that sacrifice, Mr Franco won, didn't he?' Copps rang the bell again, then got up in frustration. 'Mrs O'Brien, two teas, both white with the option of sugar, and I mean real sugar!' he yelled through the door, then sighing, returned to his seat.

'There was the other war – lots of men lost their education,' August said.

'Now that war had to be fought. Besides, Winthrop, you were not lots of men. You could have had it all, the chalice of an academic post. There was only one other boy as gifted as you in your year ... Charles ...'

'... Stanwick.' *Jesus, I was hoping he wouldn't remember Charlie, but of course he does.*

'That's right, Stanwick. You two were as thick as thieves, weren't you? Feisty chap. Quite brilliant. What happened to him?'

'Charlie died.' Not wanting to elaborate, August was curt. Again he felt the shadow of Charlie's unlived life running parallel to his own, the guilt and drive to make something of his in some strange compensation. *My ghost brother, the hangman's card.*

'So many of them have, a whole generation ripped away from their natural destinies. But you, August, you were one of the golden ones, despite the unfortunate mishap of your nationality ... Oh well, I suppose one can't help where one's born ... Although we are at the dawn of the great American empire it has to be said and like all great empires it will have its colonies, its outposts, its conquests and terrible defeats. It will be everywhere, not just in Korea; you mark my words, young man.'

The housekeeper, a portly woman in a floral housecoat and headscarf, appeared with a tray covered with a teapot, two cups and a plate of biscuits. Without a word she placed it rattlingly down on a small side table then left.

'I shall play mother. Milk, Winthrop?'

'Please.'

The professor poured milk from a small gilt-edged jug into a teacup, then handed it to August and they both sat, the cups balanced on their knees, the sunlight finally reaching the edge of the carpet. He offered August the plate of sandy-coloured homemade biscuits. Not wanting to appear rude, August took one then hid it on the saucer behind his cup while he watched the professor dip his own biscuit into his tea. The biscuit re-emerged soggy then surrendered, crumbling back into the pallid liquid. Professor Copps sighed. 'Sorry about the biscuits, it's the blasted rationing. Mrs O'Brien has been reduced to baking our own. Not the same without the butter. You were saying?'

August glanced at the older academic. In his day, Professor Copps had been considered the brightest and most erudite of his peers. A world authority on Arabic and Jewish history, he was regularly consulted by both governments and kings. But that had been twenty years ago, and time appeared not to have been kind to the academic, whose hands shook and who now, August noticed, peered shortsightedly through pebble-thick glasses.

'I wasn't,' August answered, quietly, not wanting to offend.

The overweight cocker spaniel curled at the professor's feet growled in its sleep then broke wind, and the two men sat there pretending it hadn't happened. Somewhere else in the flat a clock chimed.

'Quite. Well, my young man, now we are in peacetime

and what do you intend to do about it? A man's future is now stretched out in front of him unhindered – well, at least at the moment. Isn't it time to return to things that matter?'

'That's why I'm here. After years of research I think I've stumbled upon something that could resurrect my academic career. Something potentially extraordinary.'

As if to steel himself the professor poured another cup of tea and prodded the small dog with one foot. The dog awoke. Copps fed him the remains of a soggy biscuit then watched the animal trot off good-naturedly only to take up another sleeping position in front of the small coal fire.

'As long as you don't mention the words "The lost city of Atlantis" or "Alexander's tomb". You'll be amazed at the number of amateur archaeologists who come knocking at my door. I don't think I have the patience to substantiate another ridiculous treasure hunt.'

'This has nothing to do with Alexander the Great or Atlantis.'

'Thank God.'

'There's a philosopher, perhaps a physic, I'm trying to trace the history of – probably seventeenth-century Spain. An Elazar ibn Yehuda.'

Copps looked up, a tremor seemed to run through his body and the teacup and saucer tipped from his knees, tumbling down to the carpet. As if on cue the dog trotted over and began licking up the pooling tea. 'How do you know this name?' His changed voice was urgent and far more alert. Suddenly, it occurred to August that Copps's dithering might all have been an act masking a far sharper and unchanged intelligence. But why would the professor conceal his intellect? *Should I trust him? I have no reason not to.*

'I found it in a chronicle I've received. The name was

linked with another man, a Shimon Ruiz de Luna, who was executed in 1613.'

As if biding his time to formulate a response, Copps leaned down and rescued the teacup. Getting up slowly, he placed it back onto the small side table and shuffled over to the large Regency windows. He stayed there, looking out at the lattice of naked branches laden with melting snow.

'Elazar ibn Yehuda was not of the seventeenth century but from a far earlier period than that,' the professor finally replied, ponderously. 'He was a Jewish physician attached to the court of Caliph Al-Walid, who was made the ruler of the Iberian Peninsula in AD 711.'

'Hence the Spanish connection.'

'Perhaps. Elazar ibn Yehuda was part of the military expedition led by the infamous Tariq ibn Ziyad – invader of Spain and defeater of King Roderick of the Goths. Tariq got almost as far as the Pyrenees but then he was beaten off by the Basques.'

The professor turned back to August. There was a new vivacity to his countenance as well as an anguish. 'What do you know of the reputation of Yehuda?'

'Nothing. I'd never heard of him until this morning.' *This morning.* Already it felt as if his life had accelerated into an unexpected but exciting detour. For the first time in months nothing felt predictable. Trepidation stirred in him like a bud unfurling into leaf. *I am alive again.*

The professor, reading his face, sighed heavily. 'My dear young man, I fear someone is drawing you into a web.'

The comment only excited August further.

'Mind if I smoke?'

'Not at all, I have my pipe. As I have given up women and bridge, I consider it the last of my vices.' Copps smiled indulgently.

'Bridge I've yet to discover but the other two I know well – to my detriment,' August joked.

He pulled out the packet of Lucky Strikes and lit one up, exhaling then studying the older man before him. Since the estrangement from his father, there had been few mentors in his life. Professor Copps had been one, Jimmy van Peters another – of an entirely different calibre but one August felt had also understood his true nature; more than that – accepted it, and that had been rare in the American's life.

'Professor, I fought in Spain because of what I believed in, but to be frank, by the time the Second World War came around I knew I just liked the combat, the strategising. I guess that's why I went into the SOE. It's more than an addiction – it became a philosophy, not knowing if you would live to see another hour, another sunrise. It pins your mind back so that you absorb everything around you like it's going be the last thing you see. I guess you could call it the ultimate existentialism. Since I've returned to civilian life everything is a series of greys, of goddamn monochrome.

'Now someone has asked me to return an antiquity to Spain, to the family to whom it belongs. As a listed member of the International Brigade, I risk execution if I go back, but you know what, I would welcome it. This antiquity, this chronicle, is the key to a puzzle I mean to solve. It could be the adventure that just might save my soul.' He leaned back in the armchair, embarrassed by the grandeur of his own words. *Copps knows me, knows what I was once, how high my dreams went. The arrogant Icarus, the world at his feet.*

The academic sucked on his pipe, the intensity with which he gripped it giving away his true emotions. He had been fond of the boy, had seen his younger self in him once, the burnished mirror of possibility, and didn't want to see him sacrificed before his time. But the man is naive, suicidally so, the professor thought, while keeping his expression tight and bland.

'Be careful. Remember Aristotle said, "Fear is pain rising from the anticipation of evil."'

'Yes, but Mark Twain said, "Do the thing you fear the most and death of fear is certain",' August countered.

'Personally, I've always regarded caution as a most underrated emotion, a philosophy that has served me well, until now that is.'

August realised that the conversation had digressed entirely from the original question. Was the professor skilfully evading his query? If so, why?

'Elazar ibn Yehuda, what else do you know about him?'

Copps turned back to the window. After nervously glancing at the street, he pulled down the wooden shutters, plunging the room into a twilight. He moved to the fireplace and stirred at the burning coals with a poker.

'Yehuda was considered one of the greatest physicians of his era. The Caliph had been reluctant to let him join General Tariq's invading army but Yehuda was anxious for medical resources, and he was convinced the expedition would take him into territories that would provide wonderful new herbs, plants and trees he could use in his practices. He persuaded his benefactor and left with Tariq and his men. But halfway through the great invasion Yehuda changed. He began to neglect his medical duties and became obsessed by the possible existence of a great treasure he was convinced would unleash itself upon humanity – either condemning it or saving it, depending on how the great gift was used.'

'Did he literally mean treasure?'

'You have to understand that Yehuda was also what we would consider nowadays somewhat of a kabbalist, a follower of the early Jewish mystic text the *Sefer Yetzirah* – roughly translated as the "Book of Creation". And he was a disciple of the fourth-century great Greek philosopher and herbalist Bolus of Mendes. He also deferred to Al-Birum's *Tahfim*, which was one of the great grimoires of its day. All of this meant Elazar ibn Yehuda would have had a huge under-standing of the mystic and magical properties of plants. When Yehuda wrote "great treasure", I understood him to mean more – *a great spiritual or magical gift, an unnatural power from God* – and here he referred to both Allah and Yahweh.'

'Did he find the treasure?'

'I'm not entirely sure Yehuda hadn't simply gone a little mad – after all, the horrors he must have witnessed alongside Tariq's ruthless invasion beggar the imagination. However, when the Caliph demanded to see this great treasure, Elazar ibn Yehuda claimed it had been stolen from him. And natu-rally the Caliph, believing this a convenient excuse not to hand over the treasure, had the physician put to death – end of story. Except that through the centuries the story seems to have snowballed in its authority. There have been several fanatic movements and individuals over time that have per-ished searching for the treasure and there are still people looking today; dangerous, deluded and willing to go to any measure to solve the mystery.'

Outside, they heard the sound of a car horn and the faint ringing of church bells.

'You should be careful, dear boy. It would be stupid to throw one's life away after surviving so much.'

'I'm far too sensible for that.' August threw his cigarette into the fire. 'Can you remember the exact dates of Yehuda's life?'

'Hard to forget, I was fascinated by him for two whole years – a lifetime ago now, of course. AD 670 to 725. He was executed in Constantinople.'

Standing on his balcony, Copps wrapped his old cardigan around him and shivered as he watched August climb onto the motorcycle and drive off into the thick afternoon smog that had descended. Winthrop had been one of those rare students who'd displayed an early gift for imaginative lateral thinking, capable of insights that had surprised even him, who, then in his late middle age, had found himself drowning in a wellpool of disillusionment. August Winthrop had bought him hope, a renewed belief in the importance of the Classics, of its relevance to contemporary philosophy, thought and governance. Then his protégé had squandered it all by joining the International Brigade to fight with the American battalion. Noble but ultimately wasteful, the professor thought, and now in his late thirties, August still displayed the same rash idealism. He was the original haunted enthusiast, a doomed adventurer, his old mentor concluded. But did August have any idea how perilous a mission he'd just embarked upon? Did he even understand how powerful the object was that he might have in his possession? Copps doubted it. And even if he did, Copps had the uncomfortable feeling great danger would only inspire the American further.

As he watched the silvery wheel of the Triumph disappear around the sweep of the crescent he had a premonition that this would be the last time he would see August E. Winthrop. Dismissing the sensation with another shiver, he walked back into the apartment, closing the large French doors behind him, then picked up the telephone. To his faint surprise he found that he remembered the telephone number perfectly, and watching himself dial the number he tried to control his shaking hand.

'Olivia Henries.' The voice answering the telephone was hers, the same rich alto, the same slightly ironic inflection that always suggested profound intelligence, the same voice that he always used to find so erotic – but what he found even more disturbing was that she sounded exactly as she did thirty years ago.

Back in the studio flat in Kensington August pulled off his motorcycle helmet and searched his leather jacket for a spare shilling. He found one stuck in the lining, sandwiched between an old book of matches marked with the insignia of a jazz bar he occasionally frequented and a stale cigarette. He breathed out; it was so cold in the flat his breath misted. Stomping his feet and rubbing his hands to stay warm, he stepped out into the corridor and slipped the shilling into his gas meter. There were some luxuries he could do without – chocolate, nice soap, cologne, Jack Daniels – but not heat or cigarettes. Yet even he was tiring of the constant lack of things, a state of affairs that seemed ongoing since the end of the war. He had to face the fact that freelancing as a would-be writer and academic was beginning to lose its appeal. As they had before, the faint charms of the civil service beckoned like a middle-aged harpy on a rock, threatening to dash all his dreams.

Kneeling, August lit the gas fire. He liked being in the dark. It made him feel invisible and somehow more integral to the environment around him, whether it be forest, savannah or house. It was a trick he'd learned fighting, a way of momentarily stepping out of the chaos and conflict around him. Many times he had stood in the dark leaning against a tree to gaze down upon a burning village, preserving his sanity only by willing himself to be without thought – nothing but his senses pinned back as sharp as the night around him.

The sight of blue-green flames spluttering into life pulled him back into the room. He squatted down on his heels watching the fire flicker up. There hadn't been a message slipped under the door from Cecily. He'd half-expected one, it wasn't the first time she'd left him, but this time had felt different. Finite. *Have I lost her? Have I?* He'd never seen her so angry or distressed. Why had he slept with the Russian girl? He hadn't meant to, but she'd been beautiful and transporting – she'd broken through the grey, for a moment. The charm of the hollow man: the chase, the sex, the distraction, it filled him, at least long enough to forget what he'd become.

Could he stop? Perhaps not, at least not until he stopped running. Maybe this trip back to Spain would change him, but then he wasn't the same man he was before the war – he never would be; to try would be like catching at mirages.

Enough. He knew if he kept staring into the flames analysing the stupidity of his actions he would fall into a deep depression and he had better things to think about. He got up and switched on the desk lamp.

She stood in his doorway, her long hair still russet but she had thickened around the waist. By Copps's calculations she must be in her early fifties, even so that air of dangerous sexuality still shimmered about her, a dark vivaciousness that had always enticed and repelled.

'Hello, Severin,' she said, stepping past him in a cloud of musk. She'd used his tribal name, his secret moniker that had marked him as one of them, one of the circle.

'Olivia, still haunting I see.'

'If you're asking whether I still practise, the answer is yes,

but I think you knew that, why else would you have rung?' As
she walked around the flat her long pale fingers fluttered like
flickering light over various objects: a closed diary, a framed
photograph, an embroidered cushion, a fossil he'd taken from
a site in Egypt. He swallowed nervously, filled with a danger
that was disturbingly stimulating. He knew what she was
doing, she was reading the room, absorbing the memories
trapped inside each artefact, gleaning as much information as
she could about the last thirty years of his life.

'Why else indeed, and I'm known as Julian these days.'

Finally she settled on the edge of the armchair, the curious ring she always wore catching the lamplight – Aleister
Crowley's unicursal hexagram – to some a pretty, almost dec-
orative pattern but to those who recognised the symbol a
portal to a whole other world.

She studied him very carefully, the heat of her gaze travelling from his feet to his head. Once, as a young man, he'd
found this cool objectification arousing, and, now again, to
his deep chagrin, he discovered that his body still responded.
Her blatant sexual nature took him out of his intellect, and
he would always love her for that – nothing else did or had
since.

'You've changed.' She reached for the long heavy gold
chain that hung around her neck and began twisting a length
of it around a finger – a habit of hers he recognised. 'But I
still want you. Isn't that refreshing?'

Professor Copps sank into the chair opposite and was
silently thankful it was Mrs O'Brien's evening off.

'Is it?' he said, faintly.

'Absolutely, to know that the essence of desire doesn't
change, I would say it was positively inspiring – a kernel of
immortality, we could all do with one of those, Severin.' She
placed her hand on his thigh. Was she going to seduce him or

kill him? He couldn't decide but he was beginning to question his own motive for calling her. Was it because she was the only other person he knew who understood the great potential August had stumbled across or was it because he'd finally found an excuse to see her one last time?

'*Las crónicas del alquimista*, you think they have surfaced?'

'An old student of mine contacted me earlier today. He mentioned he'd stumbled upon a great antiquity, one that might secure his repetition as a historian, then he started asking a lot of questions about Elazar ibn Yehuda. The nature of the questions seemed to point towards the chronicle.'

'And yet you always maintained the chronicle was a mythical construct, just one of those many rumours born out of the Inquisition. How do you know this isn't just another wild goose chase?'

'He was my most gifted student and he also mentioned Shimon Ruiz de Luna. He even knew about his execution.'

She looked up sharply, an uncharacteristically unguarded movement for her. Standing, she seemed to float towards him, an effect assisted by the numerous diaphanous scarves draped around her neck and shoulders.

'And your student's name?'

'Oh, I couldn't give you that, that would be a complete betrayal,' he answered, as firmly as he could, but she had already settled astride his lap, his walking stick falling to the ground with a clatter.

'Oh, I think you could, if I was very, very nice to you,' she murmured, seductively, her heavy bosom now leaning into his chest, her scent overpowering.

Mrs O'Brien paused at the landing to catch her breath. It was past ten and she'd only just managed to catch the last bus back from Putney. She glanced over at the front door of the apartment. The professor was always in bed by nine-thirty and she didn't want to wake him. Treading carefully, she made her way to the door and slipped her key into the lock. To her surprise it was already open. She tried to push the door but something heavy seemed to have fallen against it on the other side. Panicked, she pressed her shoulder against the oak and pushed. It opened halfway before revealing a body slumped against the door. The housekeeper recognised the slippers immediately.

'Professor?' Now worried the old man might have had a fall, she pushed harder and the door gave way, revealing what lay beyond. Mrs O'Brien began to scream.

August laid out two blank sheets of paper on the desk and placed the chronicle above them. At the top of each sheet he wrote the two sets of dates: 670–725 for Elazar ibn Yehuda and 1578–1613 for Shimon Ruiz de Luna. He studied them. They were linked by region and religion, and it was safe to assume that Shimon had been some kind of follower or believer in Elazar's great mystical treasure. Was it this that had driven him to England and to King James? Had he actually found Yehuda's secret? If so, according to Professor Copps, the chronicle would be incredibly valuable to a lot of people. Just then Jimmy's account of the massacre in Irumendi surged back into August's mind. There was a detail that had been gnawing away at his subconscious ever since he heard the story, and it merited investigation. He reached for the telephone.

In five minutes he'd arranged to have lunch at the Reform Club with his old SOE employer, Malcolm Hully. A man who always seemed to be in the hub of the latest diplomatic and political scandals in London, Malcolm also possessed an encyclopedic knowledge of most military operations of the allies – legitimate or not – and he'd sounded pleased to hear from August, even if they had some dubious history. August had briefly seduced Malcolm's wife-to-be on an R & R from his spy duties during the war, but, as far as he knew, Malcolm had never found out.

August replaced the receiver then searched his desk for another shilling. If he was to have a bearable night's sleep, he needed to find more money for the meter. There was none. He glanced around the flat – there was still his collection of jazz records, many of them rare pressings and quite valuable, and also the engagement ring he'd given Cecily two years earlier, an heirloom from his grandmother – a sizeable diamond that was testimony to the old moneyed Mayflower family. It was still sitting on the mantelpiece. Next month's rent was due and he needed cash fast. A small inheritance from an aunt had been almost extinguished and he was tired of dodging debtors. He made a mental note to remind himself to ring his publishers the next morning and visit the pawnbroker – if he sold the ring, he would have enough money for almost a year. This was no time for sentimentality, he decided.

In lieu of a blanket he placed an old winter coat on top of the bed, still lying unmade from the night before, then stripped down to his boxer shorts and climbed in. The sheets smelled from the lovemaking and there was lipstick on the pillow. *This was life, the remnants of a clandestine night and the ruins of a relationship the morning after, but, heck, I still love her.*

August stared at the ceiling and for a moment was transported back to the white sands of a beach and someone's tanned legs folded up next to him. Looking across the room, he wondered how the four years he'd lived in the flat had slipped by; the rows of books faintly outlined by shadow, the portable gramophone, a battered saxophone propped up in a corner, his campaign desk, the photographs on the mantelpiece the only touchstones to a younger self. It was a poignant reminder of the reinvention that was now his life. Everything except the framed photographs seemed transient. All of his aliases and codenames danced like butterflies across his retina – Joe Iron, Tin Man, Gus, Dr A. E. Winthrop – cast-off identities, like he was a Russian doll, each persona carefully hidden inside the shell of the next, and right at the heart of him a rotting secret. *Who have I become? Who am I becoming?*

His gaze settled on the photograph of him punting on the River Cherwell with Charlie and one of his many lovers at the time. Then he remembered the man who had actually taken the photograph, from another punt that had pulled alongside – Malcolm Hully himself.

Malcolm had been older, thirty to their early twenties, and was one of August's tutors at Balliol. Defiantly English in a public-school kind of way, prematurely balding and enthusiastic to the point of irritation, he had a barking energy that concealed a far more complex persona, August discovered a few years later, for it was Malcolm Hully who recruited him into the Special Operations Executive in 1940, after August returned to England from the war in Spain.

At the time Malcolm told him he'd been scouting for the secret services at Oxford and even back then had singled out August, but socialism and Spain had stolen the American away. They'd been close during the time at the Special Operations Executive. Malcolm was his controller back in London when he was on assignment in occupied France helping the resistance smuggle Allied airmen out across the Pyrenees to Spain and back to England. Yet even then

August sensed there was a calculating aspect to Hully's personality August had only occasionally glimpsed. *Malcolm Hully was the consummate player of the great game, and had the perfect personality for espionage, but then so do I*, August told himself, a little ruefully, wondering if anyone would ever really know him, including himself. *I am a creature of shifting parts, a prism, God help those who choose to stare in.*

He rolled onto his back and looked up at the ceiling again. *Maybe Cecily is right. Maybe I am married to my work. I justify my existence by convincing myself all this research is important, as if I can find a shape to my life through tracing fables. Does any of it matter? Does one political system offer true equality over another or are we condemned to the inevitable Darwinian struggle where the talented and rich always triumph? 'Every man according to his needs' – was Marx right? Who should I stand with now?* His internal debate slipped into exhaustion then toppled over into sleep. Over on his desk, the gilded Lauburu on the cover of the chronicle caught the moonlight, and August, turning in his bed, registered change somewhere deep in his subconscious.

4

It had been a turbulent flight and the Boeing had bounced all the way from Madrid. Try as he may, Tyson could never get used to flying. It was ridiculous, he'd jumped out of helicopters into jungles, out of small planes into the ocean, yet put him in a conventional passenger plane and he was a mess. It was being out of control; Tyson was a man who hated being out of control. It unnerved him to look out of the windows down at those propellers whirling madly against the void. Night flights were the worst. There always seemed to be something profoundly senseless to them: the roar of the engine and the relentless darkness that enveloped the plane over and over.

This flight he'd hardly slept at all. Still he'd arrived, and already that dry throb of excitement, of beginning the hunt had started to thread its way through him. He wound down the window of the Austin Seven and allowed the crisp London air to peel back the exhaustion that prickled under his tired eyes.

The man sitting next to him, a taciturn, brawny presence that to anyone else might appear threatening, handed Tyson a dossier of large black-and-white photographs. Tyson pulled out the first one. It was of Jimmy van Peters standing at an iron gate of an Edwardian mansion that looked as if it had been converted into flats. The musician, although older and far thinner than Tyson remembered, was instantly recognisable, the distinctive stance taking Tyson back to that forest camp in the Basque country. He'd never hated the man, if anything Tyson had always secretly felt the kinship of the outsider with Jimmy – but the musician had simply got in the way.

'That's him, Vinko, you did well,' he told the silent Croatian. He'd rescued the university-educated Vinko from a war crimes tribunal in 1947 after Interpol had finally caught up with the former Ustashe assassin and crossbow champion. Tyson, recognising certain traits as well as a huge capacity to keep his silence even under torture, befriended the taciturn giant, then quietly made sure the charges were dropped. Within a month Vinko was working unofficially for both him and the US government. Tyson had made sure the Croatian was indebted for life and there was nothing he wouldn't do for the CIA agent.

Tyson glanced at the next photograph that had been shot through the large window of the ground floor of the same building. Jimmy van Peters could be seen talking to a younger man – a tall blond who had a bookish appearance despite his large, muscular frame. 'Who's this?' Tyson asked.

'August E. Winthrop, a minor player, ex-Special Operations Executive during the war. Before that spent some time as a hothead fighting in Spain, now drifts around in academia. A nobody who's the son of someone – Clarence E. Winthrop, ex-Republican senator now UN representative.'

'Interesting, Clary's boy.'

Tyson peered closer at the photograph. Now he could see

that van Peters was handing something to this August, this nobody. 'What field?'

Vinko frowned; this was not the question he had been expecting.

'Field?'

'Of academia, Vinko.' Tyson was careful to keep his irritation out of his voice. If there was one thing that ignited the emotionless Vinko, it was the sense that he was being patronised, and Vinko angry was terrifying.

'Classics and botany, a curious mixture. Apparently he gives the occasional lecture on the mythological use of magical herbs, a real clown,' Vinko answered in his flat Croatian accent.

Under the heavy wool coat Tyson's heart jumped, his jaw tightened as he controlled his facial reaction. He felt like a bloodhound that had sniffed the metallic smell of bleeding prey after a season of forced abstinence. 'And you tell me you've lost van Peters?'

'We think he's left the country. Paris is back on it.'

'Tag the other guy. I want to know exactly where he goes and when.'

'But he's a nobody.'

'Tag him.' Tyson's tone left no room for ambiguity.

The Reform Club on Pall Mall had, in August's opinion, its own advantages and disadvantages. One advantage was the fact that it still banned female membership, which tended to make the majestic club, with its magnificent atrium around which studies and reading rooms radiated, a little sedate and muskily male in atmosphere. But also, August found, allowed a man to focus his mind without feminine distractions. The disadvantage was that it required even visitors to wear a tie and would insist on providing one at the door if anyone was foolish enough to try and enter inappropriately dressed.

During his service with SOE, it was one of the places Malcolm Hully would occasionally lunch with the American whenever he was on leave in England. August had grown fond of its rarefied atmosphere. Bookish and idealistic, it had been started by the Whig Party – the founders of British liberalism in all its egalitarian, utopian philosophies. As an American and one proud of his country's revolutionary genesis, August felt at home sitting beneath the marble busts of like-minded individuals, all of which seemed to stare down with a kindly gaze.

They sat at one of the tables on the upper gallery that overlooked the huge atrium that ran the full height of the building and was decorated with a series of portraits of the founding members, a tray of club sandwiches set out before them. His ex-employer, now portly, still boasted that ruddy English complexion that suggested a childhood in the country. A controlled man whose inane enthusiasm would occasionally burst out untidily, Malcolm had been in charge of decoding and supervising August's operations in occupied France – all from the safe distance of the Special Operations Executive's headquarters on Baker Street.

Malcolm had had to fight hard to keep the highly imaginative, maverick multi-lingual American within his ranks, but August's intimate knowledge of the Pyrenees on both French and Spanish borders, as well as his language skills, had made him invaluable. It was a gamble that had paid off. The American's sheer bravado and reckless courage always succeeded despite extraordinary odds.

August had made four successful missions in occupied France, coordinating with the resistance – both Basque and French rebels had managed to help organise Operation

Comet, a series of linked safe houses and a route to freedom
for Allied airmen who'd been forced to bail over enemy territory. They would be led over the Pyrenees through the
Basque country then smuggled out by boat off the Spanish
coast back to Southampton.

Malcolm had ended up revelling in August's glory, but
after the war many of the old SOE operatives found themselves superfluous in peacetime. Some retired, others
returned to their previous incarnations as academics, mathe-
maticians, civil servants. The really bright ones went into
private business and even by 1950 had begun to emerge as
the new impresarios of the financial world. A few quietly
and secretly moved on to MI5 or MI6, like Malcolm, while
others got lost in the austere struggle of the post-war years of
rationing and unemployment. Malcolm had always regarded
August as one of these vanished souls. He'd fallen off the
cocktail party circuit, the embassy and business receptions,
and art gallery openings, a couple of years ago, and the two
men had lost contact. Occasionally August's name would
pop up in the social columns or at a dinner party in passing
conversation, but Malcolm really had no idea what August
had actually been doing since the war, and he was banking
on the fact that, likewise, August would have no idea about
the true nature of his own employment.

August held up one of the sandwiches.

'Real bacon, Jesus, I don't think I've seen that since 1942.'

'Canadian. I believe the club has some strong alumni connections in the Colonies. Enjoy it while you can, it'll be fish
paste sandwiches next week. So, you still engaged to that
gorgeous girl?'

'Cecily.'

'That's right, I read about it, Cecily Highton-Smith, beautiful, intelligent and rather wealthy, if I remember rightly.

Father's an ex-diplomat now in the House of Lords, isn't he?'

'Lord Highton-Smith ...'

'Well, August, you were never one for doing things by halves, but how the hell he approved of you, I can't imagine – natural charisma, I suppose. Never had much of it and never had much time for it. So, all going well?' Malcolm couldn't help but notice the American looked hungry, hungover and poor.

August bit into the sandwich, allowing the sharp flavours to seep luxuriously into his senses. For a moment the status quo of a prosperous England returned as if by magic. Malcolm Hully watched amused – on closer inspection the cuffs on the American's, admittedly once expensive, shirt were frayed and he was unshaven. He also looked like he hadn't slept in days. Already Malcolm had begun to calculate what kind of information August might offer up and how he might be able to use it to his own benefit – had his old prodigy any worthy connections with the Communist Party of Great Britain or perhaps the Soviets themselves? August always had been very left-wing, and lately Malcolm's own career had slipped into a kind of apathy. Some insight or compromising intelligence could prove to be invaluable. The atmosphere at Leconfield House was tense, bordering on paranoid both at MI5 and MI6, especially since Guy Burgess's defection eighteen months earlier. The notion that there was a mole high up in the Oxbridge echelons of the leadership was unofficially but widely believed inside both institutions, and Malcolm, as an ex-Oxford man who actively recruited in the heady political days of the thirties – when both Oxford and Cambridge were awash with passionate young men similar to August Winthrop who were attracted to seemingly egalitarian political systems like socialism, often in reaction to the rise of fascism – was naturally

suspicious. Winthrop was one of the brightest men he knew –
that kind of charm and intelligence was inevitably useful. But
Malcolm had always secretly questioned why August had
chosen the name 'Tin Man' from *The Wizard of Oz* as his operative codename. Sometimes Malcolm had wondered whether
the unusual choice hadn't indicated a flaw in the American's
psychology, a deep-seated unconscious fear that he too might
be lacking a heart. But then, an intelligent man lacking a heart
is even more useful than one with a heart, as any good spy
could tell you. Empathy was an impediment, yet why did the
women like him so much? Malcolm puzzled, thinking with
some chagrin about his own wife Marjorie and her ill-dis-
guised excitement when he mentioned he was having lunch
with Winthrop.

August finished the sandwich. 'Not exactly, in fact the
engagement was broken off yesterday. There were ... complications.' August let the last word hang, hoping he hadn't
sounded too callous.

Malcolm Hully grinned, then took a quick sip of the
rather bad port they'd been served.

'Well, as they say, monogamy is usually an activity under-
taken by two people – and usually the same two people over
a considerable length of time.'

'So rumour has it,' August retorted, also grinning. They
both burst into a chuckle.

'God, do you remember when I found dear old Bodery in
the broom cupboard with one of the FANY girls? I wasn't
sure whether to congratulate him or demote him.' Malcolm
now reminiscing, relaxed back into his seat.

'Actually I think you should have decorated her for taking
his virginity. I mean, how old was he?'

'Thirty-nine at the time. My word, those were the days.
Do you ever miss them?'

August looked away, not wanting to betray his emotions. He reached into his pocket for a cigarette. There were none, he'd run out. In an instant Malcolm was offering him one of his own, Peter Stuyvesants – only available on the black market, August noted, also noticing Malcolm's new watch and gold cufflinks. Again, he tried to remember what Malcolm's new job was. The Foreign Service in one of the administrative positions, he seemed to remember. He took the cigarette, but couldn't help wondering how the man could afford such luxuries on a meagre civil service income. He lit up and exhaled.

'Miss them? Some mornings I don't even recognise myself. The tragic thing is that I suspect I was built for combat. You know me, Malcolm, I'm not a settling man. I guess Cecily called my bluff, although she couched it in terms of psychological dysfunction.'

Malcolm glanced up, catching a rare moment of vulnerability in August's face.

'Who knows what's psychologically functional and what's not, these days?' he ventured. 'One just has to get on. We all carry scars from the war. Our generation will, you know, until our graves.'

'And you?' August asked, determined to switch the focus away from himself.

'Oh, we've settled. A nice Georgian house in Mayfair, two sons at Eton, a cottage in Sussex.'

'So the Foreign Service must be paying?' It was a loaded question and both of them knew it.

Malcolm kept his gaze steady. 'The father-in-law died and we inherited.' Now enjoying the deceit, he decided to elaborate. 'But the job does pay rather well, it's just a little on the dull side, a lot of entertaining and paper-pushing, but you know Marjorie, she always was socially ambitious,' he finished, a little more defensively than he'd planned.

'Then it's just as well she chose you and not me,' August couldn't help retorting.

The civil servant looked away, a tiny tick under his right eye flickering, betraying him. An image of August and Marjorie making love had flashed through his mind – an imagined scenario but one he knew had taken place in those last desperate weeks, the time between his proposal and her acceptance, during the tense build-up to Dunkirk.

Malcolm had fallen in love with Marjorie the moment she'd walked into his office, a small blonde who radiated an erotic concoction of vulnerability and brittle intelligence. Instinctively, he knew she was out of his range – too beautiful, too upper class and (if he was honest with himself) probably too intelligent. But Malcolm had fallen anyway and had suffered her proximity with all the pain of a martyr. Terrified of rejection, he'd stumbled around her, gruff in feigned indifference, unable to make the first move. It had only been the appearance of August, just returned from a mission in France, tousle-haired and electric with adrenalin, that had galvanised Malcolm into acting at all. He supposed he had that to thank the American for, but at the time he was secretly infuriated by the casualness with which August had set eyes upon Marjorie and, with all the indifference of the hunter, begun his standard seduction routine. The man was incorrigible. Worse still, to Malcolm's secret horror and dismay, she had responded. Luckily, just before the relationship was consummated August had been sent away on another mission. Marjorie was inconsolable, well, almost, and this time Malcolm made sure he was there to comfort her. Coincidentally, it was then that August's encoded messages from France had stopped and the department had every reason to believe he'd been captured, possibly killed. Malcolm took the opportunity to propose.

By the time August reappeared somewhere in Vichy France and his messages had been decoded, Marjorie had accepted Malcolm's proposal, but when the American returned to London they'd spent one furtive night together – something she had only confessed to Malcolm a year ago.

Looking at August now, still charismatic enough to turn heads, Malcolm hated him momentarily for the ease with which both women and the luck of survival seemed to surround him. A charmed life no matter what destiny threw at him. Again, the idea that he might be offered some hold over the American excited Malcolm.

'You know, August, I never could work out why you gave up Oxford. You could have graduated, then gone straight back to Boston, to that blue-blooded family of yours.'

'Initially it was Charlie Stanwick who got me into the party, but after I'd witnessed Hitler's ambition, I was morally compelled to volunteer for Spain. The Nazis' weaponry, their planes treating the Spanish and the Basques like some kind of dress rehearsal of bloodshed – Gernika, Madrid, Bilbao ... none of us Marxists, not the Republicans, the International Brigade, the Basque Nationalists, none of us had any illusions about peace with such tyranny. Pity the rest of the world wasn't willing to listen.'

'Well, we've all paid the price now.'

'And I'll always be grateful to you for giving me the chance to keep fighting. Nobody else trusted me, and I knew I wouldn't be welcome back in the States, not with my record of being a card-carrying Red.'

'What about now? Aren't you at least interested in going back? It's boom town there, the spanking shining dawn of industrial prosperity. Here it's the decline and burial of the British Empire – although half my colleagues are in denial, you'd think we still ruled India, China and the Middle East.'

'The Americans wouldn't have me back. Not with Senator McCarthy beating the anti-communist drum. And with Eisenhower in the White House, I'm telling you there's a new war afoot – Korea, Egypt, the Soviet Union, China, everyone is lining up.'

'Don't I know it. So what side are you on now?'

'I used to call myself a Marxist – now I'm not so sure, with all these rumours of Stalin's work camps and arrests. But I'm telling you, all hell is gonna break out when he dies. You wait. I wouldn't be packing up my fatigues just yet. Anyhow, that's all behind me now. I've spent the last few years pursuing my academic career.'

Malcolm studied his face carefully, not believing a word.

'I was wondering where you had got to. I even heard a rumour you had visited the Soviet Union at one point.' Malcolm kept his voice light and breezy.

'A conference on Georgian flora in myth.'

'That's right, you and your occult studies.' Malcolm tried not to sound sarcastic and failed, noticing August wince.

'It keeps me out of trouble, and pays the bills, kind of. And it was always my other passion. And besides, I'm an esteemed historian now, I even have a whole audience of a couple of hundred readers awaiting my second tome – *Famous Poisonings in History: The Deadly Nightshade and Other Dangerous Blooms.*'

'And you really expect me to believe that you've given up the politics?'

'Hey, I still subscribe to the *Daily Worker*, but my party days are over. I guess I'm far more politically cynical than I used to be.'

'Aren't we all. Still, considering your father is now the US representative at the UN ... '

August glanced up sharply – he hated being associated with his father.

'We haven't spoken since 1936. He never forgave me for volunteering for the Abraham Lincoln Brigade and I never forgave him for being the fascist that he was. You know he actually backed Hitler right up until England declared war? He met him once at an embassy party in Berlin in the thirties. Apparently Der Führer made quite an impression. Don't delude yourself, I'm *persona non grata* with dear Daddy and I'd like to keep it that way.'

'Pity, he could help you now.'

'Help me? He'd get me arrested. It's taken thirty years to crawl from under his shadow and I ain't crawling back now, no sirree. I hate the guy.' August knocked back the whisky he'd ordered on the Foreign Service's expense account, then regretted not relishing the malt. Talking about his father made him both anxious and furious, it was an uncomfortable mix. 'Listen, Malcolm, I'm not naive. I knew you guys had tags on me the whole time during the war, still do, right?'

Malcolm chose not to answer. Did August know whether he was MI5 or not? Now they were both playing the game.

'August, what's the real reason why you wanted to meet?'

August glanced around the gallery – there was only one other member visible, and he appeared to be sleeping behind a copy of *The Times*, a page of the newspaper undulating gently as he snored. Nevertheless, August pushed his chair nearer Malcolm.

'I need some information.' It was a sincere and disarmingly honest appeal: uncharacteristic of the American, who was notoriously self-reliant. Malcolm decided it was genuine. He steeled himself.

'I'm listening.'

'Does October 31st, 1945 mean anything to you – in relation to Anglo-Franco affairs?' The two men watched each other's expressions, both unconsciously looking for a tell, the whisper of an expression that might betray some hidden sub-text. Both men stayed grim-faced. Stalemate. August broke the silence. 'I'm figuring you might have heard something, being Foreign Office?'

Malcolm exhaled, relaxing almost imperceptibly, almost.

'Well, apart from the end of the war and the Potsdam Conference in July, it doesn't ring any kind of bell.' He leaned closer, close enough for August to be able to smell his expensive aftershave – again August wondered where he was getting his money. 'But I warn you, August, don't go meddling in Franco's affairs. The English have ghosts with Franco, just as the Americans have. Ghosts MI5 would happily silence – the ungentlemanly way.'

'Do I look like a ghost?' August replied, smiling.

'Actually you do.' Malcolm's grim demeanour did not change and August felt a faint chill brush across his skin – others might have called it fear. Malcolm rotated his port glass on the glass tabletop thoughtfully. 'Listen, you've always been my man and I've fought for you more than you know. But these are different times. There are all kinds of surprising alliances springing up every day, a new kind of mercenary thinking at the top and, since Burgess and Maclean, a new kind of paranoia. Things aren't black and white any more. We're living through a climate of moral ambiguity. One has to watch one's back.'

'So the date does have significance?'

'Did I say that?'

August shrugged, thinking Malcolm might have been avoiding answering the question. But there was something else, something just hovering under Malcolm's subliminal threat, a clue he'd let slip. August, relaxing against the back of his chair, feigned a casualness the civil servant mistook for bravado.

'Listen, August, you're still considered a security risk, now even more so because of this new Cold War. I'll help you but I can't protect you.' And, to Malcolm's surprise, it felt as if he really meant it.

Outside, August mulled over the conversation, staring into the light drizzle that had started to descend on Pall Mall. A businessman hurried by in bowler hat, overcoat and umbrella – the uniform of the denizens of the city. Tall and thin, he looked almost funereal in his black. What was in his life that propelled him along the street with such urgency? August wondered. Was he entirely as he seemed? The man, noticing August's interest and completely misinterpreting it, smiled wryly from under the bowler, and August, realising his gaff, had the decency to blush before turning away. *No, definitely not MI5*, he thought to himself then glanced back down the street. Under the rain the snow was turning to slush, yet there was something comforting in the way the grand promenade had survived virtually unchanged through-out the war. A continuity of both history and tradition. It was what he'd always loved about London.

As he gazed out the clue Malcolm had let slip took shape as he realised Malcolm had mentioned the Americans in relation to Franco, despite the fact August hadn't introduced them into the conversation. Springing into action, he pulled off the dreadful tie he'd been obliged to wear for the club and reached for his helmet, then fired up the bike.

He headed straight over Piccadilly towards Berkeley Square. There was a favour he could call in.

From the street the barge, moored in Little Venice, looked just like an ordinary long flat-bottomed boat that had been converted into a residential dwelling. There were lace

curtains in the windows and pretty little window boxes filled
with red geraniums.

Once inside, apart from a few expensive antiques like the
sixteenth-century spinning wheel that sat in a corner or the
silver candlestick holder on the table, it looked like the kind
of place a neat older woman with artistic tendencies might
live – inoffensive, perhaps even a little kitsch, but this was
exactly the impression Olivia Henries liked to present to
the outside world.

She sat at a small fold-out wooden table facing an empty
chair – the table was set for two, but only Olivia's plate had
been used. She was now studying a photograph she held in
her hand, 'Gatesways Club, 1950' scrawled in ink across the
bottom. It was of two women sitting at a table in a bar. The
younger one, dressed in a suit, a trilby rakishly tipped over
one eye, her short black hair just visible, cigarette holder in
hand, stared out of the photograph defiantly, her arm draped
possessively around the shoulder of her companion. The
older woman, lipsticked, red hair tumbling down to her bare
shoulders, was turned away from the camera as she gazed
lovingly across – their proximity allowing no ambiguity.
There was a slight fudging of the older woman's features, as
if she were in motion or some hidden light had blurred her
face, but she was still recognisable to those who knew her
well. Olivia looked down at her own indistinct face, then
traced the outline, remembering the feel of the satiny
evening dress, the eroticism of belonging to another – someone far younger, far more impatient to begin life, and
perhaps, unconsciously to end it.

'You fool, you stupid beautiful fool,' she said out loud,
addressing the empty chair, not knowing whether to scream
or to weep, then realising her fury transcended both emotions. She pulled a telephone directory off a shelf and began

poring over it – there was no entry for an A. E. Winthrop, no doubt the American was ex-directory. The only clue she had to his address was the numberplate on his motorcycle and all she'd managed to extract from the Motor Vehicle Association of Great Britain was the name of the street he lived on, no house or flat number. She knew the street and the area – it was one of the densely populated boroughs of London, filled with a multitude of one-room apartments, flats and boarding houses crowded with students, the current wave of migrants hopeful for work – not to mention the thousands of war refugees who flooded London. The street itself was four blocks long.

Resigned to a long search, Olivia pulled on a raincoat and headed out for the nearest telephone booth, situated at the junction of the canal and a bridge. Stoically ignoring the dozen business cards stuck up against the board above the phone, covered in dubious adverts like 'French mistress seeks pupil', 'Art model, well-built blonde looking for life modelling classes', 'Exotic dancer seeks patron', Olivia inserted her tuppence and dialled.

'Oh, hello, is this the central sorting office for Kensington?' she said, pitching her voice an octave higher, sounding as upper class as she could. 'It is? Wonderful. I'm trying to locate my nephew, I have a money order to send him, you see. The poor boy is quite destitute, you know how these students are. The trouble is, I have the name of his street, but not the house number ... you can? Wonderful ... the name is August E. Winthrop.'

While she waited for the postal worker on the other end of the line to locate the address, she doodled on one of the cards. Over and over she scrawled in deep black ink strokes, cutting into the thin cardboard, visualising August's face with each tiny slash, until the friendly cockney voice interrupted her. 'Flat 3, 45 Hurlington Terrace,' she repeated. 'Oh, that is marvellous, thank you so very much,' she gushed, then realised she'd turned her doodle into the image of a skull.

It was still raining in Grosvenor Square and there were still some civil servants milling around the garden square, mournfully contemplating the pigeons fighting it out over their thrown breadcrumbs. August ran up the steps of Number One, the Stars and Stripes flying over the grey stone portico of the imposing Georgian terrace that housed the US Embassy.

'Wow, don't you just love this English weather?' he drawled to the US Army guard standing just inside the oak door, trying to sound as American as possible. It worked, the guard stepped aside and August strolled up to the art deco desk that dominated the reception area.

'Can I help you?' The receptionist, severe in dark-blue serge, glowered over her glasses as August surreptitiously looked down the list of names visible beside the elevator doors, his gaze fixating on one.

'I'm here to see Mr Horatio Sampson.' He leaned over the desk smiling flirtatiously.

Unimpressed, she arched her eyebrows.

'Name, sir?'

'Mr August E. Winthrop, that would be Winthrop as in the son of Senator Winthrop.' The receptionist's expression transformed at the mention of his father's name, and August glanced at the large clock set above her – it was two in the afternoon, perfect timing if he remembered correctly. 'He's expecting me, I would suggest informing his secretary,' August told her, hating himself for stooping to such strategies.

'I will indeed, Mr Winthrop,' she simpered then picked up the telephone.

'There's a gentleman here to see Mr Sampson.' Her smile turned into a frown. 'He's not in? But it's Mr Winthrop.' She lowered her voice. 'The senator's son, that's right, Mr August E. Winthrop.' Her expression changed again. 'Certainly.' She put down the receiver and looked back up to August.

'She says you are to go up and wait in his office – fourth floor.'

'Thank you, and has anyone ever told you you have extraordinarily beautiful earlobes?' August winked before sauntering off, leaving the receptionist fondling her earlobes unsure whether she'd just been insulted or complimented.

Tyson stood in the small green park looking over at the grey façade that once held so many memories for him – this little piece of America in central London. The rain pattered gently against his raised umbrella, soothing, timeless. Vinko had done his job well, like he always did, and Tyson had had the luxury of watching his prey enter the embassy blissfully oblivious to the two men, one of whom had been shadowing him for over a day. Tyson glanced at his watch – now was the time to move.

'My God, August, have you some damn cheek!' Cindy Parsons, Mr Sampson's secretary, a tall statuesque redhead who originated somewhere south of Kansas, stood with her hands on her ample hips, feigning outrage – rather unconvincingly, as her delight at seeing August was clearly evident.

'I suppose you have no such appointment with Mr Sampson, just like I should have supposed you were never going to ring me after our night together.'

'Guilty on the second count, but not as guilty as the happily married Mr Sampson, who I correctly "supposed" was seeing that mistress of his at two in the afternoon?'

'Well, some men never change. You really are a cad.' She flounced back to her filing. He followed.

'Oh c'mon, Cindy, we had fun and why spoil a great friendship?'

'You broke my heart.'

'Really, I'm flattered. A big strong gal like you.'

She swung around and contemplated the tall man standing before her. He looked tired, a few new lines had creased the forehead, his shirt was crumpled and there was a dent in the shining veneer of his confidence. She guessed there were emotional complications that had finally spilled over into August's charmed life. It was inevitable. But, boy, did she resent the hold he always seemed to have over her whenever he was in physical proximity. Her mother was right, it was an unfair world and those who had been blessed with charm and beauty always squandered it.

'What do you want from me now, August?'

'Don't be like that. Maybe I just dropped in to say hi? Maybe ask you out for dinner?'

'That'll be a five-shilling fish and chips at Joe's café on my ticket—'

'Dancing.'

'Dancing? August, you don't dance, you smooch! Besides, I loathe jazz.'

He came up behind her and bit her neck – hard. She swooned immediately, a hot flush of memory weakening her at the knees. Their lovemaking had been good; August Winthrop was the rare combination of a handsome man and a generous lover. Damn him.

'Okay, foreplay over.' She pushed him away. 'Just tell me what you're after – I guess I might be persuaded. But don't get the idea I'm easy.'

'Easy? You!' He laughed and winked. 'If I remember rightly, you were kind of hard work.'

Cindy blushed again. 'So what exactly do you want?' she asked, curtly, trying to regain her composure.

'I was wondering whether there was any file on an operation around the 31st of October, 1945 – somewhere on the Spanish side of the Pyrenees – involving our guys?' He kept eye contact, knowing she would not be able to resist his seduction. What he was asking was highly treasonable, but if he kept his tone light and flirtatious, she might just comply. To clinch the deal, he allowed his gaze to sweep down her body – from breasts to groin – like one long lingering caress. On the other side of the desk Cindy allowed a sigh to escape her lips – she couldn't help herself.

The receptionist handed back Tyson's CIA pass. 'Welcome to London, sir, whom do you wish to see?' Her curt transatlantic accent made Tyson wince slightly. There was something lemony and acidic about her presence he disliked – nevertheless he kept the smile plastered on his face.

'Thank you.' He slipped the pass into his back pocket. 'Actually I was wondering whether an August E. Winthrop might be in the building?'

The woman looked across startled then composed herself. 'He arrived a few minutes ago.'

'Do you know where I might find him?'

'Mr Sampson's office, I believe he wanted to see him. Is there a problem?' she asked, letting slip her own anxiety about having possibly let someone into the building she shouldn't.

'No, none at all, Judith,' he told her, surreptitiously reading her name off the nameplate on the desk. 'Merely routine, his father asked me to check up on him. He's the black sheep of the family.'

The receptionist's relief was visible. 'I understand, you'll find him in Mr Sampson's office, third floor, Room 20.'

'Thank you, I won't forget it.' As he walked away from the desk Tyson checked his watch. The phrase 'Keep him just ahead of you in your gunsight, remember he doesn't even know you are here' popped into his mind: something his father told him when they were out poaching cattle – in those terrible dust-filled hungry years. He'd give Winthrop a few extra minutes.

Cindy glanced at the desk clock. She had about half an hour before her boss would be back, scrubbed, relaxed and a lot more jovial than when he'd left. That was sex for you. She turned back to August.

'I don't know, last time I "helped" you I almost lost my job.'

'C'mon, this is old history – harmless reportage – I just wanted to check on the story of an old buddy of mine. He claims he was in Spain in forty-five, I know he wasn't – I have a wager on it.' August slipped his hands down to her waist.

They felt good, large, firm and dangerously dexterous. Again she felt that tell-tale flush of warmth from her knees to her groin.

'A wager?'

'Five pounds – now that could buy you a good dinner.'

'Okay, but you've got fifteen minutes, then you're out of that office whether you've found the file or not.'

She went into her boss's adjunct office, August followed.

'No prying, stay by the door,' she instructed him, as she opened a drawer behind the large desk to fish out a small brown envelope marked 'Records office'. After taking the key out, she left the empty envelope on the desk.

'You're a trooper, Cindy.'

'Like my mamma used to say, if you're gonna fall, you might as well fall hard.'

The name Horatio Sampson was painted in small back lettering across the glass window of the office door – which, to Tyson's surprise, was ajar. He stepped in. The outer room was obviously a tiny reception area doubling as a secretary's office, the aroma of perfume lingered in the air, as well as the palatable sense that it had just been vacated. He walked swiftly and silently past the secretary's desk and into the inner sanctum of Sampson's office. A small brown envelope lay abandoned on the desk. Tyson picked it up, it was empty.

Cindy ushered August around to the records office like he was a visiting dignitary and she his guide, praying they wouldn't encounter anyone she knew. They were lucky, it was still lunchtime and the corridor was empty. Cindy opened the door with a key and left him alone in the narrow room filled with nothing but spearmint-green metal filing cabinets lined up in rows like silent sentries. The whole history of the US–European operations was kept in here – locked up for future Americans to ponder the wisdom and diplomacy of their nation.

'Fifteen minutes, August, not a minute longer.'

'Thanks, Cindy, you're a doll.'

'I'm a sucker, is what I am.'

'But a cute one.'

'Get out of here,' she joked, flattered despite her cynicism. It was hard not to be with August, he was just so damn charming. She left the office and, as an afterthought, locked the door behind her.

*

August studied the vast array of filed information, then, knowing from his previous visits, they were filed alphabetically, walked over to the file that would contain S.

He flicked quickly through until he found Spain – sandwiched between Sardinia and Suribachi. Within that file was a series of years running from 1933 to 1945. The subfile for 1945 contained twelve sections, one of which was entitled 'October'.

1st June, 1945

I feel that now the war is over we should watch Franco and any inclination of the Spanish dictator to develop expansionist ambitions like his former ally Hitler. A fascist country left remaining in Europe is a potential threat to the new fragile peace. Franco's unspoken support of the Axis during the war and his blatant exploitation of the strategic position of Spain in the European/North African theatre suggest a weak and corruptible character. Nevertheless, his ambitions cannot be underestimated. With isolated pockets of fascist battalions and movements scattered across both Western and Eastern Europe – not to mention the Soviet Bloc – now forced underground, I feel it necessary to adopt a policy to both train and 'encourage' those factions opposing the regime in Spain, with the intention ultimately to overthrow that regime and instate a democracy that would have the full support of (and be sympathetic to) both the US and its allies. It is proposed we set up a training camp for the Basque government now exiled in Paris to train both Basque soldiers and officers, with the potential to stage a successful coup. This has the blessing of President Truman.

Fascinated, August read on – so Jimmy van Peters had been right. It seemed that Truman's primary concern immediately after the surrender of Germany was the possibility that the remnants of fascism – including some of the Nationalist movements in Eastern Europe, who, at the promise of independence, had aligned themselves with Hitler – might reunite and rise up again. Franco, as a fascist leader who'd remained unconquered during the war, was an obvious candidate and Truman was not willing to take any chances.

The last page of the subfile was entitled 'Operation Lizard'. August's chest tightened in anticipation – this was Jimmy's outfit, exactly how he had described it, now lying in front of August confirmed in neat official font. The report described how the US Army had sent both arms and officers to train the remnants of the Basque Army then exiled in free France, with the intention of staging a coup, but these were withdrawn following Potsdam, when Truman, after encountering Stalin, decided Communism was a far bigger threat to the post-war world. President Truman issued orders to withdraw the Americans from the Basque camps. On the tenth page several telegrams had been stapled:

```
14TH SEPTEMBER 1945,WASHINGTON.
ORDERS FOR THE WITHDRAWAL OF ALL US OFFICERS
AND AGENTS FROM THE BASQUE CELLS WITHIN
FRANCE AND THE BASQUE REGION HAVE BEEN
ISSUED  ALL OPERATIONS HAVE COMPLIED EXCEPT
FOR OPERATION LIZARD. AWAITING COMMUNICATION
FROM THE COMMANDER CODENAME: JESTER.

18TH SEPTEMBER 1945,WASHINGTON.
STILL NO CORRESPONDENCE FROM AGENT JESTER.
THIS IS A CONCERN GIVEN THE FACT THAT
OPERATION LIZARD IS TAKING PLACE WITHIN
HOSTILE TERRITORY.
```

URGENT

4TH NOVEMBER 1945, WASHINGTON. RE: OPERATION

LIZARD

UNSUBSTANTIATED REPORTS RECEIVED OF AN

INCIDENT OF CRIMINAL NATURE ON THE 31ST OF

OCTOBER INVOLVING THE OFFICER ████ ███

CODENAME JESTER – CONSIDERING THE NATURE OF

THE OPERATIONS AND CURRENT RELATIONS WITH

GENERAL FRANCO, LEAK MUST BE AVOIDED AT ALL

COSTS. CONFIRMED THAT ALL TRACES AND POSSIBLE

REPORTAGE OF THE INCIDENT HAVE BEEN

SUCCESSFULLY CONTAINED TO BISCAY. UNTIL A

FULL REPORT AND EXPLANATION FROM JESTER

PURSUANT, PROVING HIMSELF TO HAVE BEEN AN

OFFICER AND SOLDIER OF EXEMPLARY REPUTATION,

OPERATION LIZARD TERMINATED.

Stunned, August stared down at the document – so Jimmy had been labouring under the wrong impression for all those years. The order to execute La Leona and her men had not been given by the US government after all, the order had simply been to vacate. So why had Agent Jester – Damien Tyson – ordered the massacre? To what purpose? And why go to the trouble of eliminating all other witnesses over the years?

The ancient elevator shuddered to a halt at the basement level. Tyson pulled the iron gates open and stepped out into the narrow corridor. Last time he'd been in the embassy was just after the end of the war and before he got sent into Spain – to brief the ambassador on who was to be trusted in Churchill's post-war cabinet and who wasn't. Tyson's visit had not been popular, and he'd found the labyrinth-like

corridors of the Georgian building an unpleasant but accurate metaphor for the insidious complexity of British politics.
Noting that he was probably in what was once the servants'
quarters, he felt that old sense of claustrophobia return. He
knew the records office lay to the left, beyond the end of the
long corridor. He started towards it, just then the murmur of
voices – a man berating another in broad cockney – floated
down the passageway. Tyson glanced quickly up and down –
there was a door, barely visible, set into the wall. Tyson
stepped behind it and clicked it shut, narrowly missing the
caretakers, who, unaware of his proximity, continued arguing
as they walked past outside. Standing there in the pitch
dark, Tyson fought a wave of revulsion as he realised he'd
stepped into a toilet.

August was interrupted by the sound of Cindy turning the
key in the door outside. Swiftly, he removed the last page of
the subfile and slipped it into his shirt. Composing himself,
he swung around to greet her.

'Just as I thought, the guy was total baloney. The operation he claimed he was on? Doesn't exist.'

'Glad to be of service, as usual, so dinner and dance at the
Trocadero?'

'Sure, sweetheart, whenever you want.'

Outside they heard the sound of a door slamming and
footfall. They both froze as whoever it was paused outside
the door then walked on. Cindy stared wide-eyed up at
August, and when the sound of the footsteps faded away
she hurried him to the door.

'You better get out of here.'

After he left she glanced around the filing cabinets. There
was one on the far side whose drawer was open by a crack, as

if someone had just been rifling through it. Cindy walked over. The files were dislodged like they'd just been looked at. One sat higher than the others. 'Spain 1945' – page ten was missing. Cursing her own weakness, she replaced the file hoping the next time anyone noticed would be decades away, then realised August hadn't set a time or day for their date.

Then she heard the click of the door behind her. Startled, she swung around.

'Sorry, I didn't mean to scare you.' The man – short and muscular, somewhere in his early fifties, with a shock of prematurely white hair and strangely pale green eyes – smiled at her, his capped teeth too white and too even and strangely carnivorous. He sounded East Coast – Washington perhaps – and he was wearing an expensive suit by a Manhattan designer she recognised immediately. Assuming he was some official who'd just flown in, she straightened herself, deliberately turning her back to the cabinet. 'Not at all, I was just looking up some information for my boss.'

'Your boss?' His voice was low and disorientating somehow, the tone making it difficult for Cindy to concentrate.

'Mr Sampson ... he covers all Mediterranean operations,' she volunteered then cursed herself for it. It wasn't as if she instinctively trusted this man – quite the opposite, he frightened her, there was something profoundly absent about his presence, like he had no scent or shadow, and yet she had felt compelled to answer him.

'I see.' He stepped sideways towards her, a curious almost unnatural movement. Cindy's chest tightened, she felt like screaming, yet backed up against the filing cabinet, she couldn't move.

'That's the S cabinet, isn't it?'

'It is, S as in Switzerland,' she finished, lamely.

'You know . . .' He slid closer, now she could feel the heat
of his body radiating from under the starched white shirt, the
heavy woollen suit. 'I was just outside and I swore I heard
voices in here, yours and another man's, a man who might
also be interested in S?' He smiled again, and Cindy was
reminded of a band of shark's fins circling closer and closer.
'Am I right?'

She stared at him, fascinated, still unable to move. Just
then a door slammed outside in the corridor and the spell
was broken.

'Sorry, I'm needed at the office,' she said, pushing past
him.

Pity, Tyson thought, the image of her retreating buttocks
and stockinged legs a collage of moving verticals that still
burned on his retina. Such a pretty girl, such pretty flushed
skin. What he could do with that skin. He licked his lips,
cracked and dry from the flight, then remembered a prostitute he used once on a trip to London before. He would
ring her later that night.

He swung back to the cabinet and pulled open the drawer
for Spain. It took less than a minute to discover the missing
page. He had no illusions as to why it had been stolen. So
Winthrop likes solving mysteries, he thought, recalling the
handsome confident face he'd seen with van Peters in the
photograph; an ex-spy, classicist, botanist – someone who
knew Spain better than he did, someone with a lateral mind
and more than a layman's interest in the occult, a privileged
dilettante playing at being historian. Tyson laid his hand flat
on the page and concentrated on the man, on the lingering
presence, a slow hatred forming at the back of his throat, like
a taste, an acrid tang.

Tyson had always suffered the indignation of looking in,
of belonging to that subset of humanity who through

circumstance endured the humiliation of watching others given opportunity, privilege, promotion seemingly effortlessly. He recognised August Winthrop as such a creature, born into extraordinary entitlement, born behind that imaginary window of the imaginary mansion through which Tyson felt he was always looking, no matter how successful, how powerful he himself became. It was a question of authenticity. If he was honest with himself (and he was, brutally), he never felt at ease, he never felt legitimately powerful. It was a sensation he did his utmost to hide from others, and he'd killed men for less.

A self-made son of a small-town insurance salesman who'd dragged his family around the Midwest during the dust-bowl years, Tyson had begun as a clerk in the Office of Strategic Services and finally got noticed through a propensity for languages and ruthless strategy. Within three years he had reinvented himself – then the war came and Tyson flourished. Men like him – men born without empathy – did in conflict. It was his natural habitat, his evolutionary *raison d'être*. When that war stopped he found another hidden war to operate in. Unencumbered by relationships, or even the notion of relationship, he was a good operative, his only weakness a tendency to be a little too independent of Central Office. But he was obsessive, meticulous and could kill utterly without hesitation or remorse. This trait made him invaluable to the organisation and he knew it.

He leaned against the cabinet, the cold edge of the metal digging into his back. He liked the pain; it sharpened the moment. Disparate pieces of information floated above him like cards waiting to be shuffled into exactly the right order, an espionage game of solitaire. Let him; let him be your puzzle master, your unwitting translator, was the answer that came back. He glanced down at the file with its missing page. Now he had enough bait to catch the scent of the trail.

'The trail that is going to lead August Winthrop to a place I've been looking for more than half my life,' he said out loud, then snapped his fingers as if to break a neck.

Driving back through Russell Square, then through the back of Lancaster Gate towards Kensington, August noticed a black Morris Minor following him. He checked his side mirror. The driver appeared to be a middle-aged woman, her long hair tucked under a silk scarf. She looked like an artist of some sort. *Am I becoming as paranoid as Jimmy?* he asked himself, not quite believing his eyes. He swung the car sharply into a lane that ran along the back of a neat line of mews cottages. To his horror the Morris Minor was waiting for him at the other end, parked at the kerb. After a discreet distance had opened between them the car pulled out from the kerb and started following him again.

Who was she? She certainly didn't look like any embassy official, and her shadowing skills were amateurish enough to dismiss any possibility she was MI5. The inconceivable yet disturbing idea occurred to him that she might be the mother of some girl who felt wronged by him. Was that possible? Surely not. As far as he knew he'd always taken precautions and had let his conquests down gently but firmly. Nevertheless, the mysterious woman's persistency disturbed him, and there was something familiar about her handsome but severe profile glimpsed briefly in the mirror. Where had he seen her before? Swerving, he doubled back and lost her three blocks from the apartment.

Dinner was a can of baked beans on toast with a badly fried egg on the side. August ate at the desk studying the first pages of text he'd lifted from the chronicle. The Latin had given way to Spanish, as if a new urgency had compelled the physic to turn to his natural tongue. Luckily August was still fluent in the language and, despite the anarchic nature of the prose, he could follow it.

Again, he read the pages, in which Shimon Ruiz de Luna introduced himself to the reader. Fluid and ornate, the passages listed his qualifications and skills as a physician and alchemist, but also hinted at more pagan practices and a strong belief in the occult. Here the calligraphy became a little less scrawled and more leisurely in its swirls and arcs – as though the chronicle had started its life as a personal confession.

I was but twenty-three years of age when exiled from Córdoba, my town of birth, for ten years hence. My father, mother and sisters were lost to me, tried and found guilty by the Inquisitional police, for the sin of practising their natural religion. Betrayed by a woman who ingratiated herself into my father's house to steal my family's greatest treasure, an ancient manuscript that had once been the property of Elazar ibn Yehuda, physic to the Caliph Al-Walid and medic to the moor invader Tariq ibn Ziyad. I myself escaped arrest when our dwelling was searched, by the means of a sewer. But before I fled I took Yehuda's ancient manuscript with me. My father had always told me to guard this work above my life and the lives of my family as it contained directions to a secret that would secure the fortunes not only of myself but all who followed in my lineage. And thus I fled from the cries of my condemned family with the manuscript wrapped under my cloak.

August pushed his plate away and wiped his hands on a serviette. He understood why the book's real message was so very carefully hidden. Ruiz de Luna had been concealing his true religion as well as his pursuit of Elazar ibn Yehuda's mysterious 'treasure'. In Spain in the early seventeenth century to be found to be a Jew was death sentence enough, without the added charge of witchcraft. August himself had met several Spaniards fighting in the Republican Army who revealed to him that they were *Marranos* – secret Jews – their families practising the remnants of a religion that had been forbidden centuries before. August hadn't really known what to do with these strange and incongruous confessions. It was as if they felt they could tell him, a foreigner without judgement, and not their comrades. One of the men had been killed in battle and for years August had felt weighed down by his friend's confession. Reflecting on the paradoxes and prejudices that had shaped history, he turned back to the page he'd been reading.

> *Disguising myself as a Christian, I sought apprenticeship with a medic in Gazteiz-Vitoria – a city I calculated to be far enough from my hometown to be safe. For ten long years I worked hard for this doctor and learned his craft magnificently. Then one day I returned from a trip collecting the herbs and flora required for his practice to find him in his house murdered most brutally. Terrified I myself would be found guilty of this heinous crime and my true identity revealed, I was forced to flee again. This time I chose to go to Logroño, a town of little consequence, a place where I was convinced I would be safe. Indeed, I found employment with an apothecary and within a year I hath both loved and married a Basque woman who heralded from a small fishing village, Cabo Ogoño.*

The sound of the telephone cutting through the air startled him. August swung around, his fingers still resting on the embossed cover of the chronicle. He was convinced it was Cecily, but to his surprise found himself not wanting to answer it, knowing that to do so would be to reignite the seesaw dependency that had been the nature of their relationship. If he truly loved her, he would release her – the thought was a painful epiphany. He let the telephone ring until it stopped.

It wasn't easy. Afterwards he heard the echo ringing in his head, with her whispering her name under it. He waited until it faded, his fingers blindly tracing the Lauburu, the Basque symbol. Was the chronicle a doorway back? Had someone deliberately given him a reason to face the past, find what he'd lost in that country and make himself whole again? It felt like it.

> *My wife's name was Uxue. She was wise to the old ways of her people and worshipped their ancient female deity Mari – goddess of the sky and mountains. Many sought my wife for her services. She could cure the curse of the evil eye, make sure of a good harvest and make a man love a woman he'd never seen – these were only some of her talents. And so it was, our dwelling became famous. People from other villages and town would come to visit us – my wife for her 'magick', myself for my physic skills. Soon we were both profitable and happy, then the Terror came upon the town and all was changed. I knew then it was time to turn back to my secret inheritance.*

August studied the tiny hand-drawn map on the page opposite. Under the drawing was the cryptic title written in Spanish: 'The first sacred location, as described in Arabic by the great physic Elazar ibn Yehuda.'

He picked up a magnifying glass he used in his research and ran it slowly across the illustration. It was a topographical sketch of a region he recognised from the rugged outline of the coast, situated between Bilbao and San Sebastián. The mouth and river that ran down to Bilbao and created a natural border for that corner of northern Spain were clearly marked, as was Mungia and Gernika. Further up, on the coast, sat the fishing town of Bermeo. To the right of this he could see the mouth of the Urdaibai and beyond that Elantxobe, a fishing town near Cabo Ogoño, the home village of Shimon Ruiz de Luna's wife Uxue, which was marked no doubt for this very reason. But here the map changed. It became noticeably more detailed inland from Elantxobe. August ran his eyes down the page beyond Gernika, which he could only imagine as the smouldering ruin the German bombing had left it in 1935, past Durango. To the left of a village named Mañaria, there was a far more detailed sketch of a valley. In the centre of that valley was a village called Irumendi – 'the village of the three mountains' – a reference August assumed to the three mountains that ringed it. A cross depicting a church was visible, as well as a narrow river running through it. Written in Latin were the words *'Hic primus locorum Elazar ibn Yehudae sacrorum inter betulam argenteam quercumque atque iuxta divae antrum'* – 'The first of Elazar ibn Yehuda's sacred locations lays here between the silver birch and oak near the Goddess's cave.'

August wrote down the name of the village in a small notebook then made a sketch of the original map. He pulled out a roadmap of Spain he had kept from his Civil War days. The edges were frayed and worn, and there were pencil crosses over it where he had marked the places he fought and the friends who had died. He hadn't opened it in years, and when he unfolded the sheet it was like he'd released the scent of burning grass, of orange groves and the distant thudding of aerial bombing all at once. *Roger, Juan, Xavier, Helmut,*

your names are still with me, is this the only afterlife? To live on in
the memory of the living? Or do we all evaporate into time, forgot-
ten, like air itself? He paused for a moment, his eyes shut,
willing away the faces. Steeling himself, he studied the roads
and rivers.

The cheapest way he could get there was to catch a train
from Calais to Bordeaux, then get a local train down to the
small coastal village of Saint Jean de Luc. He would have to
rely on his old Basque contacts from Operation Comet. He
only hoped some of them had survived. He still knew of
one man in Saint Jean de Luc who might be able to help,
codename Marcos. August suspected he might still be
involved in smuggling Basque Nationalists, money and
information for the freedom fighters back into Franco's
Spain.

Once over the border August planned to get a train from
San Sebastián to Durango, but from there he would have to
hitch a ride or hire a car. Irumendi itself wasn't marked –
probably too obscure and remote – but he recognised the
three mountains and the valley. On the contemporary map
the mountains had names: Alluitz, Urkiola and Anboto.

The doorbell rang, jolting him out of his study. He paused,
waiting to see whether it was for him. Outside in the entrance
hall he could hear a door creak open and the shuffle of slippers – the old widower who lived in the studio apartment
opposite his room had answered it. There came the murmur
of voices but August couldn't quite hear the conversation.
He relaxed; the old man had a sister, a retired nurse, who
would visit him late. A minute later there was loud banging
on his door. He stumbled up – the chronicle, decoded pages
and maps were all still spread out on the table.

'Hold on!' August shouted, but the banging continued.
Was it possible she had come back?

'Cecily, is that you?' He grabbed the chronicle and slipped it into a desk drawer.

'It's the police, sir, open up,' came the deep voice from behind the door.

'Just a minute, I'm not decent,' August replied, buying time.

He swept up his notes and decoded papers and slipped them under the topmost of a pile of books by the window. Just then the Mauser pistol sitting benignly on the windowsill caught his eye. Cursing, he pushed it down the back of the couch then finally turned to open the door.

A policeman and what August assumed to be a detective stood grim-faced in the doorway. For one horrible moment the thought that Cecily might have committed suicide occurred to him. *You're being absurd.*

'It's not Cecily, is it?'

The men exchanged glances, then without asking permission stepped into the room.

'Chilly in here,' the detective said, calmly, arranging himself in front of the low gas flame. The smaller and rounder of the two men, he wore his superiority in rank with a sullen aggression. In contrast, his lanky uniformed companion exuded an air of faint embarrassment. August closed the front door and turned to face them, resigned to the visit.

'Constable Jones and this is Detective Superintendent Duckett, sorry for calling at such a late hour, sir, but we 'ad no choice, see, there's been a fatality.' The policeman waved his hands around apologetically.

August's heart leaped. Had Cecily done something stupid?

'A fatality?'

'A fatality,' the detective elaborated, grimly, 'your name has been linked to. Mr Winthrop, isn't it?'

'August E. Winthrop. Just tell me it isn't Cecily.'

The policeman looked confused, and turned to his companion.

'Who's Cecily?'

'How would I know, Jones?' the detective snapped, then swung back to August, who was both relieved it wasn't Cecily and secretly ashamed that he could be so narcissistic to think she would kill herself over him. He reached for his cigarettes.

'The dead person is a Professor Julian Copps. His housekeeper claims you were the last person to see him alive,' the detective continued.

'The professor's been murdered?' Incredulous, August stared at the officers. As far as he knew Copps was well liked and his activities extremely innocuous – the only furore Copps had ever caused was because of an article he once published questioning the infamous Peace of Callias – a legendary peace treaty between the Greeks and the Persians, the existence of which had always been presumed but not proven. The idea that he might have outraged a fellow academic to the point of murder was patently absurd. No, it had to be something more arbitrary like a robbery gone horribly wrong, August concluded.

'At the moment, sir, whether it was a natural or unnatural death is open for debate. I would venture to say it was suspicious, however. Can you tell us your whereabouts at ...' The detective glanced over at the policeman, who flicked open a small notepad.

'... between four and five o'clock yesterday afternoon,' the young policeman read from his notes.

'Thank you, Jones. Mr Winthrop, the victim was discovered in his dwelling by his housekeeper, a Mrs O'Brien. The state of the corpse gave the poor woman a horrible shock, horrible. So, your whereabouts?' Both men were now staring intently at August. Stalling for time, he reached for an ashtray, thinking rapidly – he had returned directly from Professor Copps's apartment to Kensington, but the very fact that he had been alone and no one could verify his movements made him a suspect. Yet to suggest otherwise would only lead to further complications.

'I came directly home after seeing Professor Copps.'

'And what time was that?'

'I left the professor's apartment around three in the afternoon. I was back here by four.'

'Alone?'

'As you can see, I live by myself.'

'In other words you have no way of proving your whereabouts on Thursday afternoon between the hours of four and ten.'

'I guess not.'

'Write that down, Jones, suspect says, "I guess not."' The detective mimicked August's accent.

'Hold on, why am I a suspect if it isn't necessarily murder?' August sank into the leather armchair, now aware of a growing disconnect between what felt like reality and what was reality. The detective stepped forward; despite his small stature he was an intimidating man. Instinctively, August stood up again, towering over him.

'We'll know nothing until the results of the autopsy come through, which should be by the end of tomorrow. In the meanwhile, we are investigating all possibilities.' The detective strolled further into the room, his aggressive manner made August edgy; a reaction the detective was no doubt calculating on. He sat down on the couch. Immediately, August tensed, horribly aware of the Mauser hidden between the seat and the back cushion.

'The leather armchair's more comfortable,' August suggested, trying to sound as casual as possible. *Don't move, don't move.* The detective's back was about six inches from the concealed gun. If he shifted down the couch, he would discover it.

'Is it now?' The detective's voice was laced with suspicion. He glanced around the studio apartment, as if seeing it for the first time, taking in the threadbare rug, the old beaded curtain that barely hid the sleeping area from the rest of the room, the flickering gas flame.

'In some economic strife, sir, that's unusual, isn't it, for an American?' He almost spat the last word out, and August's heart sank – he was in for a long night and God help him if they found the gun.

'A temporary situation.'

The detective studied him, then shifted unknowingly a few inches closer to the pistol. 'You seem nervous. Do you have any reason to be nervous?'

'I'm just shocked, the professor was a close friend.'

'A close friend you hadn't seen for over a decade, then when you do he suddenly dies a mysterious death.'

'You can't seriously think I'm a suspect?'

The detective ignored him. August noticed he was busy scanning the titles of the book spines resting against the wall. The policeman interjected.

'This is simply a preliminary questioning, you see, sir.'

August watched dismayed as the detective's gaze settled on one particular book: *Maize Dolls and Their Uses in Haitian Voodoo.* He looked back up at August, his eyes gleaming with a new intelligence.

'One scenario is that the victim was frightened to death,' the detective said, with ghoulish relish.

'Is that possible?' August asked, knowing it was – he'd seen it happen in the prison cells of the fascists.

'Judging by the way the professor fell and the expression on his face, something came through that front door that terrified the life out of him – literally.'

'But you can't actually prove that it was murder?' August was trying to piece together the scene – Julian Copps's body sprawled out across his Persian rug, his thin white hair spread around his glazed eyes like a wispy halo, poignantly vulnerable. *How did you die and what was the last thing you saw?*

'Possibly,' the detective exclaimed, then, to August's relief, stood and began pacing the room. 'We have other circumstantial evidence that substantiates our conclusion. The questions are, who'd want to murder him and who would have access to an object that might be frightening enough to an educated man like the professor to have such a horrendous effect. And you see, that's why you, a prize pupil of his, someone who might be aware of his vulnerabilities, some secret beliefs, someone who has an educated understanding of the darker arts ...'

'Oh for God's sake, Detective, I'm a classicist who specialises in the ritual uses of plants and herbs, I'm not an occultist. In fact I am most emphatically an atheist.'

'Funny, we heard Communist.' The policeman suddenly sounded a lot less apologetic. A flash of anger shot through August: old wounds, old accusations. He glanced sharply across at Constable Jones. They must have contacted MI5; that meant he was a suspect.

'Once. I'm not so sure now.' He reached into his pocket for a cigarette. 'Mind if I smoke?'

'Oh, we don't mind, do we, Jones?'

Ignoring the sarcasm, August lit up, the blue-grey fingers of the tobacco instantly relaxing him.

'As far as I know, Professor Copps didn't have any enemies. He's been retired for over ten years and was well respected and well liked within the classicist world. And us students worshipped him. He was the best mentor you could wish for, acutely intelligent, funny, with an ability to enthuse, but most of all he always believed in his students, even when some of us stopped believing in ourselves. I dare say he saved a few lives as well as initiated a few great careers.'

'Sounds very saint-like,' the young constable ventured.

'A saint who was frightened to death. Ironic, that is,' the detective growled then glanced over at the map of Europe still open on August's desk. 'Thinking of travelling, sir?'

'I was just doing some geographical research, that's all.' August was now struggling to keep his temper.

'Good, because we wouldn't want you to leave the country until we get the results of the autopsy,' Jones clarified. 'Your sudden disappearance would not help your cause, given you have no one to verify your whereabouts during the time of the possible murder. You do understand how such an action might look somewhat suspicious, sir.'

'Of course, currently I have no intention to travel,' August retorted, maintaining the steady gaze of a consummate liar. 'But what I don't understand is what on earth could have frightened a man like Professor Copps to death?'

The two policemen exchanged glances, then the detective reached into his pocket and pulled out a small object wrapped in tissue. He walked over to the desk.

'We tried dusting it for fingerprints but there was nothing. Absolutely nothing. That in itself is decidedly odd.' He unwrapped the object and laid it out on the wooden surface. It stared up at August – the straw head was instantly recognisable to him; Professor Copps's expression of wry amusement. For a minute he thought he was going to be sick.

'It looks like a voodoo doll to me and Jones agrees, don't you, Jones?' The detective studied August's reaction.

'I do. Ugly little thing, gave me a hell of a shock when I found it.'

'Where did you find it?' August said.

'Pushed into the mouth of the victim, then left for us to find.'

'Like a warning?' August volunteered.

The detective smiled, warming to the subject. 'Now you're getting the picture, only we'd call it a calling card.'

The three men stared down at the doll. It appeared to be made of some kind of white paste – like clay – that had been baked. The body was clearly that of an older man, thin-legged, sagging at the knees, sunken-chested and with a vulnerable bulging stomach. It even had genitals. The sculpting of the torso, face, hands and feet was curiously detailed, yet other parts were clumsy and vague, as if constructed from someone's memory, and of less significance. It was grotesque in a primordial way. August shivered. Although only about seven inches in length, it was uncannily realistic in its resemblance to the professor. For one horrible moment he wondered whether it wasn't the work of an ex-lover, such was the detail. The head had strands of white hair baked clumsily into the top, framing the face that was remarkably lifelike except for the eyes. They were long pins tipped with glass black orbs that were staring back at them now. But the most terrifying detail of all was the cluster of pins that had been thrust into the heart of the doll.

'The hair is human, I had it tested. We think it might even be the victim's own hair,' the detective said.

August looked up startled, his mind spinning – in that case it must have been someone who knew Copps or at least had access to the apartment. The housekeeper? A secret mistress or perhaps male lover? August had never been entirely sure of the professor's sexual proclivities.

'The housekeeper has been ruled out as a possible suspect,' the detective went on, reading the question in his eyes.

August hesitated then decided he might as well be honest. 'I've seen something like this before, in the Pitt Rivers Museum in Oxford, when I was a student. In the section that covered magic, ritual and belief – I used to go there when I was researching my degree. It's like a voodoo totem, an effigy made in the form of the victim as a means to control or inflict pain on the subject.' *But encased in display cases, those absurd dolls were stripped of all their potency, yet this one is alive, throbbing, I can sense the danger.* Despite his disgust, August kept his expression neutral.

'I'm aware of the hypothesis,' the detective replied, dryly. 'Whether it actually works is a whole other debate.'

'Utter tosh, isn't it, sir?' The young constable glanced nervously at his superior. August and the detective, fascinated by the gawky figurine with its wispy silver hair, both ignored him. August lifted up the doll.

'What about the clay, it has an unusual texture, it reminds me of something.' He sniffed it. It smelled faintly burned and acidic. He'd smelled that smell before – after battle.

'We think it's a clay made from ground bone.' The detective stared at August, a piercing look awaiting a response, one August knew from his own military training, the policeman would read and potentially use against him. August's brain clicked into a professional detachment – survivor's rule number one.

'Human bone?' He couldn't help asking despite already knowing the answer.

'An educated guess and a correct one. But this is the

thing, sir. We think the ground bone might possibly have come from the victim himself.'

'How would you know?'

'You were aware the professor had an artificial leg – the right one from the knee down.'

'That's right, a legacy from the First World War. At least that's what us students were led to believe.'

'Ah, but that's the strange thing. We did a little bit of research and there is no record of the professor ever having served in the Great War. But suppose he knew the doll was human bone, and with his knowledge of history, myths and symbols just suppose he thought he was staring at his own death. Now that would frighten anyone to death, don't you think, Mr Winthrop?'

Olivia stood in the doorway of the small corner shop and pretended to study the paltry display of sweets in the window – a few jars of ancient boiled sweets, a box of liquorice thick with dust: remnants of a world pre-rationing. She glanced back over at the terraced house, knowing that the American's apartment was on the ground floor. Lights were on and she could see the three men silhouetted against the drawn blinds. She'd seen the policeman and his plain clothes companion enter the building and she had a strong idea why they were there. Such linear plebeian logic, she thought to herself. As if A always led to B, as if all could be materially explained. Not in her world and not when her world stretched its dark tendrils into theirs – those men standing so confidently inside those four brick walls, as though even the walls could protect them.

She should have felt fear or at least a danger of entrapment, but if anything their proximity thrilled her. It made the whole pursuit of August Winthrop more sublime. She smiled to herself then caught sight of her reflection in the shop window. For a moment she was startled, it was like seeing her own mother staring back. Good, it's what she needed, to transform her appearance. In an old winter coat with padded shoulders – a style dating from the early forties – her hair covered with a headscarf tied under her chin, her face bare, drawn and without make-up, she looked like a middle-aged housewife. Standing upright next to her was an old trolley half full of coal. There was nothing to distinguish her from a thousand other middle-aged women, a lower middle-class widow struggling with the freezing weather, her meagre coal allowance and rationing book. Utterly nondescript, she was completely invisible to them.

'I could walk through walls,' she said to herself. 'Walk through those walls and kill them all if I wished.' Her low voice frightened a passing cat that shot under a car, then crouching glowered back at her, its yellow eyes shining through the gloom. Ignoring it, she looked back across at August's windows. Would they arrest him? She didn't think they had enough evidence and it wasn't what she planned. The professor had unwittingly provided the second jigsaw piece, but more importantly he had galvanised August into action. He'd lit the fuse and stepped back. Olivia couldn't have planned it better herself.

Poor Julian. An image came back to her of him forty years earlier standing on a moor, symbols written in goat's blood across his naked shoulders, virile in his muscularity, his head thrown back against the wind. He'd been a believer then, beautiful, courageous and defiant and, in her own particular way, she had loved him. But her world did not tolerate betrayal. Not for science, not for the love of money and certainly not for academia. Funny how she'd never forgotten the shape and touch of his body under her hands – how ironic to discover the memory was still there reverberating in her fingertips after all those years.

Now the shadows were moving across the pale orange block of the drawn blinds – they were leaving. Olivia stepped back into the doorway. The front door of the terrace house opened and the two detectives appeared. They stood for a moment on the step staring out into the bleak evening fog. The policeman clapped his hands against the cold, while the detective pulled out a pipe and stuffed the bowl with some tobacco then lit up – a sudden tiny flare against the white creeping fog. Then together they stepped out into the night.

'What do you think, sir?' Jones asked, turning to his companion.

'I think he's probably innocent, but he's the best we've got so far.'

They crossed the street towards the Black Maria parked at the opposite kerb. They walked right past Olivia without noticing her. She was right; she was entirely invisible to them. The younger man turned to his superior, and in that glimpse of his wide, pale, young face, she read his personality in a split second – his anxiety over a young pregnant wife now waiting at home for him, his desperate need to impress the older detective, the drive to be promoted.

'Do you want me to set a man on the street, make sure he doesn't do a runner?' His young voice rang through the leaden air, his breath etched in white plumes.

The older detective glanced up the road thoughtfully. Despite the occasional call-out for domestic violence and the illicit homosexual encounters that occurred in the local garden square, the area was remarkable only for the aura of middle-class reserve that seemed to envelop the horse chestnut trees like a fine net.

'No, not tonight, I suspect he'll stay put. He hasn't the money to travel nor any reason. Besides, I don't want to frighten him. His expertise might come in handy later.'

'Expertise?'

'Jones, didn't you notice his pretty little collection, witchcraft, botanical voodoo and all sorts of whatnot?'

'That doesn't mean he's the killer, does it? I mean, he might have been visiting the professor about some research, like he said.'

'I've got the feeling this won't be the first and last murder of this type we'll see.'

'You think the killer might be a serial murderer?'

'Perhaps. But why Professor Copps?'

'Well, he wanted to shut him up, that's for certain,' the young policeman ventured.

'Why do you say that, Jones?'

'Because of the doll, sir. I read that as symbolic of wanting to stop the voice, like.' He faltered, embarrassed by what might be seen as an absurd flight of imagination. 'Sorry, sir, I got carried away.'

They were now at the car and for the first time that evening the detective had a sudden instinct that they were being watched. He turned on his heels and stared down the narrowing barrel of the street, already partially obscured by the thickening fog. He could see no one, only some old dear dragging a small trolley of coal. Reassured, he turned back to Jones.

'Not at all, Constable, not at all. I think you have a valid point. However, I suspect the professor was killed in pursuit of something, and I'm not convinced that the charming August E. Winthrop isn't connected somehow. The fact that he was the last person to see the professor isn't coincidental.'

He tapped the contents of his pipe against the side of the

car. The smouldering tobacco fell to the pavement. He shivered, thinking it was the cold. The arthritis in his right hand
was playing up again. I'm getting too old for this job, he
thought, as he climbed into the passenger seat. Surprised at
the sudden silence, he looked over his shoulder. His companion was still outside looking back into the fog.

'Are you coming, Jones? It's freezing.'

The constable shook himself out of his reverie. He
thought he'd seen a shadow dart across the road, but nothing
human moved that fast. Now convinced his imagination was
getting the better of him, he turned back to the car.

After they'd driven off Olivia parked her trolley against the
kerb and walked over to where the detective had emptied
out the contents of his pipe. How wonderfully careless
people were of the small personal things that defined them,
things that become imbued with their *essence*: fingernail clip-
pings, wisps of hair, pipe tobacco that still held the very
breath of the smoker, she noted, as she meticulously scraped
the contents of the pipe into a small piece of paper and
folded it up. Slipping it into her pocket, she glanced over at
August's window. The American was still up. Never mind,
she could wait. She could wait all night if she had to.

August remained at his desk until he'd heard the police car
drive off. Shock pinned him there for a good half-hour. The
image of the voodoo doll revolved slowly in his mind – both
fascinating and utterly repellent. The idea that this deeply
primitive object could have been the murder weapon of
someone as refined and intellectually sophisticated as the
professor seemed ridiculous. Was his murder linked to the
chronicle? He'd only read the first section, but it gave him a
feeling of vertigo undercut with something even more

disturbing – a sense of premonition, as if he'd unknowingly embarked on a journey that was in fact predestined. The sensation had haunted him ever since Cecily had walked out of the apartment and Jimmy back into his life, and now this visit from the police. If he wanted to escape any further surveillance, he had to act swiftly. He had to take back control. *I have to leave and I have to leave now.* The desire to move, simply to grab what he needed and run burst through him.

He leaped up and pulled down a large battered leather travel bag out of his wardrobe, one he had hauled all over Spain. He threw it onto the bed and opened an old tea chest that doubled as a chest of drawers. He lifted out two pairs of trousers, an old sweater, several pairs of underpants and a singlet, calculating what he would need for the damp chilly Basque weather. He folded the clothes into the travel bag, then threw in the rest of the cigarettes Cecily have given him – six packages in total – enough for a couple of months if he rationed himself. Then he packed his Rolleiflex camera and ten rolls of film. He zipped up the bag and after making sure the blinds and door were both securely closed, lifted the corner of the rug and prised up a loose floorboard. Hidden underneath was a small leather pouch and a bundle wrapped in an old oilcloth. He pulled out the leather pouch, blew the dust and spider webs off it and opened it. Inside were several sticks of stage make-up, powder, false moustaches, fake glasses and several wigs. It had been the disguise kit he'd travelled with during his time in occupied France. He tested one of the make-up sticks against his hand – a dark pancake he knew in minutes could transform his Anglo-Saxon appearance into one of an olive-skinned Mediterranean. The stick was still moist and usable. He sniffed the skin of his hand and was immediately transported back to a night in

Nantes in 1942, in an attic of a brothel that was also a front
for the resistance, with Germans searching the ground floor
while he, armed with a mirror and his make-up kit, disguised
himself beyond recognition, only to saunter down the stairs
past the SS officers as a drunken French sailor who just got
laid. *Maybe that's where the chameleon is most comfortable, hiding
under the skin of another.* He packed the stick away, reassured
he would have the means to disguise himself if necessary.

He placed the make-up kit next to the travelling bag then
hauled out the bundle and, sitting back on the floor, unrolled
it slowly. Inside was a hunting knife with a gleaming oiled
blade, a medal the Republican Army of Spain awarded him
for the Battle of Jarama and his Mauser semi-automatic.

He wrote out a cheque for three months' rent for his land-
lady, then a letter to his publishers requesting an advance on
his advance, then finally began a letter to Cecily. He got as
far as the second sentence – 'I have decided it would be
better for both of us if I go away for a while and an opportunity has presented itself. I know this is difficult for you . . . ' –
then realised it sounded too pompous and self-absorbed. He
pulled it out of the typewriter and tossed it into the bin. She
would just have to find the flat closed up. She was an intelligent girl, capable of drawing her own conclusions, he
decided, fighting a fierce desire to ring her.

Finally, he turned back to the chronicle. The rest of the
untranslated book seemed to stare back up at him, taunting
him, daring him to crack open those pages. He'd read so
little and yet he was already about to embark on the same
journey as the enigmatic Shimon Ruiz de Luna. He lifted
the book and felt the thick waxy pages: there was a whole
mystery trapped inside them that had been waiting for over
three hundred years to be set free – had Shimon been guilty
of witchcraft or merely political intrigue? Had he discovered

Elazar ibn Yehuda's great mystical treasure and, if so, would the chronicle reveal where it was? He would have to decipher and translate the rest as he travelled, he had no choice – like the physic himself, he too was about to be thrown into an extraordinary journey. It was either that or stay and face a possible murder charge and even more awkward investigation. He reached for the ink roller and the rest of the equipment he'd used to transcribe the chronicle, his mind made up. Outside, a blackbird suddenly began singing in the garden square opposite. Its nocturnal song reminded August of a night in the country he'd had once with Cecily.

Cecily. A sadness rose up in him like unresolved grief. Perhaps this research would be a chance to confront his own demons, demons he'd failed to bury these last fifteen years. He knew that now, his own faltering career as an academic proved it, as did the increasingly shifting, jigsaw-like nature of his own identity. But to enter Spain was dangerous, the risk of arrest and possible execution was real. He knew he was still on the list Franco held for all International Brigade fighters who had managed to escape in 1936. The question was whether his old contact from Operation Comet, a man he'd never actually met in person, would help him get over the border in Basque country without the fascist Spanish police either arresting him or preventing him from entering. Again, he felt that dry excitement, the pounding adrenalin he used to get before a battle. He felt alive.

He glanced at the clock: it was already four in the morning. If he left at seven, he should be able to catch the nine o'clock ferry to Calais. He walked over to the window and wrenched it open, allowing the freezing morning air to flow in. Outside, it was a waxing moon. Leaning out, August drank in the bluish light, illuminating the snow on the trees and ground. The ordinary transformed into extraordinary. It was ridiculous really, but he felt somehow reborn, as if he'd started stripping away everything that had kept him secretly fearful, secretly confined.

Behind him the chronicle, catching a glint of moonlight, glowed in sudden luminosity.

Tyson pulled open the hotel window and watched the traffic stream down Piccadilly. Ice crystals were already forming on the glass. It was a noisy moon that seemed to rattle the pane, its hollow bellow drilling straight into his brain. It reminded him of another moon just as demanding that had hung in another night – years ago in the hills of Biscay, where he had been told of the existence of something that until then he'd regarded as myth, an unobtainable mystery as fictional as mermaids or ghosts now made unexpectedly, palatably and thrillingly real, a mystery that could make him a god and one that later he had killed for. It was a night that had decided the rest of his life. He was jolted out of his reverie by the telephone ringing. Strolling across the Persian rug, he took his time before picking the receiver up. The voice at the other end was curt to the point of rudeness.

'He's getting ready to leave.'

'Follow him. I want every movement. I want to own him, understand.' Tyson put down the phone, heard its empty click against the papered walls. And now I will kill again for the same mystery, he thought to himself.

It was still dark when August stepped out of the terrace a few hours later. The night was just dispersing and the smell of the approaching day hung between the thawing frost that iced the grass and the black lattice of tree branches. To August, with the weight of his travelling bag slung across his shoulder and the crisp fold of his passport pressed into his jacket pocket, it was the smell of adventure.

She watched him walking towards the Tube entrance at the far end of the street. In a minute she would follow. She had prepared, she had an idea of where he was headed, but for now she would compress her presence into a faint silhouette, one that would follow at an invisible distance wherever he led her. And only when he had arrived, only when he had blindly led her to her goal in that unconscious naive manner of the uninitiated, would she make her move.

5

August leaned against the railing staring out at the vast chalk
cliffs. The sea smashed against the foot of the soaring coastline then dissolved into mist. It was an endless cycle: waves,
rocks, sea spray. Hypnotic. Infinite. The wind, laced with
salt and the smell of the diesel from the smoke billowing out
of the ferry's funnel, beat against his face and hair erasing all
thought or regret. Instead he was filled with nothing but the
sharp chill of the air and an imagined camaraderie with all
the generations of departing migrants who would also have
stared back, as he did now, at the majestic permanency of the
Dover coast. It felt like liberation.

The ferry emitted one last lingering horn blast that
echoed across the blue-grey water, then gathered speed as it
ploughed towards Calais. August tossed his cigarette butt
away before turning to go into the top deck.

Inside there was the usual milling crowd of passengers:
some tourists, English and loud, laughing and chattering
excitedly among themselves about the duty-free purchases,
the clubs they were going to visit in Paris, the frustrations at
the passport queue; while a few travelling salesmen sat along

the wooden benches in clusters of one or two. All in the cheap suits and trilby hats of their profession, some barely shaving, shiny in anticipation, as their elders slouched in seasoned resignation. Two women stood open-mouthed waiting for the tiny duty-free shop to open, the small glass shelves filled with a selection of dramatically shaped perfume bottles, silk scarves and seamed stockings – goods still hard to find in Britain. There was a young girl in a corner weeping silently into a handkerchief, slim and elegant in a well-tailored but humble dress – French, August decided, a nanny returning home perhaps, leaving behind an English lover. He was tempted to go over and comfort her but decided it was more prudent to stay as anonymous and invisible as possible – he couldn't afford any emotional complications. Behind the young woman sat a middle-aged matron studiously reading a book. Dressed in a tweed suit and gloves, she looked well-heeled, and for a moment August wondered why she wasn't travelling first class, then thought nothing of it.

He found himself a seat on a bench facing the bow. The view of the horizon and the two wings of ocean stretched across the large glass front of the cabin. It was one of those rare views of the world – devoid of man, elemental, timeless. Such sights always summoned a primal wonder in August, ever since he was a small boy staring out at the Atlantic from the family's beach house in Martha's Vineyard. He looked out, remembering how much he loved the feeling of travel, of moving forward into the complete unknown. It used to be how he reinvented himself – Cecily would say accusingly, 'escaped himself'. He stretched, shaking off the creeping exhaustion of the night before. Passport control at Dover that morning had been tense. August expected the detective to have issued a warning on his name through Interpol.

Luckily, he still had his US passport, and the travel pass he'd been given by MI6 just after the war was still valid. The passport inspector had raised his eyebrows at the American passport but been silenced when August produced the government-approved travel pass with its impressive stamp. Nevertheless, August wondered if the French would be so unquestioning.

Across the aisle the young French woman had stopped sobbing and now gazed blankly into the distance. One of the travelling salesmen had fallen into a snoring doze while his companions appeared determined to get drunk on duty-free whisky. A lull underlaid by the faint excitement of the traveller settled over the half-empty deck, now rocking gently as the ferry cut its way through the Channel. August closed his eyes and again images of both the professor's sprawling dead body and Cecily's dismayed face just before she walked out flashed into his mind. It was no good, he couldn't break free of them. He opened his eyes again, placing his hand on the travelling bag as a kind of instinctive comfort, his anchor in transit. Under his fingers he could feel the edges of the chronicle hidden inside; it was a reassuring sensation. He reached into the bag and pulled out the next pages of the chronicle he'd managed to decode in the early hours of the morning and began to read, the alchemist's words filling his head, drowning out the low rumble of the ship's engine.

My first challenge was to translate the ancient diary of Yehuda, written in the language of my forefathers, and although I had learned Hebrew from my father, to be found carrying such a document would have had me arrested as a heretic. The diary itself was incomplete, a thin collection of notes written in wild and almost illegible script – there were also maps – with strange and bizarre references to lands I've never heard of. I studied the manuscript for a year, late at night while Uxue slept. Night after night I burned the candle low, struggling with the maestro's cryptic account of his expedition – the nightmare of following the carnage Tariq's army left in its wake, the moral struggle he felt in himself divided as he was between physic and conqueror.

It appeared that Elazar ibn Yehuda hath come upon information of a great botanical secret, one that could make a man either a God or a Monster. He hath heard that the first place he needed to look was in the remote mountain valleys that made the natural divide between the Goths and the Vascones. The more he hath heard about this great treasure, the more he was determined to find and conquer its power – not just for his Caliph but for himself. Eventually, I came to understand he hath found several secret forested places within which was to be found a botanical clue leading to the location of the great treasure itself. The first of the locations appeared to be in Biscay. Then rumour reached us that the Inquisitorial guard and their Dominican masters hath arrived and they hath started arresting the innocent already.

§

Shimon sat at the simple oak desk he kept beside the window of the cottage, under the eaves of the farmhouse. The tallow in the oil lamp was burning low and despite the frosty air outside he had the small pebble glass window wide open so that the black smoke from the wick could escape into the night. Elazar ibn Yehuda's papers were spread over the wooden surface, the yellowing parchment cracked and curling at the edges. The lettering was barely visible: an archaic jumble of which Shimon could only really understand every second or third word. His transcription sat to the left of him; a labour of hours, it covered only a few pages of his chronicle. He lay down his quill carefully, so as not to waste the expensive ink, then stared out at the moon. It seemed to call him – three-quarters full, it hung low in the sky, a reddish brown, something portentous about its pock-marked visage. A bad omen, he thought, wondering about his own future. Outside, the valley below the cottage stretched out in the moonlight like a wondrous carpet. The River Ebro – a black glittering snake – wound through it with a slow majesty. Far greener and more lush than the arid southern landscape of his childhood, the country around Logroño had become precious to Shimon. As had the cottage they rented in a village on the outskirts of the town, a small building with two rooms – a front room in which they both received their patients, with the desk he now sat at and a small iron bed more for show than sleeping, and a back room with an open fireplace for cooking, a wooden table for eating (above which Uxue had hung her bunches of drying herbs) and a couch – it was on the couch in this room that they both slept. Small as it was, the cottage had come with enough land for them to grow maize, keep three cows, a few hens for eggs and a donkey. Of the two small fields they leased, one was completely dedicated to the growing of herbs and plants he used in the apothecary and the other Uxue used for her healing practices: black elder, celandine, bay, rue and sugebelarra – serpent's herb – among others.

Next to the lavish Córdoba townhouse of his childhood, it was humble and Shimon knew his merchant father would have considered it a peasant's house and would have been devastated to see how his only son and heir, an educated youth who'd once had all the mercantile opportunities Córdoba had to offer, had been reduced to living like a poor farmer. Yet Shimon had never been happier. In the five years he had lived this double life, he had learned a science and had excelled at it, he had loved and was loved, and most

importantly he had found community. Truculent at first, the
local folk were slow to win over, but once won they were
loyal for life. And there had been a great need for a physic
who was skilful and successful in his craft but who also did
not charge exorbitant money for his services. Soon Shimon
had become known as 'the people's doctor'. Often he did not
charge the very poor and was happy to make a trade with
those who had no coinage, and as a result his larder was
always full.

The cottage itself was near enough to the town for his
wealthier patrons to be bothered to visit him and far enough
away to provide them with some protection from the authorities. Both his and Uxue's businesses relied solely on word of
mouth. What else could they rely on, patronage? And as they
were both good healers, they had prospered. Soon they
would be able to afford a child. But not yet, Shimon told
himself; in nearby Miranda they had heard of the arrests in
Zugarramurdi. Fear among the communities had spread like
an infection – one carried by a fast wind. Uxue had been
especially worried; as a Basque healer who used the old
ways, she would be particularly vulnerable to suspicion. Just
then he heard the low murmuring of his wife tossing in her
sleep in the simple couch in the back room. Shimon glanced
through the open door. At the foot of the couch their dog
they'd called Little Mountain – Menditxu – a Basque hunting hound, slept, his massive head tucked between two large
paws, a thin line of drool hanging from his floppy furry lips.
How long did they have before this small pocket of utopia
was destroyed? And how could Shimon, himself a secret
heretic, protect the woman he loved? And, as an outcast,
would he ever trust his own happiness? Down on the
wooden floor Menditxu's ears twitched and his large bloodshot eyes sprung open as if he had heard or sensed

something in the distance. The dog got up and trotted over to Shimon, his ears alert and erect, his head cocked towards the window.

'What do you hear, boy?' Shimon asked, softly, careful not to wake Uxue. In response the dog growled softly, now pacing backwards and forwards beneath the window.

'Shh, Menditxu,' Shimon commanded, and the dog cowered and retreated under the desk. Shimon looked out of the window. At the far end of the narrow lane – trees on one side, the valley and slopes covered in fields on the other – the flare of torches was just visible as a group of people and horses turned a corner. Shimon watched in horror as the procession – completely silent except for the panting of the horses and the faint clanking of stirrups and armour among saddle – moved down the road. As they drew nearer he could see the brown habit of the Dominican priests who held the flaring torches, their taut arms betraying a fanatic determinism, their hoods pulled low over their brows. Wearing the crimson-and-black tunics of the Inquisitional police, with the royal coat of arms embroidered on the breast, swords tied to their waists, and grim-faced, they flanked the pitiful group of prisoners on horses as they silently rode – five on each side. And now as they mounted the crest at the top of the lane just before passing the farmhouse, moonlight flooded the faces of the prisoners themselves. Thirty, Shimon guessed, thirty men, women and children, manacled and in filthy hemp cloth, barely human, stumbling and staggering between the guards and the silent monks. Some of the men had chains around their bleeding ankles. All of them were barefoot, their hair wild and unkempt, the men bearded. All bore the marks of torture. One boy, who appeared the youngest child, about ten years of age, his face hollowed by starvation, his eyes deep set and blackened with exhaustion,

stared out terrified and bewildered. He looked like he had
lost his wits, Shimon observed. These must be the accused
from Zugarramurdi and the other villages, he thought,
noticing a hooded figure, a woman, riding a white stallion
between two guards, a long maroon cloak and hood concealing her face. As she passed under the window, her horse
reared up and the hood fell away from her face. Recognising
her instantly, a chill ran through Shimon – it was her, the
English woman who had betrayed his own family. Overcome
by terror and nausea, he pulled back from the window.
Leaning against the wall, he found he was shaking all
over.

'What is it, my love?' Uxue sat up in bed, her face filled
with anxiety.

'Nothing, go back to sleep,' he murmured, as quickly as
he could, but the dog was up again, growling and pacing
nervously, and the soft shuffling and marching outside was
clearly audible.

'What's that noise?' Uxue was now climbing out of the
bed, her long black hair spilling out behind her to the small
of her back, the white night gown gathered around her
thighs. Terrified, Shimon stepped towards her.

'Please my love, for both our sakes keep silent!'

But she was already at the window, staring out, her body
becoming rigid as she realised what she was witnessing.
Shimon slid down beside her.

'It is the witch-hunt returning, Pierre de Lancre's victims,'
she whispered, her eyes wide in horror. 'But I know some of
these people.'

'Stay silent, Uxue, otherwise you will condemn us too.'

They watched in shock as the procession passed the
window, winding itself past the farmhouses down to the
town of Logroño, the priests' faces hidden in hooded dark-

ness, the soldiers' impassive and stony-faced, eyes forward. The prisoners delirious in fear and terror knowing nothing except the exhaustion of another step on the rocky ground before them. Just then one of the men lifted his eyes and saw the two pale faces looking at him from the window.

'*Lagundu anaia!*' he yelled. 'Help me, brother!' Inside, Uxue started up, ready to answer, but Shimon wrestled her away from the window, covering her mouth with his hand.

'Are you mad, woman? Do you want to join them?'

She burst into silent sobbing and he cradled her as they both lay on the floor waiting for the footfall and clattering hooves outside to pass.

When the pale blue of the dawn had started to creep across the straw-covered floor, lighting up the veins of his wife's feet, Shimon got up and pulled shut the window. Uxue, shaking the grief from her face and shoulders, dusted the straw from her night dress, mustering courage from the stoicism she could now see in her young husband's face.

'We must leave today, this very hour if must be, Uxue. Else face arrest ourselves.'

'I know, my love. I have thought this myself, but how? We are known, we will be seen and named.'

'Those who are named are named by their enemies only. We have no enemies.'

'Some scream the names of those they love under torture, anything to save their own lives. This is human frailty.'

'We are all frail.'

'Husband, two days ago I found flax seed scattered across the front doorstep.'

'Flax seed?'

'It is what people believe stops sorceresses from flying.

Someone believes me to be a witch, Shimon.' She sounded terrified.

'We will leave at night, under cover.' He was decided.

Uxue pulled off her nightshirt, her pendulous breasts revealed in their white and red-tipped glory, the thick black bush of her sex startling against her heavy thighs. For a moment Shimon observed that his wife was thickening into an older womanhood and he loved her for it. He thought about reaching for her, and how this would push away the terror, if momentarily, but she was already pulling on a skirt and a smock and scraping her hair back into a cowl.

'I have often thought of this day and it is inescapable. I have a plan, husband.'

He walked over to take her hand. In the five years they had been together she had always been the practical one, the ballast to his dreaming.

'So?'

'So this ancient book you wish to follow, you told me the first destination that was mentioned was in Biscay, the country of my people.'

'And ...'

'We will travel there. We will flee the Inquisition, yet make a virtue of our journey, for, husband, I will not be broken by such people.' The fierceness in her voice flooded him with pride. Here was the strength he needed, here was the defiance he secretly feared he'd always lacked.

'You would do this with me? You will support me in this quest?'

'I will do more than that, I will be your assistant. I will, using my craft, assist our search in any way possible. My plan is that we are to travel in disguise. A disguise that will cause revulsion and will make people shun us.'

'How so?'

'You will disguise yourself as a priest, the kind who helps lepers. I will disguise myself as a rich young woman stricken with the disfigurement. The reason behind our travel is that you are escorting me to the leper hospital at Errenteria. With the use of herbs I shall create a mask of such hideous appearance people will avert their eyes for fear of infection.'

'Ingenious. We will take the donkey and you will ride as the rich patient. I shall don the correct robes and carry the leper's bell I will ring on approaching a village. Uxue, this is a fine and solid plan, no one will dare approach us. We pack what essentials we need and be gone by sunrise.'

'What about the dog, Menditxu?'

'He will come also. If we leave him, he will be drowned as a witch's familiar.'

§

An announcement over the intercom of the ferry told August they were due to dock in ten minutes. Absorbed by his reading, he barely heard the deep voice booming from the speakers. It was only when the other passengers started gathering up their possessions that he looked up from the sheaf of transcribed pages.

Olivia watched from behind her book, then picked up her own bags, careful not to get too close, not to appear interested or even aware of the tall American now stepping towards the exit. She was just about to follow when she became conscious of a man she hadn't noticed before on the boat. A tall Slavic-looking man, nondescript apart from the muscularity and extraordinary length of his arms apparent even hidden under a raincoat. As he walked over to follow the American she noticed a gleam of intent, of urgency, for a split second in his movement. It was betraying. August has a second shadow, she thought to herself. In the same instant a thread of fear, a sensation so intense it was almost sexual, shot through her as she realised she knew who this second shadow might belong to.

6

The rugged French coastline loomed up. It was after eleven but small brightly painted fishing boats, tugs and dockworkers still crowded the bustling harbour of Calais. The ferry docked in a flurry of shouting and ropes as August, bemused by the laconic and casual manner in which the sailors secured the hull to the metal bulwarks, waited with the other passengers while the rickety walkway was lowered down. As he stepped onto French soil it occurred to him that the last time he'd been in France he was undercover, liaising with the resistance as they tried to track down an Allied airman who'd been shot down and not captured. Now, to be walking towards a French customs and passport checkpoint felt uncomfortably dangerous and foolish. Force of habit, August reminded himself, half-expecting to see a German soldier sitting alongside a French officer with the tell-tale Vichy insignia stitched into his jacket. Fighting the instinct to break and run, August approached the glass window with his US passport and papers in hand. Oblivious to his inner turmoil, the French customs officer behind the partition took his passport politely. August watched as he placed the page with August's photo and date of birth against a list of names that would include ex-Nazis trying to escape the war crimes tribunal, possible Soviet spies and other criminals wanted by Interpol. August's stomach tightened in anxiety – he had assumed he wasn't on any list, and if he was, it was more likely because the Americans had him profiled as a Communist and had contacted Interpol. An unlikely scenario as his last official involvement with the Communist Party had been over fifteen years earlier, but old fears dictated and the officer, his face a mask of pedantic concentration, seemed to be taking his time.

'It's been a while,' August said, in perfect French. Surprised at the faultless pronunciation, the officer looked up.

'For an American you speak good French,' he remarked, his suspicion seeming to grow.

Noticing the metal badge in the buttonhole of the officer's lapel – an emblem of Free France, indicating the officer had fought against the Germans – August handed over the pass issued by MI6 to all its staff, showing he was an employee of the British government and Allied forces and as such was allowed free access to all Allied countries. He prayed the passport officer would not notice it was out of date. The officer pulled it towards him and examined it short-sightedly.

'I came in and out during the war – unannounced of course. A guest of that wonderfully French institution, the resistance,' August elaborated. 'I see you were also a member?' he added, a deliberate attempt to distract with his charm. The officer looked up and saw that August had recognised his lapel pin.

'Indeed, I fought for France, in my way.' Now he smiled. 'Nice to meet another unsung hero.' Then he stamped August's passport. 'And thank you, Monsieur, for your contribution to the liberation of my country.'

The SNCF express to Rouen wasn't leaving until two that afternoon and, after buying a ticket at the Grand Station, August walked into the town square and bought himself a soft felt hat – the kind the local French sailors wore – a pair of cheap workman's trousers and a nondescript blue jumper. He changed in the shop and, after hiding his blond hair under the hat, examined himself in the mirror. Despite his height, and rugged square jaw, he almost fitted in – he certainly didn't look so much like a tourist. The young shop assistant, amazed that a handsome foreigner like August would want to dress down, watched dumbfounded. The final touch was an old leather tool bag, the kind locals would carry to work. August transferred the camera, the chronicle and the Mauser into it then hoisted the strap across his shoulders. It was a comfortable fit, and the old excitement he used to feel adopting a new identity began to drum through his veins. Already he felt freer, as London and the turmoil of the last two days seemed to drop away.

Back at the Grand Station he found a restaurant that looked as if it had remained untouched since the glory days of the belle époque. The waiters wore white jackets, the decor was art deco, the maître d' was moustached, his dyed black hair oiled smooth to perfection, while the metal arches of the station's domed ceiling soared like high musical notes above the tables covered with linen cloths and gleaming wine glasses. The grandeur of the architecture reminded August of a cathedral – a basilica dedicated to the epicurean. It was like the war had never happened. There was even a faint glow of prosperity as the waiters bustled around the clientele, silver trays propped on their shoulders while an accordion player played 'La Mer' in the corner.

August took a table in the opposite corner and picked up the menu, which to his delight appeared to have escaped any rationing. He called a waiter over and ordered mussels, followed by steak and pomme frites. Then he sat back, contemplating the journey ahead. By his calculations he would be in Bordeaux by six, and from there a local train ran on to Saint Jean de Luc, but it wouldn't arrive until late. He would have to find a cheap hotel and approach the contact. Then he would have to convince the man of two things – his identity and his sincerity. Recalling the profile SOE had composed based on the communications sent by Marcos, August imagined he'd probably be a truculent, naturally suspicious individual. Most of the Basques he'd met fighting in Spain had been – with good cause. But the fact that August was now a maverick operating without official blessing was going to make it a lot harder to win that trust, especially as neither of them had ever met face to face. But August had no choice. He knew of at least two other International Brigade fighters who'd returned to Spain since the Civil War – one of them was still incarcerated in the notorious Carabanchel Prison and the other had been executed. It was near suicide to consider going back. *But I will, I have to.*

The last time August had any communication with Marcos was back in 1945. He owned a bar in the public square of Saint Jean de Luc – a popular venue known as La Baleine Échouée ('The Beached Whale'). Marcos had proven the perfect conduit for Operation Comet – he'd hidden hundreds of US and Allied airmen as they made their way down through Urrugne past Biriatou across the Pyrenees and over to San Sebastián. But how did August know whether Marcos and La Baleine Échouée were still there in Saint Jean de Luc? It had been years.

August looked up. Again he had that sensation in the back of his neck. He glanced around the restaurant, careful to be subtle. About half the tables were full, mainly families travelling, he guessed, south for the summer. He saw several couples engrossed in each other, and one older woman, maybe an academic of some sort, who had her head buried in a copy of *Le Monde*. No one even appeared to notice him. Was this sense of being followed another wartime legacy? The habit of paranoia? Or were the same people who murdered the professor now following him?

August took a sip of wine and turned his mind back to strategising. Marcos, Saint Jean de Luc – it made sense, he'd heard rumour the route was still used by exiled Basque freedom fighters on the French side of the border who needed to get either information or themselves into Fascist Spain on the other side. If anyone could get August safely into Biscay, it would be Marcos.

Reaching into his satchel, August pulled out a small black notebook – a travel diary covered with jotted notes, train times as well as botanical notes. He double-checked the route he'd mapped out for himself back in foggy London in the early hours of that morning. Planning on the possibility that there might be an alert out on his identity papers, he would avoid the larger cities, and instead take local trains, which was circuitous but safer. He would take the train to Rouen, then a local service to Le Mans, then through Tours, and finally onto Bordeaux, where he would change for an even smaller slower local train that would take him into Saint Jean de Luc itself. It would be a long journey, but after Copps's murder, he wasn't willing to take any chances.

A gleaming bowl of mussels, a freshly baked bread roll and a finger bowl of water interrupted him. The fragrant steam floated up from the shellfish sprinkled with garlic and parsley, each gaping. They smelled delicious. August prised one open and scooped the orange-lipped flesh out with a fork. The taste was incredible after the bland fare of British rationing. As the salty taste of the mussels filled his mouth, August felt as if he was seeing colour after years of monochrome. He sat there eating, trying to remember the last time he'd had mussels. It would have been over ten years, in another life, in another era. It was extraordinary, he reflected, how the war seemed to have accelerated history, shaping Europe in ways that were inconceivable only a few decades earlier. And with Stalin and the accelerating gulf between Eastern and Western Europe, he had the sense that they were all on the edge of a new precipice. *Would I survive another war?* It was too terrible to contemplate.

Olivia watched him over the newspaper she was holding up. Despite the rough clothes he was wearing and the hat pulled low over his brow, she'd recognised him almost immediately – she'd followed him from the ferry to the train station and had then lip-read the ticket seller's lips as he repeated the destination the American had requested.

Saint Jean de Luc.

A small resort and fishing port near the Spanish border. The question was, why there?

The rattle of the train as it passed over the tracks was like an incessant sea over which he now rode. Hypnotic, soothing. Outside, the French landscape sped past. Once they'd left Calais, the broken trees gave way to struggling wheat fields and small lines of sprouting green sugarbeet just beginning to poke up above the dark-brown earth. Occasionally, the train would whistle as it trundled past the remains of a bombed-out village – new timbered structures springing up defiantly beside the burned-out skeleton of a church or town hall – or the tumbling walls of a cottage spilling bricks like entrails. Staring out, August found the desolate images all too familiar and it was hard not to imagine the events that had led to such destruction – makeshift battles between retreating German forces and Allied troops, a betrayal of the local resistance leading to the slaughter of all the men and boys, the arbitrary bombing by both Allied and German aircraft, flattening farmhouses like paper cards. Fragments of buried memory now began to flash through his mind in synch with the spinning wheels of the train. *Don't lose control, don't lose control.* Gripping the edge of his seat, August forced himself to focus on his fellow passengers.

The second-class compartment seated six and apart from August, there were only three other people. A Catholic priest, a thin elderly man, slept in the seat opposite, rosary in hand, his face pockmarked and seemingly scarred by both harsh weather and a begrudging asceticism, a dog collar chafing his wrinkled neck. His gaunt face pressed against the leather headrest bounced gently with the movement of the train. His sandalled feet and plain cassock with crudely hewn wooden cross hanging around his neck made him look as though he'd been transported from the Middle Ages. Only the watch hanging loose on his wrinkled thin wrist placed him in the twentieth century.

Sitting next to the priest was a red-faced bellicose-looking man in his forties, wearing a too-tight cheap suit, the trousers of which were far too short. He looked like a farmer dressed for church. A handkerchief was spread on his knee in front of him and he was chewing noisily on a baguette stuffed with garlic sausage, the scent of which filled the carriage, making the other passengers' stomachs rumble and causing the small boy sitting next to August to fidget and stare longingly at the cascading breadcrumbs. The boy, ethereally blond in that transparent manner the very pale sometimes display, was with an older woman August had decided must be either his mother or his aunt. But as he watched the thin boy hungrily eye the baguette he noticed a label attached to a battered child-size leather suitcase at the boy's feet. It had the words 'DP-Lager' and the symbol for the Red Cross beside it. The woman sitting beside the boy caught August's eye.

'I know, I know, but what could I do? So he's German. He was an orphan, not even two when his parents were killed. I was working in the displaced persons camp and the poor kid was starving, and not only for food, let me tell you,' she explained, apologetically, to August in French.

'Madame, it was the Christian thing to do,' the priest interjected, now awake and nodding his head. 'It is not for us to visit the sins of the parents upon the children.'

'Indeed, Father,' August agreed, careful to pronounce his French as authentically as possible.

'What would a priest know?' the farmer cut in, gruffly, after belching a garlic stench. 'Did they fight? No, in my village the priest was the only one who kept both his belly and his gold all through the occupation. Call that Christian?'

The priest, flushed in rage, did not reply, and the matron, now visibly uncomfortable, also remained silent. August was again reminded how the occupation had divided neighbours and families between collaboration and resistance. The woman cast a querying glance towards him, but August knew his accent precluded any kind of judgement and besides he needed to stay anonymous. But then, unable to bear the huge eyes of the child any longer, he leaned towards the boy.

'*Hungrig?*' he asked.

The boy nodded shyly. August reached into his pocket and pulled out the apple he'd bought at the station, and handed it to the child, who waited for a nod from his guardian before eagerly taking the fruit.

'*Danke schön,*' he whispered then added '*Merci*' loudly after his guardian landed a small slap on his leg.

August could hear voices in the next compartment. It sounded like more than one man. Instinctively, he slipped his hand into his breast pocket to check that his passport and tickets were there. He stood and walked to the door of the compartment and saw a train guard and a border policeman, checking tickets and passports. Again, he fought the desire to run. Was it possible the English authorities had contacted Interpol by now? After all he was a suspect in a murder case. As he turned away from the door a tall balding man, wearing a leather jacket and hat, glanced casually into the compartment as he passed by in the corridor outside. It took Vinko all of two seconds to place August. Satisfied the American was now back on his radar, he continued down the corridor as silently as he had arrived. He had a telephone call to make at the next station.

The ticket inspector glanced at the middle-aged woman in front of him then looked back down at the grainy black-and-white photograph in her passport. In the passport the woman looked vivacious, wanton – there was something animalistic about the way her hair snaked down her face to her shoulders and her eyes promised plenty of trouble of the good kind. She was the type he would normally try to pick up: dangerous, a little overripe perhaps, but a good fuck for sure. And yet he wouldn't look twice at the woman sitting in front of him. It was as if she had deliberately flattened out all her sensuality and personality – the flesh and blood woman was in black and white and the passport photograph was in colour. It was this that made the ticket inspector suspicious.

'English?' he asked, as if it weren't obvious.

'I am,' she replied, in that superior English manner he'd always found faintly offensive. 'I'm on my way to see my sister in Saint Jean de Luc. She's an English teacher there,' she added, unnecessarily and entirely without smiling. Shrugging, the inspector handed the passport to the border policeman, who turned it several ways, then flicked through the pages looking at the border stamps. There were several to the Middle East – Egypt in the early 1930s, India in 1935 and one marked 'Hungary 1938', a strange destination, he thought, for one who looked so staid. He turned back to the passport photo and, like his colleague, found it difficult to associate the woman in the photograph with the woman in front of him.

'Olivia Henries?' He read her name out in English, in a thick provincial accent.

'Yes, that is me,' she replied, again in a voice devoid of emotion, too devoid the policeman thought. Besides, the name resonated with him, if only he could remember where.

'You tourist, yes?'

'Absolutely, I only intend to be in France for a month, then thankfully back to Britain. Not that I don't think the countryside is beautiful.' Her French was correct and thoroughly unappealing. Unattractive in voice as well as in the flesh, the border policeman concluded, unaware that his colleague had arrived at the exact same verdict.

The policeman snapped the passport shut, then handed it back to her.

'Madame, enjoy your stay.'

The two officials stepped back out to the corridor, about to move on, when something kept the border policeman back. 'Just a minute, Jean-Marc.' He pulled a small notebook out of his pocket and opened it to a list. He scanned down the names. On the second page he found it. Olivia Henries, neatly sandwiched between two others. *Voila*. That would be worth at least a hundred francs. He glanced back at the number of the compartment and made a note of the time, the train number and the last station they went through. He would make the call from Bordeaux before the Englishwoman caught her next train to Saint Jean de Luc. The American would be most pleased and most generous. Who cared if he wasn't exactly CIA – the American paid enough for him not to ask too many questions. Besides, it was foreign business, foreign trouble. Why shouldn't he, a Frenchman, capitalise? After all it wasn't hurting France. Happy at the prospect of the new hunting rifle he intended to buy with the hundred francs, he closed the notebook and the two men moved onto the next carriage.

'But I already showed my papers at the station.' The farmer, bristling with indignation, crossed his arms defiantly. The ticket inspector glanced at the border policeman. *Great*, August thought, *just what I need, two upset and tense police officers*. He tried not to look up at the luggage rack overhead, acutely aware of the Mauser semi-automatic hidden in his old leather bag. It would be difficult to explain why he had it if they decided to search him. *Relax, avoid eye contact, don't sweat, don't antagonise them any more*, he tried to communicate silently to the irritated farmer. It didn't work.

'What is this, a police state?' the farmer continued.

'Please, Monsieur, we are just doing routine checks, sir,' the inspector answered, politely.

'Just show us your papers,' the policeman growled, his blunt irritation galvanising the truculent farmer, who reached into his waistcoat pocket and, after pulling out his papers, held them aloft. The border guard inspected them, then handed them back. The two officials turned to the other passengers: the priest had his documents already in his hand, August noted, as did the matron. Finally they arrived at August, who promptly showed them his US passport. The policeman glanced at his face, then the passport. Time slipped into slow motion as August struggled to stay completely calm.

The other passengers watched silently. August looked nonchalantly over to the exit, calculating whether he could push past the officers and run to the end of the train to leap off. He glanced at the rushing landscape outside the window, the train must be travelling over sixty miles an hour. He wouldn't make it. For the second time that day he hoped his departure hadn't yet been noted by Interpol.

Standing over him, the border guard studied the name, August E. Winthrop, August E. Winthrop. It didn't ring any bell. As far he could remember it wasn't on any file he had – not the Interpol list or the other list, the one he got real money for tracking. He glanced at the American – just another eager tourist wanting to be jolted out of his wealthy complacency, wanting to see the 'real' Europe. Fuck the guy, he thought, and fuck his easy life, he probably thought the stupid peasant clothes he was wearing were quaint.

'Purpose of journey?' the policeman asked, brusquely, in English.

'Fishing. I hear they have great deep-sea fishing off Saint Jean de Luc.'

The guard sighed, then handed back the passport, without another word, and both officials carried on through the compartment.

'American?' the priest ventured to August, after a moment's silence.

'Jimmy Cagney,' the German boy cracked, in a bad Hollywood accent, and they all burst out laughing.

*

Malcolm bit into his Chelsea bun, then upon encountering an unusually hard raisin, worked it out of a hollow tooth with his tongue. It was a chilly morning and as the expenses at Leconfield House did not allow them decent heating, Malcolm still had his Gieves and Hawkes silk scarf wrapped around his neck. Maxine, his secretary, waited impatiently file in hand in front of the heavy Victorian desk that dominated the small office. Ignoring her irritation, Malcolm stared down at the nearly completed *Times* cross-word lying in front of him, then picked up the telephone. 'Get me D1,' he instructed the operator. 'Courtney Young, please.'

The cheery voice of the head of Soviet counterespionage came on the line.

'My frog has leaped out of the pool,' Malcolm murmured, cryptically, into the receiver, then waited.

'Spawn will fly,' Malcolm repeated, echoing the voice at the other end of the line before putting down the receiver. He scribbled the sentence in the margin of the newspaper with a pencil and stared at it. Finally, after breaking into a wide smile, he wrote the correct answer into the crossword, and ran a line down through the letters in triumph. The morning was looking better already.

'Upstairs is outside, he wants to talk to you,' said Maxine, a sensible cockney girl who disguised a secret disdain for her employer with a motherly bossiness, a pretence she found worked best with the privately educated civil servant. She held out the file as if it contained explosives.

'About what?'

'Someone you used to work with – an August E. Winthrop. Upstairs reckons he's murdered someone,' she concluded, with grim satisfaction.

Malcolm's heart rate quickened. He took the file and

immediately began scanning it. A second later he looked up to find Maxine still standing there.

'Well, usher him in and you'd better bring us another tea and another Chelsea bun. Make it one with pink icing, you know Upstairs.'

'This Winthrop fellow, one of yours in the SOE, wasn't he?' asked Upstairs, more commonly known as Godfrey Smart, formerly Major Godfrey Smart of the Lancaster Rifles. He settled his substantial bulk into the chair opposite Malcolm's desk.

'One of our main men on Comet, an excellent soldier, recruited him myself. Knew the man at Oxford.'

'But he does have some unsavoury political beliefs, Marxism and whatnot, and he's a classicist to boot.'

'Your point?'

'Exactly,' Upstairs retorted, cryptically, ignoring the question, a habit that infuriated Malcolm. 'Never trust idealists myself – flaky individuals, almost as bad as artists.' Several crumbs of icing flew from his lips as he spat out the last word, landing unceremoniously on Malcolm's shirtfront. He brushed them off, silently consoling himself that one day he would inherit Upstairs's job and it would be him doing the spitting.

'There is no doubt August is a maverick, however his service to the SOE was first class. It is also true he fought in Spain with the International Brigade, but I believe since then he's been quite bipartisan, if not an outright patriot, to Britain that is.'

'And he's not homosexual?'

Malcolm couldn't help smiling. 'Quite the contrary.'

'You can never tell with Oxbridge,' the Sandhurst man muttered, darkly. 'But then there is so much you can't tell with

Oxbridge.' It was an oblique reference to the betrayal of Guy
Burgess and Maclean, the two MI5 agents, both Cambridge
and the latter homosexual, who, since their defections to the
Soviet Union, had haunted the corridors of MI5 and MI6 like
taunting spectres. Malcolm chose to ignore the comment.

'But you've read the file?' Upstairs insisted.

'I have, actually I knew the victim myself, also from college days. A shocking way to die.'

'A very bloody strange way to die, ritualistic – something
your man Winthrop might have the imagination to have
dreamed up? It *was* Classics and Oriental Studies, wasn't it?'

'So you did research him.' Something began banging
against the back of Malcolm's mind: his survival instinct.
If they'd researched Winthrop they would be researching
him. Now he was horribly aware that his past association
with August could prove more than a hindrance. Staring at
Upstairs's bulbous red nose, he began to strategise. Was
there a way of turning this to his advantage?

Upstairs droned on. 'Him and the old professor, turned up
some unsavoury bones in the professor's cupboard – apparently he had an association with that madman Aleister
Crowley back in the twenties, admittedly brief through an
old girlfriend, and your professor was mentioned in a report
on a raid on a mansion in Kent. People dancing around
naked in goats' skins, that kind of thing, which could of
course be relevant to the method of murder.'

'Professor Copps a Magus?' Malcolm, having always
regarded his old college associate as somewhat of a bore, was
astonished.

'Possibly. Frankly, I wouldn't give a toss if he turned out
to be Mrs Simpson's secret lesbian lover, but the whole thing
has Six's nose out of joint. Turns out your professor used to
do the occasional assignment for them when he was on his

archaeological adventures in the Middle East and they've decided to take the whole thing personally. They rather fancy your friend Winthrop for it.'

'Winthrop was Copps's golden boy, I very much doubt it was him.'

Upstairs belched reflectively. 'Maybe you don't know the man as well as you think. One of our watchers sighted a . . . ' He glanced down at the open file balanced precariously on his lap. '. . . Yolanta Ashivokova leaving his apartment five nights ago, just before Copps's murder.'

'I told you, he's a ladies' man.'

'Is it a yen for the ladies or for the KGB? Yolanta's a known Russian spy, recently recruited. D Branch have been toying with the idea of turning her. She has a couple of vulnerabilities: single mother, child and mother both on temporary visas awaiting passports. A nice-looking filly, mind you, the man has taste.'

'I highly doubt that Winthrop is a Soviet spy,' Malcolm interjected, emotionally, then immediately regretted it – really, the general paranoia was setting everyone on edge.

'You do, do you?' Upstairs looked up from the file, a piercing gaze.

'And how come I wasn't told about the Ashivokova operation?' Malcolm countered, nevertheless feeling a little queasy. It was well known there was still another high-placed mole somewhere they hadn't managed to rat out either in MI5 or MI6 and everyone was under suspicion; the fact that internal information had been withheld from him meant that he too was definitely a suspect. Ignoring the question, Upstairs glanced back down at the file.

'There is also a connection to both Guy Burgess and Arthur Wynn. The union activist's been on our radar for months.'

Now Malcolm was starting to feel really bilious. He made a mental note to avoid the Chelsea buns in future.

'Winthrop was at college with Wynn, so no surprise there. What's the Burgess connection?'

'Apparently Charles Stanwick, a close friend of Winthrop's, and a noted homosexual, had a tryst with Burgess when they were fighting in Spain. You are aware that Winthrop has now fled the country?'

'He has?'

'Two days ago. He's somewhere in France. Got any idea where he might be headed?'

Malcolm averted his eyes, down to his favourite paperweight, a miniature bronze lion that sat snarling on a corner of the desk. Again, life felt as if it were offering him a great opportunity, seamlessly, organically, the chance to vent a slow and yet unexpected resentment that had built over the years, beginning with August's cavalier seduction of the woman he would marry to the recent chagrin of realising she still desired the American. But there was something else, something that now had begun to push into his burgeoning headache, an instinct, a smell, the inkling that perhaps August might be KGB after all, and if he was, the possibility Malcolm might even be able to transform his own torpid career into something quite shiny, something his father-in-law could be proud of. For a moment the lion seemed to lash its tail in a restless excitement. Malcolm reached over and picked it up, then looked slowly across at Upstairs.

'Perhaps. It could be Spain, and if so he would be taking a route he knows well, the same route we used for Comet. But I should warn you, he's a master at disguise, a true transformer. It was one of his great skills when he was working underground for us in France. But let's wait and see.'

Upstairs smiled. 'I wouldn't leave it that long, dear chap.

A little bird in Six told me there's an unusual number of OGA reps in Madrid. Seems the Yanks are cooking something up with Franco.'

Startled, Malcolm dropped the lion onto the desk. 'CIA in Madrid, do we know why?'

Upstairs found a crumb on his shirt and swatted it away. 'No, but your man might. Of course, if he has turned, it could look a little embarrassing for the department, especially you, Hully, being his past mentor. We can't have that, can we? We've lost enough credibility with Uncle Sam as it is, don't want to appear complete morons.'

Malcolm was now feeling totally nauseous. Upstairs's tone of voice left no ambiguity – not only was he himself under suspicion, his job was on the line. Damn you, Winthrop, damn you. Upstairs, reading Malcolm's visible distress with some satisfaction, pushed down on the arms of the chair and manoeuvred his great bulk upwards.

'I'll leave you to organise that and don't forget to get that file back down the registry.' He leaned over to pat Malcolm's hand – a gesture Malcolm found faintly repugnant. 'Good chap, I always knew you were a company man.'

As soon as Upstairs had left the room, Malcolm, after rubbing furiously at his hand with a handkerchief where Upstairs had touched his skin, dialled the surveillance department to organise a sweep of Winthrop's flat. If he was working for the Soviets, there had to be some evidence he'd left behind, and at the very least they could bug his phone.

7

It was after 9 p.m. by the time the local train pulled into
Saint Jean de Luc. Shouldering his travel bag, August
walked through the narrow streets to the town centre beside
the small fishing port. To his left, the dark silhouette of
Mount Urgull overlooked the French frontier town like a
malevolent guardian, as he followed the line of the harbour.
The fishing town was still lively with people, and he strolled
down the avenue de Verdun towards the main square – place
Louis XIV – where the small port and waterfront lay. Moored
fishing boats with their brightly painted hulls bobbed gently
in the water, while some were still chugging in from the fishing waters of the Atlantic. Several fishermen dressed in the
traditional clothes of the Basque – large floppy black beret,
dark trousers and working jackets – hauled nets off the deck
of a small tug, watched from across the inlet by the cream
villas of Ciboure, their sloping red-tiled roofs and bright red-
painted shutters nestling against the hill, dominated by the
distinctive stepped outline of the church tower of
D'Auvergne.

A bandstand stood in the middle of the square, which was

lined with cafés and bars, as well as the old town hall and the
mansion that in 1660 briefly hosted the twenty-two-year-old
Sun King and his Spanish bride Marie Theresa.

Small groups of diners chatted among themselves around
the café tables, some stopping to watch August as he walked
past. Above him he noticed an old woman in a black shawl
lift a lace curtain from the window of a two-storey apartment
to stare solemnly out. August tipped his hat respectfully but
her face remained expressionless. A cold breeze came off
the Atlantic and as he walked by a restaurant with red-and-
white-checked tablecloths, he was overwhelmed by a gust of
cooking smells: garlic, roasting meats, even fresh coffee, and
he realised he hadn't eaten since late morning. It was all so
normal and a million miles away from London.

Changing trains at Bordeaux had not been a problem. In
the bustling town it was easy to blend in with the transient
population of traders and visiting locals. Nevertheless, the
sense of being followed had intensified. Twice August had
swung around convinced he'd spotted the same person – a
young thuggish man he remembered from the Calais train –
following him. The second time August had turned only to
see the same youth greet his girlfriend, then disappear down
one of the lanes that led further into the town.

August had originally learned about Saint Jean de Luc
and La Baleine Échouée from a young American airman he
visited in a London hospital – the airman was one of the
many Allied servicemen shot down in occupied France and
had spent time in the small fishing town before being smuggled out by boat via San Sebastián. The twenty-year-old was
a farmer's son from the Midwest and after surviving the
perils of Operation Comet had arrived back in England only
to be diagnosed with a terrible case of jaundice. During his
bedside debriefing he told August about the week he spent

hiding in the cellar of the bar, resting a sprained ankle and gathering his strength to make the dangerous ten-hour trek to the village of Sare, then over the Pyrenees, down the riverbeds and secret mountain paths, guided by the local Basque, across the border in the early hours of the morning, past the German border guards on the French side and the Spanish fascists on the Spanish side. In a fever, the airman had described the bar and the nonchalant stoic courage of the owner, whose bravado allowed him to court the local German SS officers while hiding airmen. The American had told August that the bar was on rue de la République, a small street that ran off the square down towards the seafront and the promenade de la Plage. The young airman had described it as a four-storey building with red-painted balconies and shutters, the discreet bar itself located on the ground floor, with a mural of Basque history running over the entrance depicting the whaling of the previous centuries, the whalers' long narrow boats, rowers straining against the heaving waters of the Atlantic, harpooning the animals by hand, with a bronze miniature whale hanging over the door. 'Moby Dick,' he'd finished off saying, having deteriorated into a wide-eyed delirium. 'Who would have thought, Moby Dick in France.'

His rescue and escape had been the most exciting thing that had ever happened to the airman, and August had left the hospital wondering how the poor kid would ever adjust back to Milwaukee.

August turned into rue de la République, a narrow street that had a view of the seafront at the end. A few tourists, mainly French, sat at the tables of the hotel opposite and an accordionist played a mournful tune under a street lamp. The tranquillity of the scene disturbed him. It seemed idyllic, too idyllic. Just beyond, something swinging in lamplight caught his eye. It was the sign for La Baleine Échouée. Relief flooded through him.

The bar had a low wood-beamed ceiling. The walls were decorated with fishing nets and ceramic plates painted with the ubiquitous Lauburu, and the seats were wooden kegs set around low wooden tables. By the door stood a large birdcage with several canaries twittering softly to each other. Behind the counter was a line of framed photographs of local fishermen posing in front of the small port, staring proudly back at the camera, which dated back to the 1890s. The small Basque flag – the ikurriña – hung down in the middle. Beyond the counter, at the far end of the bar, a jukebox sat like some bizarre altar to the future, its jazzy arches and swirls of colour totally incongruous against the surrounding decor. August recognised it as a Wurlitzer, probably from the early forties. This was what he was looking for.

A thin bottle-blonde stood behind the counter polishing glasses, her cigarette burning in an ashtray. She looked up at him – she wasn't bad-looking when she smiled, he noted.

Apart from her, there was only a couple of old men playing cards in the corner. No sign of Marcos or a man who even vaguely fitted his description. August walked over to the jukebox, slipped two francs into the machine and made his selection. He waited as the record clicked down into position and the arm lowered. Immediately, the hit song 'Boom' from the late thirties sounded out. The two old men looked up, glancing at the barmaid, then shuffled discreetly out of the bar, leaving their game unfinished. The blonde put down her glass and stepped from behind the bar.

'Marcos?' August asked, smiling. She looked him up and down, then unexpectedly took his hat off. Surprised, he stepped back.

'It's customary to take your hat off in the presence of a lady, isn't it?' She spoke perfect English. August took his hat out of her hand.

'I apologise. I was trying to blend in.'

'It will take more than a hat. American?'

'Once.'

'What do you want with Marcos?'

'Just say I'm an old friend, a friend who needs help. And if that doesn't work, try saying "Tin Man" to him.'

Now she was startled. She stared at him.

'You are Tin Man?'

'Please excuse my daughter.' A tall man in his late fifties stepped out from a back door August hadn't noticed, his large face craggily handsome, with a crooked nose and distinctive large ears – a trait that was classically Basque.

'She's forgiven. I'm sorry I didn't telegram ahead but times have changed.' He watched the man's reaction to the music. 'You must be Marcos.'

August held out his hand yet the Basque hung back, refusing to shake it.

'How do I know you are Tin Man? How do I know you're not some fascist spy recruited by Franco?'

'"Boom".'

'So?' Marcos shrugged, unimpressed.

'Okay, how about Winston Holinger, the young airman you rescued in April 1942. It was him who arranged for the jukebox – a great feat of black marketeering. Before that airmen used to have to come in here and play the opening bar of "Boom" on an old piano.'

Marco lifted a bottle of cider from a shelf and placed two glasses on the counter. He began pouring it.

'So, how are Winston and his young wife?'

'Winston's fine, only he ain't married, least not last time

he wrote,' August snapped back, knowing he was still being tested.

Marcos smiled to himself. Now August sensed he'd won a little trust. The Basque finished pouring out the cider and offered August a glass.

'So you're Tin Man.' He handed August the glass. 'You know, I thought you'd be better looking,' he joked, completely deadpan. He raised his glass and August joined him.

'*A la guerre*,' he toasted. 'Of course, for some of us the war never ended,' he added, in English. 'How can I help you, Tin Man?'

August glanced around the bar. The daughter had disappeared and they were now entirely by themselves.

'I need to get across the border.'

'And why can't you get in the usual way? There should be no problem for an American.'

'I fought with the Republicans, the Abraham Lincoln Brigade. I will be arrested the moment I step on Spanish soil.'

'You and me both, *gora Euskadi askatuta*!' Marcos sat at one of the small tables by the window, indicating August should join him. 'Please.' August sat, acutely aware he was still on trial. The Basque pushed a small dish of sardines and bread in his direction. 'You know I still run people across.'

'I had heard.'

'My people, most of the Basque men who fought, are either dead or exiled from their own families. America, Cuba, Australia, here in France, everywhere but their own country, their own villages. There is no real information getting into the country except for Radio France or the BBC. Franco censors everything. We are still fighting an underground war. Many, many people rely on me to bring them news, to smuggle loved ones across, some they hadn't seen for years. So tell me, Tin Man, why should I risk all this for you?'

August stared into his cider suddenly weary from the day's travel. He knew he didn't really have a convincing argument.

'I'm on the track of something – historical research that could be hugely important if my trip is successful. But I'll be honest, Marcos, I've left politics behind.'

'My name is Joseba. Marcos was my codename.'

'And my real name is—'

But Marcos held up his hand. 'Please, I think it's better if I only know you as Tin Man. So you think I should not help you?'

August drained his glass. 'Maybe not.'

For the second time since they met Joseba aka Marcos smiled, then poured himself and August another glass of cider.

'You are lucky, there is no moon tonight. We can leave in a few hours. Do you have a good coat and walking boots?'

August nodded, finding himself speechless with relief.

'Bon, I can drive you to a place, then we will walk down a riverbed that winds its way through the mountains, maybe about four hours. Then I leave you, it will be cold, there will be snow, ice. You will walk another three, four hours. Maybe you freeze to death, maybe not. But I guarantee there will be someone waiting to meet you on the other side of the mountain. After that you will be on your own and I never met you, understand?'

'Understand. How can I thank you?'

'You don't have to, you will be carrying a parcel for me. Don't ask me what's in it because I won't tell you, but assuming you make it over to the other side you are to hand it to my contact. That's my price for helping you.'

'Fair enough.'

'So you are agreed?'

'I am agreed.'

Joseba lifted a corner of the blind that hung across the window. He glanced out at the street then swung back to August.

'There's one other thing, you've been followed.'

August turned to the window. The street looked empty – apart from the two old men from the bar who were now sharing a cigarette outside, there appeared to be only a young woman walking a dog.

'I don't see anyone.'

'My man followed you from the station. We watch all foreign visitors like yourself. An older woman got off from the same train as yours. She followed you until a street away from here. Then we distracted her. Do you know her?'

'I have no idea who she is. As far as I know no one knows I'm here.'

'Someone does. Never mind, I guarantee she won't see us leave tonight. So we have a deal?'

Now he reached out to shake August's hand.

'We have a deal.' They shook, but August couldn't stop wondering who his tail was. If it wasn't MI6, who else?

Dressed in white overalls with 'Kensington Electric' embroidered over the breast, Malcolm waited as Eddy Watkins, the surveillance man, broke into August's flat in a matter of seconds, picking the lock with criminal panache. There wasn't a door in west London Eddy couldn't get through and he often boasted he had skeleton keys to the rest of the city – a fact that had contributed to Malcolm never sleeping soundly at night. It was four in the afternoon and the building was deserted, except for the old man living in the apartment oppo-

site who'd been staring suspiciously from behind his net curtains as Malcolm and his men walked down the path. Malcolm
had tipped his cap at him making sure the insignia and the
tool bag were well visible. The old man seemed to buy the
ruse and, scowling, had retreated into the shadows of his apartment. But now standing in the neglected entrance hall with
flaking paint and the faint smell of damp, Malcolm wasn't so
sure. A run-in with the local constabulary could prove embarrassing to MI5. There had already been several humiliating
incidents, one of which a training exercise in which several
eager recruits were instructed to break into a 'safe' house and
interrogate a 'suspect'. The trouble was, they had broken into
the wrong flat and by complete coincidence had ended up
interrogating a terrified petty criminal who assumed they were
the police and confessed all. It took some imagination on
Malcolm's behalf and a ticket to Paris for the terrified criminal
to avoid a compromising situation for both him and MI5.

The three of them – Malcolm Hully, Eddy Watkins and
Eddy's soundman, Keith – stepped into the flat, carefully
closing the door behind them.

It was in semi-darkness. The curtains were drawn and
there were still clothes thrown across the bed and chair.

'He must have left in a hurry,' Eddy remarked, before
going directly to the skirting board, running his fingers along
it for unusual hollows and possible hiding places or wires.

'Man on the run,' said the soundman, a stout man of few
words – a characteristic born of the tedium of listening to
thousands of other people's recorded conversations. He
picked up the telephone and tested the receiver a few times.
'Phone's clear.'

'Wire it,' Malcolm commanded. He checked his watch.
'Well, gentlemen, we have just under an hour, let's keep
this simple and silent – anything the slightest suspicious,

photograph it and, if necessary, bag it.' He slipped on white gloves, the others followed.

'What are we looking for?' Eddy asked, already in the middle of levering open a skirting board.

'A radio transmitter, code book, secret writing, microdots, the usual suspects,' Malcolm answered, making a beeline for the desk.

Keith held up a half-eaten tin of sardines. 'If he is KGB, they ain't paying him much.'

'A man like Winthrop has political ideals, he's not interested in money,' Malcolm snapped back, opening all the drawers. The top right-hand one was locked. Fishing into his pocket, he pulled out a penknife and prised it open. Inside was an empty box that looked as if it might have once held jewellery, and a bunch of airmail letters held together by a red rubber band – letters from Winthrop's mother in Boston. Underneath them a single folded piece of paper. This intrigued Malcolm. He unfolded it, several paragraphs in handwritten Russian, signed in English at the bottom – Yolanta Ashivokova.

'Bingo,' he said quietly to himself, then ran his eyes down the lines. It looked like a poem, enigmatic enough to be code.

'Gentlemen, I think we have something.'

Olivia pressed the bag of ice against her swollen ankle. Outside, she could hear the concierge of the cheap boarding house she'd found behind the promenade de la Plage arguing with her husband about how much she'd charged the strange Englishwoman. If only that young fisherman hadn't caught the heel of her shoe with his net as she was walking – she wouldn't have stumbled and twisted her ankle. And she'd know into which street August had disappeared. As it was, by the time she'd managed to disentangle herself from the fishing net and the overly obliging arms of the fisherman, the American had vanished completely. She glanced down at the purple swelling. At least it didn't feel broken, but it would take three or four days before she'd be able to put any weight on it and she couldn't follow him on a walking stick. Suddenly furious, she tore at the lace that lay across the pillow. If she lost him completely, it could take weeks to track him down again. Leaning heavily on an umbrella, she hobbled to the window. The room was in a triangular mock-Gothic nineteenth-century building that made up the corner of two narrow streets, just below the seafront. She had chosen it for the views: from her balcony even at night she could see that she had clear sightlines of ocean, the old casino La Pergola and several of the cafés and hostels that ran along the two narrow streets behind, rue de la Baleine and rue de la République.

As it was off-season, the small seaside town that had experienced its heyday in the late nineteenth century reminded her of illicit encounters and stolen romances she'd had in similar resorts many many years before. It made her feel strangely nostalgic. She stared out at a small fishing boat battling the wind on the dark horizon as it made its way back to the harbour; remembering was painful.

August must be somewhere in the town, perhaps in one of those little hotels on rue de la République, she decided. The question was, which one and for how long? Olivia had no choice. She would have to scout the town and sit at a table at one of the cafés in the place Louis XIV, have a late dinner and keep watch. August was bound to emerge sooner or later. She became aware of a burning sensation at the back of her head, as if something or someone hostile were staring at her. She swung around, surveyed the room, then hobbled over to the head of the bed and turned the large wooden cross with a graphic plaster figurine of the crucified Christ to the wall. She had enough problems.

'So, Tin Man, you know her?' Joseba, standing in the doorway of the bar, discreetly pointed up to a mirror hidden in the alcove of a beam running over the entrance reflecting the street to the left, enabling the viewer to see clearly thirty feet beyond. Sitting at an empty café table at the next building down was a small middle-aged woman in a headscarf. She was in profile so it was hard to get a clear picture of who she was, but August felt pretty sure he'd never seen her before.

'No, I don't think I do.'

'Not the mother of some young woman you have dishonoured?' the Basque joked, again in the deadpan way August was beginning to glean was characteristic.

'I'm telling you, I don't know her.' But as he stared into the curved glass he knew he was lying. There was something faintly familiar about her but he just couldn't place it.

'This is strange but she is someone important. You know how I know? Because about an hour ago someone else arrived in Saint Jean de Luc, only he is looking for her and him I don't like. This one is a killer – an American like you, but he has a smell about him. The smell of dead men. As for your girlfriend ... ' Joseba gestured up at the mirror. 'If she is a tiger, her claws are all blunt. But this other guy ... ' He ran his finger across his throat. 'I want him out of my town as soon as you go. But tell me, Tin Man, why are you so popular?'

'I don't know. I swear no one knew I was leaving London, and certainly not where I was going.'

Joseba slipped back into the bar, closing the door quietly behind him.

'In that case, my friend, they will only know this far of your journey. I promise you.'

Around midnight they slipped out of the back door of the bar. Joseba hustled August into the back seat of his old Citroën and insisted he keep his head down until they were well clear of the narrow streets of Saint Jean de Luc and out onto the bumpy country lanes. As promised, there was no moon and Joseba drove like a madman in what seemed like pitch darkness to August, seemingly along a route he must have known by heart. The bag with the chronicle in it bounced against August's leg as the car careered over bumps and potholes. Not willing to take any chances, he'd slipped the Mauser into his trouser pocket, in easy reach in a hurry.

An hour later the Basque abruptly pulled the car up in what appeared to be an empty field. He switched off the engine and wound down the window. Immediately, they heard the sound of distant frogs, the rustle of the wind in the trees and rushing water.

'Joseba?' August ventured.

'Shh.' The Basque held up a hand and they both sat stock-still in their seats. August strained his ears and gradually from under the forest noises came the rumble of a truck. It grew louder as the truck came on, appearing to approach them. August's hand tightened on his pistol and he stared out at the mist that hung low among the fir trees. It was impossible to see the road down which the truck was travelling, but it must be near as now they both could clearly hear the sound of Johnnie Ray's 'Cry' blasting out from the truck's radio. August glanced over at his companion. Joseba's face was grim with tension – it wasn't a reassuring sight. Just as August tensed the muscles in his legs, readying to spring out of the car, the truck passed by them, its headlights arcing blindly through the tops of the trees.

August exhaled. He glanced across at Joseba. The Basque smiled then indicated they should remain silent. Finally, the sound of the truck faded completely. Five minutes later Joseba checked his watch.

'That was the border police on their way to change guards. One a.m., right on time.'

'They were close.'

'Don't worry, they have never found me yet. Okay, now we start walking. I will escort you along the river up to the plateau we use as our crossing place. We will arrive at approximately four in the morning, the time the border guards are at their most distracted, and some are even sleeping then. Here I will leave you – it will be another three hours walking before you will have crossed the border. My guy will be waiting for you on the other side. God willing.'

He got out of the car, wheeling his makila, a short wooden walking stick with a silver engraved handle and a spike at the tip used for climbing the steep slopes of the Pyrenees. August followed, pulling his bag out behind him, his walking boots sinking into the bog-like turf. Joseba opened the boot and pulled out another satchel. He waited until August had hoisted his own rucksack over his shoulders then held out the satchel. August took it.

'It's heavy.' The satchel felt like it contained a piece of equipment of some sort – August could feel hard edges pressing through the material. A weapon of some sort, he wondered, but knew he couldn't ask. Joseba took it back, pulling the bag strap tight across his own shoulder.

'Don't worry, I'll carry it until you're on your own.'

'After you leave, how will I know which path to take?'

'Don't worry, this is not difficult. We have markers along

the way. Besides, you marched in the Civil War, *non*? I trust peacetime has not made you soft?' He playfully punched August in the stomach. 'Another thing you should know, if the fascists catch you with this bag, it will be the death penalty. And, friend, it sounds as if the American Embassy would not care to argue on your behalf.'

'I don't intend to get caught.' August stomped his feet to rid himself of the spreading chill rising up from his toes. 'We should get moving.'

'*Bon*. One last thing – no speaking along the way, understand?'

August nodded. Joseba kissed his own hand then touched the Citroën for good luck. He began to step stealthily towards a small break in the trees ahead of them. August followed, careful to stick to the Basque's exact route. Somewhere overhead he heard an owl hoot.

§

It was early and an owl returning from a night's hunting glided silently overhead – its wings lazily arching against the lightening sky. The rustle of the bird had made Shimon look up, had made him yearn for the creature's unthinking freedom, an emotion he hadn't felt for years. Then, resigned, the alchemist continued walking, ignoring the dull throbbing of his feet, the gnawing in his stomach he couldn't tell was hunger or fear. It seemed like days not hours ago they'd packed all the possessions they couldn't bear to leave behind in the leather pouches either side of the mule. Now the animal plodded behind him, its ears bent down in surrender, along the narrow road that wound through the forest. They had left during the night, only hours after the parade of those condemned by the Inquisition had passed the cottage, Uxue insisting that they could not afford to risk being betrayed themselves – by some terrified enemy or even neighbour. Shimon, dressed in the black robes of a friar, had the leper's bell around his neck, the bronze tongue of which tinkled every time he had to jump a pothole. He marched in front, while Uxue, disguised as a leper, followed at a distance behind, walking silently beside the animal, her body wrapped in a stained white muslin shroud, her face concealed by a filthy veil.

It had been hard to leave the comparative safety of the cottage – itself the place of so many happy memories, the first such he'd experienced since his childhood. He glanced back at the pouches hanging off the mule. Elazar ibn Yehuda's map was hidden in one of them, wrapped up in a piece of old leather. The thought of it was reassuring, the only touchstone to the lineage he had been forced to both conceal and abandon.

'I'm hungry.' Uxue stopped beside the path. 'And my feet ache. Let's rest, just for a moment, please?'

Shimon glanced up ahead. He could hear the sound of a rushing brook. It had run alongside the path for some miles now and he was convinced that around the next bend there would be a small bridge crossing it. They'd been walking for about three hours and already the sun was quite high in the sky. The last person they'd passed had been a pig farmer herding a sow to market back towards Logroño. Upon hearing Shimon ringing the leper's bell, the farmer had fallen back, cowering against the trees. Covering his face with one hand, the terrified man had held back his squealing animal to allow the supposed priest and leper past. Shimon had blessed him as he'd passed, secretly thrilled that the disguise worked so well. But they could afford to take no risks. At the village all would notice their absence, and their sudden departure would be viewed with suspicion. Then his own stomach rumbled and he realised he too was ravenous.

'We will stop, but only for a short time.' He saw a small natural clearing between the path and the rushing brook. Sunlight filtered down, illuminating a plateau where they could sit and grass for the donkey. Shimon pointed. 'Over there. I'll tether the donkey.'

Guiding the donkey over some rocks, they reached the clearing. While he tied the reins to a tree branch, Uxue opened one of the satchels and pulled out some cornbread, sheep's cheese and apples. They ate in silence, sitting in the small pool of sunlight, the fear they felt battling the sheer exhaustion of their limbs, the constant terror of discovery hanging about them like a shadow.

Shimon looked over at Uxue. She had smeared her face with a paste she'd made of gruel and crushed herbs, and it had congealed into the kind of sores one would find in the early stages of leprosy. Again, he was astounded at the resourcefulness of his wife.

'You have never looked so beautiful,' he told her, smiling. She grinned back, the grimace cracking the stiff paste on her face.

'And you so pious.' Now they both laughed and his heart clenched in a hopeless love. He had never told her of his true identity. He had never been brave enough, fearing rejection, and yet he knew now more than ever it was this that placed them in great danger.

'There is much I haven't told you, Uxue, my wife.'

She dropped her eyes, fingering a small daisy that grew by her side. 'I know more than you imagine. I did not marry you with shuttered eyes. Tell me nothing, it is safer that way.'

'I love you.'

'And I you.'

'Are we doing the right thing?'

'We are doing what we have to, to survive. But, husband, all these past years I have seen you read that map of yours with a longing that is greater than our love, this marriage, even the love of God. And now the Inquisition has given us reason to follow your true path. One bequeathed by your father.'

Amazed, he looked up at her. Her eyes twinkled – she did know more than he realised.

'For a woman you have much wisdom.'

'It is because I am a woman.'

They were interrupted by the sound of voices and the distinctive clatter of hooves. Both of them sprung to their feet. Uxue, after retreating to the side of the tethered mule, threw the veil over her face while Shimon, stepping forward, began to ring the leper's bell vigorously.

Just over the hill a small group of soldiers on horseback appeared, five of them in the short cloaks and berets of the local constabulary. They halted and the leader – the sheriff – rode forward. He stared down at the two, glancing over at Shimon, then at Uxue, wrinkling his nose in disgust. He indicated his men to stop and the horses pulled up snorting and pawing the dusty ground. With a heavy clank, he dismounted and stepped forward cautiously.

'Who goes there?' he demanded.

Shimon, his heartbeat roaring in his ears, stopped ringing the bell.

'A humble priest and his unfortunate ward on their way to Errenteria, the lepers' hospital. My ward is afflicted with Saint Lazarus disease.'

The sheriff walked a few steps forward, suspicion travelling across his features.

'You have far to travel. From where do you herald?'

'From Gazteiz, from Vitoria, my ward is the daughter of a wealthy merchant. He was much loathed to part with his daughter, he hath bequeathed me the task of taking her to the colony. But please, good sir, do not venture any nearer, for fear of infection.'

'We come from Vitoria ourselves. I heard nothing of such matters.' The sheriff stepped closer, staring over at Uxue and the mule who had continued grazing, indifferent to the confrontation taking place around him. Shimon's mind spun as he struggled to counteract the sheriff's suspicions.

'The good merchant had concealed his daughter for the past year for fear of his neighbours' hatred and loss of commerce. An understandable sentiment, may God forgive him. I collected her in great secrecy and we left in darkness. There are few who even know of her existence, and I fear,' here, Shimon cast a dramatically sympathetic glance towards Uxue, then crossed himself, 'will never.'

Now the sheriff stood only a few feet from both of them, the insignia of the Inquisition visible on the breast of his jacket. Again Shimon struggled to retain his composure, terror fixing his feet to the ground.

'Interesting. For a physic and his wife also fled in the night, only ten miles from here. You wouldn't have seen them along the way?' The sheriff stepped closer, glancing up and down Shimon's habit suspiciously.

'We have seen nothing but a pig farmer and his herd, good sir, but please, I fear you will catch the contagion if you come any closer.'

The sheriff, ignoring him, peered at Shimon's face.

'You are unusually swarthy for a priest.'

'I am from the South.'

'A long way from home, then.'

'I go where the good lord leads me, sir,' Shimon replied, trying to stop the trembling in his voice.

'And your ward, she has rough hands for a noblewoman.' He moved towards Uxue, and Shimon, flooded with the desire to protect his wife, held his shaking arms tightly to his sides. Uxue seemingly cowered, crouched down against the grass, staring up at the official with startled, terrified eyes. Shimon couldn't tell whether she was acting or was really terrified.

Shimon, hoping to distract the man, grabbed at his clothes.

'She is much neglected and weak of heart, please do not frighten the poor creature further. I have pledged to get her to the colony alive.'

The sheriff pushed Shimon and moved at Uxue, who crouched down against the ground, whimpering. He bent over her, then reeled back, hand to his nose.

'Good Lord! What is that smell?' He leaned against a tree trunk, dry-retching. Amazed, Shimon looked over at Uxue, then realised her deceit.

'Rotting flesh, my lord,' he announced, quickly, pointing to one of Uxue's arms that was concealed by the stained muslin. 'It is the leprosy. The flesh has started to drop from her bones.'

Now covering his face with a corner of his cloak, the sheriff stumbled back to his horse, mounting it as fast as he could, while the rest of his entourage, still on horseback, backed away nervously.

'Be off with you!' he shouted back at the couple, before spurring his horse on.

As the other soldiers began to follow, Shimon ran up to the path beside them.

'*Det deus felice iter vobis*,' he chanted, blessing them in Latin as they rode past, triumph soaring through his blood. What irony, what sweet revenge.

He waited until he could no longer hear the clatter of their hooves, then turned to Uxue. She was grinning. She pulled the rotten carcass of a rabbit from under her robes.

'It was lying by the brook, I couldn't resist.'

Shimon pulled her into an embrace. 'You're a genius, woman, but you stink.'

§

They walked in a silence that stretched then contracted with each aching step. August, having fallen into a rhythm, had become adjusted to the velvety darkness of the forest and the surrounding mountain scrubland. Now he could see the silhouettes of the trees against the pewter of the sky, he had learned to discern between the thorny bushes that ran along the narrow stony path they were following and the large rocks that occasionally loomed up in his way. His bruised shins bore testimony, and his throbbing body tricked him into earlier memories of night marches through hostile territory – the sheer alertness of second-guessing the enemy as he breathes across the back of your neck.

Swallowing back old terror that rose in waves, August held the image of the alchemist's chronicle at the front of his mind. He imagined Shimon Ruiz de Luna's own journey, and felt the sense of an ancient commune with something far greater than borders, greater than political differences, the ideals for which he'd once nearly died. He had begun his journey, for better or worse, and now as the stars etched their way across the night, his own mortality seemed irrelevant.

Moving faster and with the consummate ease of someone who'd taken the path many times before, Joseba walked about ten feet in front of August, hopping over rocks and fallen branches as if he could see in the dark. August had lost

all notion of time. He knew they must have only been walking for about three hours but already it felt like days. A
sudden scurry in the bushes broke his reverie, a small
animal, a fox or a badger, he supposed. In front Joseba drew
to a halt and waited until August had caught up with him.
The Basque stood at the mouth of a small clearing. Two
large rocks marked the place where their path finished and a
new one on the other side of the clearing began. Now
August noticed the faint dark-blue flush of dawn rising up in
the west. It made him feel panicky. Would he have enough
time to get across the border while it was still dark?

'We are here,' Joseba whispered, pointing beyond the
trees. 'The border patrol's hut is about a mile in that direction.' He glanced at his watch. 'It is now nearly four, I will
have to leave you here.' He pointed to the rock on the far side
of the clearing. 'The path is marked by that rock. It is the dry
bed of an old mountain stream. In some parts there is a little
water, but not much. It runs between two checkpoints, one
you will be able to see but don't worry they can't see you.
After you cross, my contact will be waiting for you and my
delivery. Good luck.' He took off the leather pouch and hung
it over August's shoulder. It felt much heavier than it had at
the beginning of the journey. August adjusted it for comfort.

'Thank you,' said August, shaking Joseba's hand. The
Basque smiled.

'Don't thank me now, thank me when you get back out of
Franco's Spain.' Grinning ironically, he thumped his chest
then gave the Republican salute. Without thinking, August
saluted back. Then the Basque was gone, melting silently
back into the trees.

Olivia was dreaming, dreaming she was flying over a forest
looking for someone running below. She couldn't remember

exactly who she was looking for but she knew that if she
didn't find him, she would die. It was night and the trees
below were long green fingers that reached up, their tips
brushing her feathered belly. Feathers. I am a bird, she
thought, before a noise outside the dream jolted her awake.

She opened her eyes. Boarding house room, rue de
Rivage, Saint Jean de Luc, her sprained ankle. The room
was dark, only a thin sliver of streetlight filtering in through
a gap in the blinds. Faint sound of waves, a storm out at sea,
but underneath breathing – not her own. Instantly, she knew
someone else was nearby, she could feel his heat, his presence. She lay pressed against the sheets, contemplating her
options – terror was not something Olivia felt – at least not
for years, and all she could think was, who or what could
have been so stupid as to break into her room and rifle
through her luggage? Some impoverished local looking for
money or perhaps a passport? Someone who believed he was
dealing with a poor befuddled middle-aged Englishwoman.
What an idiot, and a dull joy stirred in her loins, the anticipation of the sadist, of the silent predator.

Now she identified the noise. It was the sound of a drawer
being slowly pulled open in the small enclave of the bedroom that served as a dressing room, the room that contained
her suitcase. As silently as she could, she slipped out of the
bed and, trying to keep her weight off her ankle, moved
towards the dressing room, the door of which was ajar. The
man's outline was distinctive, enough for her to know immediately who he was and Olivia froze in horror.

He was on her in seconds, his large hand clamped over her
face and mouth, the other arm around her neck dragging her
into the room. She fell, her leg catching the cord of a lamp
that crashed after her. The two of them lay like wrestlers or
lovers twisted on the ground, the smell of his sweat and

maleness acrid in her nostrils, his bulging forearm tight against her throat, squeezing her windpipe.

'Scream, Olivia, and you are one dead witch,' he whispered, almost lovingly, his mouth low against her ear. And that voice, the treacle-coated vowels devoid of emotion, sent a shock of recognition through her. Ten, fifteen years ago she had thought him dead, so many of the circle had wished it, had willed it upon him. And yet here he was as vivid as the night itself, about to kill her. She bit down into his hand, her teeth sinking into the meaty flesh, his blood salty against her mouth and tongue. He dropped her, then thudded his elbow into the side of her head. For a second her vision exploded into red and black, then she hit the ground, dazed.

He switched on the fallen lamp, the crazy light it threw jangling normalcy into a tumbled jigsaw. Staring across, she saw that he'd torn through her luggage, had strewn her clothes everywhere in a desperate search for something she guessed he hadn't found. She rolled her eyes so that she could see him. Pulling himself up, Tyson sucked at the bite in his hand. It had been about ten years but he didn't look any older – at least not in the face. He still had the even features and broad smile tailored so that he could engender trust from anyone; the pale green eyes no one could remember; the thick, prematurely white hair that had always made him look older, harmless; the cleft in the chin that made people think of certain film stars or some banker their father might have trusted in the thirties. The only characteristic that betrayed him was his physique. If one looked closer and with a practised eye, one would be able to tell that this was once a military man or at least a fighter, and certainly a killer, judging by the tight control he had over the way he moved – an economy of gesture that, if superseded, threatened to become fatally dangerous.

'What do you want?' Olivia croaked, her voice scraping from her bruised throat. She couldn't bear to use his name, as if naming him would give him more power over her.

He stopped sucking and smiled, the capped perfect teeth smeared in blood.

'What I want to know is, why are you so far away from home, Olivia? A nice homebody like yourself.' In lieu of answering, she tried to sit up but found one arm was too shattered to put weight on.

'Because you're on the hunt, aren't you? You've found something new, a map, a clue perhaps?' He reached across and gripped her injured arm, squeezing tight. Olivia, biting her lip to stop herself from screaming out, almost fainted from the pain. 'Where is it, Olivia? Where are *Las crónicas del alquimista*?'

'I don't know,' she whispered. Outside, there was the sound of footsteps in the corridor and voices. He dropped her arm and it fell limp, broken, to her side.

'But you're following someone who does know, aren't you?' He lifted her other arm, the good one, and began stroking her hand. Olivia swallowed, now frightened she might vomit.

'One broken arm is bad, two very bad. He's mine, Olivia, understand? And if you get there first or find anything I need to know, I expect you to tell me. Is that agreed?'

She nodded, a tiny gesture of concession but enough for him to let go of her hand. They were interrupted by knocking on the door.

'Madam, are you all right? We heard noises?' It was the hotel owner.

Tyson stood and kicked her.

'Answer it.'

Olivia pulled herself to her feet painfully and hobbled to

the door. 'Everything is all right. I fell over because of my ankle, that's all,' she said through the door. When she turned around Tyson was gone and she was alone again: the door to the balcony left ajar. He'd left a calling card on the bedside table with the address of a Swiss post box printed across it.

Tyson swore and pulled out a handkerchief, wrapping it tightly around his bleeding hand. He'd jumped down from the balcony into a small back alley, a narrow road that led into the town. He got to his feet hurriedly, dusting down his trousers, then adopted a casual saunter as he started walking towards the promenade de la Plage. He needed the ocean to clear his head; he needed to think. The classicist was heading towards the Pyrenees, he was sure of it. Was it possible he was visiting Irumendi? Perhaps Jimmy van Peters told Winthrop something, a clue he didn't know. Tyson was convinced the chronicle hadn't been hidden in the family house of La Leona all those years ago. He'd gone through the farmhouse, tearing up cupboards, walls, even floorboards. It had been a tense situation, the men beneath him were close to mutiny, still traumatised from what they had just had to do – they would have shot him too if they'd known why he'd taken the mission in the first place. As it was, they had nearly turned their own guns upon him, their commanding officer, when he'd given the command to shoot La Leona and her men. It had taken every possible argument to convince them he was only following orders sent from Washington. It had been easier to justify the house search, telling the men they were looking for proof the Basques had betrayed them to the Soviets. A ridiculous hypothesis but the four young soldiers believed him.

Even after Tyson realised Jimmy van Peters had returned to the camp then fled to Paris, Tyson wasn't entirely convinced Jimmy had the chronicle, or even believed in its existence. Van Peters had been so dismissive that night around the camp fire of La Leona's passionate conviction that the chronicle held magical powers – why would she give the heirloom to her cynical lover for safekeeping? Nevertheless, over the years, Tyson had arranged certain burglaries at van Peters's Parisian apartment, burglaries that had ransacked the place. He'd even had a mock electrician bug the place, but after three months of impromptu jazz sessions and noisy lovemaking with the young prostitutes the musician favoured, Tyson had pulled the surveillance. Besides, Jimmy had become paranoid and taken to changing his locks weekly, even to playing the same record over and over ridiculously loudly to drown anything that might have been said in the apartment. Tyson still couldn't listen to Perry Como's 'Prisoner of Love' – and he had never found the slightest evidence of the chronicle.

So why had Jimmy visited August Winthrop in London? There was no doubt the classicist was the perfect candidate to decipher the alchemist's symbols and maps. Pondering the connection between the two men, Tyson watched the streetlights reflected in the lapping waters of the harbour. There was no moon, he noticed. A good night to travel unnoticed. No, all he needed to do was to follow and to watch, then make his next move. A large man stepped out of the shadows. Vinko, he was early.

'Everything okay, boss?'

Tyson looked back across the ocean. To his great satisfaction, a seabird, night fishing, swooped down and caught a small fish in its beak.

'Perfect.'

Looking around him, August felt completely and profoundly alone. He stepped into the clearing. Now he could see the

glittering arc of the Milky Way and it was as if he were looking up into a window that opened out into eternity. His
eternity. He shivered – the night had arrived at that preter-
natural moment when the earth's surface had reached its
coolest. His Spanish comrades used to say it was the hour
that belonged to the spirits. Those who still walked without
knowing they had died. There were many in that war. Young
men from cities and countries, who had never seen a vineyard before, plucked the hard fruit of an olive from a tree,
felt the relentless sun burn their skin and yet they were
killed, shot down, amazement still frozen on their faces. *We
left fields of foreign ghosts. Charlie one of them. Don't think, walk*,
August told himself, rubbing his arms and legs. He had to
keep moving – determined to empty his mind, he strode
purposefully across the clearing and found his way to the
rock marking the new path, then plunged back into the dark.

The riverbed was narrow, covered in stones and small scrub
that had pushed its way through the water-worn pebbles.
Already blisters chafed at his ankles and his neck and back
ached from the two heavy bags. There was thin snow on the
ground and the temperature dropped steadily the higher he
climbed. Without warning, the path narrowed dramatically as
two walls of rock loomed up, broken only by the now extinct
stream that must have cut its way through over aeons. The
wind rustled the trees that overhung both banks, bringing with
it the faint sound of voices. It was coming from the left of him.
August froze. He peered up through the snow-laden trees,
squinting to see more clearly in the darkness. Slowly, the outline of a checkpoint tower came into focus, framed in one of
the windows the silhouette of two guards. August looked
behind him and in front. He had no choice, he had to keep
moving to make the rendezvous point. Lifting the two bags
onto his shoulders, he began to wriggle sideways through the

narrow gap between the rocks, his feet down in the thin trickle of water that was the remnants of the stream. Inch by inch, he manoeuvred forward, his arms aching from the supernatural effort of balancing the rucksacks. Just then one of his shoulders dislodged a small rock, causing a small cascade of pebbles and stones that bounced noisily against the banks. Again he stopped still, motionless, willing himself into rock.

In that instant the top of the forest was illuminated by a light coming on in the tower. Now August could see the two young Spanish border guards clearly, and with a sickening rush realised how close the tower actually was, far closer than he had calculated. One of the guards pushed open one of the windows. He peered blindly down into the forest, his rifle pointing out.

'What was that?' The Spaniard sounded young, his accent thick and rustic, some naive rookie following orders August thought. The second guard, moustached and older-looking, came up behind the first, rubbing his eyes as if he'd just woken up.

'Nothing, maybe a wolf, there's plenty around here, you know.' Indifferent, he turned his back to the window. The young guard didn't move. Instead he swung his rifle point down across the top of the forest.

'Maybe I should kill it,' he ventured, and August tensed. He didn't like the nervousness in the guard's voice.

'Why, you scared of wolves? If so they shouldn't have given you this posting, my friend.' The older guard laughed. 'Wolves are nothing. What you should be afraid of is the Basque wild mountain man – they say he has hair all over his body and teeth like a demon, and he eats Spanish boys like you for breakfast.'

'Even so, I still think we should check.' There was a click and a searchlight cut through the branches and leaves creating a band of vivid colour in a monochrome landscape. It began to sweep across the stream, falling on a tree trunk near August. He crouched as low as he could without making any noise and held his breath. If they saw him, they'd shoot and probably shoot to kill. The water had begun to seep into his mountain boots and his toes were freezing. Consciously, he took himself out of his body, allowing himself to become one with the night sky, with the frigid air, with a moth that danced inches away, a solitary acrobat drawn towards the eye of the light.

The beam now swept closer, brushing the edge of his jacket. August closed his eyes, waiting for the sharp slice of a bullet to hit him. Instead, there was silence. He opened his eyes again. The beam had passed over him and was now filtering through the branches on the opposite bank.

'I think you're right,' August could hear the young guard tell his companion. 'Just some dumb animal.'

August stayed down until the light went off again in the tower and finally when he was convinced the guards were settled again, inched his way forward and clear to the other side of the narrow ravine.

Fifteen minutes later, after climbing higher and higher, the dry riverbed petered out into a flat broad shallow mouth of pebbles, and he emerged onto a windswept plateau. A short stooped figure was waiting.

'Tin Man?' The voice was genderless, the accent Basque.

August, too cold and numb to speak, nodded. Joseba's contact stepped forward. Now he could see that it was a woman, an older woman in perhaps her sixties, weathered by poverty and hardship. She took the bag Joseba had given him, then put his gloved freezing hand into her own, rubbing it vigorously.

'Come, we need to resurrect you.'

8

There was a dull clanging. August, barely conscious, lay dozing on the hard wooden bunk bed. For a moment he forgot where he was, but the sharp cold air laced with the smell of fresh coffee, and the persistent ringing that he now recognised as goats' bells, brought the events of the night before flooding back. Remembering how Joseba's contact had guided him to a mountain hut then given him a strong glass of txakoli and a sheepskin blanket, he reached under his pillow for the Mauser he vaguely recalled hiding before passing out. The pistol wasn't there. Startled, he sat up, narrowly avoiding banging his head on the bed above him. Cursing his own stupidity he climbed out into the room. Shivering and dressed in just his boxer shorts and singlet, he pulled on his trousers and glanced around the simple mountain hut. It had a small wood-fire iron stove against the back wall, upon which a pot of coffee was brewing. Long wooden skis that looked as if they dated from the twenties were resting up against a wall and apart from the bunk beds, there was only a wooden table and bench set under a window. The Mauser lay on the table. He walked over. Someone had cleaned and oiled it, the old woman no doubt. He picked it up and cocked the trigger. The action was smooth, super smooth. It was now almost as good as brand-new. He smiled to himself and bent to look out of the window. Outside stretched a spectacular view of the Pyrenees. It was overwhelmingly beautiful.

August went to the door and pushed it open, and immediately the chilly breeze, fragrant with the smell of long grass and flowering blooms, swept across him, infusing his lungs and limbs with new vigour. On the plateau that stretched out before him new grass was springing up between patches of snow. Several goats grazed on the bright-green tufts, domesticated, judging by the bells hanging around their necks. Sitting at some distance on a large flat rock was the woman. She appeared to be staring out over the valley, standing guard over her goats, he guessed, but also looking out for intruders, unwelcome guests. He waved; she waved back but didn't move. After glancing up at the sun, he realised it was late, perhaps even mid-morning. They needed to get going. August went back inside and poured himself a coffee into a large tin mug. Bitter but warming. He pulled open his bag and took out his notebook. Here was his rough sketch of Shimon Ruiz de Luna's rendering of the first of the secret locations the Spaniard visited following Elazar ibn Yehuda's ancient map. There was the small round bulge that indicated the village Cabo Ogoño, from where Shimon Ruiz de Luna's wife Uxue came, positioned close to the fishing village of Elantxobe. Inland from that was the actual location itself. To the left of a village named Mañaria, near Gernika, was marked a small village at the foot of the three mountains – Irumendi. Underneath, August had written a translation of Shimon Ruiz de Luna's own Latin quote: '*The first of Elazar ibn Yehuda's sacred locations lays here between the silver birch and oak near the Goddess's cave.*'

August laid his hand on the sketch. He knew Irumendi must be within ninety miles of where he was now sitting. The rush of the explorer, of the researcher who places two disparate facts together and suddenly sees an extraordinary synchronicity gripped August's senses. A tentative knock on the door interrupted him. He managed to close his notebook just before the woman entered, a goatherd's switch still in her hand and a thin straight tree branch stripped of its leaves in the other, her weathered face as wrinkled as a prune.

'You have your coffee?' Her Spanish had a heavy Basque accent.

'Thank you, it is good, and thank you for cleaning my gun,' he answered, with a smile. She did not smile back. Instead, she closed the door of the hut, placed the switch and the tree branch beside it and poured herself a coffee.

'It is an old pistol. You'll need a new one if you intend to use it.'

'I'm happy with my old one. It's just an archaeological research trip. But I have history with Franco,' he lied, determined to cover his tracks.

She swung around with her coffee in her hand.

'I don't need to know why you are here. Now that you have delivered, you are no longer my responsibility,' she snapped back.

'I understand,' he said and pulled the other chair out for her. She sat down, careful to keep her eyes on the front door. 'We should leave in the next half-hour. That will give us time to get to the next village.'

'Just one other question.'

She looked up enquiringly, her eyes narrowed in suspicion.

'Have you heard of a village called Irumendi?' He studied

her face. She looked away, but for a moment August caught a glimmer of something in her eyes.

'No, I do not know of this village,' she replied, her voice guarded and low. He sensed immediately that she was lying.

'In that case would it be possible to get me to San Sebastián?'

'Donostia?' she queried, using the Basque name. 'This I can do, but I'm telling you, this village of the three mountains, it does not exist, or maybe only in American tourist guidebooks,' she added, cynically, convincing August that not only did the village exist, but she did not want him to visit it, an observation that simply fuelled his curiosity.

'We will travel as goatherds. You must put these clothes on.' She threw him a long, roughly woven hooded smock he remembered the local shepherds wearing over their trousers, and a pair of abarkak. 'If we meet any roadblocks, you are my nephew from Galicia, but you must keep your blond hair under your cap.'

August began pulling on the smock then reached for the abarkak. The soft leather fitted snugly over his feet, and he tied the lacing up over his ankles. The woman watched, a bemused expression playing over her severe features as he stood and adopted a gait he thought appropriate.

'Good, you know how to change yourself, like a demon. Maybe you've worked as a spy?'

August said nothing, merely smiled enigmatically. The less she knew the better.

She shrugged and continued talking. 'We will rendezvous with a driver who will take us into Donostia – your San Sebastián. The meeting place is only an hour's walk from here, but if anyone stops us you are not to speak. Your very presence is suspicious, there are so few men left. They have gone, either murdered by the fascists or exiled. This is a region run by women. You will be popular.' Now she smiled for the first time, a mischievous wit crackling in her black eyes.

'I'm here only for my research. I do not intend to get into any kind of trouble,' he replied, amazing himself by blushing.

The woman shrugged disbelievingly, put her coffee down and fetched the thin sapling branch back to the table. After reaching into a pocket in her voluminous skirt, she pulled out a switchblade and snapped it open with professional ease. The blade gleamed in the sunlight. For a second August wondered whether he should be thinking about defending himself, but to his relief she picked up the sapling and began whittling at it.

'When we arrive in Donostia you are on your own.' She looked up from her carving. 'Entirely on your own.'

'I understand.'

'The letter Joseba sent with you said that you fought with the Republicans, that's why you could not be here officially,' she said, concentrating on her handiwork.

'This is true.'

'Then, with respect, comrade, you must understand the danger you will bring to any Basque village if you are found by Polícia Civil. They are brought in from the South; they are Spaniards, not Basques. They watch us like hawks, they beat us for speaking our own language. We have no news coming into the country except for Franco's propaganda, so we are isolated. Be careful, my friend, but not only with your own life.' She finished carving and handed August the new goatherd's switch she'd just made out of the sapling.

August sat in the open with the ten goats they'd herded onto the truck back on the mountain slope, watching the road recede behind him. The pick-up had happened without a hitch. The truck driver took the package Joseba had sent then helped the woman and her goats onto the truck. He and the old woman exchanged a few brusque words, but in Euskara – incomprehensible to August – and the two moved quickly and efficiently in a way that suggested they worked together in this manner all the time. The driver – an old florid-faced man – glanced at August only once and that was to indicate he should pull his hood further down over his beret to conceal more of his hair.

The drive down from the mountains to the coast and San Sebastián had been beautiful, but the scars of the war and the resulting poverty were still evident – bombed-out cottages, barren fields and, as Franco had withdrawn much of the funds of the province, in many ways it looked less prosperous than the last time August was in Gipuzkoa in 1938. The most noticeable difference was the lack of men – everywhere August looked it was women, old men and boys cutting down grass with scythes, working stoically in lines as they moved through the small fields.

The country lane had become paved, then narrowed as they entered the outskirts of the port city. To the left of him snaked the majestic Río Urumea, the opposite bank lined with elegant nineteenth-century palaces and various government institutes. San Sebastián was evidently one of the commercial and administrative centres of the region. Yet it had the air of a wealthy city that had reached its zenith in the last century, and the apartment blocks along the wide avenue on his side of the river boasted balconies and ornate façades. The old woman nudged him – a sudden blast of garlic and goat.

'You know Franco has a summer house here,' she cracked, then spat over the edge of the truck, clutching the side of it as it bounced over the potholes. 'A brave man,' she added, cynically. The woman had transformed herself into a simple peasant farmer, with a traditional peaked hood pulled low over her ears. A kid goat sat in a bag she had strapped over her shoulder, its small pointed head sticking out, eyes wide in fear. All trace of the tough political fighter August had witnessed in the mountain hut were now erased.

The truck rumbled along, then they turned left at the Zurriola Bridge towards the old city centre. It passed another smaller three-wheel truck driving in the opposite direction, the back of which carried that morning's catch – a barrel of salted sardines.

'Here, the people are *arrantzale* – the people of the sea. But I am *baserritarra*, farmer of the land. Whoever you talk to, trust no one. There are Carlists and Francoists among our own people,' she advised, in an undertone. They drove down the Pescaderia, the street that led to the fish market, the streets already filling with other farmers bringing in produce from the surrounding mountains and valleys. 'Monday – market day, full of people. I take you to La Brecha, this way you disappear.'

Most of the cars August saw were at least twenty years old and the people looked impoverished, downtrodden. The truck shuddered to a halt beside the market. The old woman jumped down, August followed.

'We leave you here,' she told him in Spanish, her voice low and urgent. 'Take this.' She swung the bag with the baby goat from her shoulder and handed it to him. 'You look less suspicious with him. He will bring you luck. If he doesn't, you can always eat him. The bar you should look for is Bar de la Lamia, the bar of the river mermaid. If they let you, the information you seek you will find there. It's between Bar Eceiza and Bar Manolo.'

August swung the goat over his left shoulder, his travel
bag over his right, then turned to say goodbye, but she was
gone, disappeared into the milling crowd. He stood at the
edge of the plaza staring up at the stone entrance of the
market, the word *Merondo* arching over the top, watching
the farmers carrying in their produce: goat's cheese, sheep's
cheese, ham, tomatoes, beans, green peppers, lettuces and
sweet potatoes. August knew there was still strict rationing,
but there were still a few luxuries – chorizo, dried fruit and
strings of onions.

A row of mules and carts sat on one side of the square,
along with several small ancient trucks – nearby a group of
farmers stood smoking pipes and talking. One, noticing the
newcomer, looked over at August, his expression a curious
blend of suspicion and inquisitiveness, his gaze sweeping
over August's clothes and the kid goat on his back, as the
local tried to assess who August was and where he was from.
Just then August noticed a change fall over the group as
something caught their attention from the other side of the
plaza. He turned. Two Guardias Civiles, guns resting in their
belts and batons swinging from leather belts, had entered
the square. He turned back to the farmers; the men had quietly begun to disperse. August glanced back at the
policemen. They were loitering at a table outside a bar while
the waiter fussed over them. They hadn't noticed August
yet. As casually and nonchalantly as he could, August began
following a couple of the men down one of the narrow streets
lined with old apartment blocks and buildings, bars lining
the kerb at street level. He shuffled along at a discreet distance, adopting the gait of a shy rural peasant, eyes down, his
feet uncertain on the cobblestones beneath, the goat bleating plaintively on his back. He found Bar de la Lamia next to
Bar Manolo.

A low narrow space, with the customarily wooden counter running along one side of the room and photographs of Real Sociedad pinned up on the back wall, it was crowded with fishermen and farmers, dressed in the large black berets and checked shirts. The air was thick with pipe smoke and fragrant with the smell of rich black coffee and garlic. Several of the men were drinking salda, a fragrant chicken broth, and there was an array of pintxos, a kind of Basque tapas, displayed in the long glass cabinet that ran along the bar. As August entered, several men looked over their shoulders to see who the newcomer was and, after glancing sceptically at his clothes and beret, turned back to their coffees and pintxos, shoulders hunched over their plates. August pushed his way through to the counter.

'A brandy, please,' he said, in the thickest Basque-accented Spanish he could muster. The barman glanced at him disbelievingly and then shrugged.

'First the goat,' he muttered. August looked at him, confused. The barman reached out over the counter.

'Your goat. Don't worry, I won't steal him.'

Reluctantly, August handed the goat in the shoulder bag over to him.

'Please don't. He's the only friend I have left.'

The old farmer sitting next to him laughed, as the barman hung the bag with kid goat over one of the barrels of brandy. The animal, bedazzled by the noise and cigarette smoke, cowered. The barman poured a shot of brandy and pushed it to August.

'It's good to keep your friends close. Around here they have a tendency to disappear, usually to San Marcos, but unlike our good general, I promise I won't shoot your friend.' August, knowing San Marcos was one of Franco's notorious concentration camps, lifted his glass in a toast.

'To missing friends, eaten or shot.' He kept his gaze level and his voice serious. The room fell silent, filled momentarily by the rattle of cartwheels as a cart passed outside, and August knew he'd stepped over the border. Now it was a question of whether or not they were going to trust him – it was a huge risk. They were just as capable of disappearing him as the fascists, if they felt he might betray them. He kept his glass raised and his hand steady. Finally, after what felt like an eternity, the barman poured himself a shot and clinked his glass against August's and the tension broke like sunshine after rain. 'To missing friends,' the barman replied, now smiling, his craggy face suddenly softened by the grin.

'To missing friends,' several of the men echoed, in Euskara, raising their glasses, and as August glanced around, again he wondered at the lack of visible young men and how many exiles must have fled.

'You're not from around here – the North?' The barman indicated August's blond hair.

'No, from much, much further. But maybe you can help me. I'm here visiting Irumendi, maybe you have heard of it? I need to get there before nightfall and I need directions.'

It was like a pulse ran through the bar at the mention of the village's name. The barman glanced meaningfully towards the back of the room at one of the men, who exuded the sullen danger of a paid observer. The barman nodded, and the man, perched on a stool, slipped off the seat into a back room. August steeled himself, now fighting an instinct to make a break for the door. *Stay calm, stay calm, keep your face open, you are who you say.* The old training he used for his time in occupied France came flooding back, the techniques he knew to engender trust, to change the actual frequency, the vibration of his character.

There was a commotion at the back of the bar. The

farmers began to move aside, bowing their heads slightly in respect as an old man pushed through them. He looked to be in his eighties and he wasn't much more than five foot tall, but his shoulders were broad and muscular, probably the result of years of physical labour. His legs looked painfully wizen and thin below the contracted bull-like torso. He hobbled up and planted himself squarely in front of August. Then stared fiercely at him, his elongated countenance naturally morose. His large ears stuck poignantly out from the wispy silver hair that framed his narrow skull, giving him a curious vulnerability – in a face that was a jigsaw of scars.

'There are some places that exist on the map and some that don't, you understand me, boy?' he spat out in a gravelly, broken Spanish. August guessed that it was not a language he used often or with much affection.

August glanced around. Judging from the reverence the others held for the old man, he was obviously the patriarch, a leader of some kind. August bowed his head in respect.

'I understand.'

'So, why are you interested in Irumendi?'

At this August pulled the medal he won fighting for the Republic from inside his pocket, discreetly showing the ribbon and the metal to the old man for just a second. The old man's demeanour changed. 'I had a friend from there I fought alongside,' August told him, hating himself for the lie, but knowing he needed to get the old man to trust him and fast. 'I would like to visit his sister.'

The old man nodded in approval but eyed August suspiciously.

'It is three hours' drive from here and the road is narrow and hazardous. How do you expect to get there?'

'I have money and the goat. I need to get there, otherwise my friend the barman could lose the brand-new friend he's just made. You understand me?' August replied, not flinching from his gaze.

The old man turned and murmured something to the man next to him. A moment later another farmer, tall and pale, with a long face that looked like it had been battered by both famine and poverty, stepped forward.

'I will take you there,' he told August, unsmiling.

They were interrupted by shouting from outside, and several of the men pushed their way to the door.

'They've arrested Xabier!' one of the men yelled over the commotion. The old man bustled his way to the window, and August followed but he was careful to keep well out of sight of anyone outside.

Beyond, in the plaza, he could see the two policemen hauling a young man kicking and struggling, his arms pinned behind him, towards a police van. Men and women gathered to watch silently, the sullen hostility visible in their faces.

'Someone betrayed him,' a farmer muttered.

'Money makes mouths loose,' the old man said, as a ripple of discontent ran through the bar. The old man turned back to August.

'You see how we are forced to live, like cowed sheep. We might have lost the battle but the war continues. Send my regards to your uncle.' He winked as two tall, broad-shouldered men stepped up to escort him out of a back door.

Malcolm Hully had just pulled on his raincoat and was in the action of wrapping a scarf around his neck when the desk phone rang.

'Hello?'

''Ello? That is Malcolm 'ully, *non*?' The accent was Parisian, authoritarian, older, male. Malcolm steadied his racing pulse before answering in perfect but private school French.

'Good afternoon, Monsieur, this is indeed Monsieur Hully.'

'Interpol. We have a lead on your friend, Monsieur Winthrop.'

'Indeed, how interesting.'

'He has appeared on our system. Calais, Rouen, Saint Jean de Luc. A customs officer wired through the details. What would you like us to do, inform MI6?' The voice was slightly wry, no doubt the French officer was wondering why he'd been instructed to report directly to Malcolm and not through his superior, but Malcolm had decided to contain the information on Winthrop for the moment. There was far too much rivalry between MI5 and MI6; both departments were convinced the mole lay in the other. So he had called in a few favours from some of his old French colleagues from the SOE days.

'No, not just yet, but very kind of you to offer, Henri, isn't it?'

'Actually, it is Mathias. Henri is on holiday.'

It was exactly as he suspected. It must be Spain. August was heading straight into the lion's den. For a moment Malcolm wondered whether he should tip off any of his Spanish counterparts – he did have them – unofficially. But that would be swift and ultimately uninteresting. Better to wait and find out what skeleton the Tin Man was going to reveal. But why Spain? It must be Franco-related, Malcolm concluded, but if Winthrop was working for the Russians what was in Spain that could possibly be of interest to them? And why send Winthrop, unless it was to capitalise on his old Civil War connections or perhaps assassinate someone? And how did the murder of Copps fit into the jigsaw?

'Well, Mathias, if Interpol could just keep its eyes open along the Spanish–French border, particularly around the west Pyrenees area, we would be most appreciative. In fact ...' Malcolm rummaged through the top drawer of his desk, then found the file he was looking for. Balancing the receiver with one hand, he flipped it open with the other. 'I think we might have some information on an Algerian dissident you are interested in. Bomb attack in Marseille? A Jean-Paul Mahmet?'

'You know where Mahmet is?'

'Let's just say if you find me August Winthrop, I might just be able to find you Mahmet.'

'You have a deal.'

'*Bien, merci beaucoup*, Mathias.' But the French agent had already put down the telephone. Malcolm leaned back in the chair and stared out over Curzon Street. Below, a tired-looking prostitute harassed a potential client. Ordinarily, Malcolm would have found this mildly intriguing but today he was distracted, positively perplexed. Had the Soviets sent August in? Knowing what August faced in Spain if arrested, he could only think that whatever the motivation, the stakes must be very high indeed. What was the CIA setting up in Madrid? Malcolm knew Franco was frustrated by the NATO exclusion, as well as the denial of any of the US funds from Marshall – a scheme now hugely benefiting the rebuilding of both Germany and Italy. What did Franco have to offer the Americans that would worry the Soviets enough to send in an agent? Abruptly, he knew the answer – geography. Proximity to European airspace. The possibility of military bases for US forces. Spain was also the perfect midpoint for US planes to refuel on the way to the Soviet Union – if ever the US planned to bomb the region. All of which would make the Soviets very interested indeed. But if he was wrong and MI5 went after August, it would be personally disastrous.

For a split second Malcolm toyed with the idea of ringing a guy he knew in the CIA over in Washington, but stopped himself. The British Secret Service had lost enough credibility with the Yanks in the Burgess debacle. August, as the errant son of a highly respected ex-senator, could prove to be even more embarrassing, especially if they turned out to be mistaken about him. No, if Malcolm was to keep his job, he would have to handle the situation as quietly and as independently as possible. Who knows, it might even lead to a promotion.

There had to be someone else he knew who could confirm his theory. But who? Then he remembered an old American girlfriend of August's who was now dating someone high up in the embassy. August had broken her heart and Malcolm happened to know she was still bitter about it – if anyone would be willing to corroborate his theory, it would be her. He sat back down at the desk and in the gathering darkness of the office, picked up the telephone.

9

The two horses strained as they hauled the cart to the top of the crest. They'd been climbing for hours, hugging the side of a mountain. The road was strewn with rocks and pebbles and it would have been impossible to drive a car up it. Already cloud had descended over the surrounding peaks, cloaking them in white. They turned a sharp bend and the view of a deep valley below with a river snaking its way along the base opened up in front of them. His companion pulled the reins up sharp and turned to August.

'Look!' He pointed down and in that moment the mist cleared and a thin sheen of sunlight ran over the valley like quicksilver, illuminating a small village nestling in the fork of the river, an old church tower standing in the centre, the top of it catching the light for a second.

'The village of ...' – here his hand circled the area and August could clearly see the peaks that ringed them – '... the three mountains.' He grinned, displaying an impressive row of gold teeth – the first smile in hours. 'Now you might understand why we were reluctant to take you here. It is one of our best-kept secrets – it was one of our strongholds during the war. You can only travel here by mule and then only during the day. And it is most unfriendly towards foreigners. Most unfriendly. It still isn't too late to change your mind, my friend – I can take you back with me tomorrow morning.'

August glanced back at the mountains. The silhouette of the three peaks defined by the craggy outposts and sharp dips was distinctive set against the sky, and instantly recognisable to him. Even more extraordinary, it appeared virtually unchanged after three hundred years. The ancient physic Elazar ibn Yehuda's mountains, one of the secret places he'd described, it was astounding to August to think that Elazar had visited here in 711 and then Shimon Ruiz de Luna in 1610 and now here he was standing right in their footprints.

'I've arrived,' he whispered, in English.

'Whatever you say,' his companion cracked back in Spanish then shook the reins. Reluctantly, the horses began their descent.

He had asked the driver to drop him off with his bags and the goat at the edge of the village – it was his strategy to enter quietly, unannounced; he would need to scout out the geography and the people before he could plan how and where he would stay. Close up, the village was smaller than he'd imagined, the dwellings the traditional whitewashed steep-roofed Basque cottages with their picturesque red or green shutters. Most of the buildings looked as if they had been constructed in the Middle Ages and it appeared little had developed since then. But some looked even older, ancient – crafted from a grey-yellowish stone that, August guessed, was local. He pulled his shepherd's hood up. Walking along the narrow stone lanes, his abarkak silent against the cobblestones, the kid goat bleating behind him in the rucksack, August was struck by how quiet Irumendi was, almost as if it were a ghost town, as if some sudden disaster had mysteriously wiped out its occupants. Then he remembered that it was Sunday.

He turned the corner and arrived at a small plaza with a moss-covered fountain in the middle. Opposite stood a tiny town hall with a balcony and clock set into the façade. Beside it was the police station with the obligatory Spanish flag hanging from a pole, but the flag was ripped and did not looked loved. The police station was right next to a school, one of the walls of which had been made into a fronton – a pelota court, with bleachers to the left. A mangy dog, neglected and hungry-looking, slinked out of a doorway, followed August for a few yards, then gave up to collapse onto a doorstep.

August stopped in the middle of the plaza and looked around slowly. If there was anything more disturbing than being watched, it had to be the sense of not being observed in the centre of a seemingly empty town, he decided. There was something almost catastrophic about such profound emptiness, as if the inhabitants had been inexplicably obliterated by some terrible unseen force. Then suddenly it started, the sound of singing came from the church – the largest building on the plaza. Hymns in a language he recognised as Euskara. The voices – mainly female – floated out into the empty square, curling around the stone walls, then up across the valley.

'Extraordinary.' He spoke out loud only to have the kid goat bleat back. 'This must be one of the only services in Basque left in the country.'

He glanced up at the bell tower butted up against the Romanesque church. The belfry was the highest building in

Irumendi, and each floor within the tower boasted an arched window, some bigger than others. It was exactly what he was looking for.

He stood under the bronze bell suspended by its hinge a good nine feet above him. Steadying himself with one hand, he leaned out, binoculars in hand. The view was amazing; from the top of the tower August could clearly see back over the valley, the sweep of oak and beech forest, the tiny white line of the track he'd travelled down the mountain earlier that day and just between two of the mountains a sliver of blue he knew was the Atlantic Ocean beyond. Apart from the village itself, there were no signs of civilisation to be seen. It was just how Shimon Ruiz de Luna had described in his chronicle – down to the details of the ornaments on the church tower. August had an overwhelming sense of connection with the alchemist, almost as if it were he standing there three hundred years earlier – frantic with both hope and terror, in the middle of the expedition of his life, while being pursued by the Inquisitional police. Without warning, a bullet whizzed past, narrowly missing August's head, only to chip the stone next to him. Jolted back to reality, he ducked down, the kid goat strapped to his back bleating in fear.

'Come down! We can see you!' The man's voice came from below, in the plaza. August slid into a crouch and ventured to the opening again. Down in the square, with his arms crossed defiantly, stood the local priest, rifle in hand. Crowding around him were his parishioners dressed in their Sunday best, some of the women in the traditional Basque Gipuzkoa, long dresses covered in bright shawls, their heads in coloured and white head scarfs, across their arms neatly folded black lace mantillas; small children, old men, old women, a splattering of women in their thirties and forties, a couple of adolescents, and a couple of burly men dressed in freshly pressed check shirts and black berets – all staring up at him. August threw up his arms and smiled.

'Don't shoot again! I'm friendly. Besides, isn't it a sin to kill on a Sunday?' he shouted, in Spanish. He was answered by another bullet flying past.

When August stepped out of the shadow of the tower, the crowd was waiting. Sullen and closed-faced, they fell into an uneasy silence as he walked towards them careful to keep his hands visible.

The priest handed the rifle to a young girl of about twelve, then stepped forward. 'Who are you, stranger?' he asked, in a thickly accented Spanish that sounded almost archaic.

'A friend.' August pushed back his hood and scanned the faces, keeping his own expression open and friendly to reassure them. No one smiled back.

'We don't have friends here, only enemies living and dead,' an old woman, her chin peppered with long grey whiskers, spat onto the cobblestone.

'I mean no harm. I'm just a history professor, researching the wonderful old architecture you have here.' He tried to sound as naive as possible.

They continued to stare at him hostilely. A youth of about thirteen stepped forward.

'Then how come you speak Spanish like you come from Barcelona, you with your blond locks?'

'I am here to see the family of ...' As he was about to mention La Leona's name a shout came from the other side of the plaza and the crowd swung around. Now August could see a lone policeman hurrying out of the police station, buttoning up his jacket. He looked as if he'd just been pulled out of bed. A buxom woman with dyed blonde hair followed, her breasts free and bouncing under a thin blouse.

'Father! Father! What are you doing?' the policeman shouted across the plaza, as he ran towards them.

The old woman swung back to August. 'You want some history, here comes our *fascista* with our one whore,' she said, loud enough for the others to hear but soft enough for the policeman to miss. Some in the crowd sniggered as the policeman arrived flustered and sweating. He snatched the rifle from the girl.

'How many times have I told you folks? This is not the way to welcome visitors.' His accent placed him as both Spanish and from Madrid.

'Good to see you observe the *domingo* by resting, Commander Castillo,' the priest remarked, dryly, a comment that had the crowd laughing again and the woman – obviously a prostitute – outraged and blustering, pulling at the policeman's jacket.

'Tell him, Pepe! Tell him, he's got no respect!' The policeman pushed her away.

'Enough, woman.' He turned to August. 'So, what is your business here?'

Hoping he wouldn't ask for papers, August adopted the most refined-sounding Spanish accent he could. 'I'm here to research the house of Ruiz de Luna. I've heard it is of particular architectural interest.'

A ripple went through the crowd, several of the women looking knowingly at each other. The policeman frowned. 'But there is no house of Ruiz de Luna, is there, Father?'

The priest glanced over at August, and it was apparent to August that the villagers concealed much from the policeman.

'Indeed, there is not, Castillo Jauna,' the priest finally replied, switching to the Basque form of address – a mark of defiance to the Spanish policeman. The tension in the crowd ratcheted up a notch. The policeman paused then chose to ignore the slight. He swung back to August.

'And what kind of professor travels with a goat on his back, eh? Answer me that!' he continued, triumphantly.

'A practical one who might be hungry?' August ventured. There was a smattering of laughter among the crowd, again to the irritation of the policeman. Deciding he had better act before the situation deteriorated and the policeman was dangerously humiliated, August reached into his jacket and pulled out a letter he'd mocked up before leaving London. Written in English, with the letterhead of the British Museum visible, it declared the keeper of the letter was indeed a professor of history writing a treatise on thirteenth-century Spanish architecture. He waved it at the policeman.

'I don't mean to be disrespectful, sir, but here is my official letter.'

The policeman peered at the letter short-sightedly; it was obvious he didn't write or speak a word of English, but the letterhead was impressive enough for him. His attitude changed to that of reluctant deference.

'So where does the good professor intend to stay? We have no hotel or inn here.'

His tone was not friendly. August scanned the faces of the surrounding people; none looked sympathetic.

'I suppose I could always find an old barn or something on the outskirts of the village. I shall only be staying a few nights,' he replied, as vaguely as he could.

'Okay, okay, away with you all,' the policeman said, waving his arms, but no one moved. Ignoring them, he placed a hand on August's shoulder and the crowd began to murmur, as August tensed – was he about to be arrested? Struggling with the instinct to lash out, he let the policeman begin leading him away.

'I think I should register you at the station anyway. That is official procedure with strangers. Maybe ring headquarters. They're always interested in foreigners.'

August's chest tightened. Over the policeman's shoulder he quickly studied the square, wondering if he broke away how long it would take to escape. Judging by the mood of the crowd, he was sure he would be helped. A faint muttering of displeasure began among the onlookers, a potential arrest was an arrest even if it was of a stranger – the crowd were not happy. The policeman's grip on his shoulder got tighter. If the man checked his papers with headquarters, August would be arrested for certain.

As he was about to shake himself free, a female voice rang over the heads of the villagers.

'Enough, Pepe.'

August swung around. A striking woman, tall, pale, with black eyes and long black hair scraped into a tight bun, pushed her way through towards August and the policeman. A tall young boy, maybe fifteen years old, loped awkwardly along behind her, his protruding ears burning with shyness.

'Señora de Aznar,' the policeman said, bowing his head formally. August noticed the others around her react with the kind of reverence that made him think she was possibly the daughter or wife of a local landowner. It was only when she was finally standing in front of him that he noticed she was wearing the black of a widow.

'The professor can stay with me, I have plenty of spare rooms in the Aznar etxea.'

'That would be most kind of you. I can pay,' August offered.

'And I shall be happy to accept payment. These are hard

times, Professor,' she replied, in perfect English, to August's surprise.

'Thank you, Señora de Aznar.'

She bowed her head with a chilly seriousness and August sensed unease in the surrounding crowd. The people appeared to shrink back from the two, almost as if they carried some invisible infection, as if the woman and her child might be outcasts. It was unnerving. The boy stepped up to him and stared at him with large brown mournful eyes.

'I thought you would co ... co ... come,' he stuttered to August, in a deadly earnestness. For a moment August wondered if he was mentally impaired.

Señora Aznar, presumably his mother, turned back to the young boy. 'Gabirel, help the professor with his bags, and his goat.' The blushing adolescent took the bag with the kid goat off August's shoulders. Señora Aznar then swung back to the policeman.

'And, Pepe, we won't worry about registering the professor, will we? After all he is a guest of our esteemed village, and should be treated as such.' Her voice resonated with authority, and to August's surprise the policeman demurred.

'I suppose if he is in your good hands ... but I expect to see his papers tomorrow.'

'Expect away ...' August heard the woman murmur under her voice as she started to move back towards the milling people. August noticed that as soon as she stepped towards them they moved out of the way as if frightened, a curiously timid yet reverent expression traversing their faces. The words 'Aznar andrea' rippled across as they greeted her formally in Euskara.

August had seen such reactions before on a research trip to Haiti when he visited a local voodoo priest – it was both awe and fear.

'This way, Professor,' she instructed, and the two of them – the boy and August – followed her out of the plaza onto a broader dirt track lined with flowering chestnut trees. They walked in silence along the path that now wound up the mountain slope behind the village. As they passed one cottage an old woman standing on her doorstep crossed herself as if to warn off the evil eye.

The etxea was a large farmhouse, standing four storeys high, painted white with red shutters. It was obviously the house of a once-wealthy family, and again August wondered whether it hadn't been the domain of the major landowner in the valley. Señora Aznar ordered Gabirel to put the kid goat with the other animals in the barn, then pushed open the front door and immediately a large grey hunting dog trotted up to greet her. It growled at August and she grabbed the dog's collar.

'Nice dog,' August said, manoeuvring his way around the snarling beast.

'*Si*, he is good guard dog, but he doesn't like men,' she said, dourly, ushering him in and locking the dog out.

They walked through a bare entrance hall into a small reception room, its centrepiece a large fireplace with a carved wooden mantelpiece bearing a coat of arms. There was nothing else in the room except for two antique oak chairs sitting up against the wall and a portrait of some patriarch. Moustached and in the clothing of the eighteenth century, the middle-aged autocrat looked formidable. Señora Aznar caught August's gaze and nodded towards the painting.

'My great-grandfather. This was his house.' A flat statement that invited no further queries.

Without the youth by her side, she seemed pricklier, aggressively defensive, August noticed. She was a well-built woman, with broad shoulders and hips. Her chiselled face boasted a strong aquiline nose, a high forehead and full lips, but her eyes were the most captivating feature; large and heavy-lidded, they seemed to speak of a lineage more Byzantine than Basque. Her Spanish accent was an educated one and she had something of the aristocrat in her bearing. Although, as she reached for his jacket, August noticed her reddened hands were worn and aged like a peasant's. This was a woman who worked the fields.

'It was very kind of you to take me in,' he ventured, standing awkwardly in the middle of the small room, the space between them suddenly electric. He tried smiling. She looked back at him, expressionless, her face and eyes impossible to read. Yet he sensed some underlying vulnerability, a great brittleness. He'd seen this absence of self before in other survivors, the navigation of great unspoken loss. For a moment he wasn't sure how to respond to her, it was hard not to go on automatic, to slip into the flirtation the proximity of an attractive woman always triggered in him. To his surprise, he found that he was nervous. Señora Aznar stepped back, bristling with suspicion.

'It has nothing to do with kindness. I need the money,' she said. 'Your room is through here, please bring your bags.'

She opened a small door that led into a cramped corridor and a back stairwell with a narrow staircase winding up through the rear of the house. The old servant quarters, August assumed. Again the corridor and walls were empty, as if poverty or some sudden grand theft had stripped the house of its possessions and now it stood naked with barely a rag to cover its nudity. The war? Some familial catastrophe? August wondered, momentarily distracted by the woman's well-shaped haunches as she guided him up the uneven wooden staircase, its ancient floorboards creaking underfoot.

They arrived at the first landing and August watched as Señora Aznar swung open a low door, revealing a dim box-like room, one small window on the opposite wall. He stood while she pushed open the wooden window and shutter. Immediately, sunlight streamed in, illuminating off-white cracked plaster walls and a spare iron single bed with a dusty striped mattress on top.

'Please, don't stand on ceremony,' she told him, sternly.

Ducking through the low doorway, he stepped in, the smell of musky linen, dust and old roses overpowering, sending him into a sneezing fit.

'Sorry, it has been closed for a long time,' she said, shrugging.

A wooden cross hung off a nail on the wall above the head of the bed and an oak chest of drawers sat against the side wall, while in one corner a chipped washstand and a tin jug for water stood holding their breath as if still waiting for the previous occupant. On top of the chest of drawers lay a large ivory comb; August couldn't help noticing the strand of long black hair still wound around its yellowing teeth.

The whole room had a Spartan, utilitarian look to it. Frozen in time, it looked as if it hadn't been slept in for years, when the last occupant had left in a sudden hurry.

'My aunt slept in here, until she died. She was a very simple religious woman. So pious she didn't even dream.'

'I can't promise I won't dream, but I am neat,' he cracked. Again Señora Aznar looked at him blankly, and he made a mental note to curtail his humour.

August placed his travel bag onto the chair and sat down on the bed, a puff of dust springing up into the ray of sunlight as he did.

'I will clean it for you. It is all right?' she asked, hesitant for the first time.

'It's perfect.'

'I will bring you some water. You wash and then come down to the kitchen, and we have some wine and cheese. It is our own, there is rationing, you know.' She sounded apologetic.

'Home-made cheese sounds delicious.'

She smiled back at him, and for a moment the stern demeanour fell away, splitting like a chestnut, and he saw that she wasn't just pretty but beautiful, made more so for being utterly unaware of it. He stood, knowing that if he reached out to shake her hand she would not want to touch him. Instead, he found himself bowing his head, then felt an idiot for being so formal.

'Thank you again,' he said. Without another word she closed the door behind her.

He sat back on the bed and stared out of the window. Returning the chronicle was going to be more difficult than he imagined. The villagers were so guarded – who knew if La Leona's sister was still even alive or if any of the family had survived after the massacre? *How do I even begin without drawing suspicion to myself?* The curious reaction of the villagers at the mention of the name Ruiz de Luna came back to him. It had appeared a mixture of both apprehension and respect, and something else – a tightening of the faces. He'd seen it before in victims of atrocities. It was the deliberate blankness of those who wanted to forget.

The kitchen was located around the back of the house on the ground floor, with an iron range flanking one wall opposite an old-fashioned low stone fireplace. It appeared to be the room where both Señora Aznar and Gabirel spent the most time. A large oak table ran alongside the stove. Scratched into the top were graffiti and notches: the hieroglyphs of centuries of restless diners. A wooden ice-box was tucked against a wall. An array of cooking utensils hung off a rack suspended above the table – huge silver soup ladles, metal meat skewers, long knives and carving forks – the weaponry of gastronomes. It confirmed August's impression that this had once been the home of a family with money. Washed, with a new shirt pulled over his scrubbed flesh, he hesitated at the doorway.

Gabirel, who'd been lounging on an armchair that sat along with its battered companion, an old leather couch, in front of the fireplace, stood awkwardly, filling the room. His lanky frame seemed to knock against the low ceiling.

'Please come in, we have been preparing food.'

'It smells delicious.' August ducked his head to avoid the beam of the doorway as he went in. Señora Aznar sat at one end of the table slicing tomatoes. Spread before her on the table were plates covered with slices of sweet green pepper, a wheel of hard yellow sheep's cheese, a platter of snails cooked in an onion and tomato sauce, olives, some dried figs and a loaf of talo bread.

August's hunger gathered up and rumbled loudly through his body.

'That looks delicious.'

Señora Aznar shrugged. 'Humble fare. I apologise, there is no fish or meat, but the rabbits have been quick this last week, and it's too early for river trout. Any other produce the government confiscates and sends south. Please sit. Gabirel, txakoli?'

With the slopping grace of the deeply self-conscious, the adolescent walked over to a carafe of the young green wine and began pouring three glasses. Señora Aznar pulled out a chair for August.

'Please sit, you must be exhausted after your long journey.'

'Thank you,' he replied. Her formality was infectious and for a moment he felt like bowing.

Gabirel placed the glass down in front of August, then drew up a chair eagerly beside him, the boy's shyness radiating off him like heat.

'I've ne ... ne ... ver travelled,' he said, in slow, faltering Spanish. August wondered if perhaps the boy spoke only Euskara – some still did in the more remote areas – but then realised the boy had a heavy stammer.

'Basques ar ... are not allowed,' Gabirel explained. 'Franco thinks travel wi ... wi ... will give us ideas, but he for ... for ... forgets imagination has wings.'

'Gabirel!' Señora Aznar snapped then smiled apologetically at August. 'Forgive the lad, he thinks too much. One day he will think himself into an arrest.' She glanced over at Gabirel, a small missive of something far more complex than disapproval. August lifted his glass to break the tension.

'There's nothing to forgive.' He wanted to say more but instead looked over to Gabirel, who was now flushed with a rage August recognised from his own distant youth. 'You have a beautiful home, Señora.' As soon as it left his lips, he regretted the platitude.

'It's an empty home, Señor. Once it was full, many years ago. In a different time. My great-grandfather was a great traveller. He made money in South America, then came back. My grandmother, his daughter, was born here, then my mother, but eventually she brought a husband into this house – a Spaniard from the South. My father. She was not liked for that. There are many in the village who still have not forgiven her for not marrying a Basque.' Señora Aznar lapsed into a sudden silence that he was beginning to recognise as a quirk of her personality, the stillness closing over her, sending her somewhere else, somewhere distant.

'You are from America, no?' Gabirel broke in.

'I am indeed, from Boston. But I haven't lived there for many, many years.'

'Why not? If I were American, I would li ... li ... like to live there. Actually, I would li ... like to live there now. New York, Chicago, where the gangsters live.'

'There aren't so many gangsters there any more, unless you count the industrialists.'

'Gabirel is obsessed with all things American. He even likes their noisy music. Negro songs.'

'Jazz, I love jazz. Eddie Cochran, Charlie Parker ... I even have a record a man once bought my mother—'

'Gabirel, you talk too much, the professor is tired.'

'No, not at all. I love jazz also. I have many recordings.'

'You do?'

'Enough, eat your food.' She rapped the boy over the knuckles.

'Do you have a record player?' August asked, tentatively.

'We do, but it's very old. Sometimes I can find jazz on Radio Amsterdam on the radiogram.'

Now August noticed that the large 1920s radiogram sitting on a low table to one side of the fireplace. It was in pristine condition. Aware that radio provided the only access to real information about what was happening outside of Franco's Spain, he looked at Señora Aznar, who met his gaze defiantly.

'The radio is our only luxury.' It was a neutral statement of fact. She continued, a little apologetically, 'Much of the furniture was sold off during the war. Then, during los años de hambruna when there was only the two of us again, I had to sell many of my family's heirlooms for food. But I kept the record player, and a few basic essentials. One day I will fill the house again, I am determined.'

He studied her, recalling the bare walls, the lack of photographs, the single painting of the family's patriarch – her
grandfather. This was unusual for a Basque household,
where often a wall would be dedicated to a gallery of family
photographs, usually arranged chronologically. It was as if a
whole era of the house had been deliberately erased.

'You speak very good English, nearly faultless,' he commented, reaching for a piece of bread.

'When I was young, living in the village was an Englishwoman my mother befriended. She arranged lessons for me.
My parents had high hopes for me. In those days we had
money. The woman came from Bexhill-on-Sea – do you
know it?'

'I have visited once. It's pretty, very English.'

August felt increasingly uncomfortable. Had he stumbled
accidentally into a family he might have fought against fifteen years earlier? Had they been Carlists or Falangists –
Franco supporters? The facts seemed to point that way – the
wealthiest family in the district, daughter with a private
English tutor. But where were their privileges now? For
surely they would be benefiting from preferential treatment
or at least protection from the fascist police. If anything,
August had sensed repressed hostility from the local policeman towards Señora Aznar – the man might have feared her
but he certainly didn't respect her. On the other hand, if
they were fascists it was very likely they would be spying on
the local community and reporting back to the Guardias
Civiles. He knew well that the regime thrived on local
informants, using threats of imprisonment to blackmail
people into betraying their friends and family. But it was also
a case of divide and conquer – in every small town and village
families and neighbours were split by political allegiance
dating back to the Civil War and before. Some had betrayed

and even murdered their relatives, co-workers, people they had eaten with, sung in church with, gone to school with. After the war the winning side had prospered – the houses and businesses of the exiled and executed had been appropriated, officially and unofficially; whole communities lived on, existing over these unhealed, unmentioned scars that ran through them like the subterranean fault lines of earthquakes. It served Franco to perpetuate a local climate of constant fear and distrust this way. August had to be careful, very careful. If she were a spy, he would be in terrible danger.

'The war caused a lot of upheavals, I'm sorry you lost your family. Those were difficult days both for Spain and the Basque country.' Around him the air wound up tighter and tighter. Now Gabirel was looking anxiously in his mother's direction.

'What makes you so sure I lost my family because of the troubles?' she snapped.

'Sorry, I just assumed—'

'Assume nothing, Professor.'

'Please, call me August.'

'As far as this family is concerned, 1939 is Year Zero. Nothing existed before then. Gabirel and I would drown in ghosts if we did not believe that, and we are survivors. Isn't that true, Gabirel?'

'It's tr ... tr ... true.'

But the youth's back was rigid with emotion as he stabbed at his cheese with a fork. Somewhere in the house a clock struck two. Señora Aznar stood and began clearing the table of dishes. August sprang up to help her.

'No, please, you are our guest,' she said, insisting that he sat back at the table. She picked up an old tin bucket that sat in the corner of the kitchen. 'Meanwhile, Gabirel, you will go collect snails.' She thrust the bucket towards the boy.

'But it's afternoon!'

She glanced out of the window. 'It's just rained, they will be out. Go.'

'I'll help.' August stood. *I will get more out of the boy than the woman. She's already closed up towards me.* 'Four hands are better than two. Besides, it will give Gabirel a chance to show me your impressive grounds.'

'Farmland and forest, although much is now lying fallow,' she said, now washing dishes.

'Don't forget my vegetable garden,' Gabirel added, proudly. 'I grew the tomatoes you just ate.'

'We have a field of maize, an apple orchard and a small field for our cows, and this family is guardian of part of the mountain, nothing of historical value. That is your expertise, isn't it?' The sarcasm in her voice was evident and August wondered whether she'd already guessed that he wasn't entirely who he claimed to be. Let her keep guessing. They were equal, but her beauty was an irritant. He wasn't used to having a woman not respond to his own charms. And, to his secret chagrin, there was that old ache of desire, habitual, undeniable and now more intense as she appeared unattainable. *That's all I need now – to get involved with a possible fascist.*

'C'mon, Gabirel, let's go hunt some snails before it gets dark. I'll tell you about some of the jazz clubs I've visited.'

Gabirel pushed his chair back from the table and picked up the bucket.

The glade of ancient oak and silver birch trees was timeless. The tinkling of a nearby brook cut the air and the thin afternoon sun bathed the small clearing in a pale green light. The air washed by the earlier rain smelled both fresh and fecund with wet leaf, flowering chestnut trees and earth, and under the humming of insects there was the staccato croaking of toads. August and Gabirel were both bent over, wading through a small outcrop of ferns that edged the clearing, searching for snails, followed by the pet dog. The forest was vibrant with life, like it had a presence of its own – August had the impression the tall trees and mountain peaks were watching over him, a gaze that did not feel entirely benevolent. Just then he found several snails clumped together at the base of a frond.

'It's extraordinary. It's like nothing's changed around here for centuries,' he murmured, dropping the snails into the bucket between them.

'That's the trouble. N ... n ... nothing has changed, nothing good anyway.' Gabirel tossed a snail unceremoniously through the air. There was a clang as it hit the side of the bucket, then slid in. 'Is America beautiful?'

'Parts of it, but here you can actually hear history stretching back. It's magical.'

'Oh, there is magic.' The youth's voice was solemn, as if he were conveying a great truth. For a minute August thought his own comment might have been lost in translation.

'In English, this can mean extraordinary, as in extraordinarily beautiful.'

'I understand, but I mean it. Here we ha ... ha ... have sorcery and the old gods, they still love us. There is Mari. She li ... li ... lives in the mountaintops. I saw her once, streaking across the sky in a ba ... ba ... ball of fire, her long hair burning behind her. Sometimes we call her the Lady of Anboto. Her companion is Sugaar – he is a snake god. Then there is Urcia, he owns the sky and is responsible for the air and the clouds. And Basajaun, he is my fa ... fa ... favourite. He's big and hairy and lives in the forest. Oh and I'm forgetting the Lamia, they are be ... be ... beautiful.'

'The Lamia?'

'Mermaids who live in the streams and rivers. I've se ... se ... seen them myself trout-fishing. Here the world is older. Science and industry have not sep ... separated religion from older magic.'

August looked up from the vibrant green ferns and glanced across at Gabirel's wide face. The kid was entirely without guile, he was so certain: a chilling conviction that swept August momentarily into the same belief system. He looked up the craggy peak of the mountain above them, a lone hawk etching a lazy spiral. The landscape whispered back and August shivered despite himself.

'But I would still like to go to the Cotton Club in Hamburg just once and hear Charlie Parker maybe with a beautiful red ... re ... redhead by my side, like Ava Gardner.' The boy's voice, gruff and still breaking, brought August back to the visceral. He laughed.

'That could be arranged.'

'How? Young Basque men ca ... ca ... cannot just leave the co ... co ... country like that, you know. You have to apply for travel pa ... pa ... papers and then they never give them to you. Instead they would want to know why you d ... d ... d ... don't want to dedicate your blood and sweat to Mother Spain. Mother Spain!' He laughed bitterly, and for an instant August caught a glimmer of the man he would become.

'Doesn't your mother have important friends she can rely on, maybe a local colonel or captain?' August kept his voice casual.

'What? You think we are *fa ... fa ... fascista*!' Gabirel scowled at him, then covered the bucket with a slam. 'That's enough snails.'

He started towards a steep path that seemed to lead up

the mountain. August followed, but the boy was as nimble as a goat. Straining, August caught up with him.

'Gabirel, I'm sorry, I didn't mean to insult you.'

'And it was wrong of me to get angry. How could you know, a to ... to ... tourist like you, how it is here. I will show you!' He ploughed through some brambles. August followed him through into a part of the clearing hidden from the path.

In front of them was the low mouth of a cave buried in the foot of the mountain above them, a small open area – almost a circle – broken only by a group of ancient oak trees, the oldest of which sat gnarled, its trunk split in half by a pine tree that had somehow grown up inside it, making a chimera of the tree. The spiky pine branches fused with the lighter green oak leaves and branches. August had never seen anything like it before. It looked disturbingly unnatural, the pine a parasite on the ancient oak. Situated opposite the cave was a tiny simple stone chapel dedicated to the Virgin Mary. August knew enough about the enforced Christianisation of the region that the chapel would have been built to counteract and in many ways appropriate the old Basque paganism – a failed attempt to fuse Mari, the mountain goddess, with the Virgin Mary, to make Christian beliefs that stretched as far back as the original Cro-Magnon tribes that populated the region even before the invasion of the Indo-Europeans. He glanced over at Gabirel, who now stood hushed and awed in front of the cave. The youth's pale face was a chessboard of shadow and concentration.

'This ca ... ca ... cave is consecrated. *Akelarre* has taken place here.'

'*Akelarre?*'

'*Bruja* – wi ... wi ... witches have met here.'

'There are no witches.'

'One ca ... ca ... cannot say that they exist, one ca ...

ca ... cannot say they do not exist, but under no circumstances must you enter it. It is one of the houses of Mari and
it would be da ... da ... dangerous to you as a foreigner and
a disbeliever. A violation against the spirits of this land.'

August listened carefully, sensing the boy was committing
some great travesty by telling him about the cave at all.

'Gabirel, I promise I will be respectful. But I can go into
the chapel, yes? I am Catholic after all, admittedly lapsed.'

'The chapel is not such a problem.' Gabirel grinned,
reverting to a cheeky fifteen-year-old. August turned and
walked across the small clearing into the chapel, the cedar
pew sweetening the dusty air. Kneeling, he laid his hands
along the worn wood. In front of him behind the altar was an
ancient fresco of the Virgin Mary praying at the foot of the
cross of Christ. Judging by the naive depiction of the faces
and robes, it looked as if it dated from the thirteenth or four-
teenth century.

He looked closer. In the painted sky around the head of
Christ he could see a small flying figure, a woman in white
robes, her long blonde hair stretched behind her, appearing
to be riding a ball of fire. August stared at her, wondering if
she was an angel why she had no wings. In a flash of insight,
he realised this was a depiction of Mari, the pagan Basque
goddess, incorporated into the Christian mural. Similarly,
another figure caught his eye, almost invisible against the
foot of the cross. Crouching there was a man with wild hair
who was half snake. This must be her companion Gabirel
had talked of – Sugaar the Basque snake god. August had
seen this assimilation of local beliefs all over the world, from
the frog-princes of Bali to the Romans imposing their gods
on the deities of the Ancient Egyptians – it was a well-tried
tool of colonialism.

As August glanced back up at the simplistic and crudely

rendered round-faced Mary gazing at her crucified son, he couldn't help wondering whether Shimon Ruiz de Luna had ever been to this forest, this cave, even this chapel, for it would have existed in his time – the oak trees more slender, more hungry in their green growth back then, the cave perhaps a little deeper, a little more pristine in its mysteries, a little more saturated in the whispered entreaties of the desperate and the believing. He felt the presence of the alchemist, a fleeting shadow pressing against his consciousness, the young physic's tremendous excitement, and somehow he sensed that one of the secret locations Shimon had written about was close. A spider spilling its web descended from a rafter of the chapel like a tumbling parachutist and August's concentration was broken.

'We should keep wa ... wa ... walking before it gets dark!' Gabirel was waiting for him at the door. Without a word, August followed the boy out and back into the forest.

They sat on a craggy outpost, the snail pot between them, Gabirel's thin legs dangling over the rock face, kicking in sullen aggression, the colder afternoon air settling over them as the vast landscape below seemed to recede from under August's feet. He found the presence of the youth unsettling. Gabirel was a disturbing combination of extreme naivety and a strange precocious intelligence. August wondered if this wasn't because of the war somehow.

Down below was a clear view of the villa nestling against the hillside and the small flat grounds that stretched to the right of it, covered by an old olive grove of about ten trees and a tiny vineyard. Both the trees and the vineyard looked old and neglected; a testimony to past prosperity. Behind the villa snaked the small path the two had used to trek up the hill. It curled around a cluster of forest, sweeping left past the large rocky outcrop that, August now knew, hid the sacred cave at its base – barely visible from where they were sitting – and back around in an S shape. In the near distance on the other side of the slope he could see a small grassy incline on which several ancient burial rocks jutted out, making a circle – a prehistoric site. He'd seen cromlechs like it in Scotland.

'Have you had lots of wo ... wo ... women?' Gabirel broke the silence with an awkward intensity. August couldn't help but smile.

'A few. I guess some might think I was compulsive.'

'Compulsive?'

'You know – can't help myself.'

Gabirel frowned then worried the rock with his stick, blushing furiously. 'I thought so. You look like a man who has had a lot of women.'

'I guess that's a compliment.' Was it? August's emotional history loomed up complex and jaded next to the innocent optimism of the boy sitting beside him. *Love, and don't question the first woman you fall in love with, don't throw it away thinking there will be others – there will be, but none so bright in possibility.* The boy's hesitation brought to mind his own inability to commit – he could not disillusion him.

'What's it like?'

'More trouble than it's worth, but wonderful at the same time. You'll find out for yourself.'

'How? There is no one here.'

'That's not true. I saw a number of young girls back at the village.'

Gabirel shrugged, his underdeveloped shoulders folding under the full weight of hopelessness. 'You don't understand. We are alone in this village. Besides, even if I was accepted by the others, boys and girls aren't even allowed to dance together, not even at the fiesta.'

It was the saddest thing August had heard since he'd arrived.

'One day, Gabirel, I promise you – I'll take you to the Cotton Club and you'll have some ginger-haired bombshell hanging off your arm.'

'That's not my future.' The youth said it with such seriousness that August was again filled with unease. Wanting to change the subject, he reached for his binoculars hanging around his neck and peered back down towards the villa.

He saw several twisted olive branches and washing hanging on a clothes line, then as he swung the glasses to his right saw Señora Aznar beating the dust out of the eiderdown he'd last seen lying on top of his bed. Using a stick, she hit the quilt with an erratic rage, as if exorcising some inner anger. It was a disturbing and somehow very private sight. Feeling as if he were committing a transgression by watching, he shifted the binoculars across to the path Gabirel had shown him; there was the cross of the tiny chapel, barely visible through the trees but now, as he examined the clearing, he noticed the path of natural markers that led to the mouth of the cave. A line of boulders and the large oak tree just before it – a natural demarcation and no doubt the path the ancient Basque pilgrims must have used to find their temple as they wound their way through the forest. It pleased him that he could see it, not many would be able, but his eye was now accustomed to looking for such signs. It made him feel closer to Shimon, to the experience the Spaniard would have had looking at the same landscape.

He studied the forest beyond the chapel, away from the villa and the outskirts of the village. There seemed to be nothing but an eternity of treetops – the dark blue-green jagged edges of the pine trees broken occasionally by the softer swaying majesty of oak. Then he noticed a distinctive change in the tree line, a tiny break in the forest and the mottled angularity of something lower to the ground, something cultivated.

'What are you looking at?' Gabirel's tone was suspicious.

'Just the villa and the village.'

'If the Guardia Civil found you with these binoculars, he would arrest you for a spy.'

'But he's not going to find them, is he, Gabirel?'

In lieu of an answer Gabirel picked at a crevasse in the boulder with a twig, sending moss and earth flying. 'You're not to bring danger to my house – promise?' he asked, his face still turned away. 'Because if you do, I might have to kill you.' The boy wasn't joking. Surprised, August glanced over at him; the sense that the youth was preternaturally intelligent or intuitive prickled his skin.

'I promise, I'm a friend, Gabirel, truly. Besides, I'm only here on a research trip.'

'I think you have come to say things that we cannot say, to open boxes we are too terrified to look into.' He spoke without stuttering, his voice hypnotic, chant-like, almost that of another man. 'By the time you leave we will be changed beyond recognition.' It was a flat declaration of fact, and the youth sounded so convinced August thought perhaps he had misheard. He was about to reply when Gabirel leaped to his feet, grabbing the bucket.

'Come! I'll race you to the bottom!'

August pulled the stiff wooden shutters apart and pushed open the windows. A cacophony of frogs croaking, the distant sound of a dog barking and a moth all flew in at once. Leaning out, he let the cool night flow over him – the jagged treetops now filigree against the black, the stars high while

Venus burned yellow below the moon. Mystery pounded against his throat like excitement, like fear. He took a deep breath of the mountain air then stepped back into the room. Time to begin.

He dragged a small table in from the corridor outside to function as a makeshift desk, placing it under the open window. He stood the one lamp on top of it – the moth now flying wildly around the light, a bearing of powdered wings. August reached into his bag and lifted out the chronicle. Placing the tome reverently onto the desk, he thought of Gabirel's words about pagan magic lingering in the forests. As he stared down at the ancient book, the marks of the broken seal still visible in the cracked leather skin, August could believe it. He could imagine the same unquestioning belief in such sorcery was trapped between those ancient pages like the whisper of a seashell. All he had to do was find it and release it – the question was how to follow the charts of the alchemist's journey. He moved the lamp across, so that it flooded the pages of the chronicle in an isolated pool of light, and turned to the section about Irumendi, the description of the village written opposite the hand-drawn map.

The alchemist's sketch of the valley at the foot of the three mountains corresponded with the same geography August had seen himself, only naturally the village appeared to be a little larger than it had been three hundred years before. There were several more farmhouses and barns on the outskirts and the town hall seemed to have been a new addition. Other than that the village was remarkably unchanged, uncannily so. Shimon Ruiz de Luna's seven-teenth-century map had a simple cross to indicate the church tower and several squares for buildings – most of his drawing focused on the three mountains surrounding the valley with the river and village at its lowest point. Gazing at his own sketch, then at the chronicle, August tried to calculate where Señora Aznar's farmhouse was in relation to the mountain it nestled against. Using a piece of string, he measured the distance between the villa and the mountain and then from the centre of the village, and used a compass to work out the exact position. He knew the house was over five hundred years old – it would have to have existed in some form back then. He marked his own sketch then studied the chronicle with his magnifying glass. To his amazement he found a small circle marked in the forest near the village – which, according to his own calculations, was exactly where the farmhouse would have been located. The next challenge was to be able to find the secret location Shimon Ruiz de Luna had mentioned. He looked back down at the actual words Shimon had used to describe the location Elazar ibn Yehuda had talked of: 'The first of Elazar ibn Yehuda's sacred locations lays here between the silver birch and oak near the Goddess's cave.'

August pondered the word 'location'. The Latin the alchemist had used had several other meanings – mystery, puzzle, maze.

Maze.

The break in the tree line August had noticed through the binoculars came back to him. Was it possible? An ancient secret maze in the middle of a wild forest. Why construct such an elaborate and incongruous folly in so obscure a location? And if so, why a maze? Was it just coincidence that Gabirel had stopped him from looking down at the hillside at that particular moment? Did the boy know something? He certainly wanted to prevent August from surveying any further.

August glanced over at his Rolleiflex camera sitting on

the chest of drawers. He had to find a vantage point that would allow him to look down on the forest, somewhere he could use the long distance lens on the camera. His heart now beat with sudden exhilaration. He felt close to something, very close.

He heard Señora Aznar telling Gabirel to put out his light and go to sleep, then the soft pattering of her feet as she walked up the stairs, the footfall stopping outside his door. August held his breath; he could feel the burning presence of her through the doors, her beauty like heat. He fought the sense of wanting her, wanting her to knock, come in, to feel her long black hair tumbling across his face, his naked chest, pulling her down to the bed, to crush the sweetness of her against him.

Cursing his own absurdity, he glanced back at the door, at her shadow still visible through the crack under the door. He knew she was standing on the other side only inches away. What did she want? Was it possible she felt the same attraction? Before he could arrive at any conclusion, she'd moved on down the corridor, without a word.

That night he dreamed of Charlie, that he came to August in the bedroom, still in his ragged officer's uniform, hammer and sickle insignia hand-stitched onto the jacket, the red beret he always wore pulled low on his head, the shifting fear that had come into his eyes with the war and had stayed until it fractured his gaze into that of a madman – it was all there as he tapped August on the shoulder and woke him from a dream into a dream.

'I need you to kill me so I can sleep,' Charlie had begged, the sound of his voice so real it made August want to weep or wake. The ghost didn't seem to understand he was dead already, and August was about to tell him but found that Charlie was at the window opening the shutters, his shape dissolving in the early morning light. It was then that August realised he hadn't been dreaming at all.

Malcolm was woken by the bedside telephone ringing loudly, slicing into his sleep like an attack. He sat up, knocking the alarm clock to the floor, then, after fumbling in the dark, found the receiver. Beside him Marjorie groaned and turned over, wrapping a pillow over her head. He switched on the bedside lamp, and saw the face of the alarm clock staring up at him from the floor. Five a.m. His first thought was that his father must have died.

'Hully here.' He tried to sound calm.

'Interpol, Monsieur Hully. Sorry to disturb you, but we've had a report in from one of our agents, in relation to the man you are looking for, Monsieur August Winthrop.'

Malcolm sat up. 'You have?'

'Indeed, I rang immediately. I thought you'd like to hear sooner rather than later as the report came in south of the border.'

'Spain?'

'San Sebastián. We keep a few local eyes out there. Always useful in terms of Franco's political promiscuity, if you know what I mean.'

'Quite, so?'

'A man fitting Winthrop's description was seen going into a bar off the main market square two days ago, apparently passing himself off as Basque.'

'His language skills are good enough. San Sebastián, you say?' His mind whirled. So he *had* gone to Spain, but not Madrid – Malcolm's contact, August's old American girlfriend, had told him she'd heard there were to be some kind of negotiations between a US Army general and Franco's top military men; all she knew was that they were to be in

Madrid, but she could give him no date. So what was in San Sebastián? Why had August gone north?

'That's the dilemma, sir. He hasn't been sighted since, and our source seems to think he might have made some arrangement with the locals there to be taken somewhere else.'

Malcolm pictured the geography. He knew from his experience coordinating Operation Comet there were dozens of secluded hamlets and villages in the region, any of which would be easy to hide out in, knowledge August would also have.

'In other words we lost him.'

'I am afraid so. Do you want us to inform the Spanish? This could be the quicker way of entrapment.'

Malcolm thought for a moment. To let the local police know meant a man search, certain arrest, then possible execution and Malcolm knew it would be impossible to extradite August once Franco's men had arrested him, which would ruin MI5's chances of establishing whether he was KGB and if he was gleaning any inside information August might have leaked to the Soviets. No, better he keeps handling this himself.

'No, not yet. Keep it hush-hush until I decide when it's time to bring in the Americans.'

He put down the telephone and lay with the receiver on his lap staring out into the bedroom as the dull morning light began to creep across the floral carpet and unlit gas fire. He tried placing himself in August's skin, to fathom why the American had run. Had he killed the professor? It seemed highly unlikely, even given the bizarre circumstances of the murder, but he must know something. If the CIA was right and Winthrop was KGB, Malcolm and the department were duty bound to stop any sabotage he might be planning to

protect the US defence pact with Franco. After all he had
originally recruited Winthrop to the Special Operations
Executive. August was seen as his man, therefore the
American would also be seen as his mistake. No, if Malcolm
was to survive, it had to be him bringing Winthrop in.
Exhaustion pressed against his throbbing eyes, his back
ached and he felt old, too old for such machinations.
Outside, the birds had begun their morning chorus – it was
going to be a long day.

10

The next morning Señora Aznar made August a steaming bowl of black coffee, served up with a hunk of crusty bread covered with honey. Gabirel was already out in the fields and she seemed impatient to start her own working day.

'So I'm curious, how did you hear about this village?' She sat down opposite him and the distinctive scent of her sweat, of her hair, laced with a faint hint of vanilla, washed across, distracting him for a moment. August paused, bread in hand. He didn't want to lie but telling her too much could put her in danger.

'A friend, an American who was here in 1945, told me about it.' He measured his words carefully, and to his surprise she looked up, startled.

'There was no American living here in 1945,' she retorted.

The sound of pealing church bells interrupted her. She turned in the direction of the village.

'That's strange, it's not Sunday, is it?' August remarked.

She stood and went to the window to look down at the village below.

'They ring the bells when there is a fiesta, trouble or

someone has died, but there is no fiesta until July. We can read the bells like a book. Those bells tell of a death – of a man.' Her face was now rigid with tension. August ate some of the bread and washed it down with a gulp of hot coffee, then wiped his mouth.

'I was going to go down to the village this morning. I can find out who it is if you like.'

'That would be kind. Gabirel and I, we try to avoid going there too often, there are memories ... ' For a moment he thought he saw fear in her eyes and, more disturbingly, panic. 'You can borrow my husband's old bicycle. It's next to the mule's shed.'

With camera and binoculars hidden in his rucksack and the large black beret pulled firmly down past his ears, August cycled to the village. He planned to go back up to the top of the church steeple to look for the anomaly he saw in the tree line; to pinpoint its exact location. He needed a high lookout and the bell tower was perfect.

Bouncing over the pebbled lanes, he wove his way through the outskirts of the village towards the centre and its small cluster of local shops. The morning mist that had shrouded the mountains was beginning to lift but the sky was still streaked with grey and a light drizzle coated August's face as he cycled against the wind. The rich smell of recently ploughed damp earth and horse manure tainted the breeze, and the light rain (as well as the coffee) had sprung his nerves back to life. The squealing of the rusty pedals and his own laboured breath seemed to bounce off the walls of the buildings. August had the same illusion as when he first arrived, that Irumendi might be a ghost town, inhabited only by projections of his imagination – even worse, distorted chimeras of people he'd once known, all

those years ago, fighting in these very hills. He couldn't stop
thinking about Charlie and his visit the night before. Was
the Spain he'd known hiding in his head like a landscape
frozen in time, waiting to be ignited into scenarios of what
might have been, to be played out in those dream boule-
vards by jerking puppets of the dead? The desolation of the
empty streets did not help. Where was everybody? During
the Civil War there were only two reasons why such a village
would be deserted: invasion or massacre. How many times
had he driven into a place such as this and found the town
peppered by bullets, its houses smouldering black craters,
its men strung by their necks like strange fruit, a fascist flag
hanging from the clock tower, the pounding terror of a possible sniper blunted by his own profound exhaustion: it all
came flooding back as he cycled, all those towns, all those
battles, all those streets he marched down, his *camarada* by
his side.

The church bells began their mournful pealing again, and
August, legs straining, accelerated towards the centre. Then
the narrow lane widened and around a corner the streaking
sky yawned over the small plaza, gathering storm clouds like
a frown. August skidded to a halt and leaned the bike up
against an old stone tethering post. A group of women in
black dresses and headscarves, their shawls wrapped over
their shoulders like ravens' wings, were congregating under
the portico of the church. They turned as one animal to stare
across at August in brazen hostility. Other villagers were
filing solemnly in and out of the open church doors. A police
motorcycle with sidecar sat at the kerb, obvious, defiant and
oppressive, an indifferent policeman leaning against it smoking and watching the villagers as he chatted to a companion.
As August stood, a man in his fifties, with hunting rifle and
a string of rabbits slung over his back, walked by.

'Excuse me, friend, but who has died?' August asked. The man stopped, and after silently assessing August's working jacket, his beret and abarkak, seemed to decide to trust him.

'The *alcalde*, the mayor, dropped dead in the night. Heart attack. But if you ask me, it was the Devil coming to take back what was his in the first place.'

'And what might that be?'

The hunter glanced at the police then stepped closer.

'The soul he sold to him sixty years ago,' he murmured, without smiling. 'But still we are obliged to give our respects. In fact,' – he nodded, barely at all, towards the patrolmen – 'it will be noted if we don't. After all, the mayor was a famous man. I mean, how many men get to have a police escort at their funeral – to protect the corpse from the mourners?'

'Would you like company, friend? There is safety in numbers,' August offered, wryly.

'When it comes to this village, nothing is safe nor sacred for that matter, but if you fancy seeing evil in repose, come, be my guest.'

At which August fell in beside him and they walked across the square, running the gauntlet of whispering condemnation from the old women to step into the church. It was dim inside, the perpetual twilight broken only by the large lighted candles that stood in the four corners of the long nave. At the front, which had been cleared of pews, sat an open coffin on a simple wooden plinth. People were slowly filing around the casket, placing flowers or wreaths, then kneeling in silent prayer, crossing themselves to move on. The air was thick with burning incense, and the shuffling atmosphere took August back to the services he attended as a small boy at Trinity Episcopal Church in Back Bay, Boston. Then, as now, he was filled with the same sense of claustrophobia. In the

low light he could see the priest standing at the altar, his face
a mask of studied neutrality. The hunter fell into line, dragging his heels across the flagstones, and August followed
closely, curiosity having won over caution.

When it came the turn of the woman in front of them, she
dipped into a curtsey at the altar, crossed herself then placed
a lily at the foot of the coffin. Behind her, August leaned forward to look into the casket. The mayor, corpulent and
presidential in a suit that looked like it had been bought
especially for the occasion, resembled a rouged waxwork,
his lips and cheeks crudely made-up. The man was probably
in his early sixties and there was a faint expression of
aggrieved surprise the undertaker hadn't succeeded in erasing. The dead mayor, for all the talk of evil, appeared utterly
benign. The woman gave a furtive glance towards the priest,
who at that moment was turned away, then quick as a flash
she spat at the face of the corpse, a healthy wad of spittle hitting the top of one cheek, then beginning a slow slide down
the face like some abhorrent teardrop. Shocked, August
glanced around. No one reacted. The villagers just continued with their rituals closed-faced, while the woman, now
transformed back into a demure middle-aged widow,
stepped away.

'He betrayed her husband in thirty-six,' the hunter whispered to August, as they stood in front of the ebony box.
Dutifully, the hunter crossed himself and plucked one of
the small furry corpses from the string of rabbits still around
his neck. Kneeling, he laid the dead animal next to the small
pile of wreaths and flowers.

'Because he was as slippery as a rabbit,' he said out loud,
in Euskara, as he rose from the floor. Several of the nearby
mourners laughed.

*

Outside, the crowd was growing as others arrived from the surrounding hills. August glanced over at the tall tower rising up beside the main body of the church. It would be impossible to climb to the top now without attracting too much attention. Plus there were the patrolmen to worry about.

Stepping away from the mourners, he noticed that one of the two cafés gracing the plaza had under its red, white and green awnings framed and hung proudly on the wall a series of panoramic photographs; obviously the work of a talented amateur. Curious, August walked up to the café window and studied the pictures, which were of the village and the plaza. There were also several of the valley: two from the town itself and three from what looked like vantage points at the tops of the three mountains. The tables outside were deserted and the café appeared empty. Through the window he could see the owner, a short thin man, standing behind the counter polishing glasses. August went in and approached the counter.

'Nice photos. You do them yourself?'

'Naturally. I'm the best photographer in Irumendi. Actually, I'm the only photographer in Irumendi. I also do weddings, christenings, communions and funerals, but not that one.' He gestured towards the church and placed a glass of frothing cider in front of August.

'It's on the house, today we celebrate.' He waited for August to taste the cider.

'It's good.'

'Of course it's good, it's from my own orchard.'

'You must be the only person not in church filing around that coffin,' August remarked.

'I'm an atheist, third generation. My grandfather gave up on God when the government confiscated his land.' He laughed bitterly. 'Although, now with the mayor dropping dead, I might break family tradition and start believing again. But it would have to be Catholic of course. Did you hear it on the radio?'

August looked blank. He'd heard nothing.

'Pius finally recognised Franco. The Pope will be granting a concordat in Rome accepting him as the official ruler of Spain and institutionalising Catholicism as Spain's only legal religion. So maybe it's lucky I'm an atheist after all – if I was a witch, Jew or Communist, I'd be screwed.'

'I gather the mayor wasn't popular?'

'He was hated.' Mateo reached for a dish of salted sardines and placed them in front of August. 'When we lost the war it was him who went to Guardia Militar and betrayed half the families in Irumendi. For that honourable service they made him mayor. Tomorrow they will bury him and we will have a funeral procession around the village that everyone must attend. If you don't, they . . . ' – here he pointed to the police outside the church – '. . . will be taking notes. They watch us like hawks. So the whole village will be there, even me, shuffling behind that coffin like chained prisoners.' He poured himself a glass of wine and held it up towards the church. 'To Judas.'

'What goes around comes around.'

'In my country we have another saying: *La palabra del Alaves es como una llave de Madera* – "The words of a person from Alava are like a wooden key."'

August laughed. There wasn't much love between the different provinces. 'Alava is beautiful,' he retorted, diplomatically. 'And so is Biscay.'

'One of the best, but then it's the only one I know. I left once to Madrid but I got homesick and they all speak funny,' he joked, then downed his wine and poured himself another. The mayor's death had made everyone tense, August guessed. No doubt they would be facing a whole new power struggle with his absence. 'You're the historian staying with Widow Aznar, aren't you?'

'That's right.'

'Now that's a family with secrets. Once there were seven of them – now there are only two, and who knows who the father of the boy was. They say they never saw her pregnant. But that family, they've always been different.'

'Different, how?'

'You'll find out.' The owner closed up as quickly as he had opened. August felt he had to re-establish the intimacy between them. He glanced back up at the photographs that also lined the walls inside.

'You know I take photographs too, for my research.'

'You do? What equipment do you have?'

'I'm travelling with a Rolleiflex – with a Leica lens.'

The café owner whistled. 'What I'd do to get my hands on one of those. It's hard to buy anything here, it's all by mail order and takes months. Also it's so expensive.'

'I could help you out.'

'How?'

'I need access to a darkroom. I'll be happy to rent yours while I'm here.'

'It's very primitive.'

'All I need is an enlarger and the development tanks.'

'I have those. I'd love to look through the Leica lens.'

'It would be my honour, a talented photographer like yourself.'

The man studied him then grinned. 'It's a deal. My name is Mateo, by the way.'

'*Kaixo*, Mateo.' August welcomed him using one of the few Basque words he knew. 'There's another thing I need, a good map – one with real details.'

'A map!' The owner laughed, displaying four gold teeth on his bottom row. 'There is one, but this village isn't marked on it. Which is good and bad. Good when you don't want to be found and bad when you want friends to visit. No, my friend, maps will not teach you about these valleys and these mountains. To know Irumendi you have to breathe, eat and shit the air. Irumendi is not a whore, she doesn't just lie down for one night. People come here to get lost, they don't come here to find maps.'

'Nevertheless, I need one.'

Mateo threw his hands up. 'I trust you, fuck knows why, but you smell honest and my nose never lies. There is a map, an old map, inside the town hall. If you ask, they will let you look at it.'

'Thank you.' August poured Mateo another cider. 'This one I'm paying for.'

'*Salud*. Be careful of Widow Aznar, she is *sorgina* – and a witch, like all the women in her clan. You should be careful, but why should you worry? You're probably an atheist too. We don't believe in such things, right?'

'Right.'

Mateo clinked his glass against August's.

'But I'd watch my back. Those kinds of women, they either want to fuck you or ... ' He drew a line dramatically across his neck. 'Either way you want to wake up with your head on your shoulders in the morning. Otherwise, my friend, you are screwed.' He concluded, philosophically, 'Go back to the farmhouse, tell her the mayor has died. She should be there tomorrow for the funeral, her and her son. They have to go, they are already noticed. As for the darkroom, come whenever you like, I live above the café. But let's keep this between you and me. Here everyone talks, and I, for one, haven't lived this long to be shot as a spy.'

August glanced back through the café window, across the plaza: the patrolmen were still there. He had no choice – he would be seen immediately if he went up the tower with all the mourners milling around. He'd have to put it off until the next day. He thanked Mateo and left using a side door.

He went straight to the town hall, where he found an old woman sitting behind an austere oak table in the small reception room that doubled as the library. The woman, unimpressed by August's charms, claimed to be the wife of the town clerk, who was at the funeral, and that she couldn't help him without her husband's permission. It was only after August promised to take a photograph and a message back to England for a long-lost son who'd fled Franco that she presented the map. After ushering him over to a glass-topped reading table (the only other piece of furniture in the room), she rolled the manuscript out dramatically. It appeared to be a detailed seventeenth-century etching with nineteenth-century additions written carefully over the top – the original template of the map was in Spanish and Latin, and from the topographical and religious emphasis, August assumed it could have quite possibly served as a guide to the guards of the Inquisition. The newer additions were marked in inked calligraphy and written in Euskara. Running his finger down the landmarks, August recognised the town plaza and the church – although one of its wings appeared to have been a late addition to the original medieval construction. There were only a cluster of dwellings around the plaza and the outskirts of the village panned out into small allotments and farms. A building situated right next to the church caught his eye: a jail, and behind it an armoury, an unusual construction for such a small village. Had this been some kind of military centre for the region, some secret fortress? It was hard to imagine. The residential dwellings had their owners' names written carefully underneath the small neat topographical drawings. As far as August could tell most of the families had been living there for centuries, each generation inheriting the homestead from the next in a continuous flow. No wonder the community was so tight knit – the intimacy and policing of each other must have been extremely claustrophobic, August noted, reflecting on his own displaced nature and wanderlust. He ran his gaze to above the town and the edge of the mountains, as he tried looking for something marking the Aznar villa. To his shock, the name 'Widow of Ruiz de Luna' was written in Spanish beside the symbol for the dwelling. *Ruiz de Luna.* The same name as the alchemist. Was it possible this had been Uxue's house, Shimon Ruiz de Luna's widow, and that Señora Aznar had deliberately hidden the true identity of the family from him? It made a kind of perfect sense, especially if she was La Leona's sister – such a relationship would mean instant arrest and there would be some in Irumendi who would guard her identity as if it were sacrosanct; and there would also be some ready to betray her. Which would make it understandable that the family trusted no one.

It seemed extraordinary. The suffocating sense of predestination swept through him like vertigo. He glanced down at the bottom corner of the map. There were two dates: 1630, obviously the date of the original etching, and, written above it, 1890. August sat back, calculating – if the alchemist had been executed in 1613 and Uxue, his wife, had escaped England and somehow returned to Spain, it was possible that she could have settled back here. So in 1630 it would also be possible for Uxue to have only been in her early fifties. Could Izarra Aznar be a direct relative or had she inherited the property some indirect way? He pointed to the mark on the map.

'Widow Aznar?' he asked the old woman, who looked at him suspiciously, then answered, haltingly.

'*Si*, Widow Aznar is from the Ruiz de Luna clan. Aznar was her husband's name, she adopted it to honour him, but her father's family was Ruiz de Luna.'

August's mind spun with the implications. He looked back at the map for the area of forest he'd sighted from the mountaintop the day before. He found it immediately, labelled in bold seventeenth-century Latin with the ominous statement, 'Non-consecrated land: Pagan.' August stared at it, slowly processing the implications. He'd never seen anything written like it on any other old map he'd studied before – all land was non-consecrated outside of the churchyard, so why make a special point of marking it as such? It was like a warning.

Olivia sat on the harbour wall and looked back at the square of Louis XIV, the pretty heart of the old port. She watched a small gang of children play around the bandstand in the middle, as their parents sipped their first aperitifs of the afternoon at the café tables. She had been in Saint Jean de Luc now for three days trying to retrace August's movements with no success. It was like he'd instantly vanished or had never been there at all. First, she couldn't track where he'd stayed and second, he'd managed to leave without a soul noticing. The American certainly hadn't used the train and it was impossible to hire a car in the small town, as she herself was discovering.

A young boy chasing a small dog ran past, narrowly missing her. The whole domestic panorama unnerved her, knowing as she did the political undercurrents of the border town – the Basque refugees from the Spanish Civil War who had flooded the port in 1936, the Nazi occupation less than a decade later, the valour of the Basque resistance. Then she had an epiphany – perhaps that was August's connection to the place. He must have had friends in the tight-knit community, she decided; someone who chose to protect him, someone powerful within the town. She could tell by the manner with which the townsfolk reacted when she started asking questions – a stoic sullenness. One that suggested they'd been instructed to say nothing. But there was the other issue, the fact that she herself now had a tail – one of the few men she had ever found truly terrifying. And they were both chasing the same rabbit down the same hole. She had to find a way of finding August without betraying him to her nemesis – a man who could really destroy her. It was going to be difficult.

She had only one clue: a small tobacconist on the promenade remembered August for the distinctive brand of cigarette he'd bought there three days earlier and the fact that he'd put a branded matchbox on the shop counter while paying. The matchbox came from a café called La Baleine Échouée.

Bernadette, Joseba's daughter, was busy polishing the cutlery. It was after lunch and the café was finally quiet again. It would be until the evening regulars started to come in. The young girl was tired, she'd been on her feet since five that morning and she was looking forward to the evening beach ride on her boyfriend's Vespa. The blonde glanced up as the tall middle-aged woman entered. Despite her awkward gait – a kind of heavy-limbed clumsiness the young girl associated with the English – the woman looked friendly and well-heeled enough to give a decent tip. Bernadette perked up.

'Can I help you, Madame?' she asked, putting down the silver spoons.

The woman walked up to the counter and settled her ample backside onto one of the high stools.

Olivia glanced around the bar. It was exactly as she had pictured it, and if she closed her eyes slightly she could see the bluish imprint of the American's presence still lingering at a table near one of the windows. Interesting – as was the large cage of canaries twittering and perch-hopping by the door. Birds were useful; they were easily manipulated.

'I don't suppose it's too early for a cognac?' Olivia kept her voice warm, reassuring and a little self-deprecating. The girl fell for it.

'It's never too early for a cognac, Madame.' Bernadette smiled back, youth illuminating her thin beauty. She fetched a bottle and began pouring a glass in front of Olivia.

'Haven't you got lovely hair?' Olivia practically purred.

'*Merci*, Madame.' There was something hypnotic about the Englishwoman's voice that reminded Bernadette of her mother's voice when she was little, before her mother had died – reassuring, warm, it made her feel safe and that was something she hadn't felt for a long, long time. So when the Englishwoman reached out and stroked her hair, she wasn't surprised or affronted at all, and for some inexplicable reason, when the Englishwoman plucked a strand from her head with a sharp tug, she hardly noticed. Instead, she finished pouring the cognac, and stood there, with the bottle in her hand, smiling mutely as the woman wound the strand of hair around one of her fingers.

'I'm looking for someone, Bernadette.'

Funny, she couldn't remember telling the Englishwoman her name.

'An American, maybe you can help me.'

'Yes. Handsome, tall,' she answered, surprising herself.

'Bernadette!'

She swung around. Her father stood at the cellar door, the hook he used for hauling in the beer crates still in his hand. 'I can help this customer.'

The threat in his voice made her snap out of the warm cloud in which she felt she had been floating. She looked across at the Englishwoman and down at the bottle of cognac she was still holding. She couldn't even remember pouring the drink.

'Yes, Papa.' She returned the bottle to the shelves and retreated to the other end of the bar and Joseba led the Englishwoman to the front door.

'This way, Madame, we have nothing to discuss.' The arm he grasped felt surprisingly muscular and Joseba instantly became aware that the woman was not all she appeared. When they arrived at the door, Olivia pulled herself sharply out of his grasp, and as she did bent down and picked up a yellow feather – one that must have fluttered its way out of the cage. She sat herself firmly down at the nearby table.

'Oh, but we do, Monsieur, we have a close mutual friend, August Winthrop. Although I suspect you know him by a different name.'

'What's it to you?' Joseba remained standing, gruff, legs planted wide in hostility.

She glanced around, unfazed by his aggression. This rattled him.

'For a small bar this place is very famous in certain circles.'

She began to wind the strand of blonde hair around the feather, tighter and tighter. Behind her the canaries started to fly wildly around the cage, their song becoming more frantic. Joseba glanced down at the woman's hands, her activity disturbed him. There was something primitive yet calculating about it. Was that a strand of his daughter's hair? He felt sick. He sat heavily down opposite the Englishwoman; there was nothing about her that he trusted.

'Who are you – MI6, Interpol?' To his chagrin he sounded nervous.

'Papa, there's something wrong with the birds!' Bernadette called out from the far side of the bar. Joseba ignored her; he couldn't take his eyes off the twisting hair winding around the yellow feather.

'Neither. I'm independent, Joseba, and I need to know where you have taken the American.' The woman's voice seemed to echo from inside his head but still he fought back.

'Never. I do not betray my friends.' The sound of the canaries reached a horrifying pitch.

'Papa! They are killing each other!' Now Bernadette was at the cage door, opening it. Joseba still couldn't drag his gaze from the blonde hair winding tightly around the feather.

'Never, Joseba? If you think I'm going to be the canary, you're wrong.' Olivia smiled. The blonde hair snapped and suddenly the bar was full of screaming as the canaries flew pecking at Bernadette's face in a flurry of yellow feathers and blood.

'Donostia!' he shouted. Olivia looked blankly at him, not knowing the Basque name. 'San Sebastián! That's all I know. I took him across the border!' Joseba yelled, before sweeping both feather and hair to the floor. He rushed to Bernadette, waving and punching at the air to rid her of the possessed birds. Calmly, Olivia finished her cognac and left.

11

By the time August had cycled back up to the farmhouse it was past four and the light was fading. He found Señora Aznar hauling clean straw into the barn in the ground floor of the house. The row of three small Jersey cows turned at the sound of him, staring over their shoulders mournfully out of the dim light, still chewing the cud. Two goats now united with the kid goat he brought were tethered on the other side of the barn, bleating contentedly, and just outside the door the family's mule stood under a hand-woven rush canopy chomping at some carrots.

Hanging on the barn wall outside was a collection of steel clippers and small shears that August recognised from the gardening shed at the summer house in Cape Cod that had been one of his childhood haunts. Convinced he must be mistaken, he docked the bike against the wall and went over to examine them.

'So?' Señora Aznar startled him. She stood holding a simple three-pronged fork, its pale wooden handle smoothed by years of use. 'Who is dead?' she asked, bluntly, propping the fork against the wall.

He unhooked the string of onions and the bag of sweet potatoes he'd bought in the village from the bicycle.

'The mayor. A sudden heart attack.' He handed her the vegetables.

She smiled. 'But this is wonderful news. This means a fiesta. They will wait a few days until the Guarda Militar have gone back to Donostia but it will be a celebration. And it will be masked so that spies will not be able to betray the identity of the people. There are many who hated that man.' She clapped her hands in glee then spun around towards the small meadow behind the house, where the distant figure of Gabirel stood swinging a scythe against the long grass. 'Gabirel! Gabirel!' The youth shouldered the scythe and began to stride towards them through the field.

'A very unpopular man apparently.' August studied her, wondering when he should confront her directly on her lineage. Now the faintly oriental appearance of her eyes, set in an otherwise distinctively Basque face, the aquiline nose and full lips, these all began to make sense to him as he searched her face for remnants of alchemist Shimon Ruiz de Luna.

'A Carlist and a collaborator, he betrayed many, including my father,' she elaborated.

'I was given a message for you, by Mateo.'

'That old rake.'

'He told me to tell you to be sure to march in the funeral procession tomorrow. He told me you and Gabirel had the attention of the Guardia Civil.'

'I will think about it.' She swung away to greet Gabirel, who was now pushing open a gate, two furred rabbit corpses slung over his shoulder. August grabbed her arm.

'You must go. If not for your sake, for the boy's.'

'You think you know how we live here?'

'I know more than you think, Izarra. I fought here myself in 1934 with the Republicans.'

'*Con la brigada de Abraham Lincoln?*' Shocked, she slipped into Spanish.

'*Sí*. And you're Izarra Ruiz de Luna Merikaetxebarria, the sister of La Leona. Your mother's father's clan were Ruiz de Luna.'

He'd said it now, he'd revealed himself. The question was, would she? He glanced over at Gabirel, the boy wasn't yet within hearing range. August stepped closer to Izarra. 'Your family, they fought too.'

She glanced up at him, terrified. 'Who are you?'

August put his hand reassuringly on her shoulder. 'It's all right, I am a friend. I came here to bring you something from Jimmy van Peters.'

She gasped. 'You have seen Jimmy?'

'He gave me something to return to your family, something that belonged to the Ruiz de Luna family.'

'*Las crónicas del alquimista?*'

'It's extraordinary.' He was about to tell her about his translations when she held up her hand.

'Not in front of Gabirel. The memories stay locked in – this is the only way we can grieve. We will talk later but tomorrow Gabirel and I will walk behind that pig's coffin, only to keep suspicion at bay.'

She moved away and began talking rapidly in Euskara to Gabirel. Keeping a discreet distance, August watched the vibrant glimmers of passion breaking through the young Basque woman's stoicism, the beauty of her volatile face. But now he saw the way tragedy had bowed her shoulders, had given a defensive tinge to her gestures, the emotions buried below the surface like an underground

river that roars on imperceptibly, indifferent to the passing
of time.

The rich smell of stewed rabbit laced with garlic, tomatoes
and sage drifted up as Izarra lifted off the lid of the cooking
pot. August was famished. In silence Izarra served the stew
out onto the three plates, giving herself the smallest portion. She reached for the vegetables.

'Sweet potatoes?' She held the serving spoon over a large
dish, a small pat of butter melting on top.

'As many as you can spare.' August tried to stop his stomach from audibly rumbling. He failed, and Gabirel grinned
from across the table.

'The mountain air makes me hungry,' August said, apologetically.

'You brought the potatoes, you're entitled to eat as many
as you like,' Izarra said, with an air of sullen defensiveness. It
was as if everything was a battle with her, August noted, and
yet the tension between them had heightened as if their
very proximity had created an unintended intimacy.

'But I caught the rabbit,' Gabirel quipped.

Izarra looked at him sharply. 'Señor August is our guest!'

In lieu of a reply, Gabirel shrugged, pushing his meagre
portion around the plate with a fork. August stole a sideways
glance at Izarra. Her cheeks were flushed from the heat of
cooking and she'd undone the top buttons of her simple
cotton blouse, showing the merest glimpse of cleavage –
wanting her annoyed him. He couldn't afford to let his emotions get in the way of the real reason he was there. As if
reading his mind, Izarra met his gaze defiantly then ladled
an embarrassingly large amount of sweet potato onto his
plate.

August held her gaze until, defeated, she looked away.

As she did, he pulled over Gabirel's plate and spooned some of his own sweet potato onto it.

'Here, Gabirel, you're still growing.'

'Thanks.' Without any more ceremony the youth began to shovel the food hungrily into his mouth. August guessed that he had been starving and such a lavish meal was unusual in the household.

'Can I go to the fiesta after the funeral?' Gabirel asked Izarra, in Spanish.

'No, it will be too dangerous.' But after glancing at the youth's crestfallen expression, she softened. 'You know it is. The young people will be watched.'

Izarra took her place. August waited for her to start her meal, then began eating. The freshness and simplicity of the food was delicious. For a moment the flickering candle on the table, the glow of the fire in the hearth, the shine of Izarra's hair catching the light, as well as the poignancy of the boy's soft moustache, made August feel territorial. He had the strange impression that he had just stepped into another man's shoes and become the missing element in this family – the husband, the father, the protector. Even more disturbing was that he liked the sensation.

'You fought in the war, with the R... R... Republicans?' Gabirel asked, abruptly, barely hiding his excitement.

'Gabirel!' Izarra's voice was full of disapproval. 'How do you know that?'

'You think I'm deaf as a mule?' Gabirel spat back, then turned towards August. 'Tell me about it. You fought with the Americans, didn't you? *Con la brigada de Abraham Lincoln* – for the Republicans, our allies.'

'Gabirel, you tell too much,' Izarra insisted.

August glanced over, unsure if he had permission from her to enter the dialogue, but the boy's eager face swayed him.

'Bilbo, Brunete, Tarazona. You g … g … guys were brave, fighting for ideals like that, an abstract. My pe … pe … people were fighting for their country and their lives. We had no choice,' Gabirel continued.

'What do you know? You weren't even born,' Izarra said.

'I heard the stories, she told me.' The statement burst out of Gabirel with such anger August knew instantly that the boy meant La Leona, and that he had stepped over a boundary, revealing one of the family's unspoken secrets. Izarra brought her fist down onto the table, making the cutlery jump.

'Enough! Take your meal, you eat in your room!' she ordered, standing. Gabirel got to his feet. In stalemate, they stared at each other – the woman struggling to keep her domination over the youth, and August could now see it was only a matter of months before Gabirel would become a man. Finally, Gabirel backed down. He picked up his plate.

'You win, this last time. But I go to the fiesta,' he told her, turning back to August. 'We will talk about the war later.'

August waited until he heard Gabirel going up the stairs, then reached across the table. He put his hand over Izarra's. Instantly, desire shot between them like a bolt, undeniable, confronting. She pulled her hand away.

'Are you all right, Señora de Aznar?' he asked, quietly.

'You know my name is Izarra. Please, enough formality. You must forgive Gabirel, there have not been enough men in his life. He looks to you as a hero, and yet he doesn't even know you.'

'I'll try not to disappoint him,' he said, implying he would also try not to disappoint her.

She blushed. 'So how do you know Jimmy?' she asked, tentatively.

'I fought with him, at Teruel. He saved my life once.'

'He loved my sister ... It was a tragedy.' Changing the subject, she looked at the cooling food. 'Please, finish your stew.'

'It is delicious.'

'I was once a good cook, when I had something to cook with.' She smiled and August sensed trust opening up again between them. *I have to move quickly, win her back.*

'Izarra, the chronicle ...'

'It was an heirloom, I am happy you have brought it back.'

'I have been researching your ancestor Shimon Ruiz de Luna, an extraordinary man.'

To his surprise, her face closed down. 'I know nothing. We are just the caretakers of the book. This was our family's duty for centuries.'

'So I understand, but I have been translating the chronicle—'

'You've read it?' She sounded shocked.

He studied her reaction. He had to be so careful – any wrong moves and he knew she would retreat back into her shell. 'Why are you so interested?' she said, now sitting up, her shoulders rigid with fear. 'Who are you really?' she whispered, hoarsely.

'Izarra, please, I'm not an enemy or a spy. I'm not with the authorities. Please, you must trust me.'

'Impossible.' Now she'd closed down entirely and August knew he'd pushed too far. 'Please, no more questions, otherwise I will have to ask you to leave. With your war experience in Spain, you should understand this.' Her tone was definite. She laid her knife and fork on her plate and pushed her chair away from the table.

'When you're finished, there's an egg custard in the pantry. I will see you tomorrow after the funeral parade. I will clean up after you have gone to bed,' she told him, curtly, then left the kitchen and August found himself staring across an empty table. After a while he blew out the candle and sat there thinking, illuminated only by the embers of the fire.

Like the pied piper, the plaintive notes of the txistu started up, wailing its reedy way through the plaza. The flute was joined by a drum beating out the zortziko – the 5/8 rhythm characteristic of the region – calling the mourners to the church. Hidden in the doorway of a shuttered shop, August watched as the procession gathered itself to leave from outside the church. The txistulari, dressed in traditional white, with a scarlet waist sash and a scarlet boina on his head, held the flute to his mouth with one hand while beating a side-drum with a drumstick in the other. He prepared to lead them off, behind him ten *ezpata dantzariak* – sword-dancers – poised to begin their dance. Dressed a little like morris men, with bell-pads attached to their calves, in white with the traditional red sashes and berets, as well as the local flower, the yellow sempervivum, in their lapels, they also held swords in their hands. Their leader stood at the front, bearing a long banner-like flag. The txistulari stopped playing, a crow cried somewhere over the valley and the sword-dancers all kneeled solemnly as the flag-bearer waved his banner theatrically and dangerously low over their heads, as though giving a blessing. After the last dramatic swirl of colour, the txistulari began playing again and the sword-dancers began their dance, each clashing the tip of the sword of the man beside him as they executed small leaps and dance steps. Behind the *ezpata dantzariak* was the priest, flanked by two choirboys swinging ceremonial incense burners. They all stood in front of the funeral cart, draped in black cloth, with two muscular draught horses, black rosettes tucked into their bridles, standing impatiently, their long flaxen tails swishing against their steaming flanks. Gathered behind the funeral cart was the mayor's family – a tall, thin, pinched-looking woman and two sons in their twenties and a young girl of about thirteen. Then came a group of local dignitaries, some smoking in the early morning chill, as the rest of the villagers, summoned by the txistu and too afraid not to attend, wound their way across the plaza: small groups of them appeared from the quiet lanes that led into the square, others emerged from the dwellings on the square itself. All dressed in black and stony-faced, they assembled behind the coffin cart. Grandmothers and babes in arms, young widows and husbandless wives, the old men – their faces scowled with both resignation and anger – waited silently as the coffin was carried out of the church and placed upon the cart.

The txistulari began a funeral march and the procession took off, the wheels of the cart creaking. What struck August as extraordinary was the fact that the mayor's young sons were the only men in attendance over the age of twenty and under sixty. Carefully concealed in the shadows, he peered out and finally sighted Izarra and Gabirel walking among the villagers. They were the last of the mourners and Gabirel straggled along reluctantly, Izarra pulling him firmly forward by his arm. A police car, driving very slowly, followed at the back, its presence only adding to the oppressive atmosphere.

August waited for them to leave the far side of the plaza. He calculated he had at least half an hour before they would return. When the sound of the procession faded, he dashed across the plaza, his camera equipment slung across his back, then ducked into the empty church through the side door he knew led to the old stone spiral staircase that wound up to the top of the bell tower.

*

The morning breeze was more powerful at the top of the tower. Staring across the ravine hemmed in by the three steep mountain slopes, August could clearly see the broad bands of sunlight and shade travelling along the tops of the trees and over the snow-capped mountains as the wind chased the clouds over the valley. He leaned against the low parapet wall, his palm finding one of the many small pits that marked the stone. This high up he could smell the pine trees, their scent carried on the breeze, and the faint aroma of rosemary; early summer under the crisp spring wind. August looked down and noticed the old bullet holes made by ricocheting shrapnel, a reminder of the Civil War, even here.

His mind flashed back to September 1937 to a small village in Aragon, holed up in another church tower fighting a fascist offensive. He was back there, pressed against the sandbags, the broad shoulders of the German sharpshooter – a friend and member of the communist Thälmann Battalion – silhouetted against the narrow opening as he returned the fascists' fire, the sickening almost silent thud of a bullet as his friend's head jerked backwards, his brains a red stain on the opposite wall. In the next second August, with no thought but survival, pushed the dead body of his friend aside, to take his place at the window.

He was still haunted by that image of himself, devoid of emotion. Crouching against the tower's wall, August's senses were filled with the same stretched back alertness, the acrid odour of gunpowder, the metallic pungent smell of death, the rattling of his gun fusing with the aching muscles of his shoulder; everything narrowing down to one point – what he saw through the rifle's sights.

A sudden breeze loosened some crumbling brick. It cascaded down onto August's shoulders, jolting him back to the present. He stood slowly then with meticulous intent began assembling the tripod.

The Rolleiflex sat on the tripod like a small box-shaped cyclops, the long extended eye of the Leica lens dominating the camera like some great phallic extension. August stared down into the viewfinder. The image, criss-crossed by faint lines allowing the photographer to position and focus, was of the area of forest he felt sure contained the break in the tree line he'd seen on the walk with Gabirel. He moved the camera right and then slightly left, and the boxed-in perspective changed; now there were more trees caught within the frame. August peered closer. There appeared to be a thin white line in the treetops and trunks. He straightened up and lifted the binoculars to his eyes, looking out in the same direction, panning across the mountainside.

He found it. The same break in the forest. He looked over at the hillside, and the farmhouse – a picturesque doll's house from this distance – came into view. He glanced back up the mountain – the break looked to be at the distance he had calculated at the library. It had to be it. Lowering the binoculars, he bent over the camera and started focusing: immediately the treetops came into sharp detail, many of them mature oaks, interspersed with taller, more elegant silver birch. But what was most fascinating was the way he could now clearly see that the break wasn't just a small area of growth that had died or been burned away. It was a definite clearing. Could this be the location Shimon Ruiz de Luna had written about? The first of Elazar ibn Yehuda's sacred locations that lay between the silver birch and oak beside the Goddess's cave? He looked through the camera again, calculating where the sacred cave might be that Gabirel had shown him. It was definitely near the clearing. In which case, why hadn't Gabirel shown August himself? The youth had certainly seemed nervous when August wanted to walk down in that direction. Had he been hiding something?

August took a photograph, just for his record, and after checking again through the binoculars, took out his notebook and made a sketch of the area, marking the distance between the farmhouse and the clearing, heavily concealed by forest. *If I hadn't known where to look, I would never have found it. It was as if it had been deliberately concealed.* He wondered if any of the other villagers knew about its existence. He was so engrossed he failed to notice the sound of the txistu and the drum had returned, floating over a cool gust of wind. The procession was winding its way back through the plaza towards the graveyard at the back of the church. He had to hurry. He packed away the tripod and glanced down at the square. The snaking line of people and vehicles had almost reached the church. August gazed down the length of the procession look- ing for Izarra and Gabirel. He found them, and to his horror the boy was staring directly up at August as he walked, his gaze meeting August's straight away, as if he expected August to be up the tower looking down at them. But how? The youth's unnatural ability to second-guess where he was and what he was about to say swept through August like a pre- monition. Could he really trust Gabirel? The rest of the mourners, including Izarra, stared straight ahead, oblivious. August pressed himself against the wall, waiting for the boy to betray him. Instead Gabirel, his face impassive, dropped his eyes and continued walking. August exhaled.

§

The monk walked across the mud-caked plaza, making his way into the church to ring in that evening's prayers. Shimon didn't have much time. Watching the young priest stride past a farmer herding a small group of bullocks out of his way, Shimon smiled. There was such tranquillity in this village; it was as if it belonged to another world. He turned and stared out from the bell tower, over the town's plaza towards the mountainside. He had Elazar ibn Yehuda's manuscript opened out in front of him. The three mountains the ancient physic had written about reared up on three sides, and there were remnants of the pagan settlement he'd described established around the river that coursed through the steep valley. A settlement unmarked by the event of Christianity, Yehuda had written, a group of tall, war-like peoples who worshipped gods of the mountains and rivers, instead of Christ, a tribe that spoke an impenetrable language unlike any he had encountered in the region. The Romans had called them Vascones and appeared to have a grudging respect for the people, who had soon proved themselves both sea merchants and mercenaries. The people of his wife, Shimon thought, marvelling with some pride at the strangeness of their union – a Jew and a Basque. He turned and looked back down across the plaza and the village – here he could see the archaeological blueprint of the original settlement echoed in the buildings atop them: the church tower built on the site of the wooden tower described by Yehuda, now making up part of the wall around the settlement, the plaza where once stood the market and meeting place. It had to be the same setting.

Shimon turned back to the mountain slope. He was convinced Yehuda's sacred location was here somewhere. Bending down, he put his hand into his satchel and found the eyeglass he had bought at great expense in Gazteiz when he was working as a successful physic – a time that now felt as if it belonged to another man's life, when in fact it had been only a few years earlier.

'Shimon! Shimon!' Uxue's voice sounded up from the base of the tower. He leaned out; she stood below with a small group of women, a large basket of fruit and vegetables balanced on her head, as was the local custom. Smiling, she waved up, and he waved back, recognising two of the women as Uxue's aunt and cousin. Since arriving a few weeks earlier, she had blossomed, as free from fear as she had been in months. It was not surprising – they had been welcomed by her uncle with an immediate unspoken acceptance that involved no questions and no suspicion. After travelling for days in disguise, avoiding as much contact with people as possible and approaching starvation, the hospitality had felt like a kind of heaven and the isolation of the place made it safe – at least for a while. Uxue had even spoken about staying in the village. Her uncle owned a plot of virgin land on the slope of the mountain and he'd offered it to her. It was tempting, their very own sanctuary to spend the rest of their days in, perhaps even raise a family. But Shimon knew, even if Uxue stayed, he would have to leave sooner or later. The chronicle compelled him to keep searching, to pursue Yehuda's treasure. The search itself was now an obsession – in Shimon's mind it had become the last duty he must complete for his father, as if by solving the enigma he would put his father's tortured spirit somehow to rest. He had no choice. He had to keep looking. He had to string the clues together.

Turning back to the mountainside, he lifted the eyeglass and searched the terrain, looking for something that indicated concealment, a clue that would tell him someone was trying to hide something. The treetops appeared uniform – mainly oak and birch. But halfway down the slope, below a large jutting stone ledge, it changed. Here he could see that the trees were younger, smaller and finer in shape, and some were pine – trees that did not belong to the region. As though someone had deliberately cleared an area, then replanted. The question was why? He was interrupted by a sudden fury of wings. He had disturbed a starling, which shot by him and out into the sky – a free agent.

§

A starling shot out from behind a stone ledge almost colliding with August and his tripod. It was nearly three o'clock and the last of the procession had dispersed, the villagers heading home for their siesta. August, still at the top of the tower, waited until he saw the priest disappear into a small side door at the far side of the church building – the residential quarters of the cleric, no doubt. Now the plaza fell eerily quiet. A skinny dog with a limp half-ran half-hopped across the empty square towards the fountain and cocked its leg to piss against the war memorial. August packed up his camera equipment and began the descent down the stone stairs. If he hurried, he would get back to the farmhouse while Izarra and Gabirel were still sleeping and he would be able to set off towards the forest without them noticing.

The merchant unrolled the Arabic scroll and smoothed it down on top of Tyson's hotel room desk. He stared across at Tyson, waiting for instructions. Tyson was pleased. The merchant, an old patrician-like man with a high, domed forehead and large heavy-lidded black eyes, heralded from a once-aristocratic family in a doomed Middle Eastern country that had recently shaken off its colonial overlords and become socialist, leaving the merchant and his family with little but heirlooms and antiquities to sell. He had been one of Tyson's more reliable suppliers of *objets des sciences occultes* for a good number of years. He was almost a friend and certainly one of the few people in the world who had an understanding of just how intense the CIA operative's interest was in the subject. He was also very expensive.

Tyson leaned forward. At the bottom of the scroll was an inked stamp, an ancient seal, a drawing of a gardenia floating over a red citadel with 'Alhambra' written in Arabic underneath it.

'Are you sure it's authentic?'

'Absolutely, found in the Alhambra. The text dates from AD 810, about a hundred years after the demise of Caliph Al-Walid the First, and was the property of one of the Umayyad emirs of Córdoba, handed down to him no doubt by a disillusioned courtier. It is an account of the relationship between the Caliph and Elazar ibn Yehuda, his great physician as reported by an earlier emir.'

They were interrupted by the ring of the large green telephone sitting on the other side of the desk. The merchant glanced queryingly at Tyson, who let it ring, then, realising it wasn't going to stop, picked it up. He knew from the click at the other end of the line that it was a direct call from HQ. He turned his back on the merchant.

'Hello?' he murmured into the receiver.

'The light is green. Kissner will be in the city of the bull by Friday, high alert.'

Tyson waited for a second, calculating the US general's movements and itinerary – the meetings with the Spanish were all organised. He could afford to keep his distance.

'I will inform my end.'

'And, Tyson, keep your eye on the classicist. We can't afford any bumps on the highway, understand?'

'Understand.' He replaced the receiver, then swung back around to the merchant, who'd kept his face expressionless.

'Would you like me to translate?' the merchant asked, pointing to the letter.

'Please.'

He unfolded a pair of reading glasses and perched them on the high narrow bridge of his nose, then looked closely at the yellowed parchment over which Arabic seemed to run in a series of skips and arches, both ornate and hurried. 'This is the pertinent section I believe.' The merchant began to read, in a slow ponderous voice, '"It was said that the great physician and philosopher Elazar ibn Yehuda took his own life before the order the Caliph had made (in his great wisdom) for the physician's execution had even reached the dwelling of Yehuda. It was as if the physician had received warning or a premonition of his own execution and had decided to take destiny into his own hands. This event disturbed the Caliph greatly. He became convinced that the 'pearls of wisdom' Elazar ibn Yehuda claimed to have left across the Caliph's great conquered land of Andalusia truly existed, and that, if followed, they promised a path of great wisdom leading to great treasure. Many expeditions and soldiers were sent out to discover the Jew's path, but none proved fruitful. And so it was that the Caliph (in his great wisdom) decided the physician must have lost his sanity and that the 'pearls of knowledge that led to great treasure or enlightenment' were little more than symbolic of the great journey towards spiritual enlightenment the physician himself had aspired to, and most likely had Jewish mystical meaning both foreign and obscure to a righteous man of the Koran. Just before he died, the Caliph declared the treasure to be non-existent."' The merchant stopped and glanced across at Tyson.

'What do you think?' Tyson asked him.

'It is not my place to have an opinion. However, I can tell

you I have heard of recent discoveries in the northern town of Girona, of a medieval Jewish settlement, where they have found kabbalistic texts speaking of secret places, in which the Tree of Life has been made manifest, places where heaven touches the sky, and angels can descend and man ascend – but I should warn you that not all the angels named in those texts were good, some were fallen. One of the texts referenced the map of Elazar ibn Yehuda.'

'So *Las crónicas del alquimista existen de verdad*,' Tyson concluded, and the merchant smiled, knowing if he was to stay alive it was probably safer not to confirm or deny the existence of the chronicle.

12

August figured he had another two hours of light before nightfall. He'd left the farmhouse in his hiking boots and armed with a long knife he'd collected from the barn to use to clear his path if necessary. When he'd returned to the farmhouse it had been quiet and the shutters of the bedrooms were pulled shut. He assumed both Izarra and Gabirel were sleeping. No one had seen his arrival or his departure.

He hoisted the rucksack onto his back – it held his camera and the map he'd been composing with each new piece of information. He was confident he would find something in that clearing, but what it would actually be was another question. Shimon Ruiz de Luna had only referred to it as the first of the sacred places, the first piece in the puzzle. But August had the same sense of growing excitement he used to get before a battle – that seductive combination of fear and anticipation.

Using a young sapling he'd whittled into a walking stick, he continued along the same path Gabirel had led him up two days before. The path was narrow, almost overgrown, and August guessed only Gabirel and Izarra ever used it.

Under the canopy of branches and leaves, it was reduced to a green underworld, and it was damp. A tiny stream ran alongside, making many of the small rocks underfoot slippery. August paused, resting on the stick, and took out his pocket compass. He'd been walking north-west for over half an hour – by his calculations he should see the cave and the chapel over the next small hill.

Sure enough, five minutes later the path broadened into a natural clearing, the trees giving way to several ancient boulders, beyond which August could see the dark mouth of the cave and the stone wall of the chapel. He climbed atop one of the sarsens, and turned his back to the mountain to gaze down the valley into the thick forest where Gabirel hadn't wanted to lead him – it looked forbidden and mysterious. He lifted the binoculars and searched for contrast, for any variation in the foliage. To his surprise he found evidence of younger forest growth. The density of the trees, many of them keener in development and more vigorous than the ancient bent oak and birch trees immediately surrounding him, made it difficult to see anything. But as he was close to despairing, he came upon a chink of light glittering through the green patchwork. He checked the compass again – it appeared to be in roughly the same place as the clearing he'd seen from the tower. He jumped down from the boulder and began slashing his way through the thick undergrowth towards the light. The branches caught at his clothes and brushed his face, and he smelled the pungent scent of the cut leaves. The feeling of being both hidden and yet exposed, so very vulnerable, came flooding back to him. It was like a sixth sense, something he'd learned hiding from Franco's troops during the retreat of 1938, when he'd woken injured only to discover he was marooned behind enemy lines. For a week he'd survived, walking and hiding along the banks of the Ebro. Then he'd had to make himself an animal. Half-delirious with thirst and hunger, as well as the smouldering of a wound, he hadn't found it difficult to lose the last vestiges of what made him human. For one night he'd had to immerse himself in water, his head hidden by a floating log, waiting for a Fascist battalion to march past on the bank overhead. He'd stopped caring whether he lived or died, the last of his conscious thought plunged into the necessity of staying invisible. This had saved him.

A sapling snapped back against his face, scratching his cheek. He froze, startled, for a moment forgetting where he was and what year it was, and then he knew he was being watched, hunted, that instinctive feeling tightening his muscles in preparation. He bent his head, straining his ears, all his senses taut as he listened to the soft noises of the forest. And then he heard it, the low rustle of something moving. Something big, bigger than a fox or a badger. He span around, staring wildly into the undergrowth, but he could see nothing. A second later there was the sharp retort of a branch being snapped. Now August pushed forward as fast as he could, slashing through with his knife, knowing that it might be dangerous to stay still. Suddenly, something went past his head, missing him by inches. August recognised the sound immediately. A bullet. He was being shot at. By the time he realised it, he heard the sound of a rifle being cocked and he was thrown to the ground by someone leaping out of the bushes. The second bullet thudded into a tree directly in front of where he'd just been standing; whoever it was was pinning him down had saved his life. August pushed the man off him and rolled free. To his amazement, he saw Gabirel standing over him. The youth put a finger to his lips.

'Izarra!' Gabirel called to the forest behind them. 'Izarra! Show yourself!' August wriggled over to him, not game to stand up yet. A moment later Izarra stepped out from behind a tree, her rifle still trained on August. He froze. Gabirel began walking towards her, cursing furiously in Euskara, of which August could understand only a few words. Eventually, she lowered her rifle, the two of them illuminated by a patch of sunlight beating its way through the canopy.

Angry, August got to his feet, brushing off the leaves. 'What the hell were you trying to do, kill me?' He stepped over to her, bristling with anger. Gabirel moved protectively in front of Izarra, but August ignored him. 'When are you going to understand I am a friend?'

'A friend who tries to get secrets? Who respects nothing, not even sacred land!' she shouted back, her face red with fury.

'Who are you, Izarra, who are you really?' he demanded, all patience gone. Again, Gabirel said something in Euskara to her, his tone now adult, authoritative. They began arguing fiercely. Finally, Gabirel seemed to threaten her with something if she didn't acquiesce. To August's surprise, she softened and put her gun away, turning to him.

'Come, I will help you in your research.'

'But why?'

'Because my sister's spirit will not rest until she is avenged. Come.'

She started beating her way through the foliage; Gabirel stared at August solemnly then with a nod of his head indicated that the American should follow while he walked behind. As August stepped into the path Izarra was making, far swifter and more sure-footed than he'd been able, he couldn't remember the last time he regretted so much leaving behind his Mauser.

It was situated in a small dip in the land, lipped by the edge of a stone ledge, the result of some ancient avalanche. It was

a perfect secret place, completely hidden from the surrounding forest. August looked on amazed. The clearing had
opened in front of them almost magically. Apart from the
small chink of sunlight that seemed to dance ahead of them
as they pushed their way through thick foliage, there had
been no indication of its existence. Now August realised
why – the ancient ruins of what looked like either a Roman
or Moorish villa were almost entirely overgrown by ground
vines. It was the distinctive sandstone (not found in the
region) that delineated the original plan of the dwelling.
Only the high back wall, which ran the length of the site, was
still standing – an ancient structure in which the whitish
sandstone had been placed with remarkable craftsmanship,
each piece cut with extraordinary regularity and fitting
snugly against the next.

In front of the ruin, and this was most astonishing, rising
up in perfect symmetry, was a small maze. Perhaps only
about sixty feet across, it was in the shape of an oblong, and
had a curious design contained within it that reminded
August of a calligraphy, one vaguely familiar to him. The
walls, which appeared to be of hedgerow, stood about seven
feet tall, making it obvious that, although the maze was not
large, it was still all-encompassing enough to get lost inside.
Now the strange tools he'd seen hanging on the barn wall
made sense. He thought he'd recognised them as clippers for
topiary – his first observation had been correct. *So I was right,
but the sight of a maze here in such a setting is almost surreal it is
so wrong – why here?*

Izarra climbed down the ledge into the clearing, her
movement breaking his reverie. August followed, immediately noticing the intense scent of rosemary. At the bottom,
he saw that Gabirel was hanging back, peering down at
them, a terrified look in his eyes.

'You're not joining us?' August asked. Gabirel shook his head.

Izarra touched August's shoulder. 'Gabirel hasn't liked coming here since he was a boy.'

'It's an evil place, evil!' the youth shouted, in Spanish, the last word ringing out across the clearing.

'That's enough, Gabirel. Wait there.'

Izarra led August to the ruins. 'You are the first in a long time to set eyes upon this place,' she told him, solemnly, and with some reluctance. There was a new tentativeness about her, as if she herself were somehow cowed by the surrounds – nevertheless, he felt strangely honoured she'd allowed him this far. He walked up to the tumbled stones and knelt to examine them. Glancing across, he could make out the walls of the original dwelling. Now he could see that it was not Roman but in fact traditional Andalusian architecture, of the kind he'd seen in southern Spain, around Granada and Seville. He stood, perplexed; as far as he knew the Moors had never got this far north.

'I don't understand. This shouldn't be here. Tariq did not conquer this region.' He spoke in English without realising.

'There are many things that should not exist but do. It is only historians who squeeze history into boxes.' Izarra smiled enigmatically at him.

He began to fathom how little he really knew of the woman, how prejudiced he'd been in his projection of her, assuming she'd had no education, had never travelled. He turned to look at Gabirel. The youth was standing near the back wall of the ruins, fidgeting anxiously. Something about his stance disturbed August; it was almost as if he were frightened by the wall yet drawn to it. As August watched, he began pacing backwards and forwards, edgy and restless, like a dog defending its territory. August had the disorientating sensation that by stepping into the clearing they'd left real time behind, as if here no linear time existed; just light, air and scent hanging suspended.

'Come, let me show you.' Izarra's voice seemed to shimmer.

While Gabirel sat on the ruins waiting, Izarra led August into the maze. Now he knew where the aroma of herbs was coming from – the hedgerow was made of towering rosemary bushes. August had never seen such tall bushes; the scent was so strong it was almost hallucinogenic.

'My family were the custodians of this sacred place, for as long as my father, his grandmother and so on, could remember. At first, as the story goes, we were guardians of Mari the Goddess's cave, the one I believe Gabirel showed you. All the women in my family were *sorgina*, in English you would say "priestesses", of the traditional religion, the one that runs through the heart of the Basque. But also we had this ruin on our land, not as old as the cave, but before the time of Christ coming to these mountains.'

'The dwelling was built around the time of Tariq, the Ottoman general who conquered the Iberian Peninsula for Caliph Al-Walid,' said August. 'That makes it eighth century. It looks like a small dwelling of some sort, perhaps even a temple. But this?' He indicated the maze. 'The Ottomans liked gardens, and there was usually a religious and spiritual formality to the way they laid them out, but a maze? As far as I know, mazes didn't become fashionable until the sixteenth century, and usually as a folly.'

'I was taught nothing about either the maze or the ruins,' Izarra said. 'All my parents ever taught me was to guard the place with my life, that for it to fall into enemy hands or under the gaze of a non-believer would bring disaster to the family and the village.' She'd lowered her voice reverently as they moved to a small arch through the hedgerow that formed the entrance to the maze.

Through the arch they stood at the maze's opening, before a circular base that was ringed by high bush. She led him into the base, itself a miniature maze – a series of rings and blind looping walls creating a mini-labyrinth within the circle, at the centre of which they found an empty, round gravelled flowerbed. The walls were like onion skins, the topiary deliberately constructed to confuse. Taking his hand, Izarra walked him out of the base, confidently darting between the hidden openings and false paths, along a curved wall to another circle. There appeared to be four paths branching from the outer ring of the circular base. Izarra led him down the second path, which looked as if it finished in a dead end. It was only when they arrived at the end of the path that August realised it was an illusion – there was a hidden entrance between the thick topiary, behind which was yet another circular base also ringed by high bush and also containing a number of different maze-like rings. Again four gravelled paths (including the one they'd just arrived from) branched out from this base and, like the first base they'd entered, at the centre of it was a simple gravelled circular bed.

'There aren't many reasons why someone would build such an elaborate dwelling in such a secret place,' he said, trying to fathom the symbolism of the construct. 'They either did it for religious or ritual purposes, or as a sanctuary or hiding place.'

'We were taught never to ask such questions, just to accept this was our heritage and it was our duty to maintain the maze and protect it.' Izarra was curt, as if trying to discourage him from applying his intellect, from analysing.

They arrived at another base, again with a confusing

number of circular paths around it, and when they arrived at the centre, August now noticed that the flowerbed in the middle was also gravel, carefully raked and tended, exactly like that of the other bases they'd seen. Somehow it now seemed significant – as if it had been kept deliberately bare. The outer ring had eight different paths radiating from it. This time August sensed that he was in the centre of the maze. He turned around, disorientated, and chose an arbitrary path and began walking.

'We've just come from that path. Here, follow me,' Izarra called out, behind him. He swung around and stared down the gravel path with the towering green walls on either side, Izarra nowhere in sight, feeling dizzy from the scent of rosemary. He rested, hands on his knees. Then another figure seemed to run across the path, a figure in khaki and mud-stained boots, a figure he recognised instantly.

Charlie.

Startled, he stumbled, and the memory of that last night loomed up from the ground. The face of the Spanish Republican commander issuing him the order, the sickening feeling of inevitability, August arguing back but the commander's insistent voice echoing through him.

'It has to be you, as an example to the men. The price for desertion is death, especially for an officer. It has to be you, you know him.' Again, there was Charlie smiling at him around the corner of a hedgerow then his friend was gone.

'Come and find me!' Izarra's teasing voice rang out, sucking him back. She sounded frustratingly close. Shaking himself, August stood up fully. Then he caught a flash of ankle at an opening at the far end. He ran and swung into the right turn, cornering her.

'Not bad for a novice,' she said. 'But it's surprisingly confusing, don't you think, for such a small maze? It's the high walls and the use of herbs planted to confuse the senses, as well as the intricate designs within each circle. You wouldn't find the centre unless you were with someone who'd been taught to find their way out.'

'Like yourself?'

'We were taught that the maze is like a song. That's how we memorised the way to the centre. My mother showed me how. It was a song that had been handed down from mother to daughter for centuries. But not everyone found the way. There was a story in the family of how my great-great-great-grandmother found the body of a man who must have perished trying to get out. A foreigner, not from these parts. No one knew how he got there or how he discovered the maze. I think he must have wanted to die in the maze.'

'But why?'

'To be nearer to heaven.'

It was a curious answer. August studied her expression – her sincerity and blind belief were disturbing.

'How long have your family been in the valley, do you know, Izarra?'

'My mother's father's family have been here for ever. Then, back in the seventeenth century, around the time of the witch trials, another branch of the family moved here, at least that's how the story goes. There was much my mother didn't tell me.' They reached the end of another passage. Here the rosemary was less clipped and the beginning of a canopy was growing over their heads, reducing the light to a shadowy, scented green.

'We're almost at the next base,' Izarra whispered, as if frightened the very leaves might be listening. The path finished and they arrived at another circular base also ringed by blind curved walls and hidden entrances, and with three paths (including the one they had arrived through) leading away from it. They wound their way into the centre – in the middle the flowerbed, instead of being covered in gravel, had a small bush of vervain growing in it, with lilies sprouting from the middle, as if cultivated.

'And so you can see, no great reward or treasure,' Izarra explained. 'Just the challenge of choosing the right path along which to return.'

But August was now convinced the choice of planted herb was symbolic. He waited until Izarra's back was turned then swiftly plucked a leaf of the vervain and a lily and stuffed them into his pocket. Izarra saw nothing.

'My mother always said the maze was a symbol for life – or even ambition,' she said, swinging back to face him. 'You spend the first half of your life trying to reach a level of success, always having to work out which is the right decision, the right path, never having time to just focus on the journey itself, always thinking only of the destination. And often when you get there, it's a disappointment and just when you thought life was going to get easier you're presented with a whole new set of options or paths you have to choose.' Now she was leading him back through the maze quickly, as if she knew the path by heart. He had to run to keep up with her, knowing if he lost her he would not find his way. He had the distinct impression the design of the maze itself was perhaps more meaningful than the actual experience of walking it and that Izarra's allegory was a smokescreen calculated to confuse him. Before long they stepped back out into the clearing. August, wanting to clear his brain from the dizzying effects of the rosemary, took a few deep breaths.

'They say rosemary helps the memory, but here it is for the opposite, for the forgetting.' Izarra, watching, smiled.

'Oh, it made me remember,' he replied, grimly, the image

of Charlie still resonating, the sickly weight of guilt. She read his face.

'*La Guerra?*'

He nodded.

She reached across and took his hand.

'Izarra!' Gabirel's anguished voice broke the moment and she dropped her hand.

August glanced up. Gabirel was watching them from the ledge, looking strangely anguished.

'What is wrong with Gabirel?' he asked.

Izarra glanced over to the youth. 'He used to love coming here as a small boy, then after . . . ' and he knew she was referring to the massacre, 'after that he stopped accompanying me. I think maybe he thinks it is only a woman's place, a place for *sorgina* only, that grown men should not be allowed near.'

'Then thank you for showing me. I am privileged, doubly so as a man.'

'We have risked our lives and our history by showing you. You cannot share this knowledge with anyone.'

'I understand, you can trust me, Izarra.'

She nodded solemnly, then returned to Gabirel, and August took the opportunity to scout the outside of the maze. The design was irregular but formal and the familiarity of it teased at a corner of his mind. Glancing around, he saw a tall stout tree growing from the ledge the wall was built on. He moved towards the high wall of the ruin for a better perspective.

'Stay away from the wall!' Gabirel shouted.

'I promise I will, I just have to take a few photographs,' August tried to reassure the boy as he reached the wall. With his rucksack on his back, he began to climb the tree. Within minutes he was over twenty feet up. Below he could see Gabirel and Izarra exchange a few angry words in Euskara.

Balancing on a thick branch, August pulled his Rolleiflex camera out of his rucksack. Ignoring the argument erupting below him, he framed the shot and took several photographs of the maze from as high as he could – it was almost a topographical perspective. Here you could see the deceptively simple layout with its hidden complexity: the miniature mazes within each circular base, designed to confuse whoever was walking it. Then he climbed down to take a photo of the ruins with the wall in the background. By the time he joined the other two, Gabirel was pale, almost rigid with anxiety. Izarra put her hand on the boy's shoulder. 'It's okay, Gabirel, we will not be discovered.'

Gabirel chose not to answer, but August had the strong feeling the fear of discovery was not the cause of the youth's terror.

The darkroom was a cave drenched in red light, the infrared bulb a beacon in the small space. Two workbenches ran along two walls – on one the enlarger sitting like an oversized microscope, the frame beneath the lens ready to clip in the light sensitive photographic paper; on the other two plastic trays of developer fluid and fixer fluid. Strung across the room was string with metal clips from which to hang the film. There were also several rows of black containers to develop the film itself. Standing in the centre, August reached for one of the strips of negatives now drying on the string. The chemical smell of the developer and fixer took him straight back to his own darkroom in London and back to the hours he'd spent developing photographs alone in this artificial dusk. He'd always loved the particular solitude that was distinctively the photographer's; the darkroom a magician's workshop in which he alone had the power to conjure up images.

Mateo the café owner, grumbling about the late hour, had let him in at eight that evening. Peering at his watch under the dim red light bulb, August could see it was already past ten, and his three strips of negatives, were hung, pegged and drying. The one he was most interested in was the film he'd shot earlier that day of the maze and ruin. August looked at the negatives to see if they were ready to develop. They seemed dry enough. He had twelve images in total: five of the maze, five of the ruins and two of the wall. Careful to keep his fingers on the edge of the film, he fed it into the gate of the enlarger, excitement beginning to rattle through him like the distant roar of a train. He switched on the enlarger light. Immediately, it shone through the negative, projecting a blurry image below. It was one of the shots of the maze, taken from above. He focused the image by rotating the lens, and the shape of the labyrinth emerged in sharp detail. August bent down and examined the image – it was a near-perfect aerial shot. There was a slight angle but he could clearly see the whole design as if from a bird's perspective. Pleased, he switched off the enlarger light and slipped the photographic paper into the frame between the lens and switched the light back on, timing it so that the image was burned into the paper. After stopping the timer, he placed the sheet of photographic paper to one side and repeated the process until all twelve images were invisibly absorbed onto the light-sensitive paper.

Now he was ready for the developer. After resetting the timer for three minutes, he carefully slipped the first photograph under the clear fluid, using tongs, and the image of the maze started to appear. This was the moment of transformation August had never ceased to find fascinating, creating images from what appeared to be blank paper. He stared down into the tray; there were the tops of the hedge, the gravel paths appearing between, the details drawing together faster and faster until it was possible to see the individual sprigs of rosemary within the hedgerow. At that point, a second before the timer went off, August pulled the sheet from the tank, shook the excess fluid off over the sink, then plunged it into the fixer so that it could cement the image to the paper for ever. It was then, peering down at the floating photograph, that he recognised the shape of the maze. Not quite believing his eyes, he turned back to the enlarger and moved the filmstrip in the gate so that the next negative was lit up. He focused it. It was unmistakable – the maze had been constructed in the shape of the kabbalistic Tree of Life. He recognised the symbol from his Oriental studies. Like a square with two triangles fixed to the top and bottom, it had ten circular bases at various corners, with one at the pinnacle of the design and another fixed to the bottom.

August tried to recall the lectures he'd attended at Oxford on the subject, and exactly what each circular base meant. He remembered they were called sephiroth and represented various stages of spiritual enlightenment on the way to the top sephirot. He looked back down at the photograph. The ten sephiroth were clearly visible and there were always only ten. Now he could see that the confusing walkways he had been travelling along in the maze were the paths connecting the bases, all of which he seemed to recall had spiritual meaning, as each sephirot was considered a state of being between the manifest existence of all thoughts and the prime 'Emanation of the Creator' – each station representing a spiritual stage of evolution of the individual on his journey. Only a man with considerable knowledge of the kabbala could have envisaged such a thing. And that could only have been Shimon himself. But why go to such elaborate lengths, unless you wanted to both conceal and send a message?

Fascinated, August turned back to the photograph. Now he could trace the path Izarra had led him along. Suddenly, he noticed the last sephirot they must have arrived at, the one he'd seen with vervain and the lilies growing in it. Set against the other nine, it was far more obvious – it was the only one in the maze that had a dark centre. The centres of the rest of the sephiroth were bare and gravelled.

He looked at the sephirot at the bottom. He searched his memory, trying to envisage the diagram of the Tree of Life he'd studied years ago. It came flooding back – the bottom station or sephirot was called 'Malkuth' or 'Kingdom' and was considered the tenth sephirot – the one at the top of the tree was considered the first. But why did this Malkuth have something growing in it and the other nine were bare? Was this symbolic in itself? Was it linked to Izarra's family or to the location? August was about to begin printing the photograph when something else caught his eye. The old ruin and the wall stood at some distance from the maze. He noticed there was a strange mark on the wall, some kind of outline against it, like a silhouette. It looked like a group of people. A shiver ran through him. He'd seen people lined up against a wall like that before, back in 1938. With his heart pounding uncomfortably against his ribcage, he slipped the photographic paper into the enlarger and developed the photograph. Once more he watched the image condense and clarify in the tray. There was the shape of the people against the wall – a wall that had been completely devoid of markings or shadow when he'd looked at it with his naked eye. And there was the maze. Now he was completely convinced his first impression had been right; the maze was a depiction of the Tree of Life with its single planted sephirot. It had to be a clue, the beginning of a message calling out to him over the centuries.

Yet the image burned into the wall was a contemporary, far more sinister anagram.

There were beads of light shooting over a low horizon, somehow they were both anti-aircraft fire and musical notes, a visual orchestration that sounded out in his dream, the guttural boom of a low D followed by an E a full octave higher. Jimmy was running across a desert – a monochrome landscape – going full pelt, his body young and strong, the sand compact and solid under his feet. He knew in that unexplained unquestioning way of the dreamer that if he reached the horizon and ran straight into it, he would die. And that's what he wanted. Wanted so much and with that thought a white circle appeared in the grey sky, growing in brightness, seeming to radiate coolness not heat. Slowly, Jimmy realised it was not an imaginary moon but the ring of cold steel pressed against his head. He woke with a jerk.

'Hello, Jimmy.'

Recognising the voice, Jimmy froze. The barrel of a handgun was pushing into his forehead, pinning him to the pillow. The intruder leaned back into a strip of light that cut through the darkened bedroom from the streetlight outside. Now Jimmy could see Damien Tyson's eyes clearly. They were exactly as he remembered, utterly devoid of emotion and impossible to read. For a moment he hoped he was still dreaming.

'Hello, Damien. I was wondering when you'd come for a visit.'

'I could kill you now or we could talk.'

'If you kill me now, you'd be doing me a favour.'

'In that case, we'll talk.' With his gun still trained on Jimmy, Tyson sat on a chair. He switched on the bedside lamp, trapping them both in a tense intimacy. Jimmy began to sit up in the bed.

'Hands over the covers, else I'll shoot.' Tyson's voice was matter of fact. Jimmy, now with his back against the wall, laid his heavy gnarled hands on top of the chequered bedspread.

'I figure it must be eight years you guys have been watching me. What are you after, Damien? The operation was completed and neatly tidied up. Why, you even had the others silenced. What more could the department want with a washed-up old jazz player, who's not even a card-carrying member any more?'

'I was just carrying out orders. I'm sorry about your girlfriend, but I always thought she was a little out of your league.' Tyson was irritated by Jimmy's seemingly casual manner – he wanted more fear, he *needed* more fear.

Jimmy's fists tightened as he fought the impulse to jump out of the bed and attack Tyson.

'Easy, old fella. I'm a little trigger-happy at the best of times, but then you'd know all about that.'

Jimmy glared across the room, cursing his physical weakness.

'What do you want?'

'You went to London to visit an old buddy recently, an old socialist friend of yours. Like to tell me why?'

'I got sentimental.'

Tyson kicked over a heavy old metal microphone stand near the wall. It fell on top of the bed, cracking across Jimmy's shins, the sound resounding out as the musician stifled a scream.

'August E. Winthrop. Fought with you at Brunete, worked with the British during the Second World War and was honourably discharged, but a little birdie told us he might be in bed with the Russians.'

'Not Gus.'

'Really, because you know what, the English don't trust

him and neither do we. Then there was this little incident of a murdered professor, an old college associate of his. You still feeling sentimental?'

'Fuck you.'

Jimmy's guitar caught Tyson's eye. He glanced down at the musician's hands, twitching with pain on the bedspread.

'You still playing, Jimmy? You were good at that, serenading the señoritas.' Tyson stood and walked over to the bed. Jimmy glared up at him. His leg hurt so much he could hardly draw breath.

'Sometimes when the body fails all a man's got left is talent.' Tyson held the gun easily at his side. 'You gave him a parcel in London?'

'Chocolates for the ladies. Gus likes the ladies, and they still have rationing over there,' Jimmy hissed, choking back his fear like vomit. Tyson shot the index finger of his right hand clean off, the bullet thumping into the mattress like a tiny hammer. He lifted the gun to Jimmy's forehead.

'Where is it, Jimmy? Where's the alchemist's chronicle?'

Jimmy stared at him, the shifting pieces of the last eight years now slipping into place; Andere's face the night she made him promise to safeguard the book, the smashed rooms of the farmhouse after the murders, the order he never saw.

'It was you, wasn't it? Not HQ that ordered the killings. You were after the chronicle all along,' he managed to whisper before fainting.

Tyson glanced down at the unconscious musician, spit now drooling from the corners of Jimmy's mouth, a small pool of blood under the stump of his finger spreading through the bed like an errant blossom. It made Tyson think. He turned, scanning the flat, looking for something he knew he'd want when he saw it. It was propped up against a lamp

in the corner, an album cover of one of the jazz bands van
Peters had recorded with, signed by Jimmy himself. Tyson
walked over, picked it up then brought it back to the bed.
Lifting Jimmy's hand, he smeared blood all over the sleeve.
He waited a moment for it to dry before slipping the album
cover into his shoulder bag.

Back in his room August sat staring at the photograph of the
maze. It was past two in the morning yet he was wide awake,
his mind still racing to make sense of the images before him.
The herbs he'd picked at the maze lay beside him, the scent
of the vervain leaves and lily flower bringing back the
memory of walking through the enigma.

He pulled the photograph closer. Carefully, he drew over
the top, tracing the outline of the maze. He now had the
Tree of Life drawn out clearly – the symmetry was beautiful.
Whoever had designed it had been meticulous. Each circular station was in perfect proportion to the next and the paths
were geometrically exact. He had the same conviction that
it must have been Shimon Ruiz de Luna himself. But the
fact that the Tree of Life was visible only from above and at
some height was perplexing. Why would someone go out
of their way to create a maze that was a symbol one could
only decipher from far above – was it a way of signalling to
the skies? To God perhaps? If so, which God? It was like a
portal to the heavens. Or was it a warning to keep away?
Strangely enough, it reminded him of Mayan monuments
or Australian aboriginal land markings – structures built to
be viewed from a great height, yet made in eras when it was
physically impossible to reach those heights. And then
there was the vervain and lily growing in the centre of
the tenth base, Malkuth. What were their astrological and
magical meanings? Turning to the tracing, he filled in the

tenth base with pencil then wrote the name 'Irumendi' beside it, along with the names of the plants.

But there was something else that disturbed him even more – the unexplained configuration on the wall. August didn't believe in the supernatural. But it troubled him greatly that the silhouette had only become visible when photographed. With a sickening sense of foreboding, he began to outline the silhouette on the photograph, feeling as if the tip of his pen were actually bringing to life the horror of the image.

Under the pen the curious dark patch began to unfurl into an undeniable picture – the outline of a row of about eight people, mainly men, August guessed, from their height, lined up against the wall. He knew this atrocity, knew what his pen would reveal. Wrestling with the urge to get up from the desk or even destroy the photograph, he forced himself to continue tracing. He reached the profile of the last figure and stopped, pen poised on the paper, his hand shaking, fighting the memory of a similar horrific scene. One in which he himself had been implicated, terribly, fatally. He dropped the pen, but the trembling worsened, travelling up through his body, memories rushing through him like flashing lights.

August went to the window and pulled it open, letting in the cool night air. He breathed deep, trying to empty his mind, to push all his thinking into the visceral, into the immediate surroundings – the scent of the lilac sitting in a small vase on the desk, the faint hoot of an owl, the distant rush of a stream. *Make yourself nothing but this*, he told himself, but Charlie's ghost came floating back on a miasma of guilt. It was pointless.

He removed the chronicle from its bag. Sitting back at the desk, he turned to the page in which Shimon Ruiz de Luna

described the first secret location of Elazar ibn Yehuda's map
then opened his notebook filled with the translation of the
deciphered Spanish he had made earlier that evening. He
found the paragraph he was looking for.

*My excitement was profound when, after much climbing and
cutting through the thick forest behind Irumendi, I came upon the
first secret garden Elazar ibn Yehuda had discovered. A botanical clue located in a tiny clearing in an ancient forest, almost
invisible to the eye. It took me several hours of exploration and
viewing from considerable height before I recognised with great
surprise the first cipher. I wager I would have been the only
person in the whole region who might have guessed at its meaning or recognised that it had any meaning at all. Indeed, it had
only been after some questioning that my wife's uncle mentioned,
in a dismissive fashion, rumour of an old ruin and ancient
garden hidden in the forest. His indifference both surprised and
delighted me. It delighted me because it meant that I might be the
first to have rediscovered the site, but it surprised me that given
the local beliefs he would be so indifferent. On the other hand, he
believed it to have been Roman and therefore of an invader, a
monument not of the Basque, and as such, nothing to him.*

*The ruins looked to be a small temple and I immediately
noted that it was not Roman but Andalusian, the kind I have
seen in Córdoba. There was a small plot of land in front of the
ruined building. The garden Elazar ibn Yehuda described existed
only in its foundations, but it was this that excited me so greatly,
for I recognised the pattern the old withered beds made running
like a matrix around gravel paths that ended suddenly and led
nowhere. It is a matrix of great kabbalistic meaning, too great
and too dangerous to describe in detail on these pages, but suffice
to say it is like the first arrow pointing me along the path on
which I am travelling. And I am determined to restore it and*

maintain this botanical wonder for future seekers – no matter how incongruous it might be in the terrain. I am convinced I must keep following in the great physic explorer's footsteps, regardless of how far I must travel and to what great danger such exploration will inevitably expose me. I am convinced that transcendence lies at the end of this journey, a heaven on Earth and the possibility of Man as God. What would my father think of me now? He surely would have nothing but wonder and pride in his son. And if I should solve the enigma of Elazar ibn Yehuda's treasure? My place in posterity both as physic and alchemist would surely be assured.

August glanced back at the photograph of the site, the top of the maze the dark grey outline of the Tree of Life. Shimon Ruiz de Luna must have constructed the maze as a way of maintaining and echoing the pattern of the garden's foundations, to make a living message to the future. Stunned by the epiphany, he sat back trying to remember the words Professor Copps had used to describe Elazar ibn Yehuda – and why his rumoured discovery had fired the imagination of so many people over the aeons. 'A great gift,' the professor had said, although he'd seemed unsure about the translation from the Judeo-Arabic Yehuda had used in his writings – *a great spiritual or magical gift, an unnatural power from God that if unleashed upon humanity would either condemn it or save it depending on how the gift was used.* But Elazar ibn Yehuda was both a philosopher and a doctor obsessively involved in botanical research – for benign and malign purposes. Whatever the great physician-explorer had discovered, he certainly thought it worth dying for. August checked his notes again. Elazar ibn Yehuda had lived from AD 670 to 725, which placed the ruins roughly at the time of Tariq's invasion of the Iberian Peninsula.

But what about the mysterious outline on the wall? Why did La Leona and her men leave their shadows behind? Was it a cry for acknowledgement of their deaths? August had to find out more about the massacre.

He had to go back.

Olivia leaned forward as the taxi swung around the Plaza de Cervantes, following the harbour front down to the old fishing port, the two jetties – Mollaberria and Mollaerdia – jutting out into the bay. Fishing boats bumped gently against the buoys as Basque fishermen unloaded that morning's catch of cod and sardines. The sight took her mind back to another small fishing port she'd visited thirty years earlier, on the Cornish coast, with Julian Copps who was then her lover. They'd argued, she remembered, walking along a sweep of white sand under an overcast angry English sky, where the grey sea dissolved into a grey horizon. They'd argued about what they always argued about at that time – the esoteric texts that fascinated both of them. Despite her own vast knowledge, she'd been awed by his seemingly endless knowledge, historical and intellectual, of such literature. But even then, early on in their love affair, she had become aware of the limitations his rationality foisted upon his mind. She had seen and felt things he couldn't even imagine and her world was fragmented into those who believed and those who didn't, the ones who saw and those who were content in just being seen.

They had been talking about an Andalusian text Julian had found in Fez, Morocco, dating from the twelfth century. At that point Olivia remembered she had picked up a seashell, a small periwinkle with a black strip around it that wrapped like a thin ribbon right into the mouth of the shell. She'd slipped it into her pocket as a marker of the moment.

She still had it somewhere. The text had described the ten sephiroth that made up the Tree of Life as spiritual platforms to a ground map that led to spiritual enlightenment. 'Basic kabbalistic beliefs,' Julian had remarked, dismissively, but the text had also talked of a hidden sephirot that was a doorway or portal to Ein Sof – the state of being one with God. It had mentioned that the philosopher Elazar ibn Yehuda had proven that it was possible to depict such a doorway physically and '*be taken into God*'. It was this enigmatic phrase that they were arguing about; Olivia was convinced the meaning was literal, that Yehuda had found a way of physically as well as spiritually transcending. Julian was emphatic, in a dry academic way.

'The text was metaphoric!' he had shouted, into the wind. 'Such events were the dreams of medieval fabulists and not the thinking of a rational philosopher influenced by both Aristotle and Plato.' They'd ended up walking back to the small rented cottage in sullen silence, neither wishing to surrender to the other. But for Olivia it had been a turning point, the trigger that had led her directly to this moment in a car in 1953, as it accelerated into the centre of San Sebastián. It was the argument that had set her on a journey.

A branch broke underfoot and August stumbled, his right foot sinking into a soft layer of leaf mould and brush. Ahead, a startled woodcock scuttled across the path. He straightened himself, now feeling the weight of the small shovel and pick he had strapped to his back an hour earlier, when he'd borrowed them from Izarra's barn. He'd waited until he was sure both Izarra and Gabirel were well away from the house – Izarra at the village market and Gabirel in the orchard – before he'd left, meticulously following the path he was sure Gabirel had taken to reach the maze.

He rested for a moment against a tree and lit a cigarette. Exhaling, he watched the plume of smoke drifting up through the canopy overhead. Part of him wanted to turn back, the other was driving him forward. The sun passed out from under a cloud and sunlight streamed through the branches, and it was then that he saw it, a clearing, visible through the leaves up ahead. He was almost there.

It was an eerie feeling standing at the site. The scent of the rosemary drifting across again seemed to lull him into a mild stupor. Shaking himself alert, August clambered down to the wall. It was about sixty feet across, the large sandstone blocks only decayed at the two ends. The rest had withstood time remarkably well. There was no sign of the sinister outline so clearly visible in the photo. August walked up to the middle – it was here that the mysterious shadow had fallen against the photographed wall. Reaching out, he put his hand against the stone, as if he might intuit something through his fingers; nothing, no vibration, no locked-up echo. Just blank solidity. Close up there were no markings on the stone, just the crusty white of lichen and moss that had grown between the large blocks. For a moment August stood against the wall, his back flat against the surface, the coolness seeping tendrils through his clothes, then into his skin, as though the wall itself were trying to claim him. He broke away, then, measuring the distance, he started pacing directly away from the wall, carefully counting each of his strides. At thirty he stopped and swung around to face the wall. His mind returned to the image of the outline in the photograph. He would be looking directly at it at this point. Kneeling, he scanned the grass and broken rock around him. There seemed to be nothing but wild grass and flowers sprouting up between the sections of old stone that had once, hundreds of years ago, made up the floor of the dwelling. A sudden haunting cry above him made him glance up – in the small rectangle of sky an eagle circled hungrily, gazing downwards. August saw a flurry in the perimeter of his vision, a rabbit sitting on its haunches, grazing, blissfully unaware of the eagle above. A second later the raptor had swooped, carrying the kicking rabbit up into the endless blue as it flapped its wings lazily back towards the mountain peak. The rabbit's fate made August feel curiously vulnerable, like he too was terrifyingly oblivious of who or what might be watching him from above.

Looking back down at the cracked ground, August realised he didn't know what he was searching for, but felt compelled to keep exploring. He moved a few feet to the left. Here it seemed he was standing on the foundations of a small room, perhaps a sleeping chamber. The surface was lower than the rest and the ground appeared more disturbed by time, decay and vegetation. Just then he noticed a tiny glint, light bouncing off something metallic. He walked over and, kneeling, found the source, barely visible – the metal tip of something poking through the soil. He uncovered some more of the object with his hands. With a sickening lurch, he recognised it as the barrel of a rifle. Reaching for the spade, he began to dig, the metallic sound of the shovel hitting rock echoing out across the valley.

There were eight of them, laid out side by side in the long shallow grave. Seven men and one woman, La Leona herself, the long black hair still partly attached to the skull. Skeletons still clad in makeshift uniforms, they all bore bullet holes to the torso. Most of the men still wore the beret of the Basque Nationalist Army, the cloth badge still stitched into the rotting fabric. Two of the men had the Republican three-pointed red star sewn into their khaki jackets. It had taken August three hours of digging to uncover them all, but he had felt no emotion until now. Lying along the foot of the grave were several rifles abandoned and hidden with the bodies. Squatting, he picked up one of the rifles and brushed away the mud from the wooden stock. It was marked 'Property of the US Army'. August stared down at the marking, then dropped the gun back into the grave, and doubled over retching.

A terrible cry came from the forest nearby. Thinking it must be an animal of some sort, perhaps even a wolf, August stumbled back to the wall, but Gabirel came running erratically out from behind the pine trees. To August's horror he ran straight towards the grave. August ran at him, determined to protect the youth, and he grabbed him by the waist.

'Gabirel, no!'

For a moment the two wrestled, August trying to hold the boy back as he struggled. Finally he broke free and ran to the grave, throwing himself down beside the female corpse, moaning and weeping, his eyes swinging wildly back to the corpse over and over again. August managed to pull him away and sat him down on a rock, placing himself beside him. He threw an arm over Gabirel's shoulder.

'I saw ... I saw ...' Gabirel could barely speak, as his face twisted into a horrified recollection.

'You saw? You saw the massacre, your aunt?' August tried to prompt him gently. But the boy was inconsolable.

'My aunt?' He looked at August, amazed. 'La Leona was my mother.'

Izarra was standing in the open barn turning the handle of a corn grinder. As soon as she saw the distraught youth with August, she dropped the handle and came running out.

'What have you done?' she screamed, in Spanish, at August, then swung around to Gabirel, reaching out to touch his face.

He knocked her hands away violently.

'What is wrong, Gabirel? Tell me!'

Ignoring her, August led the boy to the front door. 'Go inside, we will be with you later,' he told him. Emotionally exhausted, the boy disappeared into the house.

August turned back to Izarra. 'Last night as I was developing the photographs I'd taken of the maze and the ruins, a strange shadow appeared on the wall in one of the pictures. It was an outline I recognised. So this morning, when you were both out, I went back to the ruins. Something, an instinct, an old soldier's hunch, call it what you like, made me begin looking and then digging . . .'

'¡Dios mio!' Izarra's face was ashen, twisting as she tried desperately to stop herself from crying.

August continued: 'There were the remains of eight of them, all soldiers, some of the Republican Army, some of the Basque, seven men, one woman.' At which Izarra let out a small strangled cry. 'I guess it was the work of an ad hoc firing squad, just as Jimmy described. They had been lined up against the wall and shot – together. Whoever buried them, buried them in a hurry, as if they didn't really fear the discovery of the bodies or perhaps any consequences.' Here, he couldn't help himself, his voice dipped into bitter sarcasm, 'After all they were only Republicans and Basques, who is there to care?'

'Stop it! Stop it!' She covered her ears.

'No, you need to hear, the time for keeping secrets is past!' He pulled her hands away from her ears. 'When I'd finished uncovering the bodies, Gabirel appeared from nowhere. I had no idea the boy had followed me. He saw the bodies and started weeping and screaming like an animal, then threw himself down ... I tried to pull him away, to protect him.'

'I thought he was too young. If I told him it hadn't happened, that his mother had gone away ... '

'So you are his aunt.'

Izarra nodded. 'Gabirel was seven. I didn't know about the massacre until afterwards, until it was too late. I didn't even know Gabirel had been in the forest that day playing. I thought he would forget, that the memory would disappear, that I could free him from it by denying it ever happened.'

'I need to know the whole story.'

'How do I really know you're not government, you're not a spy?'

August held up his finger, the one missing a tip.

'This was the work of a fascist sniper in Jarama in 1937. I was lucky – my friend next to me was shot in the eye. The scar on my face is from shrapnel as I defended Teruel. I gave four years of my life to the Republican cause. We fought alongside your people. Two of the dead in that grave are Republican soldiers – you owe me an explanation!'

She stared up at him, then placed her hand on his arm.

'Come, come inside, I will show you.'

She led him into a small upstairs drawing room. To August's surprise, there was a framed print of Franco in uniform hanging on the wall.

'It's not what you think,' Izarra said, noticing his reaction. She flipped it over and pulled out a sheaf of photographs that had been taped to the back. She placed them on a small side table and sifted through them; a couple were obviously of her parents, but several were of a striking young woman, who bore some resemblance to Izarra – La Leona.

'These are the only photographs of my sister in existence. She kept as invisible as possible.'

'I remember, even during the war I thought she might have been a fiction – a propaganda ploy to encourage the troops.'

Izarra smiled. 'La Leona burned through life like a star. When the Euzko Gudarostea, the Basque National Army, surrendered in 1937 at Santona, La Leona never forgave Aguirre. She kept on fighting, her and her men.'

Izarra pulled out a small photograph of a group of people in uniform, standing beside some trees. In the middle stood Andere, with her arm around a tall brown-haired man August recognised immediately. Jimmy van Peters, younger, vibrant and uncharacteristically radiant with happiness. Dressed in the khaki of the US infantry, he gazed down at the diminutive, strong-featured woman, herself dressed in fatigues, a black beret pushed back from her high forehead. She was smiling and looking back up at the American. There was no doubt the two were in love. August stared down at Jimmy.

'That's him. You wouldn't recognise him now – he's dying.'

Izarra, watching him, softened at this flash of vulnerability. 'I'm sorry, I liked him. I think he was an honest man.'

August picked up the photograph. In the foreground sat the two Republican soldiers – the purple, yellow and red stripes of the Republican flag stitched into their shirts, the same tattered fragments he'd seen on their corpses. One was polishing a rifle; the other stared back up at the camera warily. Smaller in physique and olive-skinned, they had the sharper features of the South – Spaniards a long way from home. In the top right-hand corner August could just make out two other men – in US uniforms in the middle of erecting a tent.

Was one of them Damien Tyson? Somehow August doubted it. Tyson wasn't the kind of man who would allow himself to be photographed, August guessed, not the Jester. He placed it back on the desk. 'So what happened, Izarra?'

'Before the Civil War we all lived together, in this house – my parents, my sister and her husband, and myself. Traditionally, it is the women who are *sorgina* and Andere and I had been instructed by my mother in how to guard both Mari's cave and the maze. But when the war came, my father, Andere's husband and Andere herself joined the Basque Army – by the end Andere was a widow and my parents were dead. Andere was older than me, and stronger. She was the fiercest, most determined person I knew – man or woman. There were some who were terrified of her. Not me. I was her sister, I had seen the human side. It was the war, the execution of her husband and all that death that had made her cold. When the retreat happened, Andere put out a rumour she'd been killed. Then she came back here, to these mountains, to continue the struggle after the official surrender.

'It was easy. This village is not well known to the Spanish, and the Basques keep it that way. There were eight of them living here, for six years, waiting and doing what they could to help the refugees, men fearing for their lives, trying to get into France or wanting to escape to fight with the Allies. Then in 1945 after Berlin fell, Americans visited my sister, officers sent by the US president. Jimmy was one of them. They said they were willing to help us, to train us, give us guns.'

The image of the file came back to August, that afternoon in Grosvenor Square.

'Operation Lizard,' he said, out loud, more to himself than her.

'You know of this?' she demanded, distrust spreading across her face.

'Only what Jimmy told me. But the more you tell me the more I might be able to help you, perhaps even catch the murderers.'

'The murderers were your government.'

'It's not that simple. Please, you have to trust me.'

'At first Andere welcomed them. They told us that now the Allies had destroyed Hitler they were worried about another insurgence of fascism in Europe. Truman felt a democratic Spain and a Basque republic might be safer for the rest of Europe. So they started working with Andere and her men. There were other American officers training with the exiled Basque government in Paris.'

'How many were here?'

'Six. Elite officers, all of them trained killers. The man in charge was called Tyson. I'll never forget him.'

'Jester, his codename was Jester.'

'Jester?' Izarra laughed bitterly. 'This is some sort of clown, no? Damien was not a clown. An actor, yes, but not a clown, although he was professionally charming like a clown. Andere put all her trust in him and his men. I've never seen her do this before, but I think she realised this could be their last hope of an independent country from Spain, and the Republicans in her group had family murdered and tortured by Franco, so surrender was not an option. So Damien and the five others set up camp in the forest behind the ruins and started training Andere and her men in the latest guerrilla warfare. All was going well. There was new hope of independence and the possibility of overthrowing Franco. And we all grew to trust and like the Americans. Andere and Jimmy even became lovers. Then secret orders were sent from Washington, to

Damien Tyson, orders to destroy the very men they had been training.'

'Izarra, this isn't true. The men were tricked into committing that massacre. They thought they were following orders.'

'Do you not believe your own government could commit murder?'

'I haven't lived in America since 1932, and I certainly don't approve of the current regime, but I also know committing a massacre is riskier than a quiet withdrawal. It would have been impractical for the Americans. The original order was for a quiet withdrawal. Tyson wanted your sister and her men dead.'

'I know this much – that day Damien Tyson tricked Jimmy and sent him out of the area on a false mission. Damien knew he had to separate Jimmy and Andere to keep Andere vulnerable. He then lured Andere and her men into a trap and had his men shoot them – all of them. I was working in the field behind the house. I'll never forget it, that sound of the rifles, one short report. I knew instantly what had happened. I called out for Gabirel but he was gone. They would have shot me, except I ran and hid in the hiding place we have in the house, built during the wars of the last century. All around me I could hear the sound of smashing furniture, drawers being overturned. It was terrifying. I crouched there in the dark, praying that Gabirel was safe. When I came out eighteen hours later, the house had been ransacked, the chronicle was missing and Tyson and his men had gone, and the bodies were buried. I eventually found Gabirel hiding in the cave. He'd been there for two days. He didn't speak for a week after that. It was only later when Jimmy returned that I discovered Andere had given the chronicle to him for safekeeping, and I let him leave with it.

I thought he would return it within a year. But now you're here eight years later with it, why?'

'Jimmy asked me. He was in my division with the Lincolns.'

'Jimmy fought with the Lincoln Brigade? He never told me.'

'There were wharfies, intellectuals, teamsters, philosophers and then there was Jimmy. He tended to show his politics in the theatre of war and not bandstanding on some picket fence. I don't know where but I always had the feeling Jimmy had seen action elsewhere. Out of all of us he was the most professional soldier. He claimed he was a card-holding party member and a simple jazz player who happened to be a believer in the free world of the worker. And boy, could he play the guitar. He was also the best rifleman I knew. And although I was this idealistic stuck-up rookie, wet round the ears, with nothing but a passion for the classical world, we liked each other from the start. He was the first to see something in me that not even I was aware of.'

'Something you're frightened of?' she asked, bluntly.

He glanced up at her, surprised by the acuteness of her observation, then realised she must have been studying him all along. He nodded gravely.

'You're right. Like him I realised that under all the dedication, all the noble self-sacrifice and fierce belief that we were there to defeat Franco and Hitler and save the world, the only time I felt really alive was on those battlefields. We were both junkies for it – the fear, the excitement, the sheer thrill. Jimmy knew it from the first; it took me all these years to figure that one out.'

'But you know now, is this such a bad thing?'

'It's not something I'm proud of. In 1938 I got captured in Perpignan. Captured and tortured. Two days later, I was sitting there in that hellhole of a cell, waiting to be shot the following morning, when Jimmy breaks me out. I still don't know how he did it. But then, at the very end of the war, we lost each other. I thought he was dead.' August looked back down at the photograph again. 'Then he appears on my doorstep a month ago with the chronicle in his hand.'

Izarra reached across her hand and slid it over his. 'And that's why you brought it back, because you owe him your life?'

'And so many others.' Even as he finished the sentence August knew it was the most honest acknowledgement he'd made to himself in years. Perhaps that's why he was now there, back in Biscay, trying to rescue his younger self. 'But there's more, Izarra. Hidden beneath the written text is a whole other story. The man who wrote it, Shimon Ruiz de Luna, your ancestor, was in great danger. Let me show you.'

He brought the chronicle, along with his notebook of translations, back into the room. Izarra unwrapped it eagerly.

'Thank God it is safe.'

He watched her tenderly lay the book on the desk as if it were sacred, not to be opened and read but to be preserved and immortalised as a holy relic. Placing his own notebook of the decoded text next to the chronicle, he opened the first page of both and laid them side by side.

'You see how the pages of the chronicle are waxed? I've inked some of them and made a pressing and managed to translate some of the pages. Izarra, the whole book is a cipher. Shimon wrote his journal in code in case of discovery. Although it presents as a harmless text on herbs and plants, it is, in fact, a guide to a far earlier and far more contentious ancient journal known as the "map of Elazar ibn Yehuda".

Shimon's family, who were then wealthy merchants and secret Jews living in Córdoba, had inherited it then passed it down the generations. Yehuda was a well-known philosopher and physician who worked for Caliph Al-Walid, the first ruler of Andalusia. He was meant to have made the map travelling up the peninsula with the conqueror-general Tariq. The map obsessed Shimon. His father had told him it was the greatest treasure the family owned if the map was ever followed and Yehuda's treasure discovered. So when the family was arrested and executed in an *auto de fe*, Shimon escaped with only the map, and then began his long odyssey across Spain, living under a false identity. Sometime in the early seventeenth century he married Uxue, a Basque from this region. Her uncle lived in this village, and in exile they came here, for how long I don't know, but I believe it was Shimon who built the maze following Elazar's map, and there are others and they are Shimon's way of safeguarding Elazar's secret. How, I don't exactly know, but I'd like your permission to find out. I want to keep deciphering the chronicle and follow Shimon's own journey.'

'It will be dangerous, very dangerous,' Izarra said. 'They will execute you if they catch you.' Her face was grim and for the first time August had an inkling she wasn't just talking about Franco's soldiers. *Who are they, Izarra? What are you hiding? Is there something about the people who believe in the chronicle that you aren't telling me?*

'Izarra, you have to understand I'm beginning to believe your sister and her men might have been shot because of the chronicle. Why else would Tyson ransack the house after their murders? Also, Jimmy was convinced he'd been watched all these past years.'

'Danger within and danger without.'

'What do you mean?'

'I knew that the chronicle was a code, but my mother always taught us that the chronicle's secrets should stay locked between the pages.'

'But Shimon wrote it so that someone, one day, would follow his words.'

'Someone did once.' Her voice was ominous and strangely formal. A chill went through August. She stood and indicated he should follow. 'Come with me, please.'

The cattle in the barn were restless, stomping and swishing their tails. They swung their heavy necks and gazed at August in a plaintive, almost accusatory manner as if he were directly responsible for the new tension in the house.

'They sense when Gabirel is upset.' Izarra climbed down from the ladder, followed by August. She walked over to a bale of hay and pushed it away from the floor, revealing a trapdoor.

'This is where I hid when Tyson was searching the house.' She lifted up the trapdoor revealing a narrow hiding place about six feet deep and ten across. 'My great-great-grandfather built it during the Carlist wars of the last century. Most houses around here have one – but we kept that fact to ourselves.' She lowered herself down into it, as August squatted by the opening. He watched as she pulled free a brick, removed a small wooden box from behind it then handed the box up to him.

'Do you read French?' she asked, hauling herself back up into the barn.

'Well enough.' He waited until she'd closed the trapdoor and hidden the entry again with the bale of hay. Only then did he open the box. Inside was a piece of old parchment – a letter written in archaic French. He began to read.

Father Bernard de Montfaucon
The order of Saint Benedict
Abbey of Saint-Germain-des-Prés
Paris, France
The first of October in the year of our Lord
Seventeen Hundred and Ten

To the Ruiz de Luna family,
I believe your family to be direct descendants of the famous
rabbi and scholar Ishmael ibn Ruiz de Luna, pupil of the
early Jewish philosopher Elazar ibn Yehuda. Forgive my
audacity in writing unintroduced, but I am driven by grave
concern. It involves the case of one of the young monks under
my care. A brother Dominic Baptise, no longer living, I
believe.

I had employed Brother Baptise, a student of mine, in the
task of translating an ancient text I had been given, discovered
in Constantinople, written in Hebrew by Elazar ibn Yehuda.
However, I never received the translation from him. Before he
finished the task, Brother Baptise, inspired by the contents of
this mystical treatise, embarked on a curious journey in search
of what he insisted would lead to the ultimate union of Soul,
Intellect and God. Naturally, the Bishop and myself did our
utmost to discourage the young monk, but he was most insistent
and left the abbey over a year ago. He was sighted in several
towns and countries over the next few months, the last being in
the Hanseatic city of Hamburg. But by all accounts he has now
mysteriously vanished from an ancient site associated with the
philosopher Yehuda.

I am obliged by Christian concern for my fellow men to
write to you, as Brother Baptise often spoke of another
chronicle he had seen mentioned that related to Yehuda's text –
by a Shimon Ruiz de Luna, who I believe was of your family.

*Please, if there are any documents written by your ancestor
that referred to Elazar ibn Yehuda's writings, either destroy
them or keep them under lock and key to save another poor soul
the same fate, for I do not believe them to be of Christian
calling but more likely the work of the Devil.*

*Yours in Christian faith
Father Bernard de Montfaucon*

August finished reading, his mouth dry with excitement.
He knew exactly who Bernard de Montfaucon was: a
Benedictine monk considered the father of palaeography –
the study and interpretation of ancient texts, in
Montfaucon's case mainly classical Greek and Ancient
Egyptian, but he had also been fluent in Hebrew, Coptic
and Syrian. It was entirely likely he would have stumbled
upon one of Elazar ibn Yehuda's manuscripts.

'All this does is make me more resolved. You have to let
me finish Shimon's journey, for his sake, for Leona and all
those other dead soldiers. You owe it to her.'

'What do you think happened to that poor monk?'

'I don't know, but I'd love to find out.'

But Izarra had already taken the box and the letter out of
his hands.

'There have been too many deaths already.'

August stood in the entrance of the barn staring out into the
night, listening to the animals breathing, the scent of hay and
manure strangely comforting. It pulled him back to normalcy,
a place where the world was divided into endless seasons,
where there were no conflicts, the complication of politics, of
man killing neighbour. The sound of music floated across
from the village. As Izarra had predicted, a spontaneous fiesta

had broken out in the village below. The wild swirling sound of the harmonica and drumming, peppered by the occasional stanza of some forbidden folk song, drifted up the valley, tugging at his feet and groin – appealing to some primal core.

He'd come here to clear his head and bury his disappointment that Izarra had not allowed him to continue researching the chronicle. It was a temporary respite. In the room above him he could hear the muffled arguing of Izarra and Gabirel, as she tried to explain herself to the youth – the timbre of raised voices rattled across the beams like startled mice, then subsided into soft reassurance, followed by the low throb of sobbing.

The truth is always healing, not matter how painful, isn't that right? Had I the right to lever open the past? I fear I have shaken the fragile alliance between nephew and aunt. Why does everything I touch break?

All of a sudden August was aware of a low whistle. Across the barn door fell a shadow – the shadow of a man with a bull's head. August reached out and grabbed a pitchfork leaning up against the door, then moved soundlessly out into the courtyard. The figure of the Minotaur man stepped out of the shadows, its great bull's head a leering masquerade of rolling eyes and horns. For a moment August imagined he had slipped into a kind of hell. He jabbed the pitchfork towards the creature. It leaped back, narrowly avoiding the sharpened tips, and pushed up the mask, revealing the face of a young man – a man August had never seen in the village before.

'Please, I am a friend,' the man whispered, nervously. August lowered the pitchfork. 'I bring an urgent message from Paris, from your friend Jimmy van Peters.' His English was good, his accent French. He held out a letter, the white envelope catching the moonlight. August took it.

'Thank you.'

'Now I should go back to the fiesta before I am missed, but I will be out of Irumendi before sunrise.' Before August had a chance to question him further, he'd slipped his mask back on and stepped out beyond the trees: a mythical figure vanishing back into the mist. August moved into the light of the barn and tore open the letter. The shaky handwriting was almost unrecognisable, as if Jimmy's health had deteriorated even further.

'Gus, I hope this gets to you in time. I've had a visitor, our friend Tyson. If you are there, you must leave Irumendi as soon as you can. If necessary take my diary with you, it is not safe. Also our friend told me both Auntie and Uncle Sam as well as Cousin Patrice are all desperate to see you. I'm well but having a little trouble with my hands, your good friend Dizzy Gillespie.'

Auntie, Uncle Sam and Cousin Patrice – MI5, the CIA and Interpol, they're all after me. How long can I run before I stumble? August leaned back against a haystack, the enclosing sense of being cornered rose up around him. *I have to leave by daybreak, to Paris with the chronicle. I have no choice. I have to see Jimmy and find out about the fate of the monk Dominic Baptise. Too late to have moral qualms now,* he told himself, the need to follow the map to wherever it led now rising up in him as intense as pain. He owed it to La Leona and her men. He owed it to Shimon Ruiz de Luna.

The dawn had begun to bleed up into the descending night. August stood on the foot guard of the truck's cabin, looking back over the village and the valley. The top of the church tower was just catching the sunrise, the red shutters of the houses around it pulled closed like eyelids in a white face. Still sleeping after the fiesta, the village looked remarkably benign, but abandoned streamers drifted across the deserted plaza and a lone balloon floated above an oak tree, its string tangled in the branches. A makeshift bandstand of soap boxes still stood beside the café tables and someone had strung the paper mask of a pig's face over the door of the police station. Now, after all he'd learned in the past weeks, August couldn't look at the plaza without thinking about the divisions within the community: the townhouse housing the police station, its Spanish flag flying from a pole above the entrance; the way the people broke from Euskara to silence to Spanish when either the priest or an official neared them; the hidden horror he'd found in the forest, compartmentalised into another time, while the people below still had to conduct their lives under the constant surveillance of an enemy; Izarra, the night before, her face torn apart by tragedy; the primal wail Gabirel gave at the sight of his mother's corpse. Just then a dishevelled-looking Mateo slapped August on the back.

'You must go, my friend, before the Guardias Civiles wake up for their coffee and the rest of the villagers with their hangovers. What a night, eh?' said Mateo, who had arranged August's lift to the fishing village of Elantxobe. August reached out and the two men shook hands.

'Remember, when you get to Elantxobe the driver will introduce you to my cousin Emmanuel who runs a small trawler, sometimes as far as Bordeaux. For a contribution to the cause, he will take you.'

'I owe you a great deal, Mateo.'

'And I intend to collect. Next time you visit, you bring me the latest Rolleiflex, agreed?' Mateo grinned.

'Agreed,' August replied, surprised at how emotional he suddenly felt.

The truck driver, already at the steering wheel, shouted a

farewell in Euskara. August hauled his rucksack onto his shoulder then pulled himself into the cabin and the truck roared off, as many unanswered questions stretching out behind him as in front.

It had been a painful process of deduction, one that required a patient and methodical mind, but Olivia had been in no hurry. San Sebastián had proved a frustrating whirlwind of false trails and dead ends, until she was approached by an old man who had watched her scout several of the bars well known for their Basque Nationalist leanings. The old man, a self-declared Carlist, warmed to Olivia when she told him she was a royalist herself, but it had still taken a hefty bribe to be told of a blond goat farmer from Galicia who had arrived a week earlier asking for a lift to a place known only to locals, claiming he had an uncle there. The old man had silently witnessed the exchange but had taken note as he thought the man's appearance and accent suspicious. Something about the old man's description of the village – a secluded valley surrounded by three mountains – resonated with Olivia. Then she remembered a mystic reference in one of Copps's books to three daughters of Mari the pagan mountain goddess who guarded a secret heart within their valley. Later that morning she paid a farmer to drive her there.

13

By the time August arrived it was already evening. He stood on the corner of the boulevard de Clichy, looking down the bustling promenade. Arriving in the city had been inexplicably unsettling; something about the intact streets and buildings disturbed him, until he realised Paris lacked the gaping scars of the bomb sites, the piles of broken bricks and the makeshift concrete bunkers that still stood in London gardens, paraphernalia of a besieged city. Like a clever whore, Paris had escaped the destruction of war.

The neon signs of the nightclubs and cabarets lit the sky above in a patchwork of garish colour. After the village of Irumendi he felt as if he'd arrived on another planet altogether. The evening crowds were beginning to congregate on the sidewalk, a combination of servicemen and civilians all intent on seeing a show or some jazz. Some were heading towards the famous Moulin Rouge, others gravitated to the seedier burlesque shows. Statuesque girls in fishnet tights and risqué costumes, legs, bosoms and buttocks shimmering under the neon, stood in the entrances of the clubs, enticing in the men. As August walked past one of the clubs he caught sight of himself in the glass window. Pale and hollow-eyed, he didn't recognise himself entirely. Something had changed about his demeanour – the experience in Biscay had finally knocked the last vestiges of youth from him. He left Pigalle and made his way over to the Latin Quarter, the bohemian area the students frequented and where the Purple Rose was located, along with dozens of other jazz clubs found in the old buildings' cellars.

The trip out of the Basque country had not been easy. The truck he was travelling in had been stopped by police on the mountain road to Elantxobe but the policemen, looking for smugglers, were more interested in the cargo in the back than the two men up front and had assumed from August's dress that he was a local anyhow. But once August arrived in Elantxobe, he found that Mateo's cousin wasn't as sympathetic as Mateo had suggested, and had only agreed to take August as far as Bordeaux for fifty American dollars – a fortune in pesos. The trip on the boat had taken a good three hours and August, forced to hide in a hidden partition behind the engine, was sickened by the lurching boat and the smell of diesel fumes.

Once in Bordeaux, he'd managed to find a cheap room to rent for the hour near the railway station and had washed, shaved and changed his rural guise for something more urbane. It had only been there, in the tiny bedchamber little more than a glorified cupboard, with an iron washstand squeezed in between the door and the window, that the ramifications of his departure fell on top of him like a weight. Part of him had wanted to stay, had wanted finally to break down Izarra's reserve, even be there as a mentor for Gabirel. *I should have stayed and protected them. Who knows what kind of attention my visit may now bring? Will the relationship between them survive now that Gabirel remembers that terrible day? I know that feeling of being unravelled only too well. Did I do the right thing morally?*

He'd stood there, staring down at a bowlful of soapy water, when suddenly white-green fingers appeared under the cloudy surface, a drowned hand, a buried memory playing tricks with his eyes, a bloated corpse in the shallows of a river. Somewhere in the hostel a door slammed and August heard the report of a gun. He jumped then grasped the edge of the washstand to steady himself. Closing his eyes, he saw Charlie in the grey of the night, his body jerking back with the impact of the bullet, and himself now running, stumbling back to the trenches. He opened his eyes and forced himself to focus on the garish floral wallpaper and the smell of frying fish drifting in from outside. Then he lifted his razor and deliberately cut his cheek, a small neat slash. It brought him sharply back. *No more memories*, he told himself, *no more past*. But the guilt of leaving so abruptly and secretly gripped him. And there was the fact he had taken the chronicle with him. He'd left a note and some money explaining that he intended to return it as soon as he had finished with his research, but none of that stopped him from feeling like a coward as he walked out into that still Biscay morning. More disturbingly, it wasn't just abandoning them that hurt him, it was the sneaking sense that he hadn't been entirely honourable. Had he been trying to compensate for the ambiguity of his own actions all those years before, was that why Charlie had now started appearing again after being locked up in his memory for so long? He tortured himself with the notion all the way to Paris.

But now in Paris there were more pressing dilemmas. He had to find Jimmy, and soon. A taxi narrowly missed a boy on a Vespa, hooting loudly, and the altercation propelled August's mind back to the street and where he was standing.

He'd been walking for over an hour, almost in a daze. He glanced up and realised he was only a block away from the club where Jimmy used to perform. Crossing the boulevard Saint-Michel, he pushed his way through a group of drunken American sailors then entered the small side street of rue de la Huchette. He could see a painted sign of a saxophone with a rose twisting around it about halfway down the street. Five minutes later August found himself climbing down a steep set of stone steps and into the jazz club.

Lit only by candlelight and a single spot illuminating a corner from which a black saxophone player was performing a haunting melody, the cellar was packed with wooden beer barrels upended, functioning as tables. The ceiling was a series of brick arches, and August guessed the venue must have once been the cellar of a rather grand building. Small clusters of intense-looking students sat around the barrels, chatting among themselves, drinking. A makeshift bar ran along the far wall and posters of various jazz artists were pinned up on the wall behind it. The barmaid was a thin brunette with waist-length hair, dressed in a pencil skirt and a skin-tight purple polo-necked top with nipples that beckoned. The air was cloudy with cigarette smoke. A harassed-looking bearded waiter in a black skivvy pushed his way through the clientele, holding a tray with a bottle and wine glasses balanced on it. August sat on a high stool by the bar, and gestured for the barmaid to bring him a glass of red wine. She brought it over, hips rolling under her tight skirt. She watched as he lit up. Taking the hint, he offered her a cigarette. She took it.

'Dutch?' she asked, in French, then exhaled a plume of white smoke across the bar.

'American. Can't you tell by the tailoring?'

'No, just that you're not an existentialist, but I won't hold that against you. Around here it's a disease you have to catch,' she answered, in English, her smile transforming an otherwise theatrically morose expression.

Encouraged, August leaned forward. 'I'm looking for someone.'

'Aren't we all, baby,' she shrugged. 'This is the human state. You look for someone, you find him, then you realise he wasn't who you were really looking for, so you go on looking.' She pushed her pointy breasts over the counter towards him; August forced his eyes back to her face.

'No, really, I am looking for someone, an old army friend, another American, around forty-five, a musician, Jimmy van Peters? He used to perform here.'

Disappointed, the barmaid picked up a glass and began polishing it.

'Oh Jimmy, sure, he's a regular. I don't know him myself very well. Agnes hung with the daddy-o, she's sitting over there – with the big guy.' She pointed to a bespectacled blonde in rapt conversation with a tall cadaverous-looking man. 'The poet with the hungry eyes. They say he's even published.'

As August started to get up, the barmaid put her hand on his. 'Hey handsome, if you don't find who you're looking for, let me know, we could be destiny.'

'Thanks, I'll bear that in mind.' He plucked her hand off his and walked over to the table. The man was in the middle of reciting a poem, what sounded to August like an ode to the electric toaster.

'Agnes?' he tried interjecting.

'Fuck off, I'm concentrating.' She didn't even bother to turn around.

Ignoring her, he pulled up a chair and sat defiantly at the table.

'Monsieur, you have broken my flow,' the man spluttered.

August didn't move. 'Don't worry, you'll get it back in a minute, I just have to borrow your girl for a moment. I have an important question, about a mutual acquaintance who may be in trouble.'

Now Agnes turned, and August realised she was really young, maybe not much older than seventeen. 'Jimmy, Jimmy van Peters,' August said, quietly.

The girl's expression softened and she whispered something into the poet's ear. Then she led August from the table, away from the crowd, into the shadow of one of the low arches. 'Who are you?'

'I'm an old friend. I fought with Jimmy in Spain.'

'You did?' August could see that she didn't quite believe him. 'What of it?'

'I need to see him. When's he in?'

'Does he need to see you?'

'I told you we're friends.'

'Why should I trust you? Jimmy has a lot of enemies. How do I know you're telling the truth?'

'Did Jimmy ever tell you about Joe Iron? About the time we hid from the fascists in the Ebro River?'

'You're Joe Iron?' Her green eyes widened. Now August could see how poignantly close to childhood she still was.

'Joe Iron was my *nom de guerre*.'

'I still don't know whether to trust you.'

'I'm staying at the hotel at thirty-nine boulevard de Rochechouart, just tell Jimmy that.' He began to walk away. She ran after him, grabbing his arm.

'Jimmy never goes out, not any more. His apartment is at fifty-six rue des Martyrs in Pigalle. But you didn't hear it from me.'

*

Situated off the place Pigalle, a notorious square lined by cafés and strip joints, number fifty-six rue des Martyrs was a narrow building that must have been quite grand in the belle époque. Once residences of the aspirational bourgeoisie, it was now crumbling and decayed. August looked down the narrow street; it appeared to be empty, apart from a couple of teenagers kissing on the street corner. Just then a young woman pushing a pram opened the front door of the apartment building from the inside. After greeting her, August politely helped her carry the pram down the few steps to the pavement, then slipped into the front door before the door slammed shut. Inside the dimly lit but elegantly marbled entrance hall there was the faint smell of cats' urine and a bicycle jammed up against a marble panel. From upstairs, somewhere in the building, August could hear the sound of a jazz record being played and, from another direction, a man and woman arguing over the thin wail of a baby. A strong smell of onion soup drifted down the lift shaft.

He checked the list of occupants beside the doorbells set just inside the front door. To his amusement the owner of the top flat had listed himself as a Monsieur M. Twain – it had to be Jimmy.

The door had a set of five locks on it. A little battered, it had seen better days. In the centre was a small brass knocker in the shape of a lion's head. August lifted it and rapped sharply against the wood.

'*Qui est la?*'

August recognised the muffled voice immediately.

'Jimmy, it's Gus,' he said, through the door. From the other side came the sound of a man shuffling across, then the clinking and rattle of locks and door chains. Finally, the door creaked open. Jimmy's shattered face came into view and

August had the unnerving experience of thinking for a moment he was looking at Jimmy's aged father, the musician had deteriorated so much in a few weeks. One side of his head was bruised and swollen, his right arm was in a sling, his right hand bandaged up – even through the bandage August could see he was missing a finger. Jimmy stared at August through a matrix of broken blood vessels. 'What are you doing here? You shouldn't have come, it's not safe,' he croaked, then hauled August into the room.

The apartment was little more than an open-plan space with a cooking ring and sideboard set against a washbasin in the corner. It was tucked under the eaves of the building and August had to duck to avoid bashing his head on the slanting roof as Jimmy led him in. Against the opposite wall was a low coffee table marked by cigarette burns, with one huge over-flowing glass ashtray perched upon it. Behind this sat a record player, while Jimmy's guitar – the most attractive object in the whole place – was leaning up against the wall. One wall was covered in posters from the early forties adver-tising Dizzy Gillespie and his band, the main band Jimmy used to play with. August put down his bag.

'What happened to you?'

'Damien Tyson.' Jimmy sat gingerly back onto the narrow rickety bed. 'Unfortunately the lousy bastard decided not to finish the job. Apparently that would have been too much of a favour. There's a whisky bottle in the cupboard under the sink and a clean glass on the sideboard. Help yourself. But don't get too comfortable, the Bureau's got to have the place staked out.' Jimmy looked terrible, his skin was greyish and his hands trembled. *The man's got weeks not months*, August thought, barely able to meet Jimmy's gaze. He went over to the kitchenette and found the whisky.

'While you're there, pour me one,' Jimmy yelled out.

'Is that wise?'

'A man's gotta die happy.'

August brought out the two drinks and handed one to Jimmy, who buried his nose in the glass and inhaled deeply. 'The smell of paradise.'

Cradling his own glass, August sat opposite the bed, sinking down into the battered leather armchair. Jimmy collapsed back on the pillows, eyes closed. For a minute August thought he might have died there and then, but then he spoke, eyes still closed. 'So you got my letter?'

'I had to come, Jimmy, I was worried. And there were other reasons I had to come to Paris.'

'What other reasons?'

'The chronicle. There was a monk in the early eighteenth century who began investigating it, then mysteriously disappeared.'

'So the chronicle *has* got its claws into you.'

'Jimmy, Andere and her men were murdered for that book, the US government had nothing to do with it. Tyson was working independently.'

Jimmy sighed. 'So I've realised. I was such a goddamn idiot, I could have killed him! I could have killed him back in 1945!'

'You weren't to know then.'

Jimmy turned painfully towards him, studying him thoughtfully. 'They're after you, Gus, all of them – the Bureau, MI5, Interpol. Tyson told me they think you're KGB.'

August held his gaze steady. 'What do you think?'

Finally, Jimmy dropped his eyes. 'Buddy, in reality I don't care, I just want you to get Tyson for what he did. And now there's talk of this defence pact with Franco – American military bases in Spain for millions of dollars, money that will finance Franco's regime for decades to come. Jesus, Gus, who did I fight for? For what? I'm telling you, a new world order is beginning to take shape. The West is terrified about how the Soviet Union will change after Stalin dies, and the Man of Steel *is* finally dying – and when he does, all hell is going to break out. America is nervous – there's Korea, South America, maybe Cuba. So if you are a spy, Gus, keep it to yourself, I could do without the grief.'

Now Jimmy reached for his whisky. He took a sip, then doubled over, his eyes watering, one skinny arm shooting out as he steadied himself against the bedhead.

'Easy.' August helped him back onto the pillows, the musician's frame under his hands painfully gaunt. 'What do you want from me, Jimmy?' he finally asked, softly.

'In truth – if I only had a day to live?' Jimmy cracked. *Gallows humour, you always were the best at it, even under fire.* August nodded gravely, Jimmy leaned forward, staring at him intensely. 'I want you to try and sabotage this pact somehow. I want you to discredit Damien Tyson. Kill him if you can get away with it.' Somewhere above their heads the plumbing rattled loudly, and Jimmy leaning back against the bedhead, pulling the threadbare quilt up around his shoulders, broke into another bout of coughing. August stared into his glass determined not to feel sorry for the man.

'Is that all?'

'August, he murdered the woman I loved and those other poor bastards, but I can give you a bit more than that.'

'I'm listening.'

'I have information that he is very well connected to the White House and close friends with Senator McCarthy. He has been one of the unofficial negotiators of this defence pact. Tyson could be your key.'

August took his good hand. 'I will get him, one way or another, I promise.'

Jimmy stared down at his hands. 'He broke my fingers and took one on the right. My days as a guitarist are over. What the heck, I got weeks left anyhow.'

He swung his legs back down to the floor then painfully got himself to his feet. He shuffled over to the gramophone player and lifted up one of the record sleeves – the album cover was Nat King Cole's hit 'Mona Lisa'. He tipped up the cover and extracted a piece of paper. He handed it over to August then put the record on. As Nat King Cole's voice crooned out, August scanned the paper. It was a list of names; some he recognised, some he didn't. He looked up at Jimmy. 'Is this what I think it is?'

Jimmy grinned. 'We're still out there, Gus, you won't be alone. This is a network of ex-International Brigade fighters scattered across Europe. It's not a large group, but these are loyal men. You can trust all of them, and they can all provide safe houses and help.'

August looked back down at the list. The names brought faces and memories back. Some had stood beside him in battle, others had gone over the top with him, shouting, willing to die for the idea of freedom, for a democracy that promised equality. And all of them had stayed on living after that moment, had had lives like he had. How had they survived?

He folded the piece of paper and slipped it into his breast pocket.

Mateo, the café owner, watched the tall redheaded middle-aged woman climb stiffly down from the cart. She looked either English or German, with that heavy frame and grace-less step. But she walked with a purpose. Two foreigners in less than ten days; this was more than the village had received for over a year. It can't be good, he reflected. Perhaps Irumendi's obscurity – a characteristic regarded as a great strength by the villagers – was on the wane or perhaps the two foreigners were linked somehow. He studied Olivia as she walked across the plaza to the fountain, then stopped to stare up at the bell tower – somewhat aggressively, Mateo noted. The observation heartened him. Perhaps she was a friend after all; any enemy of the church was a friend of his. On the other side of the square he could see several first floor shutters on the villas that lined the plaza being opened as the news of the stranger's arrival spread like a virus. Now he could see at least two old women staring out from behind white lace curtains, the village's gossips. If he didn't move now, he wouldn't be able to save the foreigner from intense scrutiny. Ah, the naivety of the stranger, Mateo thought to himself, as he stepped out of the bar, carefully pasting a smile on his face as he hurried over the plaza to greet her.

Now long past midnight, it was colder out on the street, and August shivered in his thin jacket. He pulled his collar up and began to walk briskly down the narrow lane. The lights in most of the windows of the apartments were now out, and it felt as if the city had finally fallen asleep. Yet August's mind was whirling – memories folded over experience and then splintered into dreamed fragments of information. The intensity of the past few days had pushed him into that jittering realm that exists beyond exhaustion and yet he was fiercely alert. A cat bolted out of a doorway across his path in a spitting ball of fur. He reeled back, his hand tightening on the satchel containing the chronicle, then laughed. Jimmy *had* given him a gift, he realised – he had given him back meaning.

At the end of the street a black Fiat pulled slowly away from the kerb and August had the distinctive impression someone had been watching him leave Jimmy's apartment building. He hurried out onto place Pigalle. As he turned into the boulevard, one of the side doors of a strip club opened and a burly security guard held it as a young pale blonde stepped out wearing a short white fur cape over a satin evening dress. The man shut the door behind her and she stood for a moment shivering in the early morning chill. August suddenly became acutely aware that they were the only two people left on the street. Hurrying along, he tried to ignore her.

'Monsieur!' To his annoyance she ran after him. He slowed, gearing himself to be solicited – not a prospect he savoured.

'Monsieur, can I worry you for a light?' She held out a cigarette.

Reluctantly, he got out his Zippo. 'Sure,' he answered, gruffly. 'But I warn you, Mademoiselle, I'm not interested in company.' He lit the cigarette then kept walking, but she followed, running slightly to keep up.

'Monsieur, you misunderstand me. I just need someone to walk me to my street. It's been a quiet night and I can't afford a cab, and Paris is dangerous this time of morning.' She widened her eyes appealingly.

'Where is your street?'

'Rue de Canard, it's not far from here.'

It was the next street along from his hotel. There would be no detour. Nearby there was the squeak of brakes and he glanced behind them. The street still appeared empty, but the sense of someone following lingered like scent.

'Expecting someone?' the young girl asked, coquettishly.

'No one nice,' he replied, grimly. Then they walked.

The hotel key jammed for a moment in the lock and August glanced down the corridor, a wooden floor with a cheap worn patterned runner down the centre. He could hear the sound of two people having sex in the room next door, the woman professionally vocal – *doubtless a streetwalker with a client*, he thought, as the key finally turned and the door swung open. He turned on the light. The room lay as he'd left it six hours earlier – a change of clothes flung hurriedly on the single chair sitting in front of the washbasin, a towel and a bar of cheap soap laid on the end of the small bed.

August placed his satchel on the bed and walked over to the window. After lifting the thin lace curtains, he glanced out at the street below. Under the yellow street lamps, it appeared empty, but he still had the feeling he had been watched from the moment he'd left Jimmy's apartment. Even now, as he peered out, he sensed someone's gaze. Pressing himself against the wall, he slipped his hand into his jacket pocket and felt the Mauser he had hidden there. It was a reassuring sensation. He dropped the curtain and turned back to the room. It was then that he noticed, with a jolt, a single white rose lying on the small wooden table in the corner. It hadn't been there before. He walked over and picked it up. Turning it, he studied the old-fashioned double-layered petals, an old world rose, almost Tudor – it looked strangely familiar. As he put it back down, he noticed that his fingers were sticky. Now he could see that the stem was covered in blood and a tiny thread of flesh hung off a thorn. It was like a grim symbol or warning, but who had put it there and why? He went over to the basin to wash his hands, the image of the rose before him, taunting him. Then he realised where he had seen the flower before. He dried his hands and pulled the chronicle out of his satchel; sitting down at the table, he opened the book to the page that held the hidden clues of the first maze. At the top was a detailed illustration of the very same rose; petal for petal, it was an exact copy. A chill ran through him. The sensation struck him that someone was shadowing his journey – not just across Europe but his progress as he worked his way through the young physic's account.

14

The outline of the Abbey of Saint-Germain-des-Prés loomed against the sky. It was late morning. August had overslept, the dead sleep of the exhausted, and the streets were already filling with workers making their way to the numerous cafés that lined the boulevard Saint-Germain. He stared up at the impressive bell tower. Then, after a quick glance around, he entered the abbey.

The long nave stretched out before him, the early morning sunlight glittering in through the stained glass above the altar onto the stone floor in a chequer of red and blue. Kneeling before the altar, his blond hair ablaze in the coloured light, a young monk was praying. August approached him then coughed. The monk glanced over, finished his prayer, got to his feet and walked over.

'*Bonjour*, Monsieur.'

'*Bonjour*. I wish to see the abbot if that's possible.'

The monk peered at him suspiciously. 'Do you have an appointment?'

'No, but I'm a scholar who has come far. I wanted to ask him about a pupil of the seventeenth-century scholar monk

Bernard de Montfaucon, who was an abbot of this abbey – a novice called Dominic Baptise.'

The monk looked startled at the name. He appeared to be on the verge of saying something when they were interrupted by a voice booming out from one of the side chapels.

'Francis, I will assist the gentleman.' A tall white-haired man strode towards them, robes flying. He looked more like a country squire than a priest, August noted, as he drew closer. His cheeks were threaded with the broken capillaries of the wine connoisseur and the figure beneath the cloth was stout.

'Monsieur.' He bowed his head formally at August then turned to dismiss the monk. 'Francis, there are the accounts to be finished in the priory.'

'Of course, Abbot.' The monk turned and disappeared into the shadows of a side chapel, and the abbot turned to August.

'So you are interested in the father of archaeology?'

'Well, naturally, as a classicist I know of him, but actually I was after the writings of a specific pupil of his – a Dominic Baptise?'

The abbot smiled politely and, with a hand on August's shoulder, gently began guiding him down the aisle towards the door of the abbey. 'A Dominic Baptise? I'm afraid I know of no such monk.'

'Are you sure? He would have studied under de Montfaucon around 1709 or 1710?'

They paused at the entrance of one of the side chapels, and August recognised the stone plaque declaring Descartes' tomb. For a moment he was tempted to pay homage.

'Absolutely. I am a scholar of Montfaucon myself. You have to appreciate that sometimes the learned monk hid his more contentious explanations of ancient antiquities under

pseudonyms. It is possible Baptise was one,' the Abbot
replied, somewhat patronisingly.

August glanced back at Descartes' tomb and took heart.
'No, Abbot, I am positive Dominic Baptise existed.'

'And I am positive he did not.' The abbot reached an arm
out, indicating the door of the abbey. August's audience was
over.

As he stepped out into the early afternoon sunlight, he
looked to his left. The abbot's assistant stepped out from
behind one of the stone pillars and indicated that August
should follow him around to the side of the building. After a
quick glance back towards the abbey door, August slipped
quietly after him.

They stood at the top of a narrow stone stairwell built into
the side of the abbey.

'Dominic Baptise did exist. The abbot was lying,' the
assistant told him, nervously, in a lowered voice.

'But why?'

'Because the case of Baptise is still an embarrassment to
the church. Let me show you, but please, the abbot will be
in the far wing of the building, we must keep our voices
down or risk discovery.' He began descending the stairs.
Slippery with moss, they looked as if they hadn't been used
in years. 'This is an ancient crypt – forgotten by the church,
not many know of its existence. It is only me who maintains
it now.'

Inside, it was dim and the air was chilly, the damp already
creeping into August's bones. Stone arches that supported
the foundation of the building stretched across the space,
forcing him to bend down to avoid banging his hand. The
assistant pulled a thick white candle from an ornate brass
stand and, after pulling a box of matches from his robe, lit it.

The candle flared, throwing long shadows across the low vaulted ceiling.

'This way,' the monk whispered, and began leading August through the chambers of the crypt. Under the criss-crossed arches August felt as if he were in some strange beehive, but one for the dead, the tombs suspended in a curious limbo between life and death, like egg chambers awaiting some kind of apocalyptic awakening.

'Here it is.' The young monk stopped at one of the alcoves. Unlike the others, it was empty. They stepped in and the monk held up the candle, illuminating the back wall. Now August could see that it had been inscribed both with a name and the crude outline of a man, his arms held out to his sides, his legs splayed. A word written in Hebrew ran across the figure's chest.

August stepped up, running his fingers across the engraved letters.

'"Da'ath" – "knowledge",' he translated. 'But why Hebrew?' he asked himself, as much as the monk behind him.

'This is not Hebrew, this is Aramaic – ancient Hebrew, the language of Jesus,' the monk replied. 'But you should see this.' He moved the candle across to the inscribed name, in French it read: *Father Dominic Baptise, born in the year of our Lord sixteen hundred and ninety, vanished from this Earth in the year of seventeen hundred and ten.*

'Baptise did exist,' said the monk. 'He was a brilliant student of Montfaucon, who entrusted him with translating a mystical text written by—'

'Elazar ibn Yehuda.'

The monk looked up sharply. 'So you do know.'

'I know of Yehuda,' August replied, cautiously.

'Baptise found something in the translation that sent him on a long pilgrimage across Europe, a pilgrimage that involved hidden sacred sites, the locations of which he refused to share with anyone. He was gone for two years and Montfaucon despaired of ever seeing his gifted student again, when he got a letter from the Archbishop of Hamburg telling him he'd recently received a petition from several parishioners claiming they had witnessed a miracle – the ascension of a young monk, one of Montfaucon's own order, a Dominican called Baptise. Montfaucon was what we would now call a rationalist; he believed only in the miracles of humanism, and knowing Baptise to be of a nervous and imaginative disposition, he wrote back to say he would be supportive of the petition only if substantial evidence was produced and more than five witnesses to the so-called miracle. Nevertheless, the Archbishop of Hamburg was encouraged, and an investigation followed. It was found that a single witness had seen this supernatural event, a woman with flaming red hair. The records tell us she claimed to have watched the monk disappear in a flash of lightning. But when they tried to find her to substantiate the claim, they failed. She had disappeared. Baptise's beatification was suspended indefinitely.'

'Was there anything more about the place where the monk disappeared?'

'Montfaucon's letters in the Bibliothèque Sainte Genevieve mention ornate gardens, described as a labyrinth of hedgerow.'

August looked back at the outlined figure. He could now see that it looked more like a symbol, a totemic depiction of a man, and that the placement of the word on the figure was as symbolic as its meaning. He turned back to the monk.

'Why have you told me this?'

The young monk smiled. 'Despite being a Dominican, I am a charismatic Christian. I believe in the literal truth of the New Testament. I am a believer in miracles, the manifestation of the almighty spirit in Man, both magical and humble.' He looked back at the name carved into the wall. 'Besides, he was only twenty years old, like myself.'

It was already night by the time August got back to the hotel. Once inside his room he pulled the curtains and switched off the light. After the abbey he'd visited the Bibliothèque Sainte Genevieve, hoping to track down the rest of Montfaucon's letters pertaining to Baptise's disappearance. After an hour's fruitless shifting through boxes and files the mortified librarian concluded that the letters August wanted were missing – quite possibly stolen – and that there were no copies. Again, August had the impression he was following in someone else's trail.

He threw himself on the bed and lay there staring up into the darkened room, digesting all the new information bombarding him. The fate of the monk Dominic Baptise disturbed him. It wasn't that he believed in miracles or any kind of transcendence except the very human struggle to better oneself, but he remembered a tutorial given by Professor Copps on the kabbala and medieval Christian symbolism, the academic rapt in fascination as he described how each of the sephiroth in the Tree of Life were associated with archangels, even considered to be portals to heaven in some Christian mystic circles. Had the monk been following Elazar ibn Yehuda's map? Perhaps an earlier transcription that no longer existed. Had he stumbled on one of Shimon Ruiz de Luna's mazes? And if so, what was the real reason behind his disappearance? Abduction was the obvious explanation. If Copps had been right about the chronicle attracting a following, it was quite likely the highly imaginative and possibly neurotic young man had stumbled upon a rival, another seeker – maybe he had simply been murdered.

Just then August heard a faint rattle in the corridor outside the room. He tensed then swung around. As he stared at the door a piece of paper was slipped underneath, then the key itself moved, poked at from the other side, until it fell with a tiny clatter onto the paper. He watched the paper with the key on it slide back under the door. August's heart rate ratcheted up. *Go on, go on, I dare you.* He lifted the Mauser out of his pocket and silently slipped off the bed. He moved towards the door, ready to spring. On the other side he could hear the sound of the key being turned. He aimed the gun ready to fire. The door creaked slowly open. To his surprise there was no one there. He waited. Nothing happened. He stepped quietly, carefully, to the doorway to look right down the corridor.

Then he felt a gun at his temple.

'*Hola*, August.' Izarra's voice was chilling, low and controlled. But then she dropped the gun and smiled.

Furious, August pulled her back into the room and slammed the door.

'What are you doing, Izarra? You could have killed me!'

'I'm sorry, I thought you had gone out.' She sank down into the chair. 'Besides, you're the one still pointing the gun.' August looked down, the Mauser still poised in his hand – habit of the soldier. Sheepishly, he placed it on a side table.

Smiling, she placed hers next to it.

'You thought I was out!' August studied the Basque woman, astounded. Close-up, dressed in trousers and an old jumper, she looked exhausted. 'How on earth did you get here and how did you know I'd be in this hotel?'

Izarra shrugged wearily. 'Please, do you have any water?'

He poured her a glass from a small bottle by the bed. He glanced back at her gun.

'A Walther PPK, a nice piece. I guess you're not quite the farmer I had you figured for.'

'I guess not.'

As she drank the water down greedily, August noticed that her fingernails were chipped and the walking shoes she was wearing were caked with mud. She put down the glass and collapsed back in the chair.

'The morning you left a woman came to the house asking for you – an Englishwoman, not young. She wanted to know where you were, why you had come to the village. I lied, I told her I knew nothing about an American man, a professor. But I am not *sorgina* for nothing. The moment I saw her I knew she was evil. When I turned my back I caught her taking hair from a beret you had left by the front door, looking for anything of your skin and flesh to make trouble for you. I sent her away. But that's when I decided I would help you. There will be others after you.' She smiled grimly. 'Besides, you took the chronicle and I'm not sure I trust you would bring it back.'

'What about Gabirel?'

'Looking after the farmhouse. He will be safe, a cousin is with him.'

'But how did you get into France?'

'A contact in Donostia gave me a false passport and I came directly by train. The passport is good to travel anywhere in Europe. I am here to help you,' she finished calmly, in a matter of fact tone, as if offering to launder his shirts. August stared at her, beginning to believe that she too might have been a soldier like her sister.

'It's too dangerous for a woman.'

Izarra laughed. 'I could have shot you a moment ago. It's you who needs the protection.'

He studied her. There was a new resolve to the cast of her face, a steeliness to her posture – *would she make a worthy opponent? Certainly, she knows more about the mystery of the chronicle than she has told me, but does that mean I should trust her?* 'So how did you find the hotel?'

'I went to Jimmy's club. A young girl, Agnes, told me where you were staying.'

August looked over at the white rose, still on the table. 'Izarra, tell me the truth – were you following me yesterday?'

'No, I swear this is the first time I've seen you. Why?'

He indicated the rose. 'Someone broke in last night before I got back from Jimmy's and left that here.' Surprised, Izarra looked at him to see whether he was serious. He continued, grimly, 'It was here when I got back tonight. There's blood, maybe even flesh on the stem. It's a warning, perhaps even some ridiculous hex.'

She walked over to the table and peered down at the bloom. August noticed that she didn't touch it.

'I know this rose. We use it in the Ofrenda de flores when we offer up flowers to the holy Virgin. It is the rose of sacrifice, of purity. It's suggesting that sacrifice should be, or has been, made.' Here she indicated the flesh. 'It's a warning, August.'

'Damien Tyson. I have this feeling every move I've made has been choreographed, by either Jimmy or Tyson, like I'm unwittingly leading them both somewhere.'

'Jimmy's heart is good.'

'He chose me because he knew I wouldn't be able to resist the chronicle and here I am embroiled in something that will quite likely kill me – it certainly killed Copps. I don't doubt that Tyson was behind the massacre, but am I ready to take on him, Interpol and MI6? I couldn't tell you.'

'You have no choice. You're involved, whether you like it or not. What kind of man are you?'

'I know what kind of man I used to be.'

'So be that man again, he must still be there, somewhere inside of you. And if you can't do it for him, do it for me. My sister was a great woman, a hero to her people. Her death should be avenged.'

'It won't be that simple, the great game never is. Neither is politics.'

Izarra stared at him in open disgust, then stood, grabbing her gun and her bag.

'Fine. I will work alone. I'll find Tyson and kill him, while you can procrastinate as you discover whether you still have *cojones*. But the chronicle is mine!'

'Sit down, Izarra.'

'No. I leave now,' she started, rummaging furiously through the chest of drawers. 'Where is the chronicle?'

'Sit down!' he shouted, losing his temper completely. They stood face to face. Izarra shaking with fury, glared at him, not moving. Stalemate. He pushed her suddenly down onto the bed, where she collapsed.

'There's something else you should know, before you go storming off,' he said. 'Jimmy thinks Tyson was one of the negotiators behind a defence pact between Franco and the US, one involving millions of dollars for US military bases in Spain.'

'So the rumours are true.'

'I'm afraid so.'

'If this happens, Franco will be able to stay in power longer. Decades of hardship, decades of dictatorship, who knows for how long. The international community doesn't care at all, and neither do you!'

August watched her, but all he could think about was his torturer back in that cell in 1938, the arrogance and complete belief of the fascist general arguing so coherently for Franco's regime, his calm voice murmuring on through August's pain.

And then, of all the Lincolns who had died fighting, of the
wild hopes they had discussed late into the nights, men from
all corners of life united by one belief, at the time so gloriously and seductively simple – equality for all, regardless of
class and race. And how all of them, despite the daily slaughter and the terrible odds, sitting there together – Negro, Jew,
Christian, wharfie, artist, intellectual, actor, teamster – all of
them were swept up by the searing glory of true believers.
Izarra was right, he owed something to those ideals, he owed
something to those ghosts.

'What skills do you have?' he finally asked.

'I can speak good French, my sister taught me to be a
good soldier and, most importantly, I can identify Tyson for
you. I will never forget that monster's face. I want him dead.'

'No, it has to be on my terms. He will stand trial as a war
criminal.'

Izarra laughed bitterly. 'You think the European courts
are not corrupt? Maybe you are more idealistic than you
think.'

'My way or no way.' August's face was grimly determined.

'It seems I have no choice.' She held out her hand and
they shook.

Outside, the moon was low, dawn looked to be only a couple
of hours away. August pushed up the window and immediately a fresh breeze swept through the bedroom, catching at
his tired face.

'Smell that,' he said, smiling at Izarra, now awkward at the
intimacy of her proximity. 'The lilac is fading. Soon it will be
all hot mown grass and the faint smell of gasoline. In weeks
Paris will be empty – summer's coming.'

She walked over and stood next to him, both of them staring out at glistening rooftops.

'It's a beautiful city,' he remarked, to fill the silence, horribly aware of the warmth of her arm so close to his own.

'It's a city that was never bombed. Once all cities were beautiful,' she said, solemnly, then swayed slightly on her feet. August fought the impulse to reach out to hold her.

'You should get some sleep, it's late. Take the bed, I'll have the chair.'

'What about you?'

'I'll be okay. I have some work to do. Seriously, Izarra, get some rest.'

She slipped off her shoes and, after placing them under the bed, curled up on the cover. Within seconds her eyes were shut.

He pulled the chair up to the desk and stared down at the chronicle, still open at the drawing of the small white rose. The rose itself lay above the drawing – a three-dimensional twin, its petals now curling slightly at the edges. If anything, August thought to himself, the diary seemed to have gathered presence like an invisible but powerful catalyst that had swept through people's lives – a source of both inspiration and terror, condemning some to a fruitless search and some to death. He lifted the rose, the curl of drying skin still impaled on the thorn. Who did the flesh belong to? How much was he risking by following Shimon Ruiz de Luna's path? How much was he really in control?

His expression hardened in determination. The threat the rose implied didn't frighten him. If anything it intrigued him – it was a character trait that had ended up serving him well in battle. He fed off his own fear – like a chess player who knowingly takes on a far better player just for the sheer exhilaration of pitting his wits against his opponent.

Reaching for his satchel, August pulled out the equipment he used to ink up the chronicle and began the painstaking process of deciphering the book. He'd been working on it steadily when he could, but it seemed Shimon had chosen to tantalise him. The Spaniard digressed constantly, as though testing his reader. August worked for an hour, following Shimon's progress. By now Ruiz de Luna had crossed into the South of France. Who knew where he would be leading him? August felt his eyelids start to droop. Finally, he decided just to rest his head on the desk for a moment. As he did in the distance the bells of Notre Dame began to peal six o'clock. By the fourth chime August was fast asleep.

§

In the distance the bells of the cathedral began to sound for evensong. Shimon tapped his quill against the inkpot and watched the welling ink pool and drip from the tip. He'd been writing for over four hours in the dim light of an oil lantern lent him by the innkeeper, a jovial man who, for an extra few gold coins, was happy not to ask too many questions of his Spanish guests. Uxue had just left to attend the evening prayers. Shimon hadn't wanted her to go, but she had argued that they brought more attention to themselves by not going; nevertheless, Shimon had insisted she took Menditxu with her for security. The fourth bell tolled and Shimon shut his eyes, imagining the determined figure of his wife winding her way through the narrow lanes of Avignon towards the massive papal palace – obscenely lavish for a house of God, Shimon thought, secretly uncomfortable with his wife's Christianity.

They had been resting at the inn for a week. Situated outside the city walls near the Pont Saint-Bénezet, it was small and, as a midpoint for many travellers, indifferent to strangers, which suited Shimon. The couple were exhausted, having journeyed by horse and cart and foot from the Basque village of Irumendi. The trip had taken twenty-one days and on several occasions Uxue had lost patience with her husband, worn out by the constant movement.

'We are fools to journey to the Pope's own city, we, who are sought by the Inquisition. We might as well go straight to his door and announce our arrival, and save the guards some time,' she'd challenged him.

'But Avignon is not part of France. It remains under papal protection and as such, many people, including Jews, can live there in safety, which is exactly why it is a good city in which to hide,' Shimon had argued back. 'Besides, it is the next city mentioned in Yehuda's journal.'

'In that case we go and with joy in our hearts.' By which he could not tell if she was being ironic or had simply surrendered herself entirely to his plan. But the journey was arduous and there had been plague in Toulouse that had meant they lost two days' travel. On several occasions Shimon had found himself doubting the sanity of the journey. On those nights, often sleeping out with just the stars as a ceiling, he would clasp the ancient document close to his chest, as if, by such proximity, he might imbue himself with unwavering faith. After such a night Uxue, lying beside him, had turned and simply said, 'If you lack faith, take mine, I have enough for three.' Her words had quieted his mind. Now the thought of her solemn pledge made in a ditch outside of Nîmes made him smile.

He turned back to the ancient scroll stretched out under the lantern light. Elazar ibn Yehuda, the ancient physic, had described the Roman walled city of Avignon as a colony of recent Christians and a resting house for old mercenaries attracted by the possibility of being paid by the Holy Emperor to defend the weakened stronghold. But he had also written of a secret garden, a place belonging to an old sage who he had visited and who had been most helpful in his quest. The second clue to the treasure was contained within this garden, Yehuda had written. Next to the ornate calligraphy was a small hand-drawn map. Shimon studied it – he recognised the walls of the city and saw how once, in the philosopher's time, the garden must have lain far beyond the walls, but now, Shimon calculated, it would be within the sprawling ghettos and settlements that had sprung up beyond the original Roman walls of the city. Possibly north of the inn itself. He stared into the lantern thinking, the flickering reflection of his own face momentarily unrecognisable he had aged so. It was one thing to discover the puzzles the ancient philosopher had left but another thing to preserve them from future exploitation. It was this moral dilemma that had left Shimon sleepless for nights. He could not bring himself to reveal Elazar ibn Yehuda's discoveries then leave them to be raped and pillaged by men who did not have the spiritual or philosophical sophistication to use them correctly. There had to be a way of disguising such sacred sites and saving them from such abuse.

On the journey to Avignon a Spanish servant at a summer villa that was lying empty had sheltered them. The gardener, from Seville and homesick, had walked them around the elaborate gardens of the house, describing to Shimon in a floral Spanish the intricacies of his job. At the back of the property stood a maze, the geometrical shape of which was clearly visible and easy to read from the turret of the same palace. The folly had delighted Shimon. Made from privet, the maze had both a mystery and a permanence about it that the rest of the garden lacked. Shimon had cross-questioned the proud gardener about the methods and work involved in constructing such a thing, not fully aware as to why it intrigued him so. Now it struck him as the perfect cipher. A cipher that cultivated under his hands could convey all kinds of meaning to those enlightened in the mystic arts. Newly enthused, the young physic pressed the quill to the paper and began to write.

§

The Nouvelle Athenes was filled with a mixed clientele of artisans and intellectuals, August noted with satisfaction, but the atmosphere appeared strangely muted, as if some national disaster might have taken place overnight. It was eerie. At one table a group of students were arguing furiously, but August could only catch snippets of the conversation, his ears pricking at the mention of a possible assassination, maybe even war. *Something's changed, the atmosphere has that dense sense of expectation I recognise. It's like they are waiting for a bomb raid or the sky to fall in.* As he wondered what possibly could have happened overnight, August ushered Izarra to a table in the corner, then ordered them croissants and coffee. Despite her exhaustion the night before, she looked radiant, while he felt dog-tired, having woken with his head resting on the desk. They would have to find better sleeping arrangements, he secretly concluded. A businessman in an expensive suit with immaculately pressed trousers looked across from another table. Izarra's exotic looks were attracting attention, but August knew it wasn't only that – they looked like foreigners.

'We will have to get new clothes to blend in,' he told Izarra, as the coffee arrived, steaming hot and fragrant, immediately re-energising.

'I have money, I have come prepared,' she said.

'As soon as we finish, we go over to Jimmy's. I need more information about Tyson, his psychology, where he might be based.' August bit into a croissant, the buttery pastry making him realise how ravenous he actually was. Izarra, watching him pensively, bit into her own.

'It's delicious,' she said, her mouth full. 'The last time I had a croissant was in Biarritz, with my father, a lifetime ago.' She wiped her lips. 'Jimmy is still a fighter, no?'

'Sure is.' August was distracted by the businessman – he looked Eastern European, and August didn't like the way the man looked uncomfortable in his own suit, as if he wasn't used to wearing one. He was also ignoring them in a rather pointed manner. August instinctively began calculating the fastest route to the exit.

'In some ways he is the last link to my sister.'

'He loved her, I don't doubt that for a moment and neither should you.' August was only half-concentrating. The man looked at his wristwatch – it was a Patek Philippe. No agent could afford such a watch – relieved, August turned his focus back to Izarra.

'That doesn't change the circumstances of her murder,' she answered him, coldly.

'You know he wants to see Tyson go down before he himself dies.'

'Which means we haven't very long.' She glanced around the café. 'It's so colourful here, so much visible wealth, so much freedom. Sometimes I wonder whether Spain will ever change.'

'Everything changes, it's inevitable. It's just a question of when.' She looked so vulnerable, so out of place, August couldn't stand it. He took her hand across the table. Again, there was that spark, the undeniable tug of mutual attraction running like a current from him to her. He waited: surely, she must react now. Instead she pulled her hand away.

'We are *camarada*, not lovers,' she told him, firmly, in Spanish, under her breath.

Covering his disappointment with indifference, August glanced back over at the businessman, who now appeared to be reading *Le Monde*, 'Stalin est Mort!' the headlines screamed.

'Jesus, it's happened, it's really happened,' he exclaimed, in English, forgetting himself. Now he understood the reason for the muted atmosphere.

'What's happened?' Izarra asked, also in English.

'Stalin, he's finally died.'

'And what does this mean?'

'It means the whole world is on notice. Now it will really start, the new Cold War. Everything is going to accelerate.'

Vinko looked back at the paper. 'Fuck the Russians and fuck the Soviet Union,' he said, softly to himself in Croatian, then watched the reflection in his spoon of the couple leaving. After slipping five francs under his plate, he followed.

They hurried back; on the street corner of place de Clichy the newspaper vendors were already shouting the news: 'The father of the Soviets is dead, Stalin is no longer!' August bought a paper off a boy of about twelve. Flicking through the pages, he turned to Izarra. 'According to *Le Monde*, he died late last night, but has now been declared officially dead. And everyone's speculating as to who will take over from him. I'm telling you, this is going to change the world order, you wait.'

'But is this a good thing or a bad thing?'

'I don't know, I just don't want another world war. But Jimmy will be in mourning – once upon a time he was a Stalinist.'

They reached the top of rue des Martyrs. In daylight it looked far more innocuous a street. He wondered if he had been imagining the black car he saw slip away when he'd left Jimmy's building two nights before. A teenager and his dog emerged from the building opposite Jimmy's place and walked past them. The boy, indifferent to the snarling terrier on the end of the leash, leered openly at Izarra, who ignored him. Anxious to get off the street, August led her across the road and to the entrance of number fifty-six. He pressed the buzzer. No reply.

'He's probably passed out with a hangover,' he told Izarra. But a small knot of anxiety began to tighten around his belt. He pressed the bell again. Still no reply. A small rotund man wearing an apron over a grimy vest and trousers stepped out of the building, a cigarette hanging out of the corner of his mouth.

'Please, Monsieur, I'm trying to see my friend Monsieur ... ' August glanced back at the nameplates, wondering whether Jimmy went by his real name or the one on the nameplate, 'Monsieur Twain?'

'You mean Jimmy!' The man grinned, revealing a row of blackened teeth. 'That old bastard never sees the sun until two, but here, you can try waking him.' He held the door open for them.

The lift was out of order, so August and Izarra walked up as fast as they could. August could feel her own growing anxiety. *All I want to do is protect her. How can I expect her to pursue, maybe even draw a weapon to cover me, when all the time I'm thinking about her safety?*

They stood in front of Jimmy's apartment. August lifted the knocker then noticed the door was very slightly ajar. He glanced across at Izarra, her tense expression telling him she'd arrived at the same conclusion. Heart pounding, he pushed the door open.

The curtain was drawn and the apartment was dark. Peering into the dim light, August could see only a stretch of the threadbare rug and the neck of the guitar lying at an awkward angle. He stepped into the room, the floorboard creaking beneath him – no one had attacked him so far. He reached out and switched on the light.

Now he could see why the guitar had looked so strange. Someone had smashed the body open and the strings lay in a tangled mess, hanging off a curved hip of blonde wood. The chest of drawers had been pulled open and clothes lay flung around it. Posters had been ripped off the wall and pillow feathers drifted in the breeze created by the open door. There was no sign of Jimmy. Then August caught sight of something in the bed, something covered in a sheet. History and fear plummeted through his body like lead. Not Jimmy. Not after surviving so much.

He started towards the bed, and Izarra began to follow him.

'Better stay back,' he warned her. He pulled back the sheet. The jazz musician's ashen face was covered in white rose petals, his dead eyes now clouded over, staring up blindly, his mouth twisted in a howl.

'*Camarada*,' August whispered, then buckled over, his lungs, his heart, his whole body contracting in a wave of memory: the sight of Jimmy's grinning face as the door of the Spanish prison cell he'd been locked in for three days swung open; Jimmy drunk and singing in a Madrid brothel the night before they marched to Jarama; Jimmy pulling a weeping soldier away from his dead friend moments before a grenade hit the very same spot.

'Stand.' Izarra slipped her hand under his armpits, trying to haul him up. 'You must stand, August. Lock up your sorrow. You must. This is not what Jimmy would have wanted.'

Pulling himself together, August straightened up, took a deep breath and, steeling himself, turned back to the corpse. He lifted a hand – the fingers were stiff and rigid. Rigor mortis had set in.

'He's been dead for over a day.'

'Then why didn't any of the neighbours find him?'

'Jimmy was paranoid, a hermit. I doubt he even talked to the neighbours. Besides, they might have seen or heard something that frightened them. I should never have left, I should have stayed with him.' August wiped tears from his face with a sleeve, walked over to the window and lifted it, letting in fresh air.

'August?' He swung back. Izarra was bent over, scanning the face. 'This explains the rose stem.' She pointed to a small wound, little more than a scratch, on the cheek. He joined her and crouched down to examine it. The cut bore the imprint of a thorn.

'But that means he must have been killed just after I left him the night before last and whoever murdered him was able to break into my hotel room in the time I took to get back. That simply isn't physically possible.'

'It also means whoever killed Jimmy knows that you have the chronicle.'

'But I walked straight back.'

August cast his mind back to the trip between the apartment and the hotel room on that night, then he remembered escorting the young stripper back to her apartment. Had he been set up? If so, it meant that someone was tracking his every move.

He pulled the sheet further away from the body. Jimmy was still dressed in the same clothes August had last seen him wearing. There appeared to be no visible mark or bullet hole on Jimmy's torso or head. August pushed the shirt collar away from the neck. A thin red mark ran like a band around Jimmy's neck. August immediately recognised the mark from his missions in occupied France with the SOE.

'He's been garrotted. It's a favourite with the elite operatives. Just the kind of thing a company guy might choose. Quiet, efficient, no mess.' His voice began to crack. It was harder than he thought to stay detached. 'Stalin's dead, buddy, just thought you should know,' he told the corpse as he turned the collar back up.

'Company guy?'

'CIA, Central Intelligence Agency, the guys Tyson now works for.'

'Maybe Tyson came back, maybe he was looking for the chronicle?'

August glanced over at the front door. There were no signs of it having been damaged.

'I don't think so. No signs of forced entry. Whoever it was Jimmy trusted them enough to let them in voluntarily.'

They were interrupted by the sound of a police siren growing louder as it turned into the street. August scanned the room. Outside the window, he could see the black iron railings of a fire escape. He grabbed Izarra's hand and pulled her over to the window.

'C'mon, we have to move.' He hoisted the window up and Izarra climbed out onto the fire escape; in seconds he'd joined her. As she started down the steep ladder he carefully pulled shut the window behind him. Minutes later they had climbed down and out onto a back lane that led them, past rubbish bins, straight back to the busy square of the place Pigalle and comparative anonymity.

15

'Seems like it's already getting complicated. You sure you want to come along for the ride?' Back at the hotel room August stood at the small table, sorting the information he did have into piles. It was his way of trying to contain the overwhelming sense that, after weeks of assuming he was the hunter, he'd become the hunted. He had to regain control and the only way he could now think of was through trying to second-guess Tyson's next step.

'I'm here to avenge my sister's murder but also do the best for my people.' Izarra's voice had changed: colder, more authoritarian. There was a click, one August recognised instantly. Izarra now held her Walther in her hand. Peering down the viewfinder, she was busy checking the gun.

'I assume you can use that.'

'I told you, La Leona trained me.'

'There's only six bullets in the clip, that kind of limits your choices,' he tried joking, but Izarra's face remained grim and taut. She finished cocking the gun.

'Don't panic, I'm a good shot. Tyson doesn't know I'm with you. This gives you a big advantage. Don't forget this.'

'I won't, and I'm sorry. I should treat you as my equal.'

'I am your equal, perhaps even your better.' She slipped the gun into a small holster hidden under her jacket.

'Yet you missed me that time you were shooting at me in the forest.' Buoyed by her professionalism, he couldn't resist teasing her. To his amusement, Izarra blushed.

'Perhaps I was shooting just to frighten you.'

'Congratulations, it worked, I'm still frightened.'

'Frightened or terrified? I have been told I am also good at terrifying men.' One eyebrow shot up ironically, and to his surprise he realised she was flirting. He paused, perplexed by the mixed signals.

They heard the screech of a car pulling up at the kerb. August moved to the window. In the street below two plain clothes men climbed out of a black Mercedes. They looked like police as they raced up the steps of the hotel.

'Grab your things, we're leaving,' he said.

'Now?'

'Yes, now!'

August bundled his notes into the satchel and grabbed the rucksack with his Rolleiflex and travel clothes still packed into it. Three minutes later they were both out in the corridor. They heard the shudder of the lift as it reached their floor. He looked down the hall – they wouldn't have time to get to the back stairs. He pushed Izarra up against the wall and pretended he was making violent love to her. To his relief she understood the ploy immediately, wrapping her legs around him. From the corner of his eye he watched the two men exit the lift. Stopping, one of them glanced in their direction. August buried his face in Izarra's hair, hiding his features, and the detective turned away.

'Fucking rabbits. What's wrong with a bed?' the taller one remarked, in French, to the other.

'Pierre, you need to get laid,' the other retorted then began banging at the door of August's room. A second later they had kicked it down. Once they were inside the room, August pulled away from Izarra and they moved swiftly towards the elevator.

'They are probably looking for just one man alone, so we both go back to the foyer and leave as inconspicuously as possible, just another normal couple,' he told her, as the lift descended.

Outside, August hailed down a taxi and told the driver to take them to Gare de Lyon. As they pulled away from the kerb he stared out the back window looking for possible tails. The streetscape appeared normal – there were a few people on their way to work, two students flew past on bicycles, and a cop lingered at the corner chatting to a man smoking outside a butcher's shop. A lorry collecting rubbish passed the taxi. A well-dressed matron with a small grey poodle on a lead crossed in front of them, the continuum of ordinary life unfurling like clockwork under the afternoon sun. Too much like clockwork, it made August nervous. The sense of being watched was palatable, but where were the watchers?

August turned back to the cab. With a pang of regret he remembered Jimmy's corpse, lying abandoned, probably on its way to a morgue by now. Where would they bury him? In a pauper's grave no doubt, unless the US Embassy picked up the bill, and August had a strong feeling they would not. It seemed a tragically anonymous end to an extraordinary life, but then Jimmy himself was a staunch atheist. He would have found the anonymity of a pauper's grave ironic. August made a mental note to return some day to pay homage.

'Who were they?' Izarra broke into his reverie. 'Tyson's men?'

August's mind flashed back to the detectives in the corridor, their well-spoken, even educated French – too educated for local detectives and they were definitely not CIA or Americans.

'Probably Interpol.'

'Interpol is looking for you? But Jimmy has only just been murdered.'

'I think it's related to a small mess I left back in London, but Jimmy's death isn't going to help. As an ex OSS operative, his death is bound to cause some heat.'

Izarra studied him quizzically. 'I don't really know you, do I?'

'You know enough. Besides, we just spent the night together and made wild love against a wall, who knows what the next few weeks will bring.' This time she smiled.

'Where next?' she said.

'Avignon.'

'This is to do with the chronicle?'

'Maybe.'

'You're so certain of it. Doesn't it frighten you?'

'No, it excites me. Izarra, I'm following my instinct, but I really believe your ancestor was on the brink of discovering something extraordinary. The question is, did he find it?'

She studied his profile, the mark of the old wound running down one cheek, the nose that looked as if it might once have been broken.

'The Falangists did that to your face, didn't they?'

He looked at her sharply.

'I recognise the scars.'

'Jimmy saved my life. I owe him, just like I owe those men who died beside me in Spain. Tyson will pay, for all of it, the massacre, your sister's death, Jimmy's murder.' His words emerged more passionately than he had intended, and he noticed the cab driver watching him in the rear-view mirror.

Sitting in the back seat, the two of them fell into an awkward silence. Just then the cab swerved around a corner and threw them together. To his chagrin he felt the same bolt of desire at the touch of her skin. He shifted away, embarrassed, as Izarra righted herself, smoothing down her hair that had flown across her face.

'Jimmy van Peters was a good man,' she said, softly.

'I know, I shall miss him,' he replied, now noticing that she never, ever apologised.

'But we will finish what he began. At least he has that and maybe now he is finally with my sister.'

'I wish I could believe that.'

The two detectives searched the small room carefully. The taller one pulled the small hand towel from the towel rack with the tips of his fingers – it was damp.

'He's just been here.'

The other, staring down at the rickety single bed, with its cheap side table and lampshade with a mended tear in the fabric, felt the pillow. The cover was still warm.

'You're right, but whoever this August Winthrop is, he is not an American with money. Look at this pigsty, not even my cleaning lady would stay in such a place.'

'So he's a murderer, not a bank robber.'

In lieu of an answer, the detective pulled the mattress off the bed and down onto the floor, where it collapsed, sending up a little cloud of dust, causing both men to sneeze.

Pressed against the iron grid of the bed was a bloodstained album cover. The detective held it up triumphantly. He looked at the scrawled signature on the front.

'Voilà, Pierre. The guy could not resist collecting a souvenir.'

The two men leaned over the album. Jimmy van Peters stared out from the group shot of the jazz band, half his face dyed red by the bloodstain, like an omen.

'But what was his motive?'

'We will leave that to our British friends.'

'But both the victim and the murderer are Americans.'

'Oh, the Americans are interested as well. I don't know who Monsieur August Winthrop is, but he has a lot of people engrossed in his little escapades.'

Olivia stared up at the shuttered farmhouse. It looked like it had been closed up for some time, but that didn't make sense. She'd been in Irumendi for over two days and she still hadn't discovered why August had been drawn to the place. She knew it must have something to do with Shimon Ruiz de Luna, but what exactly? The locals were under the illusion the American was a visiting professor, those who would actually talk to her, and no one seemed prepared to talk about the mysterious family he had opted to stay with, not even that idiot of a café owner. If anything, they appeared frightened, as if they were being watched. She walked thoughtfully around to the side of the house and found the barn door. She pulled it open. The barn, situated on the ground floor of the farmhouse, as was characteristic of the region, was empty, but the cow manure looked fresh and the hay had recently been raked into the feeding bins. The woman Olivia had originally encountered two days before might have suddenly gone away, but someone was tending the animals. The woman, striking and wary, had displayed a coiled violence that had put Olivia on her guard immediately and there appeared no vulnerability in her persona that might have given the Englishwoman some power over her. Yet the young Basque had lied, Olivia was convinced of it; she'd known exactly who August was. More than that she'd sheltered him in her farmhouse.

Olivia paced thoughtfully across the old stone floor. Each step brought new knowledge of what lay beneath, and there was something uneven about the floor's vibrations – a fault in the magnetic field. Her senses led her to a particular bale of hay sitting by itself, pushed up against one corner. She moved it away and found what she was looking for.

The hiding hole was cool, giving off a faint smell of damp and something more musky – mice perhaps. Olivia stood in the rectangular hole and looked up at the light filtering in from the barn above. It was the shape of a coffin standing upright on its end, she decided, fighting a faint feeling of being suffocated: the remnants of a past persecution in an earlier part of her long life. But it was a space resonant with history. She placed her hands on the cold bricks then ran them across the surface. Within seconds, she'd found the loose brick. Was this it? Was the chronicle hidden inside? Battling a great wave of excitement, she steadied her hands as she carefully removed the brick and felt inside. There was nothing but a single sheet of parchment, which she held up to the light shining weakly in from above. Squinting, she read the archaic French. It didn't surprise her – she'd known all about the missing young monk for centuries. It was one of the whispered rumours that had been carried through the generations of believers, and for good reason, Olivia had encouraged it. What was surprising was that the witnessing was reported at all – she'd never known that until now. Had they known? she wondered. The letter was a revelation but it wasn't the chronicle. Swallowing her disappointment, she replaced it behind the brick, then, after checking everything was as it was before, hauled herself back up into the barn.

At the far side she saw a ladder leading up to a door in the ceiling. It was bound to lead into the main house, Olivia noted. She could feel August Winthrop now, the echo of his presence trailing like a ribbon around the house and up the front steps. She began to climb the ladder.

Tracing the sense of him, Olivia had woven her way through four of the main rooms: the kitchen, two bedrooms and the main sitting room. Although the house had been locked up, it felt like the occupants had just left and in a hurry. There was still an apron hanging off the back of a kitchen chair, a tap was dripping and an abandoned jacket lay on a couch. She knew August had been there but there was no physical sign of him now; the only man's clothes she'd found were in a small back bedroom in a single chest of drawers; they obviously belonged to a young local. The house itself, although clean and sparse, was notably empty of furniture and Olivia suspected the family, once moneyed, had been forced to sell off their heirlooms.

She'd almost given up her search when she came across a smaller study that was an adjunct to a bedroom that appeared to belong to the young woman she'd met two days before. There was a framed print of Franco on the wall that surprised Olivia, knowing the local antipathy towards the dictator. It was this photograph that had intrigued her enough to enter. The study had a low uneven wooden ceiling and a small upright leather and wood sofa along the opposite wall, beside a secretaire. Olivia walked over and ran her hands across the top of the desk and down its wooden sides, trying to fathom the personality and intention of the last person to sit at it. Eventually, she opened the cover of the secretaire. Apart from a few bills stuffed into its compartments, it appeared empty. She pulled open a top drawer and discovered an old flag neatly folded, an ikurriña, the flag of the outlawed Basque Nationalist movement. It seemed like an extraordinary contradiction to have one of these (ownership alone was enough to have one arrested in Franco's Spain) and a print of the dictator himself hanging up in the next room. But Olivia had already gleaned that the young Basque woman who lived in the house had secrets – not all of them political.

She carefully replaced the flag in the drawer. As she did she noticed an ink blotter sitting on the desk top of the secretaire. She touched it with her fingers, feeling its uneven surface. Small indentations she recognised. Words, embossed into it as someone wrote upon a sheet of paper. She lifted it close to her face, trying to decipher the loopy scrawl. To her immense excitement, she saw that it was in English. Olivia's heart started thumping. This was the first evidence she'd seen proving that the American had been in the farmhouse. She picked up a pencil and began to cover the imprinted white letters with light pencil strokes. Soon she could read what had been written pressed against the ink blotter.

'*The Purple Rose, rue de la Huchette, Latin Quarter.*' It had to be August's handwriting.

The sharp sound of a man's whistle and the clattering of hooves coming from outside cut through her thoughts. She glanced out of the window. Beyond the back of the house a small herd of cows was trotting towards the farm. She had only minutes to get out. She pulled out the page of the blotter and slipped it into her pocket, then ran out into the corridor.

Olivia ducked out of the barn door and down the other side of the farmhouse towards a cluster of trees and beyond that forest. She moved quickly into the green twilight of the woods, then concealed herself behind a trunk and watched as a youth of about fifteen, with a dignified beauty to his face, herded a group of cows and calves into the barn, whistling and tapping them on the haunches with a switch. Stretching all her senses out towards him, she tried to get a reading. To her astonishment, she met resistance immediately. The youth's mind was a fortress; unimaginable in one so young. Amazed, Olivia stepped forward, not quite believing what she was sensing, and it was then that she heard the whisperings behind her, faint at first but definite. She froze then swung back to the forest to concentrate all her energy onto the thicket of oak and beech, the canopy of branches and leaves. Yes, the whisperings were definitely beyond the trees, lower down the valley. Fine threads barely audible except to someone like her. Pain, violence, terrible tragedy, buried under the birdsong, the nearby buzz of a bumblebee, the rush of a distant stream. But they were there, tiny wisps that caught at her hair, her throat, like fish hooks, speaking of the past, speaking of the dead.

She began to follow, taking care not to stumble or break branches, as the threads thickened and wove around the trunks, trailed down small moss-covered paths, then stopped, only to start again a foot away behind some rock. Her body tipped forward, her eyes half-shut, she drew all her senses into a sharp torch beam of listening. Soon she found herself on a narrow path, the gossamery strands converging and overlapping until she was following a rope, a shimmering silver rope, the pain of which she couldn't bear to touch or open herself to completely. It was enough to know she was walking in the right direction.

Finally, with the trees closing in, she stopped and looked back. The farmhouse and any sign of the village beyond had gone. If one wanted to bury a secret, this would be the place. But again, the whisperings, now voices, broken fragments of violence, pleasure, lovemaking and murder, audible shadowing of times past, tugged at her, urging her forward. Her hand slipped into a pocket and clutched at an amulet she had of the Goddess. It was foolish to feel fear, she told herself, the dead, even the murdered, cannot harm the living, but they can disturb. And she could sense, as much as someone or something wanted her there, there was another force that did not. She had to protect herself, if not her life, her sanity.

The path abruptly opened onto a ravine, the ground falling unnaturally away by a few feet. Olivia stopped at the edge. Facing her was the wall of what looked like an old Roman ruin and it was from this wall that the voices were pouring.

She jumped down, then, dizzy, rested against an old tumbled tree trunk. She now saw that she was standing in a natural clearing, one that would be completely hidden unless one knew of its existence. She lifted her eyes and forced herself to look at the wall again. Made of large, roughly hewn stones, it was ancient, far older than most of the architecture of the village, which was medieval. But the voices were far more recent – a cacophony of men shouting, and there was a woman among the cries. Olivia walked closer, not daring to touch it. She became aware of someone standing at the far side of the clearing between the trees. She glanced up and saw a flash of long black hair, khaki, a sliver of sunlight on metal – gun, bayonet? Gone in a flash, nothing material, nothing that was living, that could physically harm her.

She looked back down at the ground and slowly began to walk around the wall, concentrating on the event that had happened there: eight shadows, raised voices, a struggle, men in uniform, several different uniforms, the outline of someone else. A man still living, the leader. Olivia reached the edge of the wall, and with her eyes still downcast, as if not to give offence to the watching ghosts, turned the corner and began to walk the other side. She stopped halfway and shut her eyes, concentrating on the outline of the man who had given the order, concentrating on him because his energy was familiar. She *knew* him. She'd felt the shape of that evil before. In her mind's eye it wavered, tantalising her, forcing her to draw all her strength to a single point that bored into the memory-shadow of the man, his impact still burned on the fabric of time. Who was he? Why was he familiar? Now she could see the blurred outline lifting a gun, yelling orders, commanding others to herd eight figures against the wall, fury and disbelief shooting across them in sharp jagged colours. And she could see that all were now dead except this leader, this Judas, some in the next moment and the others, the ones carrying out his orders, shortly after, months or years, she couldn't tell. But this man was still living.

Now the whispering grew around her and she began to shake. Determined to envisage the whole scenario, she kept her eyes closed, concentrating until she thought her head would split or she would faint. She could see the shadowy figures begin to materialise in the outline on the wall, a row of them staring out, some terrified, others disbelieving, the woman in the middle raising her fist defiantly, and the deafening report of gunfire. Olivia's body shook as if she were taking the bullets herself; crumpling down to the grass, she covered her head with her arms and lay there with her eyes closed until the whisperings had faded away and all she could hear was the rustle of leaves as the scent of lavender drifting across filled her senses like honey. She opened her eyes and got up. It was then that she saw the maze – small and neat, the purple and blue-green hues of rosemary, a sudden enigma in the centre of the grassed clearing. But she wasn't high enough to see the actual layout of the maze. She glanced along the ridge the wall sat upon. About ten feet along, growing just behind the wall, there was a tall tree – tall enough for her purposes. Even from this distance she could see scuff marks up the trunk and one of the lower branches was broken. As if someone had climbed it recently.

She straddled the thick branch and steadied herself against the trunk then stared out over the clearing down at the maze. The perspective was perfect. The American had chosen well, she thought as she gazed down. From this height she recognised the design of the maze immediately: five circular bases visible along one side. The Tree of Life made manifest in hedge. So, Olivia thought, the legend was true. There was more than one. Ruiz de Luna had left a string of clues – botanical puzzles. But what did this first maze mean and where had it directed August Winthrop? Rosemary symbolised sun and fire and was considered a protective herb – one that could ward off evil, or any unwanted visitors. Closing her eyes for a moment, she absorbed the sudden tranquillity of this upper world of swaying branches and rustling leaves, then climbed down.

She walked up to the maze in wonder, stretching out her hand to touch it. It was extraordinary to think this had been planted and tended for over three hundred years. She knew Shimon, who understood enough about the mystical symbolism of herbs and plants, would have left a message hidden in the maze – each plant choice carried a meaning on several layers: mystical, spiritual and astrological. But by planting within a depiction of the Tree of Life – not only was it audacious, it was transgressive. Had Shimon the alchemist known he risked spiritual annihilation through such irreverence? She doubted it, as a *converso*, he was removed from the teaching of his people, his interest was more academic than esoteric or spiritual. And yet he had finally been annihilated, executed by the English for the trumped-up charge of spying. Such courage from such naivety, it was almost admirable. Almost, Olivia thought to herself. Only a desperate *man* would have resorted to such measures, or a man so convinced of the importance of what he was hiding that he felt secure in challenging the power of God himself.

In her world such a design would indicate the first step to an integration of time – past, present and future. But why construct the Tree of Life here? What had Shimon wanted to leave as a message to those he must have known would follow in his footsteps searching for Elazar ibn Yehuda's legendary treasure? Perhaps the secret lay in the centre. Olivia stood before the maze and trembled. Even to enter such a design automatically meant surrendering the amulets and shield of protection she always carried with her. Yet if she were to discover the next step and possibly what August had discovered, she would have to go into the maze.

She felt in her pockets and pulled out a witch's charm of bronze, crystal and gold inscribed with Celtic symbols and her goddess amulet. She placed them both carefully on a stone just outside then stepped under the bower of hedge that arched over the entrance of the maze. The scent of the rosemary intensified immediately, lulling her into further disorientation, a deliberate ploy, she knew, to befuddle the seeker. She made a mental note to stay alert. She was halfway down the first path when she heard the click of a gun being cocked behind her. She froze. A second later she felt the cold barrel of a gun pressed against her head.

'Don't move.' The youth she'd seen earlier stepped out from behind a leafy wall holding a hunting rifle. Olivia held up her hands, more shocked that she hadn't sensed his presence at all than frightened. How did he get so powerful? she wondered, now studying the gawky youth, who, despite the noble cast to his features, was still in the throes of a pimply adolescence.

'I'm just a tourist,' she said, in English, and tried smiling. It didn't work. The youth was incredibly tense and she was sure he would have no trouble pulling the trigger if he wanted. Now she deeply regretted abandoning her amulets. Glancing ahead, she calculated they were about ten feet from the entrance of the maze – once she got him outside, she would stand a chance of disarming him.

'This is pri ... pri ... private property. How did you even find this place?'

His English was good, she noted, despite the stammer, and he seemed to have a slight American twang over the Spanish. August's influence? she wondered.

'I visited your mother yesterday. I'm looking for someone, an American, a friend.' She watched his face for any minute tell-tale signs of emotion. There was a tiny flicker but not where she expected.

'There is no American here. You must go.' The barrel of the gun hadn't moved.

'But she isn't your mother, is she?'

'And you're not a tourist.'

'Lower your gun.'

'No.'

'Lower your gun. You're a strong young man. I'm an old woman. How can I harm you?'

Instead he pressed the gun harder against her temple. It hurt and she pulled away.

'Move,' he commanded then made her walk in front of him out of the maze, the barrel of the rifle now in between her shoulder blades.

'Gabirel, isn't it?' she ventured, remembering a cloth nametag sown carefully into a christening gown she'd seen in the chest of drawers in the bedroom in the farmhouse.

'What of it?' To her astonishment, he didn't even sound surprised she should know his name. This disturbed her. This wasn't the response of a normal man.

'So, if she's not your mother, your aunt perhaps? And where is your aunt? Not at the house, right?'

'*¡Calla! ¡Bruja!* Stop talking, witch!' His voice now held an edge of real violence and she knew she had to be careful, very careful.

They walked on back through the maze, Olivia a metre in front of Gabirel, the round stones pushing up under her soles.

'How long have you known you've been different, Gabirel?' It was a calculated guess and a risky move on her behalf, but everything she'd seen of the youth confirmed her hunch. They had reached the entrance of the maze. She stepped out and faced him; he still hadn't lowered his rifle.

'Wh ... wh ... what are you talking about?'

Now sensing a weakness, she pounced. 'You know exactly what I'm talking about. How long have you seen things others haven't? Heard voices? Had friends who weren't entirely of now?' She indicated everything around her. 'Of this earthly plane?'

'You think I'm some ki ... ki ... kind of fool? Some kind of primitive idiot?' His voice became more aggressive. She stepped back; had she gone too far?

'To the contrary, Gabirel, you're not alone. I can help you.'

'I know what you are, if that's what you mean, and this

sh ... sh ... shape you have, you have made yourself look harmless, innocent. But you can't trick me.'

'Because you have the sight. Isn't that right, Gabirel? But
what I want to know is how?'

Gabirel lifted the rifle and she saw him squeeze the trigger.

'If you don't leave, I will shoot you,' he announced,
calmly.

'You wouldn't kill me, not one of your own kind.' She
kept her voice steady, confident. In truth she was quite convinced he would if pushed.

'I am not one of you.' But his voice faltered.

Olivia decided to push her advantage. She bent her knees
and while she did she scanned the ground nearby. There
was a hidden drop a few yards ahead, where the original
foundation of the ancient villa lay a couple of feet lower than
the ground around them. Olivia noted the direction in which
it lay then picked up her amulets. Already the colours and
shapes of her world had come pulsating back. Already she
felt her powers returning.

'Wh ... wh ... what are you doing?' Gabirel demanded,
and for the first time she could see he was frightened. And
by the way he was looking at her, he could see the transformation in her himself. She stepped away from the maze. He
followed, gun still pointing.

'Tell me about the wall.' She kept her gaze locked to his.

'Shut up!' But he was still allowing her to move towards it.

'It was the wall that enticed me here, Gabirel. There are
voices.' She kept her gaze fastened to his eyes, drawing him
forward. 'One of them is calling out for you, Gabirel.'

Horrified, he moved after her, unable to pull away.
Walking backwards, Olivia felt for the drop with her feet.
They were close, only a yard or so away.

'There are no voices,' he insisted, but his voice was weaker as if he couldn't help his fascination.

'Who are you lying to, Gabirel? Yourself or me? You hear them as loudly as I do. She is screaming out your name, or should I say "screamed out your name" because this moment happened many years ago, didn't it?'

'I told you not to sp ... sp ... speak.'

They were now only inches away and Gabirel still hadn't dropped his eyes to the ground. Instead he stumbled after her, the rifle held up, still pointing directly at her chest. Olivia inched backwards feeling blindly with the heel of her shoe, calculating how far the drop was.

'But nobody heard her crying out your name because of the gunfire, isn't that right, Gabirel?'

Furious, he lurched forward. 'I said stop—' But before he had a chance to finish he stumbled heavily. As he struggled to his feet, Olivia was off, running towards the forest. He fired wildly in her direction, but the strange Englishwoman had disappeared into the thick forest.

Painfully and slowly, he stood. His right ankle was already swelling – it looked twisted. Cursing, he stared across into the cluster of trees, looking for movement between the trunks, a ripple among the bushes. Nothing appeared disturbed except for a shock of birds rising from the top of the trees. How could a woman of her age move so fast? he wondered. It was unnatural. He shivered, then crossed himself, praying silently that his aunt and his new American friend would stay safe in France. He was interrupted by the sound of his cousin calling his name across the valley.

As the train headed south the wheat fields gave way to vineyards and then to hamlets and villages. August pulled out the list of contacts and safe houses Jimmy had given him. He found Avignon, with the name 'Edouard Coutes' written beside it. A huge wave of relief swept through him. Edouard was an old colleague from the Civil War, who'd fought in the Marseillaise Battalion. They had met at Tarazona, where August had first been sent to train. Edouard, ten years older and with combat experience in the First World War fighting for the French, had been allocated rifle training for the Lincolns. A short man with an infectious energy and a short temper, always immaculately dressed even on the battle-field, he'd given August, then a young recruit, with no rifle experience except duck shooting on the Charles River back in Boston, a punishing time until he discovered they had a shared love of Dostoevsky. After that Edouard, a hardened, self-made Anarchist, had forgiven August's elitist upbringing and August had forgiven the Frenchman his constant jibes about the lack of American culture.

The train rushed through a short tunnel then emerged into bright sunlight. August looked across at the window and was distracted for a moment by the passing landscape, an old graveyard beside a small Gothic church, the grey tombstones poking up between the bright scattering of yellow and blue wildflowers. He was surprised Edouard had survived. If anyone could keep them safe, it would be a seasoned fighter like him.

'Orange?' Izarra held one up, smiling. 'C'mon, you have to eat.' She began peeling it, then handed him a slice.

'*Gracias.*' August took the orange and bit into it, relishing the tangy freshness.

He'd booked them both into the last second-class carriage of the train, thus making sure a quick escape would be possi-ble if necessary. Departure at Gare de Lyon had been remarkably easy. Too easy; he'd bought the tickets with cash and hadn't had to show his passport. *Is Tyson playing cat and*

mouse with me, just waiting until I unravel the chronicle for him?
Was it possible? It was a perturbing thought. Nevertheless,
August knew if they didn't move fast, the brief window of
anonymity would evaporate and he would have to resort to
some disguise before they reached Avignon. The man sitting opposite them in the carriage, dressed in a cheap suit and
worn, but highly polished, leather shoes, glanced up from his
book, surprised by the spoken Spanish. August noted his
appearance. He lacked sophistication, the breast pocket of his
jacket was smooth (no concealed weapon there), and his only
luggage appeared to be a briefcase at his feet. Just a curious
layperson, probably a travelling rural salesman going south for
business, August concluded. When the train had pulled away
from Paris, their carriage had been empty. The salesman had
got on at Dijon. No agent could have known which train they
were on unless they'd been spotted at Gare de Lyon, another
reason August felt confident the salesman was harmless. By
his calculations they had about twelve hours of grace before
Interpol and possibly the CIA would have a photograph of
him at all checkpoints and borders. But Izarra was the card up
his sleeve – as far as he knew, no one was aware he was travelling with a companion. Catching his eye, the salesman
smiled politely, then returned to his book.

'Last time I was in France was in 1932,' Izarra remarked,
looking out of the window. 'I was with my father. I was
twelve. We were travelling to meet an old friend of his in
Toulouse. At the time he told me it was about breeding
stock – my father had this crazy idea to create a special kind
of dairy cow, but really I think it was about antique books.'

'Your father had an interest in antique books?'

'I think it was my mother's legacy that inspired it.'
Unconsciously, her eyes slid to August's bag beside him on
the seat, and he knew she meant the chronicle.

'I remember the Frenchman was a kind of gentleman farmer. He lived in an old villa, with a huge library. My father was very polite and a little cowed. But it was thrilling to have him all to myself. It was the last time really,' she added, wistfully.

'The war?'

'He was an idealist not a soldier. He wasn't going to survive, that was obvious to all of us, especially my sister. But not to him. After his death she fought for both of them.'

August glanced over at their fellow traveller, who was still engrossed in his book. Leaning forward, August took Izarra's hand.

'Whatever happens, Izarra, remember you still have family.'

'Gabirel is all I have.' She pulled her hand away. 'What about you? Why no wife, no children? Or are you married?' She laughed suddenly. 'Funny that I've not asked you before.'

'No wife.' A sudden image of Cecily's devastated face as she walked out that morning pricked at his conscience. 'I guess I'm just the original perennial bachelor,' he finished, weakly.

'So you are frightened of something,' she concluded, wryly. He watched her face, acutely aware of how much he wanted her at that moment, her black eyes defiant and vulnerable at the same time, the smiling mouth contradicting the irony held in her gaze, the slight defensiveness of her shoulders belying the strength beneath, her muscular arms now folded across her breasts. She was right, he realised – he was a coward, still stumbling away from the battlefield, still in shock.

'I'm frightened of losing people. This keeps me distant.' Somehow the statement was easier to make in Spanish, less of a confession. He sat back in his seat, the swaying of the train a comfort.

'Me too,' Izarra murmured.

As she said it the train pulled into a small rural station, brakes screeching.

'They change porters here,' the salesman opposite explained, in French, to August and Izarra with a shrug. 'It will only be a ten-minute stop.'

As they waited August leaned his head against the wall and watched the train guards step off the train and exchange greetings with the oncoming crew. Further down the immaculately clean platform with its hanging baskets of flowers, he saw an old man pulling a cart from which he was selling baguettes, water, fruit, as well as newspapers to passengers through the train windows. As the man neared their carriage the newspaper headlines came into sight. August casually began reading through the carriage window. Under the headline 'Who is to be Soviets' New Leader?' was another smaller headline: 'American Wanted for Murder of Musician in Pigalle.' August tensed up. Izarra noticed and followed his gaze, then glanced back at him her face grim with fear. Just then the train whistle blew and they pulled out of the station.

16

They hurried along rue Banasterie. The wide boulevard ran into the centre of the old city, the light grey eighteenth-century buildings flanking them. It was early evening and the streets were still busy with shoppers and workers returning home. August felt horribly exposed, despite a broad-brimmed hat he'd bought at the station and a deliberately relaxed gait – the persona of a Parisian bourgeois on a weekend trip with his fiancée. He was painfully aware how both of them, particularly Izarra, still dressed in her simple travelling clothes, might stand out among the bustling, well-dressed pedestrians. He didn't like feeling so vulnerable. He was sure Interpol would have received an old photograph of him from Leconfield House by now, and had, most likely, circulated it among their regional offices. Now he was thankful for the presence of the Basque woman. Having Izarra by his side would work in his favour, since no one was looking for a couple. Already the chameleon's sensibility, the ability to adapt and disappear into the immediate environment, the skill that he had honed so well during his time in occupied France, had begun to drum against his brain. *Disappear, disappear, hide in plain sight, think yourself invisible.* They arrived at a street corner. He glanced at the road sign. According to his map, Edouard's place was in a small alley just around the corner. He noticed a policeman turning into the street. After pulling Izarra after him, August ducked into a greengrocers. He asked the shopkeeper for a bag of grapes while watching the policeman through the window. To his relief the gendarme took position in the centre of the junction and began directing the evening's traffic.

'C'mon, but don't hurry. Remember, we are just a couple on holiday. Try and look like my wife – they're looking for a single man,' he told her, as they stepped back onto the street. Izarra tucked her arm into his, while he carried the shopping bag, attempting to appear as relaxed as possible.

Rue de la Molière was a lane off rue Saint-Etienne, and despite its literary ambition was a rundown back alley dotted with empty rubbish bins. Number twenty appeared to be the ground and first floor of an old stone building sandwiched between a garage workshop and the back of a restaurant. The front of the garage was still pulled open and filled with mechanics in overalls busily working on several cars hoisted up in the air. A radio blared out in the car and the men barely acknowledged the couple as they hurried past.

Standing in front of the façade of the building, August pressed the bell, looking up and down the lane. No one had followed them; the mechanics hadn't even looked up. Inside the building there was the sound of footsteps running down steep stairs, then the door swung open.

'Edouard, it's me, August Winthrop.'

Edouard Coutes stared up at August, a swift piercing glance, as he instantly assimilated all the information he needed, then glanced over at Izarra. His face gave nothing away. With a quickness August recognised, he ushered them into the darkened corridor, then, after scanning the street, closed the door firmly behind him.

Once inside he pulled August into an embrace. 'Comrade, it's been a lifetime,' he said, in French, his head reaching no higher than August's shoulder.

The large room was filled with an old printing press, the inked rollers still turning, spitting out large sheets of printed paper. The noise was almost deafening. August and Izarra stood at the entrance and waited while Edouard, pulling on a large lever, turned off the machine.

'Come in, come in, you look exhausted, my dear, come rest,' he told Izarra, then turned to August. 'Nowadays it's not often I get to shelter a fugitive. We should celebrate with some burgundy and then we talk.'

Izarra threw herself onto a small couch at one end of the room while Edouard, moving with that characteristic energy August remembered from years before, took a good bottle of burgundy from inside a cupboard. He balanced three glasses on a table covered in magazine proofs.

'I heard about Jimmy's murder on the radio. I assume that's why you're here?' he asked August, as he concentrated on pouring the wine.

'He gave me the list, the night before. I promised to complete something for him. He was investigating something and—'

'He wanted you to take over. Don't worry, my friend, I knew Jimmy was dying. And I am correct in thinking you were not the one who hasten his fate?'

'I'm being set up, Edouard. The question is why and by whom?'

'The same person who silenced Jimmy wants to silence you perhaps.'

He handed August a glass then took one over to Izarra. He held his own up.

'To the struggle, may we fight for ever, *salud*.'

'*Salud*.' August drank; the wine was strong and fortifying.

Edouard smacked his lips in satisfaction. 'Is good, no? Not only has this burgundy legs, it has thighs.'

Now August had a chance to look about him, he noticed the newly printed pamphlet appeared to be about a local historical society. Edouard caught his gaze.

'This used to be a printing press for the resistance. I ran it all during the war. Nowadays I'm just a whore to whoever pays, but I cover my rent.'

'You don't seem surprised to see me, Edouard.'

'August, I am delighted to see you, but surprised? Why should I be, your name is all over the radio. You are wanted for Jimmy's murder, and I think some murder back in London. A professor ... '

'Copps.'

'That's the name. Such celebrity is dangerous, my friend.'

'The two could be linked. Jimmy had an enemy and I have something that enemy wants.'

Edouard threw up his hands. 'Please, too much information is dangerous. I trust you and I trusted Jimmy. It is enough he sent you to me. How can I help?'

'We need somewhere for a few days. I have some research to carry out in Avignon. I'll also need a disguise.'

Edouard glanced in Izarra's direction. 'And the woman?' he asked, softly.

'Connected and committed to helping me. Edouard,' August lowered his voice, 'she is La Leona's sister.'

Edouard whistled. 'So royalty, then.'

'This mission is for both the Republic and Euskadi.' August couldn't remember the last time he'd sounded so serious.

Edouard turned to Izarra. '*Kaixo*, I am honoured, Mademoiselle. I was a great admirer of your sister.'

For a moment Izarra glared back at August, furious he'd given away the identity of her sister, but she also knew such knowledge was galvanising for anyone who'd fought with the Republicans in Spain.

'Thank you. Your Euskara is good.' She smiled politely back at Edouard.

'I had a grandfather from Irún. But please, allow me to feed you both and then we talk.'

They sat in the back office, a small room dominated by an old desk and one large leather chair. Spread out on the table was the food Edouard had brought in – a hunk of bread, tomatoes with the vine leaves still on them, a large round of white goat's cheese and several slices of ham. He watched amused as August and Izarra ate ravenously.

'Sorry.' August wiped his mouth. 'We haven't had a proper meal since yesterday lunchtime.'

'Don't worry, my friend. Besides, I think it was I who taught you an army marches on its stomach.'

'Didn't stop us starving in Spain.'

'Ah, but we starved in style. Remember that time you found the jar of caviar in the Ritz Madrid during one of the raids? Only after we'd eaten it did you discover it had belonged to the Soviet general Emilio Kléber. That night we had caviar on stale talo.' August laughed, but the Frenchman continued: 'But you were extraordinary. A light in all that chaos. A true idealist, it was because of that I feared for you. That and your terrible shooting. It still depresses me, all those young men and I was given ancient Soviet rifles and less than a week to train them.'

'You did your best.'

'It was a slaughterhouse, a fucking abattoir and, when André Marty accused my commander Delasalle of treason and had him executed, I'm sorry, for me that was the end of the Left. The Butcher of Albacete they called him – you know I believe he killed more of us than Franco! And there is no doubt in my mind now that Gaston Delasalle was framed by Marty. But imagine if we had won? Imagine if the Republic had beaten Franco, Hitler, Mussolini. Maybe then Hitler would not have been so encouraged to invade the rest of Europe – perhaps the world would not have gone to war.'

'Without the support of any of the major Western powers, the Republic was never going to win. It was David without his sling against Goliath wielding a brand-new club.'

'And now, with Stalin gone?'

'A new world order perhaps, but not without a war.'

'Do you really think that?'

'It's possible, but I'm hoping it's too soon. Europe's still exhausted and America is caught up in Korea, but Eisenhower is nervous, very nervous. One thing's for sure: they will keep the partition of Berlin now, maybe even carve the country into two.' August pulled out his cigarettes and lit one up. He had only about ten left. 'So Edouard, I can't afford to stay for more than a few days. We have to move fast. I am attracting more flies than a dead cow.'

'What are you looking for?'

'An ancient villa, located south-east of the city along the river.'

Edouard looked surprised. 'This is what you are risking your life for?'

'It's a key to a massacre.'

'The shooting of my sister,' Izarra added.

Edouard looked from one to the other then nodded. 'In that case it is more than an honour to help.' He turned back to August. 'I have a close friend who is a local historian. I can get you several old maps to study. I'll make up some story about wanting to publish a piece on historical sites. But you can't go out like that, both of you look foreign. Avignon is a fairly sleepy town, apart from the usual petty crime. Nothing much happens, but the chief of police likes to keep an eye on old anarchists, especially me, ever since I exposed him as an ex-collaborator.' Edouard clapped his hands in glee. 'Not a popular move, but then I have never wanted to win a popularity contest. I have an old soldier's uniform, it should fit you.'

Izarra glanced up at August's hair. 'Some black hair dye and scissors would help.'

'Certainly, and I will also bring a good French dress. I don't mean to offend, Madame, but in those clothes you look like a renegade.' He still managed to sound charming, but as he turned to the door Izarra grimaced. August, amused, couldn't help grinning.

'Come, I'll show you your quarters, follow me.' Edouard gestured for them to follow.

After collecting up their bags they went back out to the printing press. He walked them to the middle of a wall, then pushed a small table away from it, revealing a trapdoor set into the floor. He hoisted it up and immediately a steep wooden ladder appeared leading down into a cellar. Edouard kneeled and, after sticking his arm into the trapdoor, found a switch fixed to the cellar's ceiling. Electric light flooded the steps.

'This was used by the resistance during the war to hide Allied fighter pilots. No one in Avignon knows of its existence except me.'

They climbed after him down the narrow ladder, Izarra first, then August. Once he was standing on the concrete floor, August whistled in amazement. The basement was large, larger than the floor above; there was an iron bunk bed in the corner, a washing stand, a camping stove, several large bare tables and a wood burner in the corner.

'It extends under the street, which was useful during the occupation, I can tell you. See that disk set into the ceiling?' Edouard pointed up to a circle of wood above their heads. 'That leads into a manhole that takes you out into a side lane. We used it a couple of times, when the SS searched the printing house. I apologise for the cold, but once we get the burner going, it will warm up in no time. It's not exactly the Hotel Inglés, but it'll be comfortable enough for a week.'

August had already placed his bag on one of the tables and was busy unpacking his notes and the chronicle.

'It's perfect, thank you, Edouard.'

'There's one running tap, cold water, but there's a kettle you can heat up on the stove. During the day you don't have to worry about making too much noise, the printing press is so loud above you, no one will hear anyhow. As long as you're gone by nine in the morning and back after five, it is unlikely anyone will see you.'

'Can you get me the disguise and the hair dye and possibly the old map tonight?'

'Absolutely. Anything else you need?'

'I'll need the use of a darkroom, in a day or so. Any local photographer you trust not to ask questions?'

'My wife, you can trust her. We met in the resistance.'

'Excellent.'

Edouard turned to leave. Calling out, August stopped him. 'One last thing – do you have a friend in the hotel business?'

Edouard grinned. 'You are disgusted with my accommodation already?'

'The accommodation is perfect, but I need the use of two
hotel rooms for a couple of hours tomorrow – say at six? I will
also need a fake receipt for a single passage on a ship from
Marseille to Port Said and a map of Marseille.'

'I think I understand. The hotel is L'Hôtel de Pont,
eighty-six rue Victor Hugo. The owner is a close friend, discreet. We tell him it is for some unusual tryst.' Edouard
winked at Izarra. 'And he will not bat an eyelid. And for two
hours, he will make a trade, maybe fifty brochures. The
receipt for the ship's passage and the map of Marseille, now
that is easy.'

'Good, make it rooms fifteen and sixteen. There's one
other request, Edouard. I need to make a telephone call to a
trusted friend back in England. It would be a big favour.'

'Don't worry, the telephone is not tapped. But I have only
one in this building, upstairs in my office.'

August waited until Edouard had stepped out of the office,
then he sat down at the large old art nouveau desk and
picked up the heavy handset of the telephone. After dialling
the operator, he requested an English number in French.
The operator, cool and efficient, patched him through in
seconds, but the phone rang for ages. August checked his
watch. Eight o'clock in France, seven in London – dinner
time. Just when he was about to give up, Malcolm Hully's
voice sounded at the other end of the line.

'Hello?'

For a minute Malcolm's detached and terribly English
voice disorientated August, sweeping him straight back into
his previous life in Kensington, the comparative safe
anonymity. *Cecily, she must have heard by now. What would she*

make of it all? Would she believe I'm a murderer, a wanted criminal? Was it morally reprehensible to have involved her in my complicated life? Well, she's free now. In the background August could make out the sound of children's voices and the faint drone of a radio. It made what he was about to do feel almost criminal. *What happened to you, Malcolm? Was our friendship so cheap? Or is it that now we're fighting a far more complex war in which friends will betray friends and enemies assist enemies for the right price or ideology?*

'Hello? Is anyone there?' Malcolm persisted.

'Malcolm, it's August.'

There was a pause at the other end, during which August could hear the sound of a door being closed then footsteps across what sounded like parquet floor as Malcolm returned to the telephone.

'Where are you?' Malcolm waited, amazed the American had made contact at all, and if he was a Soviet spy, why now? Was it possible he was working independently? He was maverick enough.

'Never mind, I can't talk for long but I need some information.'

'August, you should know people are a little edgy here, and they're extremely interested in you.'

'Great, nice to know I'm still wanted.'

'Oh, you're top of the hit list. I give you two weeks on the outside. First Professor Copps, your old mentor, found murdered, a terrible thing, such a nice innocuous old chappie. Then this Jimmy van Peters murder, some retired OSS operative living in Paris. The Yanks are most upset – seems you're the only common denominator. It doesn't look good.' Malcolm kept his voice deliberately light, reeling the American in with an outraged friendliness

'Listen, I'm being set up. There's a CIA operative called

Damien Tyson who was responsible directly or indirectly for
both murders. He's an old colleague of Jimmy's from the
OSS. Can you pull some discreet strings and find out as
much as possible about him?' *Take the bait, take the bait.* If
Malcolm Hully was working with Tyson, he would now
realise August knew the identity of his pursuer. It was a dangerous ploy but effective.

At the other end of the line Malcolm stared down at an
old paperweight he'd inherited, a scorpion suspended in
glass. This was getting interesting. He'd heard of Tyson.
On the other side of the Atlantic, he had the reputation of a
viper, bloodless, near invisible, and deadly if he didn't like
you. Malcolm also knew Tyson's playground was the Iberian
Peninsula, sometimes even as far north as Paris, but why
Tyson? And, if August was with the Soviets, why would he
want to plant Tyson as a suspect? Was it possible August
knew that Malcolm was MI5 and might be playing him?
Malcolm contemplated all the ramifications. The situation
had more layers than an onion, but he was determined not
to be taken for a fool. He decided to play along – for now.
'I'll do my best, but the Americans have become totally
paranoid since Stalin's death, very edgy indeed, I'm afraid.
Start of a new big chill, I fear. We are all suspect, my dear, do
be careful.'

'Thanks, Malcolm, I really appreciate this. I'll ring you
in a couple of days. Another thing, would it be possible for
you to wire some money? I will be at L'Hôtel de Pont,
eighty-six rue Victor Hugo, Avignon, room fifteen, tomorrow,
at 6 p.m. precisely.'

'Not a problem, but take my advice: trust no one.'

'Advice taken.' *Starting with you*, August added, silently. In
the distance the cathedral bells began to chime 9 p.m.

'Where are you now?' Malcolm asked. To his ears, having

grown up with a father who was a local bell puller at the village church, the bells sounded loud, substantial, quite possibly those of a cathedral. But before he had a chance to hear another peal the dial tone clicked into the void. Malcolm stood staring down at the phone then scribbled the address of the hotel and the time August had said on a notepad. He was pretty sure August was now back in France as the American had seemed unsurprised to hear about Jimmy van Peters's death, which meant he might have been in Paris himself at the time of the murder. But Malcolm was convinced he would have fled the city by now, there were many cities in France that had cathedrals. Avignon was just one of them. Should he believe the Tin Man or not? Malcolm sat down at his desk and began making a list.

When he'd finished he picked up the phone and dialled the direct line through to Upstairs. He got him straight away. 'The Winthrop situation – I now have a strong lead, sir, but I think it's time we talked directly to the OGA.'

'Are you sure we have to go to the CIA? You do realise that is tantamount to relinquishing control?' Upstairs did not sound happy.

'I suspect we have already lost control, sir.'

On the other end of the line Upstairs fell into a dense silence, which Malcolm, if he was honest with himself, found terrifying.

August stared down at the telephone, then lifted up a corner of the blind pulled down low over the window. Night had fallen and the lane was lit by one old iron lamppost, streaking the cobblestones in yellow.

Somewhere in the shadows they were waiting.

*

August towelled dry his newly dyed hair, the shorn feeling alien to his hands, then peered into the broken piece of mirror perched on two nails over the washbasin. The short black hair set against the scar on his face and his crooked nose made him look gaunt, more sinister. He lifted the false moustache he'd packed from his kit and stuck it carefully over his upper lip. Immediately, he was transformed into a soldier, an officer, older, arrogant, probably served with the Vichy government, the narrative already spinning out in his head. He threw back his shoulders and gave his spine the rigidity of a man used to salute and duty, a man who was a traditionalist, who most likely grew up in the northern provinces, rural originally, once desperate to leave the poverty of his father's provincialism. Reaching over, he put on the soldier's jacket Edouard had left hanging over a chair. The weight and fall of the cloth felt right. Invigorated and now in character, he clicked his heels.

'You're frightening me. I think you have let another man's soul into your body.' Izarra was staring at him from the other side of the room.

'Antoine Bools.'

'What?'

'Antoine, that's my new name. I had a Belgian father, something I don't volunteer. This has made me even more patriotic. I don't really like Charles de Gaulle but I don't advertise the fact and I'm hoping that my marriage will help me get promoted next year.'

'Who's your fiancée?'

'You.'

'You're very confident I would have said yes.'

'If you'd said no, Antoine would have simply said *au revoir* and immediately begun looking for the next candidate, he's that kind of man.' August then started to walk around the room, practising. He introduced a kind of stiffness to his upper body, then a characteristic: a nervous habit of striding with his hands held behind his back.

'Extraordinary. You are unrecognisable,' she said, fascinated.

'You see, to really disappear you have to let the artifice become your reality, even under interrogation. The trick is not to be a good liar, but a great believer.'

'I can believe you.' She blushed suddenly then glanced down at the blond locks scattered around his feet.

'You were better looking before.'

'Don't worry, I can change back.'

'But don't expect me to marry you.' Izarra stifled a yawn while he stifled a grin then checked his watch. It was late, past 1 a.m.

'Izarra, catch some sleep. I have to work for a while.'

She glanced over at the bunk bed. 'You prefer upstairs or downstairs?' she asked, seriously, not knowing the term for bunk bed.

August laughed.

'I'm fine sleeping on upstairs. And don't worry, I don't snore.'

'Actually, you do,' she retorted. 'Don't stay up all night, you will need to be alert in the morning.'

She picked up her bag and carried it over to the bed and placed it on the lower of the two. August turned to take off his jacket. As he did he caught the reflection of Izarra undressing through the broken piece of mirror; she was pulling her trousers and top off, her breasts pale half-moons cupped in a black bra, a swirl of feminine curves that made him ache. He tactfully glanced down at the basin, the image still burning against his loins.

*

There was the sound of a log exploding inside the wood stove. Ignoring it, August looked down at the old eighteenth-century map Edouard had borrowed from his historian friend. It was a delicate web of villages, rivers, farmland, roads and streams, over which August could imagine the future shadow of modern Avignon and its surrounds.

Behind him he heard Izarra turning in the bunk bed. It was late, his eyes stung with exhaustion, but he was determined to find the location that night. They had to move on as fast as possible. He turned back to the chronicle, a newly translated page of his transcription set against the original diary entry from Shimon Ruiz de Luna.

Elazar ibn Yehuda hath spoken of a place where the sky met two rivers, and that it were in this fork that the next sacred location lay. I have to confess as I sat studying the philosopher's cryptic words in the small lodging-house where Uxue and I had taken refuge, it was overwhelming. I had not the slightest notion of where I should begin my search.

§

Shimon stopped writing and looked across at the tiny fire flickering in the grate. To write the truth would be to condemn his wife and yet not to write the truth struck him as a moral compromise. He was not a compromising man. He stared into the flames, pulling the old horsehair blanket tighter across his shoulders. Uxue had not yet returned from a market where she hoped to find some abandoned fruit and cheese to feed them. An ember flared up as a small twig caught light. Shimon, closing his eyes, tried to fight the vague memory of three nights before, but failed and allowed the images to flow over him like water.

It had been near dawn, the smell of the night evaporating away with the first warm breath of the day. He had been sleeping, wrapped in the thick dance of a dream in which he was sitting down to a Shabbat dinner with his family, his sister, a languidly beautiful girl of eighteen, turning towards him, a bowl of roasted chickpeas in her hand, when he was woken by the feel of a breeze across his skin and a low murmuring. He'd lain there half asleep, not knowing whether he was still dreaming or not, his eyes half-open, adjusting to the darkness of the bedroom, the image of his wife, her dress open and about her waist, her breasts uncovered, the window behind her open, the dawn sky bleeding up from the horizon. Unaware of his gaze, Uxue appeared to be smearing herself with a thick green paste that looked to be made of herbs, her voice a loud singing in her native tongue, as slowly, rhythmically, with the ritual of a priest, she applied the ointment.

'*Sasi guztien gainetik eta odei guztien azpitik* – "Above all the thorns and through the clouds",' she chanted.

Shimon, wondering whether he was actually awake or whether his dream had shifted into a new reality, shut his eyes, only to hear a cock crow thrice. When he opened them she had gone, the curtains of the window billowing in a sudden gust. He rolled over and returned to his dream.

A few hours later he woke to find her asleep and naked by his side. Later, she had told him, in exacting detail, of the place Elazar ibn Yehuda had described, a place where the sky met the water. She had also told him how to travel there. But how? How had she known? He had heard stories of *bruja* smearing themselves with flying ointment in order to travel over the fields. Was this what he had witnessed? Or had he just imagined it? He glanced back at the half-written page of his chronicle; he loved his wife – he would lie to his reader to protect her.

*But just then Uxue returned from evening song and told me she
had made a friend, a woman who was also a healer, a local,
who knew the surrounding lands and fields of the town. I asked
her if her new friend might be able to help us find this place, and
my wife, ever resourceful, agreed to ask the woman in the
morn ...*

*The next day the woman arrived at the dwelling house. When
I had described the place I was looking for, she told us there was
a place she knew that was good for gathering herbs, outside of
the city. Below Avignon there was a small peninsula sandwiched between the River Durance and a smaller stream where
the two joined and then descended a small waterfall. It was possible, she told us, to stand amid the long grass and rushes and
look out over the waterfall and there it was as if the sky met the
water. She then turned to Uxue and whispered something – the
kind of confidence that only happens between womenfolk. Later,
Uxue told me the old healer had said that this place was
rumoured to be of great energy, haunted by a great magi who
had visited hundreds of years before. The next day she led us
there.*

§

August looked back at the old French map. No doubt the
suburbs of Avignon had spread south in the last three hundred years and swallowed up such a rural location. It was
even possible the smaller stream had been made into a city
drain, but just maybe ... He ran his finger down the map,
tracking the course of the Durance. There were several small
streams that fed into it. The question was, which one led
into a waterfall?

'Could I help?'

Izarra stood behind him, wrapped in an old shirt. The

scent of her hair, now loosened and falling over her shoulders, and the sight of her long bare legs were an instant distraction.

'I was trying to find the location of what I think might be another maze. In the chronicle it's described as the place where two rivers meet the sky, a kind of junction of two waterways leading into a waterfall,' he told her, a little more perfunctorily than he intended, but he was trying to disguise his feelings.

Izarra bent down over the desk, her hair sudden black silk across the page, the arc of her back tantalising. August closed his eyes for a moment, trying to will away the swelling erection he tried to hide under the table.

'The voice of my ancestor. It is extraordinary to me to think he sat somewhere in this foreign city and wrote this,' Izarra murmured, looking down at the marked paragraph on the transcribed page. 'It is as if we are travelling along his words, making the same journey.'

'We are ... From what I can glean he seems to be an honourable man, driven by a legacy he is compelled to carry through – not just for personal gain but as a kind of redemption, a way of avenging his father's murder. You know his family was executed by the Inquisition for being secret Jews.'

'They were *conversos?*'

August nodded cautiously. Knowing the pride many of the Basques took in their nationality, he was a little concerned about how Izarra would take this news.

To his relief she smiled wryly. 'I always thought we might not be pure Basque. My mother's mother had some interesting customs, for example she always refused to eat pork and would insist that the family have a large meal together on a Friday night. But it is strangely comforting to think that

Shimon Ruiz de Luna and myself share a legacy – our families were both murdered and we are both seeking revenge.'

She was now leaning up against the edge of the desk, her
legs inches away from him. Glancing up from his chair, he
wondered whether she consciously realised how provocative
her stance was, but her expression was serious. Fighting the
impulse just to reach across and wrap his arms around her
thighs, he decided his only hope was to move away. He got
out of his seat and walked over to the wood stove, his hand
thrust into his pocket. Izarra noticed nothing.

'But tell me, I know why I'm here but why are you,
August? Is it just the allure of the great secret of the chronicle or something else you are keeping hidden?'

Staring down into the little glass window behind which he
could see the red flickering flames of the burning wood, he
struggled for an answer, one he could live with.

'I was drawn back to Spain because I had left something of
myself behind back in 1939. This is my last chance to make it
right.' He thought he sounded inarticulate, guarded. Like
with all the other women he'd cared about, he was finding it
impossible to be completely honest with her. Was it fear that
she would think him a monster? Or was it that he'd been so
successful in obliterating the memory that only when he was
drunk and in the throes of the transient intimacy of a one-
night stand did the compulsive need to confess override all
his rationality, his cool justification? He looked back up at
her. To his relief, she smiled, albeit a little sadly, at him.

'We all lost something of our souls in that war. In some ways
it made us a little less human,' she said. Then, sensing that he
didn't want to elaborate, she started studying the map again.
'The place "*where two rivers meet the sky*"... Here, August,
there's a village south of the city called La Rivière Rencontre
le Ciel – "The River Meets the Sky" – Skywater?'

August joined her at the desk. He looked down where her finger was pointing. There it was, a small village on a peninsula between two rivers, in exactly the direction Shimon had described in the chronicle.

'Jesus, you might be right.'

The fontaine Médicis in the Jardin du Luxembourg was one of Tyson's favourite locations for a drop. There was something about the baroque romanticism of the fountain, at the end of a small oblong pond, that provided a deeply ironic setting to the squalid and very unromantic business of espionage. It also had the advantage of being secluded and a little removed from the Parisians who frequented the gardens. Tyson was a few minutes early and, after checking his surrounds for any suspicious onlooker, he sat on a wooden bench opposite, tipping his pallid face to catch the sunlight. Then he watched a duck swim in the shallow pool at the base of the reclining figure of Polyphemus, while its mate, the drake, waded listlessly at the base of the fountain. The figure looked on two lovers immortalised in stone, who were apparently oblivious of his gaze. Was he the husband or perhaps some voyeur? Tyson could never decide, but he liked the cool detachment of the observer that the reclining figure embodied. It was decadent, uncaring. He related to the character's isolation, the self-containment that appeared to be both aloof and superior. He looked back at the duck. The creature perplexed him, swimming in small circles as if puzzled by such a shallow body of water that appeared to have no fish in it. Such stupidity irritated Tyson; it seemed to go against the grain of nature, the expediency of evolution. A bird like that deserved to starve, he decided.

Choosing to ignore its mate, the drake began waddling hopefully over the pebbled path towards Tyson, obviously

used to being fed by the tourists that frequented the ornate
gardens. Tyson checked his watch then touched the brim of
his trilby, an unconscious nervous habit – his contact was a
minute late. Another plane of his world slipping out of control. He looked around. Except for a couple of tourists that
had appeared at the head of the pond, the place was empty.
Leaning forward, he kicked the drake, his foot catching the
bird across the breast, and after an indignant squawk, half-
staggering and half-flapping, it flew off. He glanced back at
the tourists and the woman shot him an appalled glance,
before hurrying off with her husband. It was an immensely
satisfying moment Tyson noted happily to himself. Then he
felt a tap on his shoulder.

'The Diamondbacks are having a challenging season,'
said the contact, a grey-haired man in his mid-forties, his
face lightly beaded in sweat, also in a suit, carrying a folded
newspaper under his arm. He sat down beside Tyson.

'My money is on the Rockies,' Tyson replied, delivering
the coded greeting. The contact glanced around the park,
then slipped off his jacket to cool down. 'Hot, isn't it?'

'Pleasant enough.' Tyson stayed friendly, but this wasn't
his usual contact and that augured badly.

'You should know we have questions.'

Tyson kept his eyes forward, maintaining the illusion that
they were complete strangers.

'This guy Winthrop, you know whose son he is?'

'So, he hates him, the guy's awol.'

'If Winthrop was heading for Madrid, he'd be there by
now.'

'The Soviets are cleverer than that. He's biding his time.
There are other means of sabotaging General Kissner's talks.'

'We sure he's KGB?'

'C'mon, he fought in Spain, he's a dedicated Marxist.

Besides, I found evidence in van Peters's apartment. Winthrop's KGB,' Tyson insisted. The contact breathed in sharply, both men careful to maintain their gazes out towards the fountain.

'Hard evidence?'

Tyson folded the newspaper he held across his knees. 'In the drop.'

'Again, if there's any information that could potentially embarrass the US government, given the timeframe on this pact, we need to know now, not in a few weeks, understand?'

Tyson nodded, the slightest of gestures.

'Good, because if there's a screw-up, it's on your watch, understand?'

Tyson made no response – physical or verbal. The contact slid across the newspaper he had under his hand. In an instant the two had swapped newspapers, both of which looked identical.

'Van Peters, Jesus, that was a mess. Was that you?' the contact asked, sharply, a veiled threat in his voice.

Tyson scanned the horizon. There didn't appear to be a living thing near them, except a red squirrel ten metres to the left beside a tree. Tyson doubted it contained a hidden microphone. Breaking basic protocol, he turned to the contact and met his eyes, memorising the face in a flash.

'Interpol is convinced it was Winthrop.' He smiled.

'Fuck you, Tyson.' The contact stood. Tyson stayed sitting.

'Do I still have Winthrop?'

'For now.' The contact started walking away.

'Do you know where he is?' Tyson's voice was just loud enough for the contact to catch. In lieu of a reply he stopped and bent down to tie his shoelaces. 'It's in the drop,' the contact directed back at Tyson over his shoulder.

*

After Tyson had watched the contact disappear down the path toward the boulevard Saint-Michel, he opened the newspaper. Inside, embedded within an article about the French fighting in Algiers, there was a series of letters circled in red – together they made up the word 'nongiva'. Tyson ran it backwards in his head – Avignon. He checked his watch. If he hurried, he could be there by sunset.

Early the next morning Edouard bought August a blank fake French passport and took a photograph, promising he would have the new passport ready by the end of that day. By sunrise August and Izarra were on the road, driving along the bank of the Durance on an old motorcycle Edouard had lent them. Sunlight cut through the plane trees that lined the road like a strobe: black, white, shadow, light, the polarity flashing across August's face, obliterating all thought except the feel of Izarra's arms wrapped around his waist, the warm air streaming past them like hope and the beat of his own excitement drumming against his ribcage.

About ten kilometres outside the outskirts of the city the signpost for La Rivière Rencontre le Ciel loomed up on the side of the road. Minutes later they roared into the small village. August, dressed in the soldier's uniform with his black hair and fake black moustache, and with Izarra wearing a smart skirt and wool jacket, was convinced that they looked like a visiting French soldier and his girl out for a pleasant rural weekend. He pulled the motorcycle up at the local bar, set in the small square. In the middle of the square was a small green, upon which several older men were playing bowls, while a group of women, their wives presumably, sat in the sun, watching and talking among themselves.

'Wait here,' August instructed Izarra, then walked over to the women. He took off the officer's cap he was wearing and politely bowed to the women, who watched him suspiciously from under their headscarfs and black shawls.

'Good morning,' he said, in French. 'I wonder if any of you lovely young ladies would be able to help me?'

The women's faces puckered into grins, displaying a variety of broken and blackened teeth; not one of them appeared to be under the age of eighty. One of them piped up, her huge bosom resting on a massive stomach, sitting in the centre with some crocheting spiralling like a spider's web across her lap.

'Depends what kind of help you need, handsome,' she replied, in a broad rural accent, at which the rest of the women burst into gales of cackling laughter. August glanced back over to Izarra, who was watching, amused. He swung back to the women.

'I was hoping to take my fiancée somewhere special and I've heard there's a place near here where it is like the sky touches the water.'

The women turned to each other, then, after a rancorous debate, the elected spokeswoman turned to August.

'I think you mean the old villa on the other side of the village. Used to be grand before the Germans ...' and here she spat onto the pavement, '... burned it down. At the bottom of the grounds there's a place where if you lay down – or something a little more naughty ...' She glanced meaningfully at Izarra, then back at August and winked to his great amusement, ' ... and look over where the two rivers meet, you see nothing but the sky and the water. I've had three children conceived there and I'm a great-grandmother now!' she concluded, proudly. The other women broke into laughter again. 'Follow the riverbank, then veer left, you can't miss it. And *bonne chance*!'

*

The villa, a solid nineteenth-century bluestone building, had three walls standing and one tumbling out into an overgrown driveway in front. There was only a small section of the roof remaining, blackened from soot, the rest a charred skeleton of rafters yawning out against the azure sky. As August turned off the motorcycle engine, immediately the rushing cascade of a waterfall became audible and there was a fresh crackle to the air – the negative ions of colliding water – that was instantly invigorating. They disembarked and stood in front of the ruin before the remnants of a garden where lavender and roses sprung up between the tumbled stone and an old bent lilac tree was in the last stage of blooming. Izarra handed August his camera.

'C'mon, let's check around the back, I suspect that's where most of the grounds would have been,' he said.

They walked around the wrecked building, disturbing several doves nesting in the eaves. The tranquillity of the landscape disturbed him. He had the unerring sensation that in some way the house was still occupied and he couldn't rid himself of the sensation that he was trespassing or even that the house, with its broken windows, was watching him. Noticing that Izarra was also taking care to tread carefully through the overgrown weeds and grasses, August wondered if she felt the same unease.

'Do you have your gun?' Izarra asked, quietly, as if reading his thoughts.

He nodded.

'Good,' she told him. 'There is something wrong here. I don't know what, but I feel it.' She paused, August glanced across the grounds. Here the overgrown grass was almost waist-high, easy to hide in – not a reassuring sight.

'Stay close behind me,' he instructed her, in a low voice.

As they made their way around, the full extent of the old

grounds opened up before them. It had once been a grand garden – set on a gentle slope flanked by converging rivers on either side that led into a point at the bottom, where the two bodies of water met. Rising up out of the centre of long grass was what looked to be a tumbled mass of overgrown topiary, roughly in the shape of an oblong.

'Do you think that was the maze?' Izarra asked, pointing.

'Possibly. I have to get closer.' The ruined house was now behind them. August realised he would have to get an aerial photograph to get a clear topographical view of the maze, assuming that was the maze. He looked along the fallen walls of the ruin; they weren't high enough.

'I'm going to check whether the location matches Shimon's description,' Izarra told him, then began striding through the long grass towards the end of the peninsula, startling a pheasant that was ground-nesting along the way. August watched her receding figure then pushed on towards the tangled ancient shrubbery he suspected was the remnants of the maze.

The wall of hedgerow was at least fifteen feet high and had vines of ivy and honeysuckle growing through it and over it. It was impossible to see whether it was the wall of the maze or whether there was a maze lying behind it without climbing over the hedgerow itself, and there didn't appear to be an entrance.

'August, come!' He swung around. Izarra's figure was a silhouette against the dark river behind her. She stood at the bottom of the slope, gesturing wildly for him to join her. 'Please! You must see this!'

Reluctantly, he pulled himself away and, pushing through the long grass, joined her.

She was standing at the edge of the riverbank. Opposite and below there was a whirlpool of white water as the two rivers met, beyond which August could now see a small waterfall where the water cascaded over.

'Look! It's exactly how Shimon described!' She shouted, excitedly, over the roar of the rushing water. August stared out over the churning pool. It was true that the water did appear to meet the sky as the landscape receded from the edge of the waterfall, but the bank below the waterfall and the trees flanking it were still visible.

'I can't really see it. Are you sure this is the point?' August ventured.

Izarra crouched down, looking out over the water's edge. 'You have to see it from a particular perspective. It only happens at this one point,' she explained then gestured that he should squat down beside her.

August, unconvinced, crouched and peered along her sightline. From this perspective it was magical, the illusion of two elements cleanly meeting each other – the aqua plane of the water and the sapphire of the sky – filled his gaze. It was like looking into infinity and for a moment August was almost overwhelmed by a sense of vertigo. Still in that position, he turned his head to look back up the slope at the house and the maze. Suddenly, he gripped Izarra's arm.

'Look!'

Staring along the same sightline, it was obvious there was an entrance to the overgrown maze, a small low arch – not more than a crawl space – that curved out as if it were originally the half of a planted circle, the rest hidden within the maze. The first sephirot, August guessed.

'It's inverted. The entrance of the maze is facing away from the house, designed to be seen only after the place where the sky meets the water is discovered.' August's words came tumbling out in his excitement.

'So this is really Shimon's work?' Izarra spoke in an awed whisper, as if in church.

'If that's the case, who has kept this maze alive all those centuries? We know your family tended the first one.'

'It must be someone who understands the importance of the symbolism.'

'But wants to keep it hidden.'

They heard a sudden splash behind them, startling both of them. August reached for the gun hidden in his soldier's jacket. He swung around.

'Don't worry, its only salmon.' Izarra put out her hand to steady him, then pointed to the river at a flash of silver belly, a spray of water hitting the air, then another one as the salmon leaped upstream. August glanced back to the darkened entrance to the maze. It was hard to see, shadowy with a greenish light filtering down through the thick hedgerow growing overhead, and yet the lip of the tunnel had been clipped quite carefully. It wouldn't be easy crawling through to the other side, and he hated the idea of placing himself in such a defenceless position, but he had no choice.

'I'll have to go in.'

'I thought you might have to, so I brought this.' She held up a ball of string. 'I took it from the printer's shop. It's an old trick we used ourselves as children when we first went into the maze. Here, take it. I'll be at the other end.'

August dropped down to his belly and, using his elbows, began crawling along the tunnel entrance, overhanging twigs and roots brushing against his back. At the end he could see sunlight illuminating gravel. *Shangri-La, the forbidden land, it is like I have become a character in a bizarre fairy tale, the soldier hero.* The ball of string threaded through his trouser belt unravelled behind him as he inched along. He reached the end and wriggled out onto a gravelled path and into the secluded world of the maze. Even the light looked different to him as it bounced off pieces of flint hidden in the gravel path, glistening like jewels, the walls of the hedgerow arching high up around him, clipped and manicured, a disturbing contrast to the deliberately overgrown exterior. The thought of these invisible gardeners or guardians unnerved August. *Where are you? Who are you?* Staring across at the pruned branches, he felt more than a trespasser, he felt like he was committing a religious sacrilege. Was it possible they might be responsible for the rose left in his hotel room, the same rose that had been embedded into Jimmy's corpse? Were they willing to kill to keep their secret? The sense of being cornered swept across him, as he fought both fear and claustrophobia.

'Are you all right?' Izarra called from the other side. Already she sounded as if she were miles away. August swung his legs out of the tunnel and stood blinking in the sudden sunlight, dusting down his clothes. The tunnel had led him to the outer ring of a sephirot he now recognised as Malkuth, or 'Kingdom'. After weaving his way through the winding inner walls of the sephirot, he finally reached the centre. It was gravelled, unlike the one at Irumendi in the first maze, where it had been planted with lily and vervain. Frustrated, he took note, marking it mentally in his mind, as he searched for hidden meaning, then made his way back to the outer circle. The three definitive paths, one straight in front of him and two at sharp angles left and right radiated out from it. The whole design of the maze had to be the Tree of Life again, it had to be. The string attached to his waist tugged urgently.

'I'm fine,' he yelled back to Izarra. 'Stay where you are. I'll need you if I get lost!'

He turned back and contemplated which path to take –

this time the maze walls were made of yew, clipped and dense. There was something far more sinister about both the darkish colour and the height of the maze, which made it almost funereal. He envisaged the shape of the Tree of Life: the ten circular stations of spiritual enlightenment, the middle stem broken by four circles, the two other stems running parallel, on either side, each with three sephiroth, and the matrix of paths that individually linked each, symbolising the various paths of enlightenment a man could take to reach the highest plane of spiritual integration – Kether. Only in this living rendition each sephirot had its own maze designed around each centre. Casting his memory back again to his student days, he recalled Professor Copps giving an impassioned lecture on the various schools of esoteric philosophies that had sprung up around a single debate: which path would take the individual to the highest plane of enlightenment the fastest? From sephirot to sephirot, which was the correct path? From Shimon Ruiz de Luna's lineage, the Spanish medieval kabbalists, to the Christian alchemists of the Middle Ages, right through to more contemporary witchcraft and the mystic beliefs of Aleister Crowley. The Tree of Life even had symbolic associations with Hinduism and Buddhism and was most certainly the hidden true meaning of the Tree in the Garden of Eden, August now remembered Professor Copps telling the class most emphatically. But which path should he take now? Would that affect his chances of finding the next key to Elazar ibn Yehuda's journey?

August decided to take the left path. As he walked the string spun out behind him. It was surreal. He felt dwarfed by the towering dark green walls of leaf, and strangely vulnerable, as if he no longer walked in the physical material world, but in another metaphysical dimension.

To anchor himself he took the rough string and allowed it to burn a painful sense of reality between his fingers as he proceeded cautiously down the narrow path, the gravel crunching under his boots the only noise punctuating the thick silence. Above him, a raven circled in the thin strip of sky, enclosed yet isolated.

A few feet on and the path abruptly opened onto the next circular base – the sephirot known as Hod – meaning 'Splendour' or 'Glory'. Again, the sephirot was designed with a series of confusing circular paths around the centre. Now August was beginning to realise that each sephirot in each maze was designed in a unique maze pattern, making it impossible to memorise a simple path through to the centres.

August looked across the carefully gravelled circle, empty of all symbolic planting. Here, as in all the sephiroth, the walls of the maze circled the bed and arched over each path's entrance in leaf bowers. There were four paths confronting him, including the one he'd just arrived from. He decided he would take the one directly in front which, by his calculations, ran up to the next station, Geburah. This way he would be travelling around the outer edge of the maze – along one side of the Tree of Life. Then he would come down the other side, he decided, before venturing into the middle of the maze.

He walked between the dark walls, winding his way right around the outside sephiroth – all of them unplanted – back to the station that sat opposite Hod – Netzach or 'Victory'. He was now facing back towards his starting point, the entrance of the maze, the sephirot Malkuth. Standing in the centre of the barren Netzach, gravelled like all of the other sephiroth he'd walked through, he knew the path ahead of him would lead him back to where he began. From the outer ring he took the next path along to the right. By his calculations this had to take him to the second sephirot in the middle branch of the Tree of

Life – Yesod or 'Foundation'. Just then it occurred to him that the mini-mazes contained within each sephirot were designed to make it impossible to look clearly down any of the paths (or branches and trunk) of the Tree of Life. Once inside the maze one sephirot was obscured from another. It was genius.

When he reached the centre of Yesod he saw that, in this maze,Yesod was a living sephirot. The circular flowerbed in the middle of the circle of maze was planted with two herbs – anise and a low flowering bush he recognised as the purple bloom of the mandrake root. It was well tended like the rest of the interior of the maze, hidden as it were by the shell of wild overgrowth. The scent of the mandrake filled his head and he crouched down for a moment, overwhelmed, burying his face in his hands, as the world closed around him and he was back in that night, in that forest outside Belchite, and there was Charlie walking in front, the white of his shirt dancing in front of August as they moved through the young saplings stretching up around them as if yearning for the sky. He felt that sense of terror tightening his throat while Charlie, his army trousers loose on his skeletal frame, talked out into the dark, a stream of incessant words, from one who'd been silent for weeks, as if he were determined to fill the ever-accelerating void between them. And August, his trembling hand wrapped around his gun, hidden deep in his jacket pocket, could not stop shivering despite the sticky summer heat, could not stop the encroaching horror of what he had been ordered to do. And still, seemingly oblivious, Charlie chatted on, as if they were simply taking a walk in a forest, the two of them, in that moment of their toppled youth. Small talk. August could barely concentrate to make sense of this babbling chatter. There was memory – the river, their rooms, the passionate arguments that always finished in drunken self-congratulatory diatribes; the quiet Oxford lanes and Charlie's broken loves; there were the dreams they had shared; the time in Paris when they were waiting to be smuggled into Spain and into the ranks of the International Brigade; and then there was the fear. And in the middle of this, one small sentence glistened apart from the others: 'Don't look so worried, Gus,' Charlie had said. 'I have always looked after my own fate.' And then, after launching into another reminiscence, he began walking again, before August, his wild red hair a beacon of sacrifice. And August now wanted to run after him, to reverse what he knew was coming, but the flashback faded as quickly as it had appeared.

He came to his senses, his face still in his hands. He had never recalled that night in such detail before – it had always been too overwhelming, too profoundly distressing, but now he had Charlie's strange little sentence hanging in his head. It was an armature he could build something upon. *Do I really know what really happened? Do I?* A bee buzzing around his head landed on his arm. He brushed it off and stood, now fully in the moment. *The maze, how to decipher the layout.*

He would have to get a topographical shot of the maze to really decode it, and the question was how. Just then he felt a tug on the string. He looked up. To his utter amazement floating overhead, quite low, was a hot air balloon advertising Dunlop tyres. Dropping the string August began running towards the path he knew would lead him out of the maze.

17

'Where are you stationed?' The balloonist hauled up the last of the anchoring ropes, then sent another blast of flame up into the billowing silk above them. The basket lifted off from the ground with a lurch and they ascended over the grassy slope and the maze.

'Up north, a small coastal town. You wouldn't know it!' August yelled, over the roaring gas. The balloonist glanced at him sceptically. For a moment August worried that the man might have recognised him from a newspaper or the radio descriptions that had been broadcast, but the balloonist merely broke into a grin. 'That would explain the accent!'

'What?'

'You have a funny accent!'

August smiled blandly back, while inwardly cursing his French grammar teacher he'd had as a child in Boston – who was in fact an aristocratic emigrant.

'My father was Belgian!' he lied, over another blast of flame.

'Well, we can't all be lucky.' The balloonist shrugged philosophically. A thin, energetic man, dressed in a black canvas jumpsuit, he had originally thought August was waving him down to the ground for some illegal geographical transgression he might have unwittingly made. The balloonist had travelled off course – his usual route was along the roads and over the village square to advertise his sponsors, but the wind had sent him inland. It had, therefore, been comparatively easy for August to negotiate a ride over the maze as the balloonist, greatly relieved that he wasn't going to get charged with trespassing, was more than happy to oblige. Above them the burner expelled another huge blast of flame and the balloon rose several feet. Down on the ground Izarra, leaning against the motorbike, waved up at them and the balloonist waved back enthusiastically.

'Pretty girl, your girlfriend?' the man asked, with obvious intrigue.

'My fiancée,' August replied, firmly, extinguishing any further interest. 'Just a short ride over the garden would be wonderful, you could land over there in the field,' he instructed. He leaned over the edge of the balloon's basket. Below he could see the top of the ruined burned-out villa, the blueprint of the architecture now clearly visible – an inner courtyard and the outline of five large rooms that fanned out from what remained of the roof.

They were now nearing the maze. August pulled out his camera and leaning over started to try to focus.

'Is that legal?' the balloonist asked, jolting August's elbow, his voice ringing out in the sudden silence that occurred after another blast of flame.

'Don't worry, it's just a harmless hobby.' August tried to contain his irritation at having his photograph ruined. 'Besides, I am a decorated officer, you know,' he added, hoping that pulling such rank might shut the man up. The balloonist gestured apologetically.

'In that case, Officer, would you like me to take you lower? You're bound to get a better view then.'

'That would be superb, *merci*.'

August looked down again. Now he could see the maze perfectly from above. The outer walls were like a tangled wild shell, built deliberately high enough to conceal the meticulous cultivation within. It was an ornate and beautiful depiction of the Tree of Life in hedgerow. The ten circles joined by straight paths all in perfect proportion, all of them containing a circle of blue-grey gravel – except for the second sephirot in the middle trunk, one up from the bottom, the sephirot Yesod, which had a circle of green in the middle. Yesod. He sounded the name out in his mind, feeling the leaves of the anise and mandrake he had hidden in his pocket. *Nine blind grey eyes staring up at me, with one living green one. But why wasn't any of it visible from outside of the maze. It really was a hidden symbol, decipherable only from above as if God himself were to be the only witness.* For some inexplicable reason, August found this terrifying. Quickly, he fired off a series of photographs, snapping the maze first in its entirety then in stages as they descended toward it. The balloonist leaned over beside him.

'Crazy, eh? Why have a secret garden no one can see? Some folk have noodles for brains. But not me,' he confided.

August sped along the bank of the Rhône on the boulevard Saint-Lazare. Although it had begun to cloud over and the sun was sinking behind the island of Bagatelle, there were still small fishing boats and speedboats on the river. He swung left into rue Banasterie, now roaring towards the old city centre, Izarra's arms wrapped tightly around his waist, the camera and the herb safely in his satchel. The cathedral bells were tolling four o'clock, the schools were emptying

and the locals, festive in their summer clothes, had started to
stroll home from work. There was a deceptive air of normalcy about the city, the faintly festive ambience of day's
end, and waiters had started to set out the café tables on the
squares for the evening diners. As much as August would
have loved to have stopped at one of the cafés and sat and
drank, he dared not succumb to this false sense of security.
With the warmth of Izarra's body pressed against him, it was
easy to imagine another life, that they were just a local
French couple returning from a day out in the country, the
scent of crushed grass still lingering on their clothes.

He drove past the old Palace of the Popes, then glanced
into his side mirror at a red Citroën that had been following
him for the past ten minutes. He turned sharply into a side
lane to lose the car. The motorcycle bounced over the cobblestones, then out into another square that was filled with a
group of religious pilgrims; Italians, mainly, being ushered
around by several priests. In the centre of the square a
merry-go-round spun slowly, the painted horses moving up
and down, each with its own small rider screaming in pleasure atop it. August navigated his way through the milling
crowd and street carts, narrowly missing one man pushing an
ice-cream cart. Ignoring the man's shouts, August checked
his mirror again. It had worked – he'd lost the tail. He
checked his watch. He still had over an hour, so he swung
the motorcycle around and headed towards the rue Victor
Hugo.

18

L'Hôtel de Pont was a small place sandwiched between a café and the administrative offices for the Collège J. Vernet. It was an inconspicuous building, the kind of hotel an executive might take his mistress for an afternoon tryst, a place that made a virtue out of discretion, not luxury. August thought it perfect. He parked the motorcycle out of view behind a pissoir.

'What are we doing? I thought we were going back to Edouard's?' Izarra looked up at him, perplexed. Avoiding a direct answer, he pressed the satchel with the herbs and his camera into her hand.

'Listen, I want you to walk to the next square and wait for me at a café. I'll be an hour, no longer.'

'No, I stay with you.'

'Izarra, I have some business. It won't be safe.'

'So you think I'm a coward? I come with you.' Her lower lip was jutting out in that determined way he'd learned meant there was no point in arguing with her. *Okay, have it your way, but I will not be responsible if you get hurt, I will not.*

'Okay, if you insist, but we play by my rules. You do exactly what I say, understand?'

She nodded reluctantly. He started striding towards the hotel trying not to let his irritation show, Izarra now running to catch up.

'But what are we doing?'

'You'll see. It's an old Bostonian hunting trick, a way of flushing out the rabbit.'

'Rabbit? Huh! You should try hunting wild boar.'

'Well, let's just see what we flush out. After all that's the objective of the game.'

August pushed his way through the glass door into the hotel and Izarra followed silently. The lobby was small, chintzy in decoration, with a panorama of Gay Paree along one wall, a faded red velvet chaise longue and low wooden coffee table, a balding middle-aged man squeezed into a tight suit sitting awkwardly at one end of the chaise, radiating embarrassment as if he were being kept waiting by some woman sadistic in her tardiness. Edouard stood at the counter, talking quietly to the proprietor behind the desk. They both turned as the two walked in. As August and Izarra approached them, Edouard smiled while the proprietor, a sober ruddy-faced man of about fifty, held out two sets of keys.

'What I don't know cannot kill me,' the proprietor told him in French, shrugging.

Without a word August took the keys, then turned to Edouard, who handed him an envelope.

'I'll meet you back at the printing press at seven,' August murmured. 'Until then you should disappear.' He headed to the elevator. After a questioning glance at the two men, Izarra turned on her heels to follow him.

The proprietor leaned towards Edouard. 'You didn't tell me he was a soldier?'

'He's not, at least not of that uniform.'

'In or out of uniform, a man like that will always have

women,' the proprietor conceded, ruefully, at which Edouard could only grunt.

Inside the tiny elevator August tore open the envelope. Inside was the fake passport, the fake receipt for a passage on a ship called *La Veuve Joyeuse* bound for Port Said from Marseille, and a map of Marseille. He flicked through the passport – it appeared authentic enough, and he didn't recognise the intense black-haired moustached man staring up from the page as himself. *The perfect forgery*. Satisfied, he tucked it into his back pocket.

'Edouard, you're a genius,' he said, quietly.

Izarra glanced nervously at the documents. 'You planning to abandon me?'

'Watch and learn.'

The elevator shuddered to a halt on the third floor, the doors opened and August pulled back the iron safety grid. Now he realised the lobby was in fact the most palatial part of the hotel. The narrow and claustrophobic corridor, painted a hospital green, had no such pretensions. It was lit by a blinking light, and at one end, August noticed, had a small service cupboard. He checked the tags on the keys – rooms fifteen and sixteen.

'C'mon.' He headed towards the service cupboard, picked the lock and within three minutes had handed Izarra a cleaner's white coat and a vacuum cleaner.

'We haven't got much time,' he told her. She took the coat, then wheeled the vacuum cleaner obediently behind him as he made his way to room fifteen.

He switched on the lights and the room spluttered into a dreary palette of browns and maroon. The double bed with an embroidered bedspread that had seen better days dominated the room. A small chest of drawers with a mirror stand sat squeezed against the wall while a framed poster of *Le déjeuner sur l'herbe* hung on the opposite wall – a misguided attempt to bring some colour into the room. August walked over to the window and dragged the curtains back. Outside was a tiny balcony, just enough space for a man to stand. He pulled open the French doors and stepped out. As he had predicted the balcony for room sixteen was right next-door – less than a foot away.

Climbing over the iron railing, he took care not to look down at the street, a staggering four flights down, and swung his leg over the balcony of room sixteen, the satchel over his shoulder. Once there, he opened those French windows and placed the satchel on the bed then let himself out of the hotel door and rejoined Izarra in room fifteen.

He threw the bedspread back. 'Get into the cleaner's coat and tie your hair back,' he ordered. While she slipped the coat on he got into the bed fully dressed and rolled around in the sheets until they looked sufficiently well used. He then went to the small shaving bowl, poured some water from the china jug beside it, made it cloudy with soap and splashed it about a bit. He took off one of his socks and left it tossed on the threadbare carpet. Outside, the cathedral bells rang a single peal indicating it was half-past five.

'We haven't got much time – they'll be coming for me at six.'

'They know where you are!'

'They think they know where I am. All I'm asking is for you to keep your nerve. You're the chambermaid. You will be vacuuming the corridor. If anyone talks to you, you don't understand a word of French, understand? You might recognise them, but they won't recognise you. Believe me, in that uniform you're less than wallpaper.'

'I understand, where will you be?'

'Watching from the balcony.'

'But they'll find you.'

'Don't worry, they won't.' He checked his watch. Now they had less than fifteen minutes. Reaching into his pocket, he placed the receipt for the ship's passage to Port Said on the side table by the bed and the map for Marseille beside it, then he put a couple of the pillows under the bed cover so it looked as if a man might still be asleep under the quilt.

'Okay, time for you to start vacuuming. Start at the far end of the corridor. Don't look directly at the men when they arrive. Keep your eyes down until you're sure they're not looking at you. Concentrate on the job as if you're irritated and just want to get finished as soon as possible. When you're sure they've left and are not coming back, join me in room sixteen. Oh, and lock this door behind you.'

He climbed back out onto the balcony and drew the curtains, leaving just a small gap through which he could see the room, then pulled shut the French doors.

The vacuum cleaner was upright and had a light shining in its base reminding Izarra of some curious growling one-eyed monster, as she pushed the heavy machine backwards and forwards across the corridor carpet, the thumping of her heart feeling as if it were eclipsing even the roar of the machine. Behind her there came the rattle of the steel cage of the elevator as it arrived on her floor. Someone pulled open the gate with a bang and a silent menace rolled out of the lift and down the corridor. Through the corner of her eye, Izarra watched two heavy-set men who followed – they were not the same two who had raided August's room in Paris.

Through the crack in the curtain August watched as the door opened slowly. Immediately, the long snout of a revolver fitted with a silencer appeared around the door, and he heard the thud of two rounds fired into the shape under the bed cover. August winced; it was as if he could feel the vibration of the impact through the floor of the balcony.

Fuck you, Malcolm, you've just had me killed, you bastard.

He tried pushing the emotion down, down through his feet, as if pushing the actual event of the shooting back into the minute before, into the moment when there was still a modicum of trust left in the friendship. *Now I'm dead. No entry, no attempt at interrogation, no effort to gain information. They don't want me, they want my corpse.* The drive to beat them, to survive rose in him like a huge anger.

Just then the two men slipped into the room, legs bent, guns raised ready to fire at any sound. Professionals, August noted – this wasn't Interpol. These were trained mercenaries, hired killers and they looked like CIA. *Who are they? Tyson would want me alive. Who are these guys and how is MI5 involved?* One man, squat, muscular, hair shorn tight against his skull like the fur of a predator, had found the receipt of the ship's passage. He scanned it then handed it silently to his partner, while he picked up the map of Marseille, no doubt searching for a marked destination. Meanwhile, the other assassin had moved to the sideboard, his finger running across the splashed water around the base of the shaving bowl. A minute later he turned towards the window curtain. That was enough for August – in seconds he was over the balcony and into room sixteen. Izarra was waiting for him, her face grim with tension. They waited until they heard the slam of the door of room fifteen as the men left, and then the clang of the elevator door being pulled shut and the elevator descending. Beside him August could hear Izarra exhaling. 'So now you know you are hunted by wolves, wolves who care only to kill,' she told him.

*

It was dark by the time they reached the house. As August turned the motorcycle into the street he noticed a man standing opposite, looking over at the printing press. Not willing to take any chances, August drove straight past him and into the side lane and pulled up beside the drain cover.

'Why did you do that?' Izarra asked, as she climbed off the motorcycle.

'The building's being watched.'

He pulled a tyre iron out of the motorcycle's basket, then levered up the manhole cover. Izarra, clutching his satchel, climbed down the ladder below and August followed, only after checking the lane was still empty and pulling the manhole cover over.

'What did he look like?' Edouard stood in the centre of the cellar, coffee pot in hand.

'Small, thin, swarthy. Like he might have been sleeping on the streets,' August answered, as he carefully placed the satchel on the table.

'So no relation to the thugs who visited you earlier?'

'None. This guy doesn't look like a professional of any kind.'

'Well, he's not there now. Hopefully, he was just some local kid hanging around for a job, maybe at the garage.'

'Maybe.' August paced the room. 'Are you sure no one can see us from the street?'

'Positive. But maybe we move you tomorrow, just to be on the safe side.' Edouard watched August thoughtfully as he unloaded the camera.

'So, was your research trip successful?' he asked, before pouring the coffee. August glanced up. He wanted to tell Edouard more but for the Frenchman's own safety the less he knew the better. Yet without Jimmy as a sounding board,

August yearned to run his strategy by someone who'd worked in both espionage and underground. The sense of urgency and of always having to be one step ahead of his pursuers weighed him down. It was a lonely feeling.

'Perhaps. I'll know when I've developed these, but in other ways I don't know yet. It's like fishing. I have the bait dangling out there but I'm not sure yet whether I have a nibble. The line twitches and then it doesn't. Trouble is, this fish is just as likely to haul me into the water before I haul him out.'

'And the fish?'

'He's not a fish, he's a shark.' Izarra unbuckled her jacket and pulled her revolver out of the pocket. She unlocked the safety catch and emptied the barrel with professional ease, then placed the gun on the table. August watched bemused. He hadn't even realised she'd taken the revolver with her for the trip. She was proving to be a worthy companion. Catching her gaze, he ignored the caution in her eyes and decided he owed Edouard his trust.

'There was a US operative working with Jimmy in 1945. He betrayed Jimmy and a group of Basque fighters they were training up. He wants something I have and I want him. The complication is that he still works for the CIA and he's set me up as a target. They think I killed Jimmy for some kind of information, maybe to do with the KGB.'

Edouard whistled. 'You really have stumbled in the shit.'

'It was this man who murdered my sister,' Izarra interjected, her voice intense with hatred. Edouard looked from one to the other. Suddenly he felt old, too comfortable in the little world he'd spun for himself since the war. The sense there was something bigger to strive for, something more grand and far-reaching swept through him. For a moment he envied them the adventure. 'And how are you going to catch this shark?'

'What I am investigating is like an ancient puzzle, the secret of which he has already killed for, many times over. I solve the puzzle, then he will come to kill me for the answer.'

'Only we kill him,' Izarra added, passionately.

'I prefer the idea of bringing him to justice,' August insisted.

'Such evil is beyond justice. Besides, he is not the only one following you. There is the *bruja*, the one that turned up at Irumendi.'

August glaced sharply over at Izarra. Did she really believe in witches? It was a disturbing thought. He turned back to Edouard. 'She's right. I have another nemesis after me. She could be Interpol, MI5, I just don't know.'

'No, I don't think so,' Izarra answered, thoughtfully, busy cleaning her gun. 'I think she is either freelance or independent – or working with him. Either way, she's pure evil, like him.'

'I don't believe in pure evil. Everyone has an agenda, a moral compass,' August argued back.

'*¡Basta!* You are a romantic, weak.' She replaced the bullets and cocked the gun. 'I will have to kill him myself.'

Appalled, August stared at her. 'You will do no such thing. Here you are under my command, you understand? We work together or not at all.'

'This is not the army! I have my own agenda!'

'We work together, Izarra.' August could barely contain his anger. He was conflicted. Part of him would like to kill Tyson, but he also thought he should stand trial, and even more disturbing was how beautiful Izarra looked flushed and enraged. His attraction to her compounded his annoyance.

Now both of them were glaring at each other. Sighing, Edouard stood up and placed an arm on each of their shoulders.

'*Oh l'amour, l'amour,*' he sighed, dramatically, a comment

that made both Izarra and August back away instantly with embarrassment.

'I told you before we're not lovers,' August insisted.

'No, of course not,' Edouard said, soothingly, then began walking them over to the small table where the coffee sat waiting with a couple of baguettes. 'One thing I have learned to understand in a life that is a little longer than yours, is that what we call evil is when a man lacks morality altogether. Such an individual cares for no one but himself. This is not malice but a handicap, like being blind or deaf – a profound lack of empathy. Such individuals are born not made and they are the most dangerous of all. They are not afraid of death, their own or anybody else's. They simply do not care. When such a man lacks vision, he makes a great mercenary, but when he has vision he will become a great dictator or fanatic, or possibly start simply murdering, because he discovers it elevates a certain emotional flatness. He discovers that it gives him pleasure.' Edouard sat them both down at the table. 'I have had the misfortune to have known such men in Spain, in occupied France, as I'm sure you have, August. Every war has them. It provides a legitimacy for such behaviour, gives such monsters a place in society they do not merit.'

'So you do believe in evil?' Izarra interjected. Edouard chuckled, putting his hand over hers. 'I do, my dear. I think, for whatever perverse reason, it is something nature throws back at us, with each new generation, with each new war. Perhaps such men are born for a purpose, to spill a little blood, to show us what base clay we spring from.'

'And you think we should kill him?' Izarra concluded, triumphantly.

'*Bien sûr, ma chérie*, if he doesn't kill you first,' Edouard replied, then held up the sugar bowl. '*Du sucre?*'

*

The photographic paper floated on the surface of the developing fluid for a moment, like a leaf on a pond then sank slowly as the clear liquid eased its way over the top until the photo sank to the bottom of the shallow tray. August plucked it out with a pair of tongs and slipped it into the stop bath for a minute to make sure the image didn't fade in time.

'Are you okay in there, Monsieur Iron?' Edouard's wife, a friendly middle-aged woman whose bourgeois demeanour August did not doubt hid both a political ferocity and a loyalty that would be formidable to cross, enquired through the darkroom door. He looked up from the tank, his profile hawkish and sinister in the infrared light. Madame Coutes's use of his *nom de guerre* in French made him smile. Edouard had introduced him as Mr Joe Iron, a visiting party member from England who needed to develop some photographs for a Communist magazine back in London. Impressed, she had been most obliging.

'I'm fine, Madame Coutes. It's a well-organised darkroom,' he yelled back, careful not to bump his head on the low ceiling. He pulled the photograph out of the stop bath then slipped it into the fixer tray. The compact darkroom was really a large cupboard situated under the stairs of their house. Everything he needed hung from the wall, neatly labelled. It was the work den of the obsessive compulsive and as cosy as a womb. Smiling to himself, August wondered about the Coutes's love life. Such control did not bode well. But he remembered how Edouard's extreme adherence to discipline had kept both him and his troops sane in the face of sheer chaos – perhaps the Frenchman had found his natural mate. Behind August a timer pinged three minutes and using the tongs he lifted the photograph out, dipped it into a tray of water to clean it, then shook off the water and pinned it up to dry with a wooden peg Madame Coutes thoughtfully kept in a white cloth bag marked for the purpose. He sat down at the small workbench and in the netherworld of the infrared light examined the clues he had spread out before him: a photograph of the first maze – the Tree of Life clearly visible as a whole aerial pattern. In the photograph the sephirot Malkuth, or 'Kingdom', at the base of the tree, the first one he discovered that was planted, was a dark circle against the other unplanted sephiroth, which were all blank, flat gravelled circles. The contrast between the empty beds and the planted one was dramatic, but what did it mean? The plants he'd picked from the first maze were pinned to the back of the photograph. Lily and vervain. He stood and unpegged the drying photograph he'd just developed, then laid it flat beside the first photograph. Now it was clear that in the second maze it was, as he'd seen from the hot air balloon, the second sephirot Yesod that had been planted, this time with anise and mandrake root. But what was the connection with the first maze, the herbs and the chronicle? He remembered from his reference books back in London that the Spaniards used to think that, if eaten, lily petals could restore a person who had been transformed into a beast to a human, while vervain was considered a witch's herb, used to enhance dreaming. As for those found in the second maze in the sephirot Yesod, anise was used in clairvoyance and for psychic protection, whereas the mandrake root was a common ingredient in magical practices.

What was the alchemist Shimon Ruiz de Luna trying to communicate through such symbolism?

Increasingly, August felt there was a message to be discovered in linking the mazes together, one written in code that if deciphered would tell him where Elazar ibn Yehuda's great mystery lay. But the alchemist had not made it easy. There was the symbolism of the sephiroth within each planting and then the symbolism of the herbs themselves. Layers of meaning that when woven together gave one clear direction; the question was how to interpret the symbols. He looked back at the anise and vervain. Psychic powers and dreaming – could these be the connection? Was Shimon trying to tell him that Elazar ibn Yehuda's great treasure was metaphysical? If so why would a man like Tyson want it so much? What kind of power did it hold to haunt so many people over the aeons? August shivered – a chill had swept in from under the door.

§

Shimon held up the sprig of dried vervain against the flickering flame of the lantern. The heat warming the crinkled leaves released a strong lemony scent. He breathed in then closed his eyes, trying to remember. He could not, but he noticed, with his eyes still shut, the faint scent of orange blossom and jasmine, the rich incense that burned in his family's house, the thick Turkish carpet under his bare feet and when he opened his eyes his father's ghost, smiling and oblivious to its own ephemeral presence, stood before him, those large olive-skinned hands Shimon remembered so well resting on the desk.

'Yesod, Foundation, Shimon, that is the most important sephirot. You must remember my teachings. These will help you understand the words underneath Elazar ibn Yehuda's great secret wisdom. You remember the legacy of your forefathers, the hidden meaning of the Book of Exodus, Ezekiel's vision and the Four Worlds that descend from Kether, the Crown, each more complicated by governing laws of the universe, each a further removal from the Divine presence. The first level we link to fire is the realm around

Kether and embodies the will of man – the calling. Remember, Shimon, this I have taught you. The second realm is that of the intellect and is associated with the element Air – this is the Divine creation. The third realm, the realm of Water, is emotion and how it expresses itself in the ebb and flow of forms – the Divine ... forming ...'

And here, Shimon, forgetting his father was dead entirely, leaped up as eagerly as he had when he was twelve in that grand study in Córdoba, the shelves piled high with rolled scrolls and leather-bound books.

'I remember! Abba, the fourth realm, in which the sephirot Malkuth, Foundation, exists, is the realm of Action, it is of the Earth, and symbolises the Divine and his making.'

'So, was that so difficult?' said his father. 'Elazar ibn Yehuda's chronicle is both an allegory and a journey. His journey was his lightning bolt through the ten spiritual stations, the sephiroth, leading to his perfect unification with the Divine. It destroyed him as it will destroy you, but, child, life is death and death is life, we are reborn as light and we die as light.'

Outside, Shimon could now hear Uxue's footfall on the narrow stairs of the inn. 'One minute, Uxue,' he called, but by the time he turned back his father's ghost had vanished. He glanced down at the blank sheet of parchment then lifted up his drawing square. He had an idea, a notion of perfect concealment, and one that could talk through the very elements themselves across the centuries. That would be his legacy, Shimon Ruiz de Luna's message to the future.

§

The sound of scraping and footsteps above him woke August instantly. For a second he lay there not knowing where he was before the familiarity of the cellar, the ceiling only inches above him came flooding back. He heard a loud thump, followed by a scurry of footfall. August reached for the Mauser under his pillow.

'Did you hear that?' Izarra whispered up from the bunk beneath.

'Yes.' August kept his voice low and swung his legs from under the cover and slipped down from the bed. He could hear Izarra cocking her own gun as she, too, climbed out from the bunk, the white of her shirt catching the dim light filtering in from the crack in the trapdoor above them. August gestured for her to keep quiet then follow him as he began up the ladder. Above them he could hear the sound of somebody creeping across the creaky floorboards.

August lifted the trapdoor a sliver, just enough to peer around the printing press. In the stripe of streetlight falling across the floor he could see a small slim figure standing over a set of office drawers at the far end of the room, rifling through them furiously, his back to August. He looked back down the ladder to Izarra and gave her a quick nod, both of them tensing in expectation. She nodded back, ready for anything. He swung the trapdoor open as quietly as he could and with his Mauser trained on the intruder climbed out. The intruder, absorbed by his task, noticed nothing. Izarra followed, gun in hand.

They both crept silently towards the intruder, August in socks, Izarra in bare feet. When they were about a couple of metres away, Izarra accidentally knocked a discarded ink roller with her foot. The intruder swung around and sprang at August, pushing him down to the ground. The two men rolled and wrestled on the floor, but the intruder, who August now recognised as the man he'd seen loitering in the lane earlier that day, was physically much slighter. August managed to pin him to the ground and a second later Izarra's gun was at the man's temple.

'Don't shoot, don't shoot, I'm harmless!' he yelled out in English, in a broad cockney accent, much to August's amazement. Now he could see the man clearly. He looked young, not much more than twenty – a thin, narrow-skulled youth, with large terrified black eyes, aquiline features and a week's growth of beard. Wearing an old belted overcoat that looked too big for him, he cowered against the floor. August hauled him to his feet then pushed him down into a chair, while Izarra kept her gun trained on him.

'Who the hell are you?' August demanded.

'Jacob Cohen, from Stepney, don't hurt me, I didn't mean you no harm! I didn't think anyone was here. I was just after some information!'

August exchanged glances with Izarra. 'What kind?'

The youth swallowed, his Adam's apple bobbing in a scrawny neck. 'Can't say unless I know who you are first?'

'Listen, kid, I'm the one with the gun. Who sent you?' August demanded.

'No one sent me.'

'C'mon, you've been watching this place for a day.'

Izarra pressed her barrel against the man's temple.

'I work solo!' he squeaked.

'I don't think so. I think you've been following us for a while. I think you killed a close friend of mine back in Paris.' August stepped forward threateningly.

'I didn't kill Jimmy!'

'So you do know Jimmy.' August tilted the lamp so that it illuminated the young man's face and eyes; he didn't look like he was acting and certainly from the incompetent way he'd tackled August, he appeared to have had no military or police training. 'Damien Tyson, does that name mean anything to you?'

Cohen averted his eyes; it was obvious he knew something.

'Listen, you can trust me!' he began to argue, hysterically. 'Do I look like a trained killer? Blimey, I can't even kill the chicken me mum brings back from the market. I'm probably looking for the same thing you are.'

'Which is what?'

'I'm a Nazi hunter working solo, all right? I went to see Jimmy because he had information I needed. We're on the same side. But this business of having a gun pointing at me head is making me nervous, I've only got one brain and they tell me it's a good one.'

'Stand up,' August ordered and the young man stood as August patted him down. He was clean. 'It's okay, Izarra, time to put the guns away.'

Izarra lowered her revolver.

'Thank God for that.' Cohen crumpled with relief, then turned to August. 'Got a fag?'

August offered him a cigarette and he took it gratefully, then lit up from August's Zippo. He inhaled deeply and immediately started coughing, stopping only when he'd thumped his own chest. 'American?'

'Once upon a time. So, Jacob—'

'Jacob to you. Back home they call me Big Jacov,' he snapped. August couldn't help smiling – at five-foot-nothing, Big Jacov looked more like a boy than a man.

'So, Jacob, what do you know about Tyson? And don't make me ask Izarra to get her gun out again.'

Cohen shivered, then looked around the room. 'Listen, I'm 'appy to talk, but I've been standing out there in the freezing cold for hours. Is there anywhere I can thaw out?'

*

Now down in the cellar, cradling a mug of hot coffee Izarra had made for him, Jacob rocked backwards and forwards as he spoke, as if the movement were somehow anchoring the intensity of his diatribe. August had the impression that if he stopped rocking, he would be propelled out of the chair by his own pent-up energy.

'I've been hunting Nazis since I realised no one else was going to do it. Post-war governments have short memories. One day a man's a war criminal, the next he's a bureaucrat cash-up and squeaky clean. Me, I remember. Some things can't be forgotten. You could say – not that I will – that the Allies don't give a monkey's about the victims of war, especially the four-by-twos, which is my tribe.'

'What are you, a child detective?' August cracked. Izarra laughed, while Jacob stayed grim-faced.

'What I am is a maverick, paid by no one, disliked by most. I hold up the mirror no one likes looking in.' It was obvious he was insulted by their laughter and August couldn't help respecting the strength of his convictions.

The three of them were huddling around the potbelly stove; Jacob in a plain wooden chair, Izarra with her knees and legs now tucked up an old woollen jumper, August's lanky legs astride a stool. 'So Jimmy put you onto Tyson?' August asked.

'Not at first. I kept running across this German codename, Der Pfarrer – "The Priest" – in Russian transcripts of interviews of arrested SS officers recorded in the days following the fall of Berlin. One of these interviewees indicated that the Priest might have been an American, a Nazi sympathiser working within the US war machine. That's where Jimmy came in. I met him in Paris when I was on the trail of a Vichy collaborator. He was playing at a club I'd gone to, we were introduced and got talking. When Jimmy told me that he'd worked for the OSS, I mentioned the Priest, hoping he'd have some leads.'

'Der Pfarrer is Tyson?'

'I think so, and I'll tell you this much, he is definitely one of the brokers behind the US pact with Franco. I believe Tyson is close to a Basque exile rumoured to be working for the Americans – Jesús María de Galíndez. The rumour is that the US is going to sign with Franco in Madrid in September and it's worth billions. Ugly, it's got my uncle, a paid-up member of the party, most upset.' Jacob looked over at Izarra for her reaction. She spat on the ground, cursing Franco in Euskara.

'We have been betrayed by everyone. First the Pope with the concordat of the Vatican this month and now this. I tell you, next the UN will make Franco a member,' she concluded, passionately.

'Never,' August retorted. He turned back to Jacob. 'We know all about Tyson's involvement with Spain. Tell us something we can use.' August was losing patience – morning was only a couple of hours away and he had a strong sense the safety of the hideout had been compromised. Jacob got up and started pacing, his hands gesturing wildly.

'This sounds crazy, but that codename kept niggling at me. One transcript referred to Der Pfarrer having been paid with antique artefacts instead of hard cash. With Nazi gold taken from all over Europe – from the Iberian Peninsula and from Russia – raided from some of the most influential Jewish families. Kabbalistic artefacts, medieval, a couple were even ancient Egyptian. Now, my German is good but when I saw that I thought it must have been a mistranslation. I mean, what kind of spy gets paid with occult trophies? Not a sane man is what. Then I get this other lead, evidence that Der Pfarrer spent time in England in the early thirties and had been an associate of Aleister Crowley. Spiritual bedfellows, one could say. Finally, eureka, the penny drops.' He looked pleased with his own detective work. 'It's obvious when you think about it – Der Pfarrer is a reference to Tyson's black magic practices. In his mind he *is* the High Priest. Turns out our Mr Tyson or Der Pfarrer to the Huns is—'

'Jester to the Americans,' August cut in, beginning to see a link in Tyson's choice of codenames. He thought about Malcolm Hully – who was playing whom? Until now he'd assumed he'd had the upper hand. Now he wasn't sure. He looked over at Jacob. 'What proof do you have that Tyson played the English too?'

'Nothing substantial yet, just an ugly rumour and one or two unbelievable coincidences. Why, have you heard something?'

Both Izarra and Jacob looked at August questioningly. The queasy feeling he might have endangered them both unwittingly swept over August. 'No, but we're moving out of here as soon as it's daylight.' He felt cornered. He knew all too well how organised MI6 could be in locating people, especially with American help. The bloodied white rose left for him in the hotel room came to mind. Was he being played? If so, why? And who was the woman who had visited Izarra?

Jacob sighed then took a long sip of coffee.

'What you have to understand is that the Priest's been involved with all sorts of black voodoo, all really unkosher. He's been collecting magical artefacts for decades like a saner man might collect stamps. I mean, he really believes. Don't know about you, but that scares me.'

Izarra and August exchanged glances. 'So the Germans exploited this fact?' August ventured, carefully, not yet willing to divulge his own information.

'There's been a link between fascism and black magic for a long time. It's well known that Hitler believed in hogwash like that, and when they liberated Berlin they discovered "black" Tibetan priests that had been housed by the Führer. The Nazi regime was sympathetic to such beliefs, or, should I say, an American double agent with the same beliefs as the Führer would have been attractive to them. Your friend believes there are ways of manipulating people, external ways through the practice of the occult and for a man obsessed by power that's a seductive conviction. You and I might not share such beliefs but that's irrelevant.' Jacob stopped rocking and leaned back in his chair. The cellar was beginning to fill with a faint light, seeping in from the floor above, and there was the sound of a dawn chorus of birds filtering through the blocked-out window. Jacob stared down into his tin mug mournfully. 'My coffee's gone cold.'

Izarra got up and put another small pot of thick black coffee on top of the stove.

'Tell him,' she instructed August, still with her back turned to the two men. She swung around, her face an open book. 'He deserves to know the truth.'

'What truth?' Jacob asked, looking from one to the other. August searched Izarra's face.

'Are you sure?'

She nodded solemnly.

'Izarra knows Tyson from a US black operation training a cell of Basque fighters at the end of the war. A black op that ended in a massacre Tyson ordered. Her sister was the commander of that cell. She died with her men.'

'From a family of six, there are only two of us left – myself and her son,' Izarra said, standing in front of Jacob, and now August could see she had recognised something in Jacob he

himself hadn't seen, something she shared with the slight
youth – a familiar grieving.

'I'm sorry for the death of your sister, I know what it is to
lose your family,' Jacob replied, suddenly older and wiser
than his years. Then he got out of his chair restlessly. 'But
the fact that Tyson ended up running that black op wouldn't
have been a coincidence, he's a cold-blooded calculator –
there would have been something else that brought him to
that village, something linked to his obsession with power
and black magic.'

August and Izarra exchanged glances again. Reading her
expression, August decided to hold back on the information
about the chronicle.

'That might be, but tell me, how did you find us? You said
you'd seen Jimmy in Paris a week ago, so why come to
Avignon?' August ventured, while wondering how much he
could actually confide in Cohen.

'I've been on Tyson's trail since he flew in from
Washington to London about a month ago. I followed him to
Paris. I'd managed to alert Jimmy. I thought he should know
his nemesis was in Europe, then Jimmy gave me a list of
contacts—'

'The same list he gave me – a network of ex-International
Brigadiers – those who survived,' August interjected.

Jacob's face flushed with a sudden revelation. 'I know
who you are,' he told August. 'You're Joe Iron, Joe fucking
Iron.' He grabbed August's hand.

Embarrassed, August stood there, feeling like a fool, while
Jacob pumped his hand up and down vigorously. Izarra
looked on, amused.

'Who is Joe Iron?'

Jacob turned, amazed. 'Who is Joe Iron? You telling me
you don't know who you're sleeping with—'

'Jacob, she's not sleeping with me,' August, further mortified, interrupted, over Jacob's loud, emphatic voice, but the young cockney ignored him.

'He hasn't told you about what he did at Jarama? Or the time he tricked a whole Falangist squadron into marching the wrong way at Quinto? Or the courage he showed at Belchite?'

August looked at Jacob aghast; so Jimmy had told Jacob about the firing squad, that terrible day.

'Enough about Belchite!' He swung back to Izarra. 'Joe Iron was my *nom de guerre*, and you knew I'd fought in the Civil War, the details are not important!' Only when he noticed the shocked faces of the other two he realised he'd lost his temper, something he never allowed himself to do.

'But you were a hero?' Jacob looked perplexed, aggrieved at August's outburst.

'A hero? That war was lost,' August replied, now dangerously calm. Trying to steady himself, he reached up to sweep back his hair, a habit of his – then remembered with a shock that it was now shorn and black. Turning away, he lit a cigarette and took the opportunity to collect himself. He turned to face Jacob, something knocking against the back of his mind.

'You followed him here, didn't you? Tyson's here, isn't he, in Avignon?' As soon as he said the words, August felt the thrill of anticipation – the fish was on the hook, so close.

Jacob glanced nervously over at Izarra, then back at August. 'About two days ago, just after you arrived, then I lost him.'

'You lost him!' August burst out in frustration.

'It's not like tailing a normal man. You get this uncanny feeling he's choosing when he allows himself to be seen and when not. It's like a tease, like he's watching you but without his eyes. When I lost him I panicked, I had this horrible feeling he was now after me and that bloke is worse than a mercenary. Mercenaries killed for money, he kills for pleasure. So I came here. Jimmy promised I'd be safe here.' Jacob was interrupted by the roar of a car outside. They all froze, waiting for the car to pass. Only when the sound of the engine faded did August venture to speak.

'Do you think he's still in Avignon?'

'Without a doubt, something is keeping him hungry, something apart from closing the pact with Franco.'

'Good, he's taken the bait. Now we just have to reel him in.'

Jacob was looking at him curiously, as if he'd just had an epiphany. 'Winthrop, why is that name familiar to me?'

But August had moved to the table where he had his map laid out. 'Let it go.' There were some things he knew he needed to keep from Izarra, if he wanted to retain her trust; Cohen had already exposed too much.

'I never let anything go, that's why I'm good.'

'I said let it go!' August wheeled round, threatening, but Cohen didn't move. He remained defiant. Now August could see why he might be an irritant to so many people.

'Got it. Clarence Winthrop, the American UN representative, any relation?'

August glanced over at Izarra, who was now staring back at him – he had no choice but to be honest.

'He's my father.'

'*Mazel tov*. I'm guessing you were the black sheep of the family, or should I say pink?' Jacob cracked.

'Pink sheep? You have pink sheep in America?' Izarra asked, now totally befuddled by the English banter.

' He's making a joke, Izarra, a bad joke.' August turned to Jacob. 'My father and I haven't talked in years. His previous incarnation as a right-wing republican senator and close buddy of Joe Kennedy aka the Nazi lover was a little hard to swallow.'

'But he could be our only chance.'

'What are you talking about?'

'We have to expose Tyson and alert your father so that the UN can do something to stop the pact from going through.'

'Not a hope in hell. He disowned me years ago and I wouldn't be surprised if my father was in on the deal.'

But Jacob was lost in concentration. 'But we can use him and get him to help us arrest Tyson for war crimes. That would discredit Tyson and draw more international condemnation towards the defence pact. Just let me talk to him?'

'Not a good idea. You're definitely not one of Senator Winthrop's people, if you understand me.' August couldn't bring himself to use the word "anti-Semitic", but the look on Jacob's face told him he'd got the message.

'August, you have to try. Listen, the general assembly is sitting in a few weeks in Geneva and I know Tyson is one of the American delegates who will represent the case to instate Spain as a member. This could be our chance!' Jacob's hands moved through the air emphatically.

'But I don't want Tyson to stand trial and serve a sentence. I want him dead.' Izarra was adamant.

'Well, that could be arranged as well,' Jacob offered.

'Stop it. Both of you.' Exasperated, August thumped the table. 'Is there anything concrete on Tyson? So far we haven't actually got any witnesses to the massacre. Jimmy might have testified but he's dead.'

'There's Gabirel,' Izarra suggested, tentatively.

'He was seven at the time; the court could dismiss it as fiction. We need more, something official that places Tyson there.'

'I've heard there's a classified file on Tyson, one that might contain real evidence of his involvement in the massacre,' Jacob interjected.

'How do you know that?' *Who is this guy? How come he's so well informed? How much does he really know about me?* August's sense of the clandestine began to prickle. 'Befriend everyone, trust no one' – it was one of the first things they'd taught him in training for espionage work. Jacob met his gaze openly and did not flinch.

'There are people who dislike him within the CIA, and besides,' said Jacob, grinning cheekily, 'not everyone disapproves of my covert activities.'

August studied the slight youth before him, then, taking a leap of faith, decided to trust him. 'I found mention of the black op and an operative codename Jester in a file in the American Embassy,'August said, slowly and clearly. 'The only way the CIA would have anything is if they've been tracking him since the war. But I have contacts within MI5.'

'So does Tyson,' Jacob added. 'I have evidence the British bribed some of Franco's generals to dissuade them from joining forces with Hitler during the Second World War. There was mention of a US operative with fluent Spanish who was in with a couple of Franco's generals, codename Magus.'

'So Magus was his English codename?' August said, before Izarra interjected.

'And you think the Jester, Der Pfarrer and Magus are all the same man?' She leaned forward.

'Possibly. Tyson played everyone off against each other; I suspect it made him feel powerful, superior. August, if you really want to trap him, you have to have something he wants. Politics and espionage is only the top game; there's another game Tyson is playing on an occult level – that's the one he really cares about.'

August glanced over at Izarra and she nodded almost imperceptibly. He stood. 'I have something I have to show you.'

19

The photographs of the two mazes as well as the chronicle were spread on the table like pieces of an obscure puzzle. The other two watched in silence as August laid out the pages of his transcription of Shimon Ruiz de Luna's chronicle.

'The text is allegorical. It is impossible to work out what the mazes mean, which I'm beginning to think Shimon had built at each location as a means to both conceal and represent, like a secret code. I haven't had time yet to translate all the chronicle but I know there are others to explore and I suspect the answer will appear when images of them are put together.'

Jacob picked up the chronicle reverently. Lifting it to his face, he sniffed at the leather, then caressed the embossed cover, then murmured a blessing in Hebrew. Feeling as if he were intruding, August looked away for a moment.

'Amazing to think this is over three hundred years old,' Jacob commented, handing back the book.

'Written in 1609, four years before Shimon's execution, but he was following a far older book.' August wrapped it carefully up in the canvas bag.

'Hitler managed to burn more of our history in twelve years than all the other zealots from the time of the Romans, and yet this little diary survived.'

Izarra smiled. 'My family have been the guardians of the chronicle since Shimon Ruiz de Luna entrusted it to his Basque wife. It has not once fallen into hostile hands.'

'On behalf of my people I thank you,' said Jacob and he gave a little bow, which delighted Izarra. Cohen turned back to August's transcribed notes. 'You know, in my religion a book – when it contains the name of God – is never destroyed, it is always buried like a man would be. This chronicle would be considered holy. As for the mazes, the designs are of the Tree of the Sephiroth, more commonly known as the Tree of Life. In kabbalistic and occult terms, this is literally a depiction of the map of creation. Both kabbalists and members of the occult believe spiritual beings can descend the tree to Earth just as human beings in an advanced state of meditation can zigzag up the tree to the top sephirot Kether and move into a state of enlightenment.'

'So I believe, but why make a physical manifestation of a spiritual map?'

'Like you suggested, perhaps because it's the perfect code, or messenger.' Jacob pointed to the top sephirot in the photograph of the Avignon maze then wrote a Hebrew letter down – 'Kether' – 'Crown'. 'This is a spiritual attribute above consciousness.' He pointed to the next one to the right and wrote the Hebrew name down beside it.

'This is "Chokmah", "Wisdom". This is also considered to be a spiritual state that floats above consciousness. Then we move down the tree into the next plane, which is considered conscious intellect. Here we have Binah, Understanding; and Chesed, Kindness; Geburah, Severity; and finally Tiphareth, Beauty. The lowest four sephiroth are considered to be conscious emotions – Netzach,Victory; Hod, Splendour; Yesod, Foundation; and finally Malkuth, Kingdom, from which all action springs. The sephiroth themselves are like spiritual attributes through which God, in Jewish mysticism known as Ein Sof – 'The Infinite' – reveals himself as he continues to create the physical and higher metaphysical realms or worlds.'

'How do you know so much?' Izarra asked.

'My *opa*, my grandfather, insisted I knew the basics of the Tree of Life, just as his father had before him. Hebrew was my first language back in Germany.'

'You're German?'

'I was sent to England in 1938 on the Kindertransport. I was nine. I never saw my parents again. They perished, along with my grandfather, in the camps.' To August and Izarra's surprise, Jacob's voice now dropped into a thick Berlin accent. '"*Was mich nicht umbringt, macht mich stärker.*"' Nietzsche, somebody else my grandfather admired. Life has made me a chameleon; it was the only way to survive.'

'Now I understand why you might be so driven to hunt down Nazis,' Izarra observed, quietly.

'Yeah, well, I'm a persistent sod and it keeps me off the streets, London streets, that is,' Jacob cracked back, reverting to the deceptively cheerful cockney façade. He picked up the photograph of the Basque maze. 'It's interesting that only the Malkuth is planted in this one, the first Shimon mentions, right?'

'Correct.'

'Because that suggests by entering the first maze you have begun something – brought into action – intentionally or otherwise, a journey you cannot stop. This could be spiritual, psychological or physical. The beginning of an unravelling.' Jacob looked over at August and August had the uncanny feeling that Jacob could read a lot more of his psychology than he was comfortable with. Averting his gaze, he glanced at the photograph of the first maze. The planted sephirot seemed to look back at him defiantly. *Was that unravelling you, Charlie? Waiting for me behind that wall of hedgerow? What were you trying to tell me? That I can't deny you any longer?*

'But I'm afraid I can't help you with the symbolism of the herbs, I know nothing about nature.' Jacob's voice brought him back to the cellar.

'There are the magical aspects of the Tree of Life. Didn't Crowley use it in his rituals?' August asked, remembering something he'd read once.

'I have heard this, but all that stuff is mumbo-jumbo to me. But I can see why Tyson would be obsessed with the chronicle.'

'What I don't understand is why these particular mazes are mentioned in the chronicle with only a single sephirot planted each time?'

'The paths you take to reach the Kether are as significant as the sephiroth themselves, more so,' Jacob replied. 'It could be that Shimon is indicating that he has discovered the most direct path possible to Ein Sof. The Hebrew translation is 'without end' – this is a manifestation of God, a state of grace, to be one with the Infinite. This could be another key to Elazar ibn Yehuda's great treasure.'

'So Shimon was sending a hidden directive on several levels: transcendental, literal and physical. Like a secret map that if you find it, then follow it, you will go on a spiritual odyssey that eventually leads to a material treasure,' August elaborated.

'How do you know the treasure is material? From what you've told me I'm guessing Elazar ibn Yehuda was a great philosopher and most probably a magician in the classical kabbalist sense as well as a great physic. This treasure of his could very well be metaphysical or even a metaphor of some sort,' Jacob suggested.

August stared down at the chronicle, recounting Shimon's words in his mind, the way the Spaniard had described how the treasure would be liberating for mankind in some way, how Shimon's father had emphasised to his son that it could save the family. It hadn't sounded like the description of something ethereal or abstract; it had sounded solid, something material you could offer a king. The idea caught at his imagination like a hook – had that been the reason Shimon had gone to England? A perilous trip for both a Jew and a Spaniard. The court account had mentioned Shimon demanded an audience with King James, that he had something to offer the king. Surely such a treasure would be something King James would have been able to use in some fashion – not an abstract philosophy or some nebulous spiritual insight, but a powerful tool.

'No, I don't think it's a metaphor. It's real. Real and potent enough for Shimon Ruiz de Luna to endanger both his wife and his own life. Real enough for Tyson to kill for. There has to be something else about the mazes, something behind the reason he chose the Tree of Life as a design.' Then August remembered the curious Hebrew word inscribed over Brother Dominic Baptise's memorial in the crypt of Saint-Germain-des-Prés, the young monk who had mysteriously vanished researching a clue left by the same philosopher-explorer Shimon Ruiz de Luna had been inspired by. He looked at Jacob.

'Does the word "Da'ath" mean anything to you?'

Jacob studied the photographs, frowning as he concentrated. 'Da'ath?'

'I believe the translation is "knowledge".'

Jacob clapped his hands in excitement. 'You're right. Opa did tell me about Da'ath. It's a hidden sphere – like another sephirot, but invisible.'

Eagerly, Jacob started drawing on a piece of paper, sketching out a rough picture of the Tree of Life. Under the top sephirot Kether he drew another circle. August watched fascinated.

'Da'ath is the hidden sephirot that floats in a whole metaphysical realm of its own. It has huge significance in the occult,' Jacob concluded, triumphantly. He then wrote the Hebrew for the sephirot underneath. August recognised it instantly. A drum of intense excitement began beating in the pit of his stomach. 'I have seen this before, written on a memorial plaque for a monk who disappeared researching the same maze.'

'Dominic Baptise? He really did disappear?' Izarra was almost whispering. August nodded. Jacob leaned forward and rested his hand on August's arm.

'August, you don't have to continue on the physic's journey. There's no shame in stopping now.'

'I can't stop, I don't want to stop.' He picked up the two photographs of the mazes and held them up to the lamplight. 'Besides, there's no evidence Da'ath exists in these mazes.'

'Haven't you got others to explore, when you've deciphered the locations?'

August touched Jacob's drawing of the Tree of Life, his finger resting on Da'ath. In broken pencil strokes it did seem to float above the other sephiroth, a Shangri-La of enlightenment – for good or for evil. Either way, he had to get there before Tyson.

'Come with us, Jacob, we can help each other.'

Jacob shook his head. 'I'm flattered. But I don't plan to go anywhere yet. Go on without me. I'm going to stay back and track Tyson when he follows you.'

'How do you know he will follow us?' Izarra asked.

Jacob held up the chronicle. 'Trust me, Tyson would follow this into hell.' He glanced over at August. 'But then so would you.'

The small stone office in the refectory in the abbey of Saint-Germain-des-Prés was unheated and despite the warmth of the sun falling across the flagstones, Olivia found herself chilled to the core. How much of this was her intense discomfort at being inside a house of Christ and how much of it was genuine cold, she couldn't decide, but she'd had no choice. She studied the young monk sitting before her. He had the smoothness of feature that betrayed a limited emotional experience, as if sheltering in the abbey had preserved an innocent banality to his face. Some might see it as purity, but all Olivia saw was a fear of the world in all its visceral complexity. Stifling her contempt, she took the young monk's hand and stroked it like it was a cat.

'Father, I understand the importance of protecting the knowledge, the ascendance of Father Dominic Baptise is a delicate matter, but it is an ascendance we ...' she paused here, momentarily wondering whether she should elaborate on the nature of the collective she belonged to, then wisely deciding it would be safer just to emphasise there was a collective, 'we, and there are many of us – silently united in this belief – are profoundly committed to. Naturally, we are all curious as to which angel he surrendered his earthly form. But just as important to us, in terms of worship, is the exact location of this miraculous event. I have heard rumour it happened in what we now know as Germany.'

The assistant's face lit up, thrilled to have such a respectful and captive audience. 'Indeed, Madame, it occurred on the outskirts of Hamburg, in the year of 1709, I believe. It has been hard to get an exact date but my research suggests the 31st of October of that year.'

'And you have evidence of the location?'

'Well, now that you mention it.' He turned and pulled out a small drawer of an austere wooden campaign desk, retrieving an old manuscript. He rolled it out carefully, weighing down the opposite corners with two clear paper-weights.

'This is one of several letters from the Archbishop of Hamburg to Father Baptise's abbot Father Bernard de Montfaucon. In this one he tells of the last sighting of Dominic Baptise as being just outside the city of Hamburg, by the bank of the Elbe. Actually there was a witness, a woman described as having auburn hair.' He glanced for a moment at Olivia's own red hair, marvelling at the coincidence, then dismissed the observation as fantastical whimsy. 'But when it came to locating her later to collect evidence to support Baptise's sanctification, she was nowhere to be found.'

Olivia locked eyes with the cleric for a moment. It still disturbed her that a written account existed at all. This wouldn't do at all; she was not a woman to leave clues. She glanced down at one of the paperweights. It was made of glass and heavy, heavy enough to brain a man if necessary.

'May I take a closer look at the manuscript?' she asked, sweetly.

20

The three of them waited as the morning light – a thin bluish square escaping down through the trapdoor – had travelled across the concrete floor like a sinister sundial from another world. That night as August translated, Shimon had finally revealed the next location: Hamburg.

Izarra sat on the edge of her bed, dressed, with her packed bag beside her; Jacob, a little less gaunt in the face after four hours' sleep, his eyes closed, sprawled in the battered armchair, his thin legs thrown across the worn leather like some strangely aged boy in the embrace of an old bear; and August stood statue-like, beneath the trapdoor, staring upwards. He'd been standing there for over forty-five minutes, poised, waiting. It was past seven o'clock and Edouard had not given his usual knock, the signal that it was safe to ascend into the printing press. Now counting the minutes, August turned to Izarra.

'Something's wrong, he should have knocked at six, as arranged.'

Jacob opened his eyes, while Izarra stood, swinging her bag over her shoulder.

'His staff will be here in less than an hour,' she said, softly, August's anxiety reflected in her face. Jacob was already on his feet. August pulled his gun slowly out of his jacket.

'We're going up.'

Something heavy was blocking the trapdoor, a dull leaden weight. August, balancing on the top of the ladder, butted his shoulder up against the wood and pushed. On the other side he could feel something slip, a slight give in the pressure.

'Jacob, give me a hand,' he instructed. Cohen climbed up behind August as close as he could and together they heaved against the trapdoor. Again, it felt as if something rolled slightly but not enough to clear the hatch completely. The two men fell back.

'Okay, on the count of three. One, two, three,' August commanded, and they pushed with all their strength. The weight rolled away and the trapdoor suddenly swung open, throwing them into the light of the floor above. August was the first to climb through.

Edouard's half-naked body lay there, his jacket and shirt torn off, his neck twisted at an unnatural angle, his face squashed against the floor, his eyes wide open and milky, staring across the room with almost an aggrieved expression. The red mark of a garrotte ringed his neck.

'Oh no, please God, not again.' August, horrified at the sight that met his eyes, climbed out and kneeled beside Edouard's body. The others followed in shocked silence.

August rolled the body over, revealing the bare chest and forehead; odd-looking symbols had been scrawled in lipstick across his body and forehead.

'He must have died hiding the trapdoor from his killer,' said Jacob, kneeling down next to August.

It was hard to imagine how, but he had.

'He died saving us.' August closed the corpse's eyes, then stood, a vision of Edouard playing before his eyes, sixteen years earlier, laughing and getting drunk with August in a field in Aragon; a black-and-white image jerking like a piece of film stuck in a projector gate. He just couldn't link that man – so vibrantly defiant of death, fate and other concepts the Frenchman had always regarded as 'bourgeois abstractions designed to confine the spirit' – with the broken corpse lying before him. 'We should never have come here.'

Izarra put her arms around him. 'He knew the risks, August. For him the fight was not over.' Furious with the absolute waste of it all, August pushed her away.

'You don't understand. He was one of the lucky ones like me – nothing could kill him! Two wars and an occupation, nothing! And now? What about his wife, his sons?' Distraught, August slammed his hand against one of the presses.

'This is not your fault,' Izarra pleaded, grabbing his shoulders. She stared into his eyes, trying to calm him down. 'We have to stay strong, we have to keep moving.' Her stern tone brought him back. He glanced over at Jacob, who was busy examining the body. It lay half on its side, the right hand hidden under the hip.

'So, was it Tyson?'

'I don't think so. The garrotte is a little tidy for his handiwork. Tyson likes to make more mess. Spilt blood is his signature, if you like.'

'What about the signs? They make it look like a ritual killing or sacrifice. Why write the sign for Pluto on someone's forehead?' August gestured towards the red symbol daubed on the corpse's face – the lipstick now bleeding into the white skin. Jacob looked startled, then pointed to another scrawled sign on Edouard's naked left shoulder. 'That one is?' he asked August.

'Saturn.' August then indicated the one written on the right shoulder. 'Aquarius.'

As if he had joined some macabre guessing game, Jacob placed his finger on the symbol written in the centre of a circle in the middle of the corpse's chest. 'And that would be the sun. The next one down – on his stomach – the moon, and on the left hand Mercury, and I'm guessing the right one will be Jupiter.'

August lifted the right hand from under the hip. The fingers were curled around the crushed stem of a red carnation, and scrawled across the knuckles was the sign for Jupiter. August pulled the flower out from between the fingers. The carnation – the flower inscribed over the first page of the chronicle. August's second calling card.

'The carnation is a reference to the chronicle, but how did you know the symbol would be for Jupiter?'

'They are the astrological signs associated with each sephirot from the Tree of Life. The one on the forehead, Kether – Pluto. The left shoulder Binah – Saturn, and so on. The whole corpse has been marked as if he is a Tree of Life himself.'

August reeled back on his heels, nauseated.

'The murder must be a message, a message for me. Whoever killed Edouard knows about the mazes, and the occult. I remember reading that for occultists the Tree of Life is a system, a way of arranging and associating mystical, magical and spiritual properties. Even Crowley used it in rituals.'

'But I still don't think it's Tyson. Interesting that the tenth astrological sign for the tenth sephirot is missing. Malkuth – Kingdom. Astrologically, Malkuth is associated with Earth,' Jacob pointed out.

August gazed at the three signs running down the middle of Edouard's body. He began pacing from the corpse's lolling feet in a direct line, tracking the floor. It led him to the far wall. He stopped, facing the blank wall, then looked up and found himself looking into a hung mirror. Drawn on the glass, again in lipstick, was another sign. It framed his face precisely, as if whoever had drawn it knew his exact height. In the reflection it ran across his forehead, a sinister mirroring to the zodiac sign written on his dead friend's face. Only whereas Edouard's sign symbolised Kether the Crown, the one reflected back across August's forehead symbolised the Earth. He stood transfixed by the image then shivered.

Jacob walked up behind him.

'Malkuth – Kingdom. The murderer didn't leave it out after all,' August told him, still staring into the mirror.

'It's a code. The astrological sign for Malkuth is the Earth. I think whoever killed your friend is letting you know they intend to bury you next – in the Earth.' Jacob paused, looking at August's reflection. 'There's someone else apart from Tyson who's following you, isn't there?'

August's face was grim with tension. 'Maybe.' He swung around to the room. He hadn't wanted to tell Jacob about the woman he suspected might have been tailing him since London, his instinct being to hold back information that might prove compromising later.

Jacob whistled. 'You mean someone else as well as MI5, Interpol and the CIA?'

'Nothing like being the life of the party,' August retorted. 'What you have to understand is that I'm on the trail of something hundreds of people before me have tried to discover, and someone out there in their parallel world of symbols and magic and psychological manipulation,' he gestured toward Edouard's body, 'as well as terror, knows it.' He was interrupted by the sound of jangling. Izarra stood over Edouard's jacket, holding his car keys aloft.

'We should move,' she said.

Appalled, August moved towards her and snatched the keys from her hand.

'No, we're not thieves.'

'It's what he would have wanted,' she insisted, her face expressionless.

'You haven't got time for sentimentality,' Jacob reminded August. 'If you're really playing bait, you need to move fast, really fast. I can send you a telegram, telling you the whereabouts of Tyson as soon as I've located him. I'll send it to the central post office in Hamburg, addressed to Joe Iron.'

August looked back over to the body, painfully aware of the others waiting for his response. In the street outside they could already hear the sound of the garage opening up next door, the cheerful banter of the mechanics as they arrived at work: normal life, the world without bizarre murders, without the running. August started to move. 'Okay,' he finally told Izarra. 'We leave for Hamburg – now.'

The rain fell in sheets against the window of the Fiat, making watercolours of the fields that flanked the narrow country lane. August, at the wheel, leaned forward to peer out of the windscreen at a sign looming on the side of the road.

'That must be the turn-off for Dijon,' he told Izarra, who had a map of Europe unfolded across her lap. She looked at the map.

'Fifteen kilometres.'

'We'll have to change the plate before we reach Dijon. The police will have traced the car by now.'

'I can arrange that.' Izarra smiled over at him. 'An old trick my sister taught me.'

The turn-off came up and August swung left, and the road immediately broadened into a four-lane highway.

'Pull over there and park just behind that tree,' Izarra instructed. He drove the Fiat off the road, the car bouncing across the gravelled side lane, and parked behind the long trailing branches of a weeping willow.

'Do you have a pocket knife?'

August nodded, wondering what she planned to do now. She bent the rear-view mirror towards her and produced a tube of lipstick and mascara from her pocket and to his amazement began to apply them – he'd never seen her wear make-up before.

'Good, stay out of sight until I get to the truck. When I get in, run out and unscrew his numberplate. Got it?'

'What if I haven't enough time?'

Izarra grinned. 'You'll have enough time – don't worry, I'm practised at this.'

For one horrible minute August thought she might be about to prostitute herself, but before he had time to stop her, she'd climbed out of the car. The rain had just stopped and a few beams of sunshine emerged like some celestial torchlight from behind the grey clouds, illuminating her hair and face. She looked, he realised with a jolt, remarkably unmarked by time and experience, as if the face powder had blanked out her history. He had to fight the impulse to leap out of the car to protect her.

He watched through the window as she walked to the side of the road then held out her thumb as if hitch-hiking. Set against the ploughed clay of the field behind her and the sudden light travelling across the wet, glistening road like a slice of colour in a black-and-white photograph, she resembled some strange pilgrim from an earlier time; the plait-waisted skirt, the sensible shoes and stockings offset by the obvious sensuality of her now loosened hair and slash of crimson mouth – whore and saint, Madonna and Jezebel. He didn't like it. He didn't like leaving her there vulnerable. *She's as much of a soldier as you are. Besides, she would never forgive you if you stopped her. You have to learn to trust her. But have I ever really trusted any woman?*

A car drove past. It slowed then sped away, indifferent. Ignoring the rebuff, Izarra stood stoically by the kerb, her thumb still out. Another car, a battered Renault, two older women in the front seat, cruised by slowly, the passenger turning to stare disapprovingly as they passed.

Inside the Fiat, August was beginning to feel increasingly uncomfortable with the whole plan. He was about to climb out and call the whole thing off when he caught sight of a small truck turning the corner into the road. An advertisement for a meat supplier in Lyon was painted on the side, and the driver, a red-faced man in his forties, was visible at the wheel. The truck stopped just past Izarra and the cabin door swung open. Without even turning to look back at August, Izarra raced up and climbed into the cab.

August slipped out of the Fiat, taking care to stay out of sight of the driver's wing mirror, and raced around to the front of the truck. As fast as he could, he began unscrewing the numberplate with his penknife. Only two screws held it on and it took him all of three minutes to get it off. He scurried to the back of the truck and unscrewed the rear plate, wrapping his jacket around both plates. After which he ran to the car and replaced Edouard's plates with those of the truck. He threw Edouard's plates into a ditch then glanced over at the truck. In the steamy cabin, under the yellowish interior light, Izarra appeared to be sharing a cigarette with the driver, smiling and chatting. The man's rotund face, flushed with possible conquest, looked particularly venal, and August steeled himself against the impulse to run over and simply haul Izarra from the truck. Noting he had at least another few minutes, he tightened the screws on the new plates then got back into the car.

He looked into the rear-view to check how Izarra was going. Now she appeared to be having some kind of argument with the driver, waving her hands around dramatically. August's stomach tightened and he wondered whether he would, after all, need to rescue her. But then she climbed out of the truck, slamming the door behind her, her face angry. She waited until the truck screeched off, then slipped back behind the willow and into the Fiat.

'So what did you tell him, that you were a novice nun?'

'Something like that,' she said. 'But we got the number-plate, didn't we?' She was delighted as a child.

'That will buy us a little more time,' August grunted, in response.

Amused, she glanced back at him. 'You weren't jealous, were you?'

'If he'd touched you, I would have killed him.' He kept his face on the road, not wanting her to see his expression.

Izarra chuckled. 'You wouldn't have had to. I would have done it myself. He wasn't so bad. He just supported the wrong football team.'

August pulled the car out from the lane and with wheels spinning hit the road.

'I plan to dump the Fiat in Hamburg, as soon as I hear from Jacob.'

'Good idea, they must have discovered Edouard's body by now.'

'Don't worry. We'll be in Germany by nightfall.'

'Malcolm, can you hear me clearly?' August stood hunched over in the phone booth, the receiver pressed to his ear. He was watching Izarra standing by the Fiat, as a young Frenchman filled the car with petrol. They were on the outskirts of Dijon, where farmland had given way to small industry. The gas station was sandwiched between a brick factory and a rundown poultry farm. The booth's isolation made it safe to use to call London. There was a crackle, then Malcolm Hully's booming voice echoed down the line.

'August, exactly on time. What a surprise.'

'A feat, I can tell you.' *And you know just how much of a feat, you bastard.*

'I can imagine. You should know both Interpol and the CIA are on your tail, and I'm afraid Her Majesty has officially disowned you.' Malcolm sounded genuinely concerned.

'That's disappointing. Remind me to write to my local MP.' August kept his voice neutral.

'Seriously, August, the word is that they're not particularly fussy about who brings you in or the state of health they bring you back in. Black code, my friend, not so much *persona non grata* as *persona mortis.*'

'Ouch, I am in trouble. And that money wasn't at the hotel, Hully, what happened?'

'Yes, sorry about that, bureaucratic problems my end, old man,' Hully replied, smoothly.

August's hand tightened on the receiver. He wanted to punch him now. *Play the game, don't show your cards, not yet,* he told himself. It was disturbing how good an actor Malcolm actually was. August began to doubt the whole premise of their earlier friendship. What had been the real reason why Malcolm recruited him to the Special Operations Executive? Had Malcolm ever really trusted him? *Sometimes Englishmen were so damn difficult to read.* Then August clapped his hand over the receiver lightly enough just to muffle the sound and, in passable Arabic, shouted out, 'Please, my luggage.'

Then, smiling, he removed his hand and Malcolm's voice, now bright with anxiety, sounded out of the receiver.

'Where are you, the Middle East?' Malcolm asked, falling for the ruse.

'Never mind. Tell me what you've learned about Tyson.'

'He's ex-military, now working mainly in Spain. He's with OGA, a company man, and the Yanks regard him as a valuable asset, so, August, you should let it drop. Interestingly enough, Tyson's Spanish counterpart, the man he talks business with, is General Cesar Molivio.' Just the mention of the name gave August the impression the ground was tilting. There was a pause at the other end of the phone line, as if Malcolm knew exactly the impact he was having. August pushed back against the booth, fighting the sense of vertigo sweeping through him, his knuckles white as he tried to steady himself. He put his hand over the mouthpiece, took a couple of breaths to calm down, before putting it back against his ear.

'Molivio, are you sure?' He kept his voice low and steady.

'Why, do you know him?' Malcolm's voice was innocent, empty of emotion – a counterattack on his behalf? August was convinced of it. He'd never shared any of his experiences in the Civil War with his old supervisor, but if Malcolm was with MI5 it was possible someone had accessed the information. *They want to disorientate me. They want me to betray myself.* The image of Molivio smiling gently at him as electrodes were applied to his testicles flashed through his mind, making his body jolt in memory. It was hard to forget the insidious psychology the Spaniard had used, befriending him, then torturing him in an attempt to extract the names of all of the Lincolns under his command, information August knew would condemn at least a dozen fellow Americans.

'Small world,' he said, tightly – but was it just chance

Tyson was working with Molivio, another connection to him?

'Other than that, Damien Tyson is rumoured to be a little of a loose cannon, but the Americans respect him as a hard man and one who has a direct line to Franco. Give yourself up, August. He's a killer with no scruples. You don't stand a chance.'

Turning from the gas station, August looked across at a farmer working a field opposite, the heavy plough turning the earth red as the farmer, tugging on a harness, encouraged a huge carthorse with short whistles, the animal's shoulders rippling with the effort of pulling the old plough, breath steaming from its nostrils into the chilly air. August suddenly felt terrifyingly isolated – Jimmy murdered, Edouard gone and now Malcolm's betrayal. What trap was he leading Izarra into? But the coincidence of Tyson's relationship with his old torturer was too extraordinary, it had to have meaning – the way his past had abruptly surged up like a tidal wave impossible to outrun. Yet perhaps this was exactly the reaction MI5 was calculating on.

Outside, Izarra was now paying for the petrol. August noticed the gas station attendant looking over, with sudden curiosity, at the blue Fiat, as if he'd just remembered something; their cue to get moving. Just then a flock of geese flew low overhead, honking loudly as they passed.

'There's something else. Has a man called Jacob Cohen been in contact with you?' Malcolm's voice was tinny at the other end of the line.

It was disturbing hearing Malcolm's clipped English accent saying Jacob's name. The sense that every move he made was being tracked closed over August like a suffocating heat. He stared out at the attendant. Ruddy and long limbed, the man was chatting innocently to Izarra. Life looked so normal, it was hard to believe they were probably being watched. Jacob's words about Tyson possibly being a triple agent came flooding back. What if Tyson was still in contact with MI5? And how did this reflect on Malcolm? *Play him, play him as hard as you can.*

'No, never heard of him,' August lied, smoothly.

'Apparently, he's obsessed with Tyson. Cohen is regarded as both paranoid and a fanatic, and is marked as a security risk. My advice would be to steer clear if he does reach you.'

August knew that if MI5 had a file on Cohen, Jacob's investigation must have enough factual basis for them to take it seriously. If anything, August regarded such condemnation as an endorsement.

'Thanks, Malcolm. I have to go, the medina has just opened.'

'But where are you—' Malcolm asked, but August had already put down the receiver.

Malcolm turned to the small grey-haired man who'd been tapping the conversation.

'So, what do you think? The intelligence is that he's either in Marseille on the way to Port Said or in Port Said.'

Nesbit Norris, a psychologist and operative for MI5, allowed his pale blue phlegmatic eyes to flicker briefly over Malcolm's face. 'He's still in France, but he's on the move. North,' Norris said, in a hard, flat voice.

Malcolm repressed a shudder. *The man is so reptilian,* he thought to himself, *as cold as a lizard,* but then again, *that's why he is good at his job.*

'How did he take the Molivio lead?' Upstairs interjected, tipping forward on his chair, his halitosis drifting across the desk. Malcolm couldn't stop himself from grimacing. 'I think he swallowed it, but I doubt whether it will bring him out.'

'Why not? According to our records, Molivio damn near killed the man, and Tyson is very close to the chap. Surely Winthrop would like to take a shot?'

'I don't know. When he was working underground in France for me, he was good, one of the best. August doesn't do anything he doesn't want and he's suspicious as hell.'

'But did he feed you anything?'

'He tried to get me to think he was in North Africa. Like he was in Port Said already. I think he knows the welcoming reception at the hotel was ours.'

'We have to keep playing him, but he's definitely not in Egypt. *La Veuve Joyeuse* hasn't docked yet. I checked.'

Malcolm thought for a moment then swung around to Nesbit. 'Why north?'

'I heard geese. Geese begin to migrate north this time of year – from Africa to northern Europe – Scandinavia, Denmark and Germany. He's also lying about Cohen. They've been in contact,' Norris concluded, leaving no room for debate. Norris looked across at the map they had pinned on the blackboard. Every major cathedral town in France was circled in red. He picked up a piece of chalk and with one long sweep drew a line from the bottom of Spain up through France curving east over Germany.

'From the cry I'd say it was Barnacle geese. They have a preference for Holland and northern Germany. Get the Germans on the phone,' he instructed Malcolm. Malcolm didn't move.

'I didn't know you were a birdwatcher, Nesbit,' he remarked, coldly.

'Ah, but I know you're a sentimentalist, Hully,' Norris retorted, then picked up the phone himself, pausing, receiver in hand. 'What was the colour of Edouard Coutes's Fiat again?'

§

The ship lurched again and Shimon reached out to stop his inkpot from sliding across the table. The sound of the sailors racing over the deck to secure the sails ran across the low ceiling as the beams of the small merchant vessel creaked and groaned with each new wave, the guttural Dutch sounding through the tiny cabin. Shimon sighed then lifted the bouquet of cloves to his face, breathing in the heady scent in an attempt to quell his seasickness. I am from a desert people, he told himself, my stomach shall never make peace with the sea. Just when he thought he might have to vomit, the inhalation worked and the nausea subsided. Steadying himself against the edge of the desk, he opened the chronicle at its last page and began writing furiously, calculating he had only a short time before the next heave of the ship would distract him.

The sound of the cabin door opening broke his concentration.

'Husband.' Uxue's voice seemed to float across the surface of the parchment, but for a moment he ignored it.

'Husband, I have fear.'

Shimon swung around. Uxue, her face chalky pale, her legs spread to steady herself, stood in her plain travel dress, her full womb now visible under the hessian weave.

'Uxue.' He got up and navigated his way to her, using the corners of the fixed wooden bed, their travel chest fastened by ropes to the floor, and the edge of the desk. Then he took her in his arms.

'We will be safe. It is just a small storm – it will pass.'

To his surprise, she pushed him away. 'It is not the storm I am afraid of, husband. It is you and your stubborn will. You will have all three of us condemned and executed. I know it!'

She sat heavily on the bed, her face grim. 'Why England? An enemy of Spain. Why risk all to seek an audience with the King, you, a simple physic? This is suicide, Shimon.'

He sat next to her and picked up her hand. It was freezing. Absentmindedly, he began rubbing it. 'Why the misgivings now, Uxue, when I have explained all to you before?'

'Because maybe I find that I am not as noble as you are. I want to live, Shimon, I want to live and be happy with my child.'

'And you will, Uxue, I promise.'

'And with you.' She was staring wide-eyed at him, knowing if anyone could promise this, it would be him. He turned away, unable to keep looking into those questioning black eyes. He got up again. He had to move, to throw himself into his own determination.

'I've told you. I'm on a mission for peace. This is greater than us, than our child. The great treasure I have found will stop a future war – one more widespread than Europe has ever known, a religious war that will tear brother from brother. It will help broker peace between Catholics and Protestants, both in England and in Germania and eventually France itself. But I have to begin with a tolerant monarch, one who still wavers. King James is rumoured to be a secret Catholic. He will give me an audience, especially when he hears what I have to offer.'

'Husband, there is no war between the Protestants and Catholics.'

'But there will be, a long war that will fall like a shadow across Europe, one that will last for decades, hundreds of thousands will die. I can prevent this, Uxue. I have the power.'

Furious, she struck out at the straw pallet. Straw and dust rose with the blow. Startled, Shimon stepped back. He had never seen her so irate – was it the pregnancy? he wondered, but was wise enough to say nothing.

'So we are sailing to England for you to talk the King into preventing a war that hasn't even started? Shimon, I have stood beside you this whole journey, believed in you and your great search, but now I have my doubts.'

'You are human and fallible, this is only natural.'

'If I did not love you, I could leave,' she said, almost as if telling herself and not him.

He kneeled on the hard wooden floor and laid his head in her lap, the swell of her full womb a warm curve against which he buried his ear.

'Do you want me to release you? I believe we have enough money. You could return to Irumendi and start a life there without me.'

Her fingers crept through his long black hair. Without him knowing, she started to cry silently.

'You couldn't release me even if you wanted to. We are woven together; words of the same song.'

'Indeed.' But still he dare not lift his eyes to her.

'But, husband, tell me how do you think a single man will stop the birth of a war?'

'Faith, Uxue, and the miracle of a legacy.'

On the other side of the room a sudden gust of wind ruffled the pages of the chronicle.

21

There was a bitter wind coming off the Alster. After spending the night sleeping in the car at the side of the road they had driven for hours, winding their way through the bottom of Germany, crossing into the country from Saarbrücken, then up towards Cologne, skirting around the main town, through the devastated medieval city of Münster, then Bremen and finally into Hamburg. The cities, caught in a frenzy of rebuilding, still bore the tell-tale scars of the intense Allied bombing, much of which had transformed historical Gothic centres into skeletal ruins, leaving vast empty lots stretching between the surviving buildings – the incongruous end of a terrace, the blank wall once attached to a whole row of houses, now a mute witness to unimaginable destruction; the tall industrial brick chimney left standing like a curious totem pole, the only remnant of some nineteenth-century factory; the spire of a church emerging like a single note from a pile of rubble. The sight had reduced August, no lover of the Nazi regime, to silence.

August and Izarra stepped out of Hamburg's central post office. They had waited in line for a good half-hour, nervously scanning the milling crowd for uniforms or anything indicating possible MI5 or Interpol presence and when they'd finally reached the counter there had been no telegram from Jacob – a worrying sign, although August was determined to hide his growing anxiety.

'Now what?' Izarra asked, shoulders hunched, as they walked back to the car through the wind-driven drizzle.

'We go see a friend of mine.' August tried to sound as confident as possible, but he knew they stood out as strangers among the odd clusters of grey-coated pedestrians that hung around the edge of the city square, some walking purposefully through the drizzle, others loitering in a listlessness around the stalls selling bratwürst and hot pretzels.

As they drove through St Pauli great swathes of flattened ground, interspersed with the odd old red-brick tenement, came into view.

'Fifty thousand dead in one night, it must have been hell,' August said, as much to himself as to Izarra.

'Death is death,' Izarra retorted, bitterly. 'But when I look at this, all I can see is Gernika.'

'Not all Germans supported Hitler.'

'Perhaps, but the collective always pays no matter what.'

They drove down Grosse Bergstrasse, where he could see cheap barracks-like buildings had been constructed, no doubt to house the many made homeless at the end of the war.

A Jeep passed them, slowing to check the numberplate, a small Union Jack fluttering from the aerial. August was careful to keep his gaze straight ahead.

'British?' Izarra asked.

'The occupying forces. The British have Hamburg, the Americans Bremen. Both are dangerous for us.'

The Jeep turned at the next corner, to August's relief.

'Where are we going?'

'Speicherstadt, the old warehouse district, to one of Jimmy's contacts, and an old friend of mine, Karl Haardt. He was one of the founding members of the Thälmann Battalion – a brigade made up of German Communists and resistance that fought in your war, the Spanish war, many to the death. He was a close and loyal friend. We had a few things in common.'

'Like what?'

He glanced over, smiling wryly. 'You really don't want to know.'

'Yes, I do.'

'Women, chess and jazz. Not necessarily in that order. But all three got us through Aragon, Madrid and the siege of Bilbao. Although Karl wasn't so lucky.'

'How so?'

'He got hitched. Although I'd lay money he's no longer married. Anyhow, the main point is that he's a Hamburger born and bred. There ain't nothing he doesn't know about this city. The good, the bad ...' They had now turned into the Reeperbahn, its garish neon lights advertising strip shows and burlesque glittering through the evening mist like aberrant lighthouses. A particularly fat prostitute came into sight, resplendent in a tight pencil skirt, flesh rippling over the waist, and a tight spangly top, cleavage gleaming like the underbelly of a whale. She had cornered a diminutive man in a suit, at least six inches shorter than she was. 'And the grotesque,' August concluded, inexplicably cheered by the sight. On the other side of the road he noticed the Ernst-Merck Halle was advertising an upcoming concert by Lionel Hampton.

'That's new; Hitler banned jazz.'

'Franco's not keen on it either,' Izarra said, dryly.

They drove on alongside the rows of warehouses that
backed directly onto the broad canals, the car gliding across
the wet, glistening pebbled lanes through the back alleys.

'Speicherstadt, we're here.' August pulled the car up at a
street corner and looked up at a broken street sign.
'Zippelhaus. From what I can see from the map I think we
have to turn at the bridge here, Kornhausbrücke. Karl is
working in a warehouse on Holländisch.'

There were only workers, poorly dressed in old heavy
jackets and the flat caps the local sailors like to wear, walking
home in small groups scattered through the narrow streets,
the Gothic warehouses towering over the streets like a relentless wall of mercantilism. A surprising number had survived
the bombing.

'The Allies concentrated on the port – where the battle-
ships and U-boats were being constructed. They flew down
the Alster using the Church of St Nicholas as a landmark and
dropped most of their bombs on commercial areas like
Steinwerder and around the fish market, and onto St Pauli
and Altona – heavily populated working-class districts. Hitler
did the same to London during the Blitz.'

'How come you know so much?'

'I've been here before, for a week in 1948. I had some
cleaning up to do for the SOE, bringing in an agent who we
originally thought had gone missing. The whole place was
bleached honeycomb back then. I'd never seen a city so
devastated.'

They pulled up outside a warehouse. The sign over the
door read: 'Importeur von exotischen teppichen'. August
looked down at Jimmy's list he held in his hand. 'This is it.
I think Karl is the foreman here.'

Just then a thin Arabic-looking man dressed in a kaftan
and fez with an old fur coat pulled incongruously over the

top stepped out of the large oak door, one hand holding his fez against the wind. He looked as if he were leaving for the night.

'Go out and just ask to see a Karl ...' August scanned the list again, '... Haardt, and use that charm of yours on him, the one you save for strangers, but not so much that he mistakes you for a whore.'

'I'll try my best,' Izarra quipped back then checked herself in the rear-view. 'In what language? I don't speak German.'

'Try English. If he asks any more questions, tell him you're a friend or relative of Karl's first wife.'

'First wife?'

'He was married to a Spaniard for two weeks. I told you he likes women.'

Izarra adjusted her lipstick, then stepped out of the car and approached the thin dark-skinned man, smiling. Within seconds he'd escorted her to the front door of the building and had yelled out Karl's name. August watched from the car as the tall, craggy-faced German appeared at the warehouse entrance. Time flashed back as he recognised the lanky stance, the loose-limbed stagger that had not disappeared in the older man. Karl Haardt's face was more battered and there was a new hollowness to the broad cheekbones, the high patrician nose and deep-set eyes. He was also walking with a slight limp, but the essence of the man appeared unchanged. The two men exchanged some words, then the younger businessman – obviously Karl's employer – handed some keys to Karl and, after kissing Izarra's hand, walked swiftly into the night.

Karl and Izarra watched him disappear, then the German, after glancing in both directions, strolled over to the Fiat. August stepped out of the car and they embraced.

'My friend, you are alive.'

'You too.'

'Gus, I wasn't sure I'd ever see you again.'

'But here I am.' When August finally managed to free himself from the embrace he couldn't help noticing Karl had tears in his eyes. The grey afternoon was now changing into evening and there was a thin veil of mist settling over the canals. August glanced down the empty street. He felt a prickle of awareness, standing there. Then it was gone.

'*Mein Gott*, Gus, I would not have recognised you with this black hair – you look terrible, like a Slav stevedore. Come, I understand you need to get off the street.' Karl ushered them both into the warehouse.

The front showroom, deceptively plain from the outside, was lavish inside. The walls were hung with imported Arabic rugs and, in a small reception area, there was a brand-new desk with a modern leather chair behind it, in stark contrast to the evident poverty that surrounded the warehouse.

'We import from Morocco to America. The Brits also help us with the English market – with the army base here there's a lot of shipping now to Britain,' Karl explained, as he hurried them through into the back warehouse. Apart from an apprentice who was busy hauling a crate of goods up from the canal using the crane jutting out from the top floor, the building appeared deserted. Karl ordered the youth to finish up as soon as he could, then led the others into a tiny office.

It was a box within a box, a hardboard cube built into the corner of the huge warehouse space. Karl pulled a cord and a naked electric bulb illuminated an old chipped table pushed against one wall, a wooden chair pushed neatly underneath it. A stack of American magazines and some German papers sat on the desk; behind them, hanging from a nail in the wall, was a Betty Grable calendar dated 1950, and a certificate in German announcing Karl Haardt's election as representative for the union of shipbuilders.

'Humble headquarters, but it's a job and they're hard to find in Hamburg.' Karl began pouring out three small glasses of Schnaps while August pulled out the chair for Izarra to sit on, then rested against the edge of the desk, almost stumbling over a large artillery shell that sat end up on the floor, its bronze casting seemingly unscathed. Karl chuckled. 'A souvenir from Operation Gomorrah in 1943, two hundred and seventy-seven houses flattened in one night, seven thousand dead. It has *Made in Sheffield* inscribed on its bottom, and luckily for us it's been defused.' He handed the Schnaps to Izarra and August. 'Your beautiful friend here tells me you have driven all the way from Avignon. So first we drink, then I take you to a nice little hideaway I keep for such occasions. You will be safe there. It is so obscure not even my wife knows where it is, which ... ' Karl nudged August, '... has been very useful when I am entertaining some nice lady friend.'

'You're married again, Karl?' August queried, grinning.

'Since liberation, Bettina has been a comrade in the party. She was on the outside during the war and helped smuggle food and messages into the labour camp. Liberation made me sentimental. I proposed the day after Hitler killed himself. So *danke schön*, Adolf. It's been useful. In the ensuing chaos I got myself a new identity. And if you're British military, I have been dead for at least ten years. So you see, you have to be nice to me.' He winked suggestively at Izarra. 'I am not in good health,' he concluded, robustly, thumping his vast chest as if to emphasise the point. 'But tell me, how did you know how to find me?'

'Jimmy van Peters.'

Karl skulled his Schnaps, then steadied his piercing gaze on August. For a moment August panicked. *He knows about Jimmy's murder and he's heard the reports that I am the killer.* August fought not to flinch.

'Murdered, I hear – is it true?' Karl asked, his voice friendly and level.

August glanced across at Izarra. Jimmy and Karl had been close; he had no choice but to trust the German.

'I'm sorry, Karl, it's true.'

A flash of pain travelled across Karl's face, then he poured himself another drink.

'Every week there is one less of us. Soon Europe will be devoid of its idealists, soon there will be nothing but mercantilism and Coca-Cola. *Viva el capitalismo*,' he added, cynically.

'I believe he was killed by the man I'm pursuing. But they're trying to frame me for his murder.'

'I know, I have a radio. Congratulations, Gus, you must have done something to really rock the boat.' Karl downed the Schnaps as August stepped closer.

'This man, he's possibly a double agent, maybe even triple.'

Karl looked at August; a searching gaze. Finally, he spoke. 'I've seen Jimmy once or twice since the end of the war. I know a little about his nemesis, August. This is not a man to be played with.'

'We know what we're doing.'

Karl sighed then looked at Izarra. 'You know, by the time we were forced to surrender, Gus and I had begun to think of ourselves as the invincible ones, magical men marked by some invisible sign of fortune. As our comrades fell we always escaped unscathed, no matter how terrible the odds, how ill-equipped we were. We thought we were gods, that no man would pull us down.'

'I'm far more of a realist these days,' August retorted.

'That I don't believe. You always thrived on hope and imagination.'

'You too, Karl.'

'And women, my friend, don't forget the women.'

'But in the end it wasn't those things that kept you going, Karl. After all you survived Franco, Camp de Gurs, Hitler's labour camps.'

Izarra looked up. 'You were in Camp de Gurs?'

'The French bastards put us on beaches – whole families, women and children, starving and desperate for fresh water, forced to dig holes in the sand for shelter. I finally escaped, then worked underground in Germany for a while until my arrest in 1941. The Nazis put me in with several of my Communist comrades in Neuengamme, then in the last week of April 1945 they started shooting us one by one. So many of the resistance were executed that month because the bastards knew surrender was just around the corner. They issued orders to execute all Communist Party members and anyone they thought would prove useful and sympathetic to the incoming Allied forces. They executed seventy-one men and women in the Neuengamme camp, on the 21st and 23rd of April alone. So many great people died that week. I was lucky the morning of the day I was due to be shot, the news of the fall of Berlin came through. I stood in the concrete yard waiting for my death but no guards came. They'd all fled. But I tell you, Gus, by then I was ready to die, I had no hope left.'

'And now?' Izarra couldn't help asking.

'Now Stalin is kaput, the Allies carve up East Germany and Berlin like they were a Sachertorte and the same lawyers and judges that served the Nazis are now passing so-called judgement on them. It is hard to stay an idealist in such circumstances. So instead I have become a hermit.'

'You've given up politics altogether?' August ventured.

Karl smiled. 'Not entirely.' He indicated the certificate on the wall proudly. 'I am the district's representative for the Steinwerder. It is a great honour.' He checked his watch. 'But come, we have to hurry. We need to get to my bolthole before Tommy starts his night patrol. Is the car safe?'

'For now – we changed the plates.'

'We'll dump it tomorrow. It's not as safe as you might think here. Interpol and MI6 regularly come through on the obligatory search for ex-Nazi officials and war criminals, although I have noticed every time I try and give them some real leads they're not interested. They prefer to root around the old working-class districts – what's left of them – Altona, St Pauli, always avoiding the obvious routes out and the hideaways. The number of Nazis who pretended to be refugees and left the country courtesy of the Red Cross was sickening. It seems Interpol like making their own mistakes, but I don't underestimate them. Why do you think your man might be in Hamburg?'

'Because I'm here now.'

Karl looked over at Izarra, who shrugged innocently, then the German burst into laughter, throwing an arm around August's shoulder.

'As I thought, you haven't changed a bit, my friend. You still hanker for that rush as the bullets whistle past your ear. You have become one of those sad men who only feel life when they are confronted with death. It's psychosis.'

'Karl, I want this guy – he's a murderer, a traitor and a war criminal. I will have him no matter what.'

'Then why not just go out and find him? Why play this dangerous game of hide and seek? Better to be a simple predator. You and I know that from Spain.'

'This war isn't that simple, and there's something else at stake.'

'There always is.' Karl turned back to Izarra. 'Are you sure you want to stick with this loser? He'll get you killed for sure, whereas Uncle Karl is dependable, better looking and, by all accounts, a better lover,' he flirted, grinning.

'But you're married,' Izarra deadpanned back.

'So?'

The three of them walked back through the warehouse. The showrooms and storerooms were now empty, the crate they'd seen earlier dangling from the crane now sitting neatly in the centre of the wooden floor. At the front door Karl pulled out a set of keys.

'I hope you don't suffer from claustrophobia or seasickness,' he told them.

'Why?' Izarra asked.

'You'll see,' he replied, with an enigmatic smile.

The small Fiat was buffeted by the wind coming off the Alster as they drove following Karl's motorcycle, his dark-blue helmet catching the streetlights like a flare. The squat brown-grey body of his BMW R75 hugged the road as he sped ahead, the empty sidecar bouncing over the broken tarmac. The two vehicles wound their way back over the cobbled lanes of the Speicherstadt, then into the wider streets of the city itself, some still pitted with potholes.

They drove north, past the massive sheds of the fish market and the old customs office. Untouched by the war it stood like a sentry from a bygone era. As August glanced to his right, south of the river, he could see the bombing patterns of the Allied planes more clearly – it had intensified the closer they got to the commercial shipping yards and lanes, where the Nazis built their navy.

Ten minutes later they arrived at the entrance of the Alter Elbtunnel, then plunged into the chilly artificial light of the old tunnel that took them under the river south towards the shipyard district on the opposite bank. August drove, his shoulders hunched over the wheel, acutely aware of how vulnerable the car was – if they were being followed, the tunnel would be the perfect opportunity for an ambush. Izarra must have been feeling the same because she glanced behind them, just as an army delivery truck passed in the opposite lane, the impassive blank face of the driver illuminated momentarily by their headlights, making her jump slightly. Apart from that one truck, the tunnel was eerily empty save for their car and Karl's motorcycle, the roar of which bounced off the curved walls, which only made August feel more conspicuous.

'You trust this man? He could be taking us anywhere.' Izarra looked around anxiously.

'Completely. Don't worry, the tunnel will take us out to the south of the Elbe, to the shipping yard district. It will be deserted around there at night, and Karl knows it like the back of his hand.'

'So we spend the night in his hideaway, then what?'

'We look for the third maze tomorrow. Somehow I suspect the fate of the monk Baptise is linked to the reason why Tyson wants the chronicle so much.'

'You really think he's going to come after you?'

'That's what I'm calculating on.'

'So am I. Don't let me down,' she finished, soberly, as August accelerated the car out of the tunnel up into the dockland itself.

They drove alongside the water: a geography of broad shipping canals, flanked by cranes, a couple of US and British naval ships and a minesweeper. With a burst of exhaust that hung in the mist like a black feathery plume, the BMW accelerated in front of them and together they sped past warehouses and offices, many newly constructed, interspersed with the bombed-out shells of older buildings. Karl still drove on and the shipping works began to give way to more and more destroyed buildings, turning into an industrial wasteland as the canals narrowed and split. Finally, he pulled up beside a derelict jetty, a concrete structure that arched over a canal. One end of it had broken away, the rusting steel girders poking out like ancient bones. August parked the car beside the motorcycle. There was not a building or house in sight.

'Well, it's remote enough,' he remarked.

'Remote enough to be disappeared and never heard of again,' Izarra retorted; August noticed she'd slipped her hand into her jacket pocket, no doubt to wrap her fingers around her revolver. He placed a hand on her wrist.

'I told you he's trustworthy.'

'That doesn't mean I should trust him.'

'If you trust me, you trust him,' August insisted, a slow anger beginning to burn within him. He wasn't going to let her sabotage anything through paranoia. 'This isn't Spain, Izarra. Karl has nothing to gain from helping us and everything to lose, including potentially his life.'

Angrily, she pulled her hand away. 'Just remember, we're here to get Tyson, that's the most important thing. The chronicle can wait.'

'I promise you, I solve the final maze – you get Tyson.' Fighting his own temper, August climbed out of the car, slamming the door behind him, and Izarra followed.

They joined Karl who was waiting helmet in hand by the entrance of the semi-derelict concrete construction built over the canal. Intrigued, August stared up at the building, trying to work out whether it was a shed or some kind of shelter. Karl, reading his confusion, chuckled. 'I found this little treasure at the end of the war. Seemed like the Nazis had captured a small Soviet reconnaissance submarine in the harbour, moored it here, then forgot about it.'

He walked them into the shell-like structure and the sound of water lapping bounced off the thick concrete walls. It was like being in a tunnel with the distant glow of a city at the far end. Without warning, the bunker was flooded with light as Karl switched on the power, revealing the U-boat, its grey-black metallic body sinister in presence.

'Isn't she a beauty?'

'Is this your hideout?' Izarra stared across the submarine, amazed. Karl stepped up on the wooden walkway leading to the deck of the U-boat.

'The Nazis built concrete bunkers over all their sub-marines in a futile attempt to prevent the Allied bombers from getting to them. The U-boat was originally moored in a larger canal further in the Steinwerder, but I had a couple of shipyard mates tow it out here. The bunker conceals it from the outside and the whole place looks so derelict no one ever comes here.'

'Genius.' August whistled.

Karl helped Izarra step onto the wooden ramp that led onto the body of the submarine.

'I've always liked to think of it as a personal gift from Stalin himself, for services rendered to the Party, but of course now, with his recent passing, I get to keep it,' Karl joked, then mounted the tower and swung open the heavy metal hatch to the submarine. 'In service it would only accommodate a crew of about five, but that's big enough for me. C'mon, I give you the grand tour. Ladies first.'

Izarra began climbing the short metal rungs welded into the tower. The two men watched her ascend.

'Nice legs,' Karl observed, in an appreciative undertone as she disappeared down into the entrance. August followed and Karl paused to glance back along the bunker and out to the panorama of lights illuminating the cranes and vast hulls of the stationary ships. Out on the water there was the sudden cry of a gull. It was a desolate horizon of some industrial underworld, hauntingly eerie. Satisfied the surrounds were empty of any unwanted onlookers, Karl followed the others, slamming shut the hatch behind him.

The three of them stood in the cramped command bridge of the sub, the two men with their heads bent to avoid bashing them on the myriad of pipes, dial controls and machinery that ran like arteries up and down the corners and walls of the tiny space, which was dominated by the thick metal column of the periscope in the middle of the circular cabin. The air was pungent with the smell of diesel fuel. Karl, catching Izarra's grimace, smiled.

'The air is always foul in a U-boat. The longest dive time they could survive without surfacing was three and a half days, poor bastards – stinking hot, horrible air, no space. Still you and I,' he slapped August on the back, 'would never have qualified – too tall.'

'What happened to the crew?'

'Caught and executed in 1943, I believe, but don't worry, the place is not haunted. At least I hope not.' He pushed open the heavy circular door of the next compartment, stepping over the protruding metal frame and into the section. The others followed tentatively. A pin-up poster of Jane Russell in a bikini hung over a control panel, while facing the buxom starlet on the opposite wall was a small flag of the hammer and sickle.

'Eclectic decor, Karl,' August observed, dryly.

'You can't imagine how great it feels to be able to hang what you like where you like,' Karl replied.

'I can,' Izarra said. 'In my country, everything is censored – the papers, the radio, you can't even speak your own language without the risk of being arrested.'

Karl looked at her sympathetically. 'My consolations, comrade. We never intended to leave Franco still in power. But I sense his days are numbered.'

'I am not your comrade – I am a Basque, not a Communist,' she snapped back.

'In Spain we were fighting for our countries, you for independence, me for free Germany,' he countered. 'We both got tyrants.' For the first time Izarra smiled at Karl, and August relaxed a little, relieved that she appeared to trust the German a little more.

'But here everything has changed. I even saw Louis Armstrong play the Max Ernst theatre recently, the crowd went crazy,' Karl continued, moving forward in the sub. 'Ten fucking years of Hitler telling us jazz was deviant, primitive music. Germans have a lot to catch up on.'

Izarra and August followed him, picking their way carefully around and over the machine parts and cables that stuck out from every corner and panel.

It was hard to imagine a more unpleasant work environment, August thought, as he squeezed his tall frame around the sharp metal corners, fighting a growing sense of claustrophobia. Karl paused and they came to a standstill in single file along the passage. 'There's not much room, but I adapted it so that it was at least comfortable for two – three at a pinch,' he said, as if reading August's mind.

The next compartment was filled with rows of batteries, more complex machinery and a tiny scullery off the main passage that ran down the centre of the submarine. Karl led them into the scullery. Behind a small glass window was an icebox, a vinyl-covered bench and a wooden table that looked as if it folded back into the wall. A small metal sink and camping stove sat beside it. Two wine glasses and a portable record player sat in the corner. A Communist paper lay thrown across the table, a half-smoked pipe atop it.

'Very cosy, Karl.' August smiled at the German, who shrugged.

'I told you I use the place to entertain sometimes. There's some coffee, a little liverwürst in the icebox, but little else.' He turned to Izarra. 'I'm afraid you will have to go out for supplies.' He turned back to August. 'They don't know she's travelling with you yet, right?'

'As far as we know.'

'Good, we will use this to our advantage. Meanwhile, I can speak to a few friends inside the British compound. I should be able to get some information for you before the night is over. Let me show you the sleeping quarters. The captain's cabin is down near the torpedo room.'

It was a space that was less than seven feet by four. A curtain separated the bed, more like a sleeping shelf set into the wall, from the rest of the tiny space that had room for one fold-out wooden chair, a writing area and a radio in the corner. Over the writing space, beneath the small metal lamp protruding from the wall, was an old black-and-white photograph, a group shot of smiling young men in uniform clustered around a trench of rocks, two of them playing chess in the middle, one strumming a guitar, a couple of the others resting with rifles slung across their backs. Behind them the tell-tale eucalyptus trees – naked trunk and sparse branches – and dusty ground under their feet. August recognised it immediately.

'The Thälmann Battalion, was it Las Rozas?'

'*Ja*, that photograph was taken just outside, around the 6th of January 1937, just before we went into battle.' Karl pointed to one young face. 'He died the day after this photo; him too; Franz a week later from injuries; three others also. The rest in internment camps – out of the eight in this photograph only two are still alive. I am one of them. Throughout all the hell of those years I managed to save this picture. It's the only thing I have left, except for the memories. They are a legacy for these men.'

Izarra looked closer. 'So young.'

'There is something else, Karl.' August reached into his rucksack and pulled out his gun, now wrapped neatly in the oilcloth. He uncovered it and held it out to Karl.

'Recognise this?'

Karl's face lit up. 'My Mauser! You kept it after all these years?' he exclaimed, struggling to keep the emotion out of his voice. He caressed the gun, weighing it in his palm. 'A C96, such a sexy gun. A real beauty and she still looks good.'

'Do you remember the night you gave it to me?' August asked him.

Karl sat on the edge of the bed, August at the desk, Izarra stayed standing, framed in the doorway. 'It was in Madrid, in that brothel – what was it called again?'

Karl smiled. 'El Toro Bravo. If I remember, the madam was quite bipartisan—'

'You mean she let the Communists in the front door while pushing the anarchists out the back?' August joked.

'There was even a rumour she was a favourite with José Millán Astray when the Nationalists were in town,' Karl elaborated. 'She had this saying, "Red, blue, black, in the end the politics mean nothing – all men have one thing that they wave harder than a flag!"' The two men broke into raucous laughter. 'I gave you the gun because I couldn't bear to see you with that piece of First World War Russian rubbish.'

'Then that little Mexican bastard stole it while I was with Rosa!'

'Now I remember! You ran out naked, screaming, "Where is my gun, where is my gun!" The girls were most impressed. While you were inconsolable.'

'The gun's been good to me all these years, Karl.'

'Of course, it's German. We make great fascists and great guns, even better than the Americans. Was Rosa that redhead from Carmona?'

'That's the one. Jesus, the number of nights I crept out of base to see her.'

'Fantastic breasts, if I remember correctly. But the best one at El Toro Bravo was Cochinta. What she could do with her mouth could make a corpse stiff.'

At this the two men doubled up with laughter again.

Disgusted, Izarra hauled her bag and placed it beside Karl on the bed.

'When you two boys have stopped reminiscing, we should make some plans, then rest,' she said, soberly. August pulled himself together.

'Izarra's right. We have some travelling to do tomorrow. Karl, I need the use of a darkroom. Would that be possible?'

'Sure, the party's HQ has a darkroom out the back. Anything else?'

'A good map of Hamburg, and you mentioned earlier that you might be able to get some information on whether Interpol or any of my other friends have followed me here?'

Karl checked his watch. 'If I leave now, I can still catch my friend at work. In the meantime I suggest Izarra goes to the local store – there's a small illegal market in the ground floor of one of the temporary housing blocks about three

streets from here – coffee, milk, bread, cigarettes, all you need.
Do you have American dollars?'

August nodded.

'Excellent.'

'But is it safe?' August asked.

'For her, yes.' Karl glanced at Izarra. 'If anyone asks, you
just tell them in English you're a refugee with the English.
That will frighten them off. I'll only be a couple of hours.'

'I can take care of myself,' she told him, patting the gun
concealed in her trouser pocket. Karl frowned, then held out
his hand. 'No weapons.' Reluctantly, Izarra took out the gun
and handed it to him. He placed it on the table. 'If Tommy
catches you with that, he'll arrest you and question you. Try
and stay as inconspicuous as possible. Naturally, this is difficult for a beautiful woman,' he concluded, a little
patronisingly.

'You insult me.' Izarra stepped forward and August, anxious to stave off another argument, came between them.

'Izarra is a seasoned fighter.'

There was a beat of tension then Karl turned back to
August. 'Maybe, but here being invisible is more important.
Remember this is an occupied city, under constant surveil-
lance with a curfew.'

Karl led them out of the cabin back to the scullery. He
showed them a large water bottle under the sink and pulled
open the icebox.

'There's cups in the cupboard and the camping stove has
gas if you want to cook. Feel free to make as much noise as
you like, no one can hear you. I'll leave the map for you then
I'll be gone till early tomorrow morning.' He swung his jacket
over his shoulders. 'I'm going to leave you the BMW in case
you need it. It's less noticeable than the car and it has German

plates. Just don't crash it. She is my first love and maybe my only true one. I'll take your car. That way if anyone is following you, I will create a false lead. Be good, you two.'

Back in the captain's cabin August ran his hands along the edge of the work surface that folded out from the wall. Then he rapped his knuckles against the top to check. Sure enough, it sounded hollow. He took out his Swiss Army knife and prised open the edge. There was enough room to slide the wrapped chronicle into the space, which was the perfect hiding place. He pushed the wooden end of the desk back into position. No one would even notice. He switched on the small lamp that stretched out from the wall like an aberrant branch and slipped on the white gloves he always wore to examine his rare books. Then he began to unwrap the chronicle. Now that Izarra had gone for supplies, the submarine felt eerily empty – strange distant clanking noises seemed to come from inside the pipes and the occasional electronic blip sounded out randomly in the thick silence that filled the confined space. It was hard to dismiss the sensation that the absent crew, who seemed to have left invisible trails of past activity like comet tails, were not about to step around the corner of some steel portal or cabinet.

'Hello, old friend,' August told the chronicle. The remark hung in the air before being swallowed again by the oppressive atmosphere. It was cold comfort. August smiled to himself; it was absurd that someone like him, who'd happily gone into battle, fought close combat against ridiculous odds, should be scared of ghosts. And yet even his very seat, on which the Soviet captain must have sat and wondered during dangerous expeditions and dives if he had made the right decision or if he had unnecessarily endangered his own men, even this seat seemed imbued with the presence of the executed sailor. The whole ambience of the sub reminded him of a time during the Civil War when he was commanding a unit of the Lincolns. There was an out-post – a deserted nunnery with a tower that looked out over a small town – that had changed sides several times before August's men finally retook it from Franco's troops. The tower itself had been witness to a number of killings as each wave of riflemen were slaughtered by the incoming army. It offered the ideal outlook but a rumour had started among both the Republican and Nationalist troops that the tower was haunted by one particular ghost, a young fascist who had sustained a wound that left him disembowelled but alive, barely alive, when his battalion had to evacuate the tower, leaving him to die a particularly nasty and lingering death. The story was that you knew the ghost was there when you felt the slithering cord of an intestine slip around your neck. August was always careful to post two men up there, but one night he was forced, due to a lack of troops, to post only one rifleman. The young sharpshooter from Wyoming was found the next morning at the foot of the tower, having thrown himself off the top in the middle of the night. After that August always took ghosts seriously.

He was just about to open the chronicle when the sound of footsteps resounded over the hull. He froze, listening. The sound came again, of clanking and the definite creak of footfall. After slipping the chronicle into his jacket pocket, August reached for the Mauser and got out of the chair as silently as he could, gun held ready. He stepped into the passageway, dimly lit by pools of dirty yellow light shining down from a string of naked bulbs. Looking up, he tracked the footsteps above as they walked the length of the craft, picking his way carefully over the metal ribbing so he didn't trip and betray himself. A sudden gust of air ruffled his hair

and shirt collar, a draught running down the centre passage
of the U-boat. The tower entrance must have been left open.
August tensed. There was no way Izarra would have been so
careless and if it hadn't been her – who had? August felt
thankful that, after Karl had left, she'd insisted she take her
gun with her. At least she was armed. Every shadow seemed
to harbour an intruder and several times he swung around
expecting to see an assassin at the ready.

He reached the command bridge and as quietly as he
could, stepped onto the first rung of the steel ladder leading
to the surface. Now he could feel the wind whistling in from
the open hatch of the U-boat, prickling against his skin.
Knowing he was utterly vulnerable to attack, he continued
up. If someone was waiting, he would be an easy target once
he reached those top rungs. Cautiously, he climbed up until
his head and shoulders were just through the open hatch. He
looked out over the hull. It was hard to see, there was a
heavy fog beyond the entrance of the bunker and it was dark
in the recesses of the building. He quickly crept out onto the
hull, grateful for the rubber soles of his boots. Suddenly,
there came a bloodcurdling howl from the shadows. Startled,
August stumbled back, skidding on the slippery metal. He
fell, catching at a handrail with his left hand, and hung for a
moment from the side of the submarine, holding the Mauser
in his right, ready to shoot. Just then a rat bolted from the far
corner of the bunker and scurried along the wooden plank to
the jetty. It was followed by another unearthly yowl and a cat
leaped out of the dark after it. The cornered rat jumped into
the filthy strip of brownish water glinting between the hull
of the U-boat and the canalside. The cat, spitting furiously,
glared down at it, then looked up at August and bolted into
the fog. By the time he peered back down at the dirty brown
water the rat had disappeared. Cursing his own stupidity, he

hauled himself up and clambered back onto the hull. Still with his gun at the ready, he walked over the plankway and switched on the light in the bunker. Apart from the rusting machine parts and boat engines littering the sides, the place was empty and yet it felt as if someone had just been there. August stared out into the fog. He could just see as far as the edges of a yard opposite. Everything appeared shut down, devoid of people. There was no sign of Izarra. Where was she? he wondered. He checked his watch; she'd been gone for less than an hour.

After telling himself not to worry, he switched off the light in the bunker and returned to the submarine.

The lamp was still on in the captain's quarters, now shining down on the tiny, empty wooden table. Only now, where the chronicle had been only minutes before was a single magnolia, droplets of water still shimmering on its petals – completely incongruous in the compact and utterly industrial surrounds. Its thick scent filled the little cabin like a dream. August gaped at it in shock. So someone had been there, but what was this? A symbol? A warning? He turned, almost expecting the intruder to be standing right behind him, but there was nothing except the arched metal entrance he'd just stepped through, framed by bolts, with the array of wiring and pipes running along the corridor behind it like the spinal cord of some robotic centipede. How was it possible for someone to enter so silently and swiftly without him seeing them? It could only have happened while he was out by the mooring. Even they must have exited from the other side of the U-boat. *How could anyone move that fast that quietly? Nothing human, that's for sure.* Determined to stick to a rational train of thought, August pulled out the chronicle and opened it at the next chapter – the one marked 'Germania'. Just as he thought it would be, the flower that headed this section was a magnolia – identical to the one he held in his left hand.

'I bought some pumpernickel, cheese, some sausage, a couple of apples and some beer. It's freezing out there.' Izarra unloaded the bag onto the scullery bench. August was sitting at the kitchen bench, nursing a vodka having found a hidden bottle, trying to regain a sense of control, his brittle sense of security utterly violated. Surprised by his silence, Izarra glanced over at August.

'What's wrong? You look like you've just seen a ghost.'

'We had an intruder.'

'What do you mean?'

'They left a signature – a magnolia. It's identical to another one in the chronicle. August held out the journal, the magnolia lying along the spine, its large flat petals mirroring the illustration on the page opposite the '*ancient and beautiful abode of the Hanseatic burghers of Hamburg*'.

Shocked, Izarra sat down, her eyes wide with disbelief. 'It's him.'

'If it were him, he would have killed me and taken the chronicle.'

'So who is it?'

'I don't know.'

'And why haven't we heard from Jacob by now. He was meant to contact us to let us know where Tyson is.'

'It's too early. Give him a day or so.'

Izarra pulled the lid off a beer bottle and drank from it. 'August, you are making the mistake of assuming you are more intelligent than Tyson. I know this man, I saw how he was with my sister. Using the chronicle to trap him is not going to work. You are just being sidetracked. The real reason why we are here is to kill him.'

'I told you before, he is going to stand trial as a war criminal. If we kill him, we become him.'

'You are him!' She slammed her fist onto the table. 'You're just as obsessed by the chronicle as he is! That's the real game here—'

'You're being unfair!'

'Then tell me why aren't we going straight to Geneva to talk to your father? We know Tyson has to go there sooner or later.'

August was at a loss for words. Was she right? Had Shimon's obsessive quest hijacked his perspective? And yet he felt compelled to find the next maze. He was too far in. He'd risked far too much to abandon the hunt now.

'Izarra, you have to understand,' he tried to sound as convincing as he could, 'the chronicle holds the key. You want to know why your sister was murdered? Why Jimmy wanted me to have the book? Why your ancestor was executed? We will get Tyson, but right now the chronicle is more important.'

'More important than the liberation of my people? More important than trying to stop a deal that will fund Franco for decades? There isn't anything more important.' Furious, she swung around to leave. August grabbed her by the arm and pulled her towards him.

'Izarra, I'm sorry. I just can't let go right now, but I promise—' He stopped, their faces only inches apart, her mouth tantalisingly close to his, the beauty of her black eyes an utter distraction. She stared up at him, furious, but she didn't pull away. Abruptly the anger turned and they were upon each other, pulling off each other's clothes, lips clashing together hungrily, hands fumbling with buttons, zips, tearing at scarves, all rational thought having fled. August, his thighs trembling, could barely think. All he wanted was to be inside her, weeks of desire having risen and broken through any constraint. His hands reached into her jacket for her breasts, the soft full warmth of them, the large nipples hard against his palms, her sex, hot and wet against his fingers. They fell against the edge of the table and an apple broke from a bag and rolled down to the floor forgotten, like an escapee from a parable.

Izarra, wrapping her legs around his hips, drew him down to her lips, her mouth. For a second August hesitated.

'Izarra, maybe this isn't a good idea.' But, flushed with lust, her eyes blazing, she pulled him back towards her.

'*Sí, sí*, it is good. I hate you,' she whispered into his mouth, in Spanish, her hand reaching for him, the shocking touch of her on him, on his cock, the undeniable fact of his desire. He lifted her up and carried her out of the scullery down the narrow corridor and into the captain's cabin. He lowered her onto the bed, then banged his head as he bent down to join her and the two of them burst into laughter.

She lay curled in his arms, her sleeping face pushed against his chest, her long hair scattered across his forearm, her aquiline profile and lips, the bottom fuller than the top, eloquent in repose, her curved eyelashes fluttering in dream. They had made love like animals, like saints, like thirsty people who hadn't drunk for a month and the intensity of it had shocked him to the core. He couldn't remember being so openly sensual with anyone, not even Cecily. But the feeling was as much emotional as sexual. He had been himself with Izarra. There had been no pressure to pretend to be someone a little gentler, a little more civilised, someone who had never lived nor tasted the edges of life, which was the man he'd always felt women expected him to be before now.

Was that why he'd never told Cecily about Spain, about so
many things about his past? He'd been so careful to present
an acceptable construct, the urbane man who would never
commit murder, legalised by war or anything else. The
charming rogue, always ready with a joke, with ironic banter
that deliberately skated across the surface of darker issues.
This was the man he presented to the world. But Izarra?
Izarra knew all, or nearly all of it. He wondered what her
reaction would be if he told her about Charlie, or the massacre he himself had been forced to order at Belchite –
would she condemn him? Or understand the terrible paradoxes war made an ordinary man face? He looked at the
sweep of her back and hip, her broad shoulders defenceless
in repose. And in that moment he thought that he would
always want her, because she made him feel whole. The
stunning simplicity of the revelation shocked him. He imagined she would accept the truth of him, say nothing in that
profound way of hers and yet understand everything. After
all she had fought in the same war, seen the same unmen-
tionable things. Was it just this that made her different from
the others? Or was it more – a shared instinct, a common sensibility?

He traced the curve of her breast with the tip of a finger,
the warmth of her rising and falling with each breath. She
wasn't manicured or perfect; her body was a working body,
the strong legs, almost as muscular as his own, the large
breasts peppered with a shower of moles, the thick black
pubic hair, fecund, lush. Her sexuality had an uninhibited
primal drive and it had liberated his own. Swept away, he'd
placed his own pleasure first and, to his profound delight,
this had only excited her further. Their lovemaking had felt
like an act of worship to a dancing God who had filled
August's head with some resonant song, or note, a melody

that took him away from conscious thought, from the limitations of himself, of his past. For a moment it felt as if he had been offered a whole possible future, one he would never have conceived of a mere month before. It had felt like hope and, even more disturbingly, he found himself wanting to stay. To be with her. He rested his head against the bedhead, the warmth and scent of their two entwined bodies rising up, an oasis of intimacy in a sea of hard metal edges. He could not believe how intense his emotions were. Here was a man undone, he thought smiling, thankful she was asleep – the great icicle melted, and yet he was finding it hard to trust what his heart was telling him. Where was the usual sense of panic, of sudden suffocation he always felt after making love? The immediate desire to leave, to shed his post-coital body like a shell and flee the moment? He stared down at Izarra. If anything, he found himself more terrified that she would be the one to leave him. The strength of her resolve, the singularity of her existence, meant she had no need for him. She was not someone who needed protecting, or even supporting – she was as resilient as he was, her past as dense and complex as his. She might have wanted him but she certainly didn't need him. It was a painful observation.

Izarra rolled away from him in her sleep. Carefully, he shifted his leg from under her, making sure he didn't wake her, then, after slipping on his trousers and a sweater, went to the desk. The chronicle still lay open atop it, the magnolia on the page. He began reading the text he had translated only hours before.

We arrived in the Hanseatic port of Hamburg by means of a postal coach. It hath been a long and hard journey and I feared for Uxue's health, for I knew she was with child. Once in the city, I sought refuge with a wealthy Jewish silk merchant who hath sought the services of a physic for his young son. The child had but a fever and, with the help of Uxue's herbal remedies and my own skill, the fever broke within two days and the child was robust again. The merchant, a kind but illiterate man, whose intellect hath been swallowed entirely by his mercantilism, was embarrassingly grateful and thinking I hath saved the life of his only son, asked how he could repay me. When I told him I needed to construct a maze, the man was astounded, but after I explained the folly was to be in service of a great mystic power that would enhance his reputation as a pious man, to his immense credit he declined to ask any further questions but instead supplied me with both labour and a plot of land in a pleasant fishing village that was advantaged by being a great distance from the city gates and its harbour. Built on a steep slope along the banks of the Elbe, it was used as a point for the barges that ferried people across the river. It was well positioned and afforded a broad view of both the river and the pleasant industry of the passing Hanseatic League ships – pretty with their sails and painted hulls. The grounds the merchant hath offered up were themselves at the foot of the garden of his own summerhouse, a retreat he hath called the House of Sweet Water, as once it had a well famous for its sweet spring water. The gardens were of a generous size and I hath voiced my reluctance at such an imposition on his own private estate, but he hath reassured me he liked doolhof and hath seen such botanical labyrinths on his travels in the Netherlands, pledging he and his family would keep the maze safe and intact in its design. We began work almost immediately, as our passage for England hath been booked and our departure was now weeks away. These were happy times, for the city, used to foreigners through trade and shipping, welcomed both myself and my wife. Although one morning while at the market I thought I saw my nemesis again, the betrayer of my family, her long red hair and stature was unmistakable, but just

as I had become convinced she hath followed me to the city, she
disappeared from sight. Again, I found myself wondering
whether what I'd seen was my terror made manifest or whether
she really hath followed us from Spain. I could not sleep that
night. I now am secretly resigned to leaving Europe altogether. I
dare not tell Uxue.

Izarra groaned faintly, momentarily distracting August
from his reading. He got up and pulled the blanket over her
shoulders, then went back to the chronicle. He stared down
at the transcribed words, trying to remember the geography
of Hamburg. *A small fishing village on a steep slope once visited*
by ferries. Shimon's description resounded in the silence of
the cabin broken only by Izarra's breathing. He unfolded
the map Karl had left for them, tracing his finger over the
Elbe to the west of the city. Othmarschen was too near; the
next suburb along, Nienstedten, was a possibility, but it still
felt a little close. Then he remembered Karl describing
Blankenese as a place full of large country houses traditionally owned by the rich burghers of the city. Was it possible
the physic's maze still existed in the garden of one of those
mansions? It would be extraordinary if that was so, but not
inconceivable. Running his eye along the bank, he found
the area, further along the river; the perfect location for a
small medieval fishing village.

After replacing the chronicle into the hollow of the desktop, he grabbed the Rolleiflex, the Mauser and the helmet
Karl had lent him and stepped out of the cabin.

Malcolm Hully looked out of his office window down across
the rooftops. Sandwiched between two sections of guttering
a blackbird perched on the edge of a nest was busy feeding
a fledgling. With a jolt Malcolm realised somehow the

season had changed without him being aware of it. August
Winthrop had hijacked his waking hours and he had the
unpleasant sensation that if the case were to end badly, it
would fall on his head. He sighed, then paced the tiny
office, two steps to the door, two steps back, thinking. Why
was August obsessed with this Tyson character? He'd managed to glean some information from his friends in
Washington, but after a few vague snippets the Americans
had closed ranks. Tyson was either very high up or very
embarrassing. Malcolm couldn't get an indication either
way. Ever since Burgess and Maclean, the Americans
regarded the British Secret Service as little more than a
bunch of upper-class buffoons playing at amateur hour.
There were times that, frankly, Malcolm could only concur;
even so, MI5 couldn't afford this situation with August to
become yet another international embarrassment. One
thing Malcolm had found out was that Tyson had held close
ties with Spain for over a decade and he'd been there in
1945, on what Malcolm was now beginning to believe was a
black CIA operation the British knew nothing about. But
how did this link to August? Had he known Tyson from the
Spanish Civil War? August was out of Spain in 1945, and if
he was KGB, why would the Soviets have been interested
in such an operation?

Malcolm stopped at the wall and rested his forehead
against the plaster. He'd had the language department translate the Russian note they'd found in August's apartment.
He couldn't get two stanzas of the poem out of his head:

> But I will go
> Though a scorpion should eat my temple
> But you will come
> With your tongue burned by the salt rain.

He was convinced the stanza was code for a mission – but what mission and what code? How was August going to sabotage the defence pact? Would it be violent? A surprise bombing of the US Embassy in Spain? An assassination attempt? It was a horrific thought. Malcolm repeated the stanza to himself. The pattern matched nothing they knew of the code the KGB was currently using. Perhaps the fact that Lorca had been a Spanish Republican poet murdered by the regime was symbolic to the mission somehow?

One thing was certain, August was on an operation to either destroy or sabotage the US cash for military bases deal with Franco. The question was, how and when would he hit? They had no idea where the American was now, but sooner or later he would have to go to Switzerland.

Malcolm picked up the phone.

'Maxine, get me Upstairs, I want to know who we have in Geneva, preferably in the UN itself.'

The sun had just started to streak its thin way through a violet-grey dawn. Winding his way along the Elbe on the BMW, August left behind the built-up areas of Hamburg and the streetscape widened into leafy suburbia, the neatly sloped roofs of the Teutonic middle classes. The river, a broad grey band running along the left side of him, seemed also to have changed character the further he rode from the port itself, taking on a gentler more rambling nature as the river traffic thinned to the occasional ferry. August had packed the map, his gun and his Rolleiflex before leaving Izarra, still curled up and sleeping. Looking down at her, he'd tried to stop a great wave of tenderness that shot up from the soles of his feet. It was something about seeing such defensiveness and strength momentarily at rest, the childlike way she had bent her arms above her head, laid out on the pillow, an unconscious gesture she'd probably made since a baby. Her face was devoid of the sorrow and the air of acerbic brittleness she always seemed to carry with her and it was profoundly moving to see her looking so unmarked both by time and experience. For a moment he'd been tempted to lean down to begin to make love to her while she was still sleeping, if merely to observe that flush travel across her cheeks again like some sudden aberrant sunrise, but he knew he should leave and this time without her. So he'd walked away from the steel bunk and, after carefully closing the cabin door, left the U-boat, ensuring that the entrance was securely locked behind him.

A rabbit darted across the road, jolting him back into the fresh morning air. Already the day was heating up. Twisting the throttle, he tried to lose his emotions in the icy wind. *I must not get involved, I must not.* His hair streaming back, the sun burning his face, the thought beat on like a tattoo and he realised Izarra, her taste, scent, the echo of her body, had fastened hold, sending tendrils through him like strata in a rock.

Behind him he thought he heard the sound of a car back-firing. He looked over his shoulder – there was nothing but the lane receding behind him in the morning haze. He hadn't encountered another vehicle for at least twenty minutes and the road felt eerily deserted. Unnaturally so, and he couldn't shake off the sensation of being followed, or watched, like prey in an open field. Was Izarra right? Was Tyson three moves ahead of him? Did he know about the existence of the mazes and if he did, why hadn't he attempted to assassinate August and steal the chronicle yet? What was he waiting for? For August to do the groundwork for him? Had he been unwittingly leading Tyson to exactly where he wanted to go? Was he just a pawn in a bigger game?

August couldn't shake off the niggling sensation that he might be.

He arrived at a fork in the road and following a sign came to the crossroads of what must have once been the village of Blankenese, now swallowed up by suburban surrounds. He parked the BMW against a tree and glanced around for someone who might know the area. It was still early, the shops had just pulled up their shutters and he saw only a few pedestrians on the street. He walked around for a good ten minutes before he saw an old postman delivering letters from a large sack across his back, and went up to him.

'Excuse me, sir?' he asked, in German. The old man turned around, his long face thin-skinned, his forehead bulbous with knotted veins, the eyes, pale blue and red-rimmed, peered out suspiciously.

'*Ja?*' he retorted, brusquely.

'I am looking for an old house in Blankenese, which was once known as the House of Sweet Water, a long, long time ago. I'm sure no one would know the area as well as a gentleman like yourself. Have you heard of it?' August hoped that his schoolboy German didn't sound too ridiculous. The postman, obviously concluding August was a foreigner, crossed his arms defensively, his eyes narrowing.

'I'm not a gentleman, I'm a postman,' he told August, firmly, in that candid German fashion.

'Exactly,' August replied, having decided the best tactic was to reply with similar bluntness. 'Which is why you are the best person to ask.'

'Funny, because you're the second person to ask about that house in two days.'

August tried to hide his surprise. Feigning casualness, he joked, 'Really, you must be getting sick of us. Was he an American perhaps, like me?'

'No, a woman, not a young one either. But there was something about her eyes . . .' The postman's voice trailed off for a moment, then his focus came back. 'Maybe someone has published something about this house in a tourist guide?'

'No, nothing like that, just coincidence,' August reassured the German, who he felt was less likely to volunteer information if that was the case. August's mind whirled. Who was the woman? The same one who followed him to Irumendi?

'Well, you're lucky, because I have also spent my entire life in Blankenese. Of course, back then it wasn't even considered part of Hamburg. There wasn't even a bus you could catch to get here—'

Frightened he would ramble, August interjected: 'The House of Sweet Water?'

Deliberately ignoring him, the postman looked closer at August's jacket. 'Are those American cigarettes?'

Taking the hint, August offered him one. The man lit up and sucked gratefully. Exhaling, he continued: 'I suppose you are one of those ghoulish tourists who collects war memorabilia? Looking for something to take back to the folks back home, a souvenir of the monster Hitler to put on the mantelpiece?'

Confused by the man's aggressive tone, August stepped back. 'Sorry?'

'The Well House. You're after the Well House, isn't that right?'

'It should have a large garden – grounds, even, at the back. Are we talking about the same place?'

'We're talking about the same place all right. The House of Sweet Water used to be known as the Well House. There was an old story that a miracle happened there many, many years ago, maybe hundreds. A young priest vanished into thin air. My grandfather once told me it used to be visited by pilgrims, but we're talking about the same place only in this century. As I was saying, before the war it was known as the Well House, then after that the Well Academy for Hitler Youth. The original owner was a Jew, you see, and the Führer, in his wisdom, "confiscated" the building in 1939. After that it was used to train Hitler Youth, and then, when they started to send them to the front, some as young as fourteen, the boys I used to see training in those gardens, they were getting younger and younger, lambs to slaughter they were. Not that I'm saying it was wrong or right. But it happened, don't let anyone tell you otherwise.' The postman paused, finished his cigarette with one long drag then ground the butt under his heel. As he looked up his face clouded over with some distant terrible memory. 'When the Russians came everyone, everyone who was still standing that is, surrendered, except for the academy. They might have been boys but they still knew how to use a gun. They held the Soviets off for two nights and two days, until there were fewer than twenty boys left shooting. When the Russians finally got in, the place looked like an abattoir. When they found that some of the boys were as young as six it was said that even the Russian soldiers wept. No one has gone into the house since. On a quiet night they say you can still hear the boys singing their patriotic songs. And now here you are, a souvenir hunter.' He spat into the gutter.

'My friend, trust me, I am not here for souvenirs. I am interested in the architecture of the building itself, and it is old, isn't it?'

'Over a hundred years old and there has always been an estate there. The gardens are even older, now all overgrown.'

'So can you direct me?'

'If I do, I can't vouch for your safety. It is haunted, you know.'

'I can take care of myself.'

Reluctantly, the postman pointed to a small lane.

'It's toward the Elbe in the Treppenviertel. It's like a rabbit's warren down there. I will draw you a map. But if you meet an eight-year-old ghost called Werner, say hello. He was my sister's boy.'

The Treppenviertel turned out to be a labyrinth of narrow lanes and steps set on a steep slope that ran down to the bank of the Elbe. They wound down between the mansions and houses, all of which were set on large plots of land that broke up the hillside in a series of terraces. Following the postman's handwritten map, in pencil on the back of an old envelope, August found himself in a lane flanked by high hedgerow, the glistening flagstones underfoot slippery with morning dew. He followed the path down to another set of stone steps, the vista of the Elbe and the flat horizon beyond dipping tantalisingly in and out of view like some distant paradise below, with each new twist of the path. Finally, he arrived at a high iron gate, the footpath beyond almost entirely overgrown with linden and chestnut trees. The gate, white paint peeling and rusty, was fastened with a heavy lock and chain. It looked like it hadn't been opened for years. A wooden sign, part of it vandalised beyond repair, proclaimed 'Die Akademie für die Jugend von Hitl—'. Careful not to catch himself on the spike railings, August climbed over the gate. Under a canopy of branches and accompanied by the sound of creaking tree trunks moving with the wind, he followed the path, barely visible through the weeds that poked up between the paving stones, down to a terrace. Heavily overgrown, the area looked as if it had been deliberately planted to conceal the path and the top storey of the large stone three-storey mansion that now appeared, visible on the next terrace down. Beyond the house lay yet another terrace further down the slope towards the river. This, August could see, was once tended grounds – landscaped and manicured – now overgrown like a sharp photograph that had lost focus. And it was at the far edge of this terrace that he thought he could see the high topiary of a small maze.

She leaned against the cool red brick, gazing out over the grounds below. The mansion was noisy to her. There were the more recent whisperings that seemed to reach out to her like arms extending down the long whitewashed corridors that reminded her of a hospital. She knew it had been a school of some sort during the war. There were the rows of iron bunk beds lining a once-grand room that must have been a ballroom – the proletarian utilitarianism startlingly ugly against the peeling gilt grandeur. And there had been children. She'd come across a crumpled football, hopeful in its faded chequered expectancy, waiting like an obedient dog, by a door, lost in time. But what disturbed her most was the faint singing, strange patriotic songs she half-recognised, that rose up like reeds wrapping themselves around her ankles. Still, she knew she was in the right place, the place where he would come, soon. She felt him. She'd followed him and now she was waiting.

She glanced back down at the overgrown lawn that sloped back towards the next terrace. She wouldn't even have to go looking for him – he would find her and then she would save him, from himself, from the obsession that had hijacked him like so many before him and hopefully from the malevolence she was certain was shadowing both of them. The only question was, was she too late?

The mansion was a Gothic mausoleum, a classic example of nineteenth-century aspiration reaching back towards a medieval fairy tale landscape. There were turrets, fake ramparts running between them, an arch of stone over the massive front door and grimacing gargoyles at the corners of the roof beams. A lawn, now peppered chaotically with weeds and wildflowers, stretched out before it, a broken archery target still standing at an angle like an old war veteran at the far end. August could feel the mansion – its windows glinting in the morning light like a dozen eyes – draw him toward it. Come to me, come to me, it whispered, like a petulant woman moaning from a bed. He resisted. He had to find the maze first – the house could wait.

At the end of the lawn, the grass had become a moist sponge under his boots. He reached a low brick wall that edged the terrace and clambered down, some ten feet, to the next terrace. This was an entirely different terrain. Completely neglected, without a remnant of landscaping, it looked as if it had been derelict even when the academy was functioning, unless, August noted, the Hitler Youth were using it as a rehearsal ground for forest reconnaissance or underground resistance. Brambles had sprouted everywhere, climbing and running between young saplings that had shot up among the established birch and oak. Using a knife, August slashed his way to a small clearing and climbed on top of an old tree stump. Through the branches he glimpsed part of an old stone wall set in the far right-hand corner of the terrace.

He fought through the rest of the brambles and found

himself staring at a wall of about eight feet in height. He followed the wall around, carefully examining the base, looking for a tunnel under or a door. There didn't appear to be one. The wall seemed to enclose a courtyard, one completely invisible from the upper terrace he'd just climbed down. It was a perfect concealment. Was it a maze? One that had been completely bricked in? He looked back into the tangled undergrowth. Near a corner of the wall was an old tree that had died and fallen against another. The felled tree was only feet from the wall. Using all his strength, August pushed it towards the wall and it fell against the stone, dislodging some of the large grey stones from the top. Using branches for footholds, he climbed up the trunk. At the top of the angled tree he swung his legs over to the top of the broad wall. Catching his breath, he gazed over. The curved edges of a maze were instantly recognisable. From where he was sitting he could see the three round stations of the left side of the Tree of Life, with their inner rings of maze encircling the centre of each sephirot: the sephirot of Geburah was immediately opposite, Binah to his left and Hod to his right. The start of the design, Malkuth or Kingdom, must be to his far right, he noted, as a way of orienting himself. He slipped a hand into his jacket pocket and pulled out Jacob's drawing of the Tree of Life. Holding it up, he compared it to the maze before him. His calculations were right – he now knew his exact position, facing the left side of the maze. The living wall, made of woven willow, grown over with ivy, looked somehow forbiddingly impenetrable. After securing his camera around his neck, he jumped down onto the maze side of the wall.

There was only a gap of a few feet between the maze's topiary and the wall. August began edging around towards the start and base of the maze, to the sephirot Malkuth. He found the entrance, over which grew an arch of wild roses. He stepped into the outer ring and made his way to the centre. In this maze the centre of Malkuth was grav- elled, filled in, blank, like a closed eye, August observed. Which sephirot would have its eye open to God this time? he couldn't help wondering. He felt as if he were walking on a massive code card with some of the symbols punched out, some left blind – all he needed to do was to lay the cards over each other and together each punched-out letter would make a word. It made him think of the mathemati- cians the SOE had employed during the war to decode the German transmissions. He could really use one of those guys now.

In the first maze it had been Malkuth, the lowest in the tree and the tenth sephirot, that had been planted. In the second maze Yesod, the next sephirot going up the main trunk of the Tree, had a symbolic herb growing in its centre. Therefore it would be logical to assume that the next circle up the middle – Tiphareth, or Beauty – would be planted. Or so he rationalised.

August turned so that he faced the top of the maze, directly opposite the entrance. He was now looking down the middle path, one that should lead to Yesod. Checking Jacob's map, he realised it was marked as path thirty-two. Jacob had explained that each path had a spiritual meaning, symbolic of the emotional and psychological transformation the devotee would undergo through taking that path – another step towards enlightenment and to Kether, the Crown or the top of the Tree. What path should he take? he pondered. Had he already triggered some psychological transformation in himself by stumbling blindly down these paths before? It was an intriguing thought. He started down the path, the hedgerow thick and towering on either side. It led directly into the outer ring of the next sephirot, Yesod. The centre of the sephirot, as he suspected, although open to the sky, was unplanted, a bare, scrubby patch of gravel. After winding his way back to the outer ring of Yesod, on a whim August took the left path. This led to an opening in the hedge and beyond that the complexity of Hod. The centre of this sephirot too was unplanted. Radiating from this sephirot were five paths (including the one he had used to get there). Visualising the design, he took the fourth path along, planted with thistle and orchids. To his immense satisfaction, it led to the centre sephirot – Tiphareth. Finally, in the centre of this sephirot were planted two simple bushes – one of laurel and one of bay, ringed by a group of stones that looked ancient. He plucked a small twig from each of the bushes then made his way to the edge of the sephirot. He looked across at the path opposite that he knew would lead to the top of the maze, the Crown of the Tree of Life – Kether – and noticed something glittering in the sunlight now filtering in from above. He checked the number of the path from the map – nineteen. After slipping the sprigs into his pocket, he started up the path. Halfway along he discovered a flat stone flecked with flint set into the path and set into this stone was the clear imprint of a set of footprints of naked feet – as if a man had once stood there. Scratched under the footsteps was the inscription:

Dominic Baptise 31.10.1709.

Amazed, August dropped to his knees, running his hands across the surface of the worn stone. The imprints were a geological impossibility. It was as if the young monk had stood there, perhaps naked, and somehow marked the rock for centuries with just the touch of his bare feet. It was then that August noticed something buried in the gravel by the inscription and the edge of the stone: a tiny white head. Digging carefully, he scraped away at the surrounding gravel and pulled free a miniature statuette of an angel, wings unfurled, a primitive almost demoniac depiction. The whitish clay it had been modelled from looked familiar. August realised with a shock where he knew it from – it was made of the same material as the statuette that had been thrust into the mouth of Copps's corpse. Bone, human bone.

Horrified, he dropped it on the path. *I've got to get out, I have to.* Panic flooding through him as swiftly as nausea, his vision darkening, he found himself back in the Spanish forest with Charlie, walking into the clearing he'd visited alone the night before, a place he had chosen for its isolation and soft soil easy to dig into. The trees had opened up above them and there was the moon; that thin pock-marked crescent looking down at him that now seemed to mock him, August's heart roaring its pounding fear in his head and there was Charlie as real as ever, turning and smiling.

'Look at me, Gus, look at me. I'm about to be freed,' he tells him, and skips, no, dances into the centre of the clearing and, as August's fingers tighten around the hidden revolver, begins to spin in the faint moonlight, his face tipped up to the loud stars that pour down on him, and he is beautiful, his tall thin figure a whirling dervish, and August is aiming his gun, is aiming for the heart ...

August came to. He was crouching against the foot of the wall of hedgerow. *Keep a grip, stay in the here and now. All else is an illusion, August, an illusion.* Cradling his head in his hands, feeling disorientated, he allowed the blood to rush back into his brain before standing. Then he brushed himself off and, using Jacob's map, navigated as fast as he could back to the place where he had climbed over the wall and into the maze.

He studied the wall before him. He had to cover ten feet to reach the top, where the trunk still rested. The wall was worn and there were a few potential footholds. He picked a loose rock from the ground and chipped away at the footholds until there was space for him to slip a toe in. Then he hoisted himself up, his left foot resting precariously in the first foothold until he swung his leg up the wall and found another gap for his right toe. He was close enough to reach the top of the wall with one hand now. In seconds he had climbed to the top and sat astride the wall. Looking back over the maze, he realised he didn't have enough height to take an aerial photograph. He turned back to look at the upper terraces and the mansion. It was then he noticed the turrets.

Ivy had run into the windows and threaded its way across the old parquet wall like hungry fingers. August had climbed in through a large shuttered window that had fallen in on the ground floor. To his surprise light streamed in from an open hole in the roof at the top of a grand central stone staircase that dominated the entrance hall. The boys had assembled here, probably every morning, August imagined. The remnants of a shredded banner still fluttered from its pole at the top of the stairs. He saw them all standing there saluting the swastika, unquestioningly, shiny in their enthusiasm. He shook the vision off and looked around. To his right through a huge oak door that hung off its hinges he could see into the banqueting hall where there were still rows of long wooden tables, some with battered tin mugs on them. The walls were peppered with gunshot. To his left, through another set of half-opened doors, there appeared to be an office, with a typewriter still sat on the desk, pieces of paper, curling and brown, scattered across the floor, intermingling with dead leaves and ivy. It was unquestionably creepy. A strange smell permeated the air – mould, rotting wood and something faintly metallic August couldn't quite place but was convinced he had smelled before, in battle. It unnerved him.

Determined to put the postman's stories of ghostly singing out of his mind, he stepped onto the staircase and a board cracked with a loud resonating snap under his weight. He froze. His entrance had been silent until that point and he liked to think of himself as an invisible observer, undetected by the dormant house and its ghosts; now he had been betrayed. Moving quickly, August climbed the rest of the stairs and made his way through the upper corridors. The ceiling was lower here and he was sure he would find a door to the ramparts and a turret. Yet he felt the growing awareness of something other than him. It was like he was being watched. It wasn't just the old portraits, hanging from the walls (many of them defaced and torn) but the dark recesses around each half-closed door and entrance he came across. Instinct told him he wasn't alone. It was a sickening sensation and he held his gun low and ready by his hip. In an enclosed space like this he was an easy target.

The walls of the corridors were marked with graffiti – *Elvis Presley Regein! Die Briten können unsere Frauen nehmen, aber sie brachten uns bunte taschentuche! Klaus liebt Birgit* – local poetry from teenagers who must have broken in, August assumed. At the end of the corridor he found a door with the key still in the lock. To his surprise it still turned. He stepped out onto the ramparts, the sun now high in the sky and the morning brightening up. In the distance stretched the river, the two lower terraces clearly visible. He leaned over to get a clearer view of the overgrown terrace with the maze in the far corner. He could just about see the faint rings of the sephiroth set out in that distinctive design he now knew so well, but he still wasn't quite high enough to get a good photograph. He looked back down the ramparts. The turret was set at the end and looked to be at least ten feet higher than where he was standing. Just then there was the noise of scuttling. He jumped back and flattened himself against the ramparts ready for an attack. Two doves, obviously disturbed from their nests, flew past missing him by inches. Relieved, he made his way to the turret.

The turret was a perfect stone miniature tower, a nineteenth-century imitation of a Saxon rampart. August wondered at the nature of the rich burgher who must have commissioned the building – why had he left the maze intact? Was it possible he was a direct descendant of the merchant who had helped Shimon? August stepped up into the stone arch, open to just a foot above the turret floor, and looked down over the terraces. Now he could see the maze completely from above, the centre sephirot Tiphareth clearly a green circle against the nine other empty ones. He lifted his camera out of the bag, removed the top of the case and the lens cap, and began carefully lining up the image in the viewfinder.

He heard a rush of air and felt an arrow shoot past his left shoulder, catching the fabric of his jacket. He ducked and, still crouching, scrambled down from the arch, then, to his greater shock, found himself thrown to the floor by someone who had jumped from above. He lay winded for a second, pinned down. The man on top of him, at least he thought it was a man, was hooded and smaller than him, but surprisingly strong. He hauled August to his feet and then pushed him backwards hard towards the arch in the turret wall, where August tottered for a second, almost losing his balance as the back of his legs hit the low wall below the arch, the dizzying sight of the ground fifty feet below snapping into focus over his shoulder. His attacker came forward again, to apply the final push, but August managed to find his feet and wrestled the man to the floor of the turret, where they rolled in a tangle of struggling limbs. August, assuming he was fighting a youth, was shocked at his strength. Although slight, the attacker was surprisingly muscular and well balanced, regaining some purchase on the flagstone floor and pushing August back once again towards the open arch and certain death below, when another arrow thudded into the assailant's side through the open arch on the other side of the tower. The youth fell into August's arms. Another arrow flew just over their heads and August lowered him to the floor hurriedly. He pushed the hood back and was shocked to see the face beneath was that of a woman – and one he knew.

'The arrow, it's silver-tipped,' Olivia murmured, struggling to raise herself, staring up at August.

'Keep still, I'll get help.' His mind whirled as he tried to remember who she was – London, Oxford? Spain, even? But he couldn't quite place the features.

'It's no good, silver kills me. I am to die. At least I saved you.' A thin streak of blood ran from the corner of her mouth.

'Who are you?'

'We've been watching you for years. You have an extraordinary talent, pity you waste it in the flat world.'

'The flat world?'

She was now fighting for breath, her hands involuntarily jerking.

'The mazes are an anagram. They tell of a shortcut – a shortcut to enlightenment.'

She was dying. It was obvious to August, holding her hand. He wondered whether she was still lucid. Or was she hallucinating?

'Did you kill Professor Copps?'

'Julian?' she whispered, and something passed across her features, softening her pained expression. 'We were lovers once. I'm not sure you could call it murder, as much as seduction ...' Her voice was failing. She tried to pull him closer, her hand clawing at his jacket. 'Listen to me, the chronicle ...'

'The chronicle, you are after the chronicle?'

'The chronicle is sacred. Shimon's message must remain unspoken.'

'You're working with Damien Tyson?'

'Once, not now. But he is a Magus, the most powerful, and Wicca, as we are.'

'We?'

The woman managed to smile and suddenly August recognised the face – from years before, from his student days, from those hours he'd spent in the Pitt Rivers Museum in Oxford, studying the tribal masks and ritual objects. She was the curator of his favourite exhibition room in the museum – 'Magic, ritual, religion and belief'.

'Olivia Henries?'

She nodded and another arrow flew inches from August's head to ricochet against the wall behind him. Olivia reached up, her bloodstained hand clawing at his jacket.

'You must go, he will be here soon. He will kill you.'

'Tyson?'

'He turned, like the sun, to dust, such power ...' Her hand fell to her side. She was fading fast. 'Take my pendant and put it between my lips so I may die with the name of the Goddess as my last word. Hurry,' she whispered.

'Olivia, I have to know, what happened to the priest, what happened to Dominic Baptise?' But now her skin was ashen and her lips had started to darken. He reached down and from under her jacket pulled out the pendant she was wearing, one etched with the same symbol as on the pendant Jimmy had given him, ripped from the throat of his attacker in the Paris catacombs.

'The other assassin who attacked van Peters, she was—'

'My lover. Shimon never understood the power of Elazar's gift, but you could. He was a fool, idealistic,' Olivia murmured, her eyes now rolling back. Her breath was laboured; he had seconds.

'How do you know that?'

She smiled – an amusement that shimmered under the pain. 'Because I was *there*.'

He stared at her, remembering the description of the woman Shimon had written about in the diary, the woman who had betrayed his family to the Inquisition, who had mysteriously appeared in Avignon. As if reading his thoughts, she nodded slightly, then her head fell back, lifeless. August held onto her body for a moment. That last look of hers had almost been one of affection. How could she have known so much about him and yet he had barely been aware of her existence?

He placed the copper medallion between her blue lips and lowered her body to the floor. Keeping his head down, he began to inch his way out of the turret and along the ramparts. He peered over the top. Below, the deserted driveway looked surprisingly tranquil – a blackbird hopped across the sparse blades of grass that had shot up between the gravel, its head cocked quizzically up at August as if it intuited his gaze. Apart from the bird, he could see nothing moving.

August scanned the panorama; in the centre of the derelict grounds was an old fountain, with a large seated bronze figure of Neptune flanked by a couple of Teutonic-looking nymphs. A shallow pool of greenish water surrounded the centrepiece. As he looked, August noticed movement reflected in the smooth surface of the water to the side of the statue. Squinting, he could just make out the reflection of someone behind the statue, someone tall, someone holding an odd-looking weapon. It had to be Tyson or one of his men. Whoever it was, the man was professional, as the reflection revealed a modern cross-bow equipped with viewfinder.

August crept further along and slipped over a low wall to a roof beneath. From there he dropped onto a terrace, then climbed down a drainpipe to the ground, at the side of the house. He hugged the wall and looked around the corner – the man came into view. He'd stepped out from the fountain and was walking slowly, crossbow raised, towards the front of the house, looking hard at the turrets above for his quarry. August lifted the Mauser, steadying his wrist with one hand. Aiming carefully, he fired.

The bullet hit Vinko in the side of the head, killing him instantly. He swayed for a second on his feet, then toppled backwards, the crossbow falling to the ground. August listened for anyone else but he heard nothing, only the faint cawing of crows and the distant hum of a shipping barge on the river. In front of him was a mass of brambles and overgrown roses. Then there was the sound of a passing car – the road must be beyond the brambles, higher up the slope. Without stopping to examine the body, he raced across the open lawn, then dived into the brambles, beating his way as fast as he could to the top of the terrace and freedom, half-expecting gunfire to cut him down any second.

Seven minutes later he emerged from the overgrown garden and burst out onto a tarred road he calculated to be the main road running above the Treppenviertel towards the centre of Blankenese. He saw the motorcycle parked twenty metres away, back down towards the steps that led to the mansion. He ran down, and, after leaping on the bike, swung it around and headed back towards Hamburg as fast as he dared drive, leaves and brambles flying from his hair and shoulders as he sped away.

As August turned towards Hamburg-Mitte he found himself behind a school bus, with a garbage truck approaching in the opposite lane. As he waited to pass he glanced in the wing mirror and saw a black Mercedes turn into the crossroads from the same direction he had. August watched it cruise his way in the mirror. It was following him. He gunned the BMW up onto the sidewalk, narrowly missing a couple out for a stroll. He overtook the bus, dropped back onto the tarmac, then went straight through a red light, outraging the bus driver who pushed down on his horn. But by the time August had swung into the next street it appeared he had lost the Mercedes. Crouching lower in his seat, he hit ninety miles an hour, the R75 smooth under his grip, the Elbe flashing past on his right like a brown snake, and for a moment he was swept away by the exhilaration of the chase. Then the Mercedes re-emerged, only about thirty metres behind him. The built-up streets of the city loomed up on either side. Each time he tried to lose the car it reappeared, as though telepathic. As he hit Altona, he took a hard left, then another, squeezing by a lorry unloading, which baulked the Mercedes. He roared towards the narrow streets of the Speicherstadt, then up onto a loading barge that threw off its moorings just as the Mercedes pulled up fast at the kerb.

The barge took him down to the south side, where he disembarked and threaded his way through the docks and down the canals to the bunker, the U-boat and, most importantly, Izarra.

22

August knew something was wrong the moment he entered the bunker – the entrance hatch to the U-boat had been left open and all the lights in the submarine were blazing. He scrambled down the submarine ladder as fast as he could.

'Izarra!' he yelled out, wanting her to be there waiting, perhaps even to rush down the narrow steel-ribbed corridor to greet him. Instead his own voice bounced back at him in the ominous silence – she hadn't even called back to him. His heart started to pound uncomfortably. Had he made a huge mistake leaving her alone? Had whoever pursued him visited here first? August bolted down to the captain's quarters. The cabin door was swinging open. The bed where they had made love had the covers pulled back and was rumpled as if she had just stepped out, but there was no sign of her clothes nor her bag. Not daring to think about the implications, August rushed to the desk and pushed the end of the desktop off one hinge. It swung open revealing the hollow interior. August reached down into the desktop, and felt a wave of relief sweep through him as he touched the wrapped package of the ancient manuscript. But where was Izarra? He looked back at the bed, at the indentation her body had made in the mattress. His first thought was that they had abducted her. Cursing himself for leaving, he sat down on the bed and punched the pillow in frustration. It was then that he noticed a note left under it, the scrawled handwriting in Spanish. His stomach lurching, he picked it up:

Dear August, I went to the central post office and found a telegram from Jacob – he is in Geneva. He says Tyson is there and the agreement between the US and Franco is imminent. I have gone to join him. I'm convinced this will be the only way we can catch Tyson and sabotage the pact. Izarra.

Furious, August crumpled up the paper.

'Bird flown the coop?' Karl's voice boomed out, and August swung around, startled.

'Jesus, you scared me. I didn't think anyone else was here.'

'Sorry, I learned to walk without making a sound in prison. Invisibility was a good way of surviving – I perfected it.' He glanced down at August's shirt. 'You're bleeding?'

Surprised, August lifted his sleeve. It was stained red from Olivia's blood, from when he had held her dying body.

'Not my blood, someone I tried to save. I've just been fired at, strangely enough by a crossbow, over in Blankenese.'

'An arrow will still kill. They didn't follow you here?'

'I lost them in the Speicherstadt.'

'Good. I would appreciate it if you didn't leave too many dead bodies behind you. One I can explain away, two gets a little difficult.' He glanced at the letter August still held. 'So, your Basque woman has gone, my friend?'

'To Geneva. I can't blame her, it's probably a better strategy.'

Karl glanced critically at the rumpled bed.

'And I'm guessing it's no longer such a platonic work arrangement?'

August smiled ruefully. 'She's a good woman, Karl, courageous, strong-willed.'

'Pig-headed? They're the best, the women you can't control. What's in Geneva apart from UN and a few Swiss banks?'

'A UN resolution is going to be passed on the impending US defence pact with Franco. I promised Izarra I would do what I can.'

Karl turned towards the desk, noticing the end of the desktop hanging off like a hinge. 'I have bad news. I made a few enquires – both Interpol and the Americans are after you. But what is more of a concern is that none of this is official, you're off the radar.'

'That would explain the professionalism of my pursuer.' August stepped up to the desk and extracted the chronicle. Karl smiled knowingly. 'So you must have some information they want very badly.'

August held the chronicle close to his chest. 'Or I have information they don't want exposed.'

'Gus, who is the man you're after?'

August glanced over. It wasn't that he didn't trust the German – he couldn't afford another death, not of an individual who had defied so many odds, a fighter with an almost supernatural aptitude to survive.

'If I tell you, they will kill you, like they killed Jimmy and Edouard.'

Karl sighed. 'I understand, but I would have liked to have helped. Things have got a little quiet around here since liberation. Of course there's always East Germany and Berlin – that will be interesting now Stalin's dead. Everyone has got

so wonderfully jumpy. It is going to be a real funfair ride, Gus.'
He grinned then slapped August on the back.

'You've helped enough, but meanwhile,' August pointed
to the Rolleiflex sitting on the bed, 'I have some photos to
develop.'

The photographic paper floated in the tank, the image
unfurling in a growing palette of greys and blacks as the
developing chemicals worked their magic. Now the distinctive design of the kabbalistic Tree of Life emerged like a
matrix. Smaller than the other two mazes, and ringed by the
stone wall, the Blankenese maze's topiary was still distinct
enough to see the pattern clearly. August pulled the wet
photograph out with the tongs and pegged it up to dry next
to the other two shots he had taken. Outside, he could hear
Karl and the young Communist who ran the centre arguing
in angry, guttural German over who would be the next Soviet
leader.

Shutting his mind off, August stared across at the drying
image, the centre sephirot. The third circle up from the base
of the design was spectacular against the others, dark in its
foliage, while the others stood bare and empty, white circles
surrounding a black. It was like Morse code, a cipher that
related to the placement of the other planted sephiroth. He
sat down at the small worktable and under the infrared light
studied the images of the other two mazes. An anagram,
Olivia Henries had told him, as she was dying. He'd translated enough of the text now to know there was another maze
mentioned further along in Shimon's book, but the pages of
the last chapter were missing, torn off. Yet the three mazes he
did have images of made up a line of planted sephiroth –
that had to be the main clue. The line could be a symbolic
way to reach enlightenment, he guessed, remembering

Jacob's words. Perhaps Shimon had discovered the most direct, fastest route to enlightenment knowing how much significance both kabbalists and occultists attributed to the thirty-two different paths one could take to reach the highest spiritual plane.

So far it had run directly from the base Malkuth/Kingdom – the first sephirot to be planted in the maze in the Basque country – to the next sephirot up the central trunk Yesod/Foundation – planted in the Avignon maze – and now to Tiphareth/Beauty, the third base along the central trunk. It was too simple and too easy. But unless he had an aerial photograph of the fourth maze, it was impossible to know which way the line would run from Tiphareth. It could go to the right – either up to Chesed/Kindness or down to Netzach/Victory – or it could go to the left – up to Geburah/Severity or down to Hod/Splendour. Was it possible that the Hebrew letters that began the name of each sephirot could make up an anagram that translated into another message? And he still didn't understand the significance of the plants so carefully tended and cultivated in each planted sephirot. They too had mystical meaning – were their linked names an anagram? And how did Olivia mean the mazes were sacred? Whatever their power, it was obviously sacred and secret enough for her to have sacrificed her life. But why to save him? The idea that he might have been pulled into a role that had been preordained somehow had begun to tug at the edge of his mind. How much real control did he have over all this? Was he falling prey to the same obsession that drove Shimon and perhaps the young monk Baptise to their deaths? Did Tyson have the upper hand? Was he being manipulated in some way he was unconscious of? August glanced over at the photograph of the German maze. The black branches of a tree in the foreground reminded him of Izarra's hair spread on the pillow the night before. The idea that without realising he had led her into danger filled him with self-loathing. But what should he do? Follow Shimon Ruiz de Luna's journey to the fourth maze and the next clue to where Elazar ibn Yehuda's great treasure might be or switch tables on Tyson and actively pursue him back to Geneva and join Izarra and Jacob?

That evening, after ridding himself of his moustache and donning a pair of glasses, he caught the express train to Geneva.

Tyson stared out at Lake Geneva, standing next to a line of bathers sunning themselves along the wooden pier of the Bains des Pâquis. He took solace in the variety of bodies lying out on deckchairs, from the robustly middle-aged to svelte long-limbed beauties of both genders naively oblivious to the power they held over others. It was all so human, so animal. He liked that; he liked to observe the flaws, the shifting undercurrents of attraction and repulsion that ran, like electricity, between the observed and the observers. Perhaps that's how the world really ran, he mused; perhaps it was only the way one is perceived by others that actually gave definition to one's existence. If so, who was he? A large presence, he liked to think, imagining with relish how Olivia looked as Vinko's arrow pierced her. One could almost say he was like a god with the power to give or take life. He checked his watch – he had two hours before he had to meet the Spanish general, two hours to strategise. The conference at the UN tomorrow promised to be the apex of all his hard manoeuvring, all of the negotiations he had so carefully set into play. He didn't like how one passion now threatened to destroy the other. The chronicle was not meant to intrude into the Spanish alliance. If the vested interest came to light, he would be court-martialled or perhaps even terminated. Fuck Winthrop, he should have had him killed at the maze. At least he could have saved Vinko. But he couldn't get the antique dealer's words out of his head. *Angels good and bad.* He'd climbed into the maze after August had left, had found nothing but a bunch of circular flowerbeds, all unplanted except one and in the centre of one of the paths those strange engraved footprints. What was he missing? Perhaps he shouldn't have ordered Olivia's killing after all – she would be able to answer those questions. However, patience serves the hunter, Tyson reminded himself. He sat down in one of the deckchairs, tipping the attendant an extra franc, dismissive of the incongruity of his large frame swathed in a tailored Fifth Avenue suit amid the sunworshippers. He watched a ferry chug its way over to the left bank of the lake. There was really no rush. He checked his watch again – the night train from Hamburg came in at nine-thirty and he'd received a wire earlier from a friend at the British base in Hamburg informing him that Winthrop had been sighted boarding it. Yawning, he relaxed into the deckchair and let the warmth of the sun beat a pattern across his sunglasses; the classicist really was so predictable. Time to pay Winthrop senior a call.

August stood outside the Gare de Cornavin. The streets of Geneva, untouched by war, were bustling with a kind of old world opulence and it was hard not to go into cultural shock. The train ride had been tense and he was relieved to discover that the fake passport Edouard supplied hadn't appeared to be registered with Interpol. The Swiss border police had been perfunctory, efficient and polite. They'd studied the passport photograph and smiled when, making a joke, August had taken off his glasses to make perfectly clear it was him in the photograph. And now with his bag with the chronicle in it tucked safely under his arm, he felt strangely invincible, as if his luck increased with each escape from the authorities. It was a dangerous illusion and one he knew well from the battlefields of the Civil War – 'the luck of the blessed, the blessed undead', they called it in the brigade.

Geneva was warmer than Hamburg and the whisperings of summer were evident in the blossoming flowerbeds in front of the station. After circling around the block, carefully scanning the milling pedestrians, he began walking in the direction of Les Pâquis district – an area famous for its cheap migrant hostels, nightclubs and red-light district. It was also conveniently close to the Palais des Nations and the United Nations building. If Izarra would be staying anywhere, it would be there, he decided.

Les Pâquis was a warren of cheap apartments and boarding houses for poor Italian workers and other refugees. August tried at several hostels, but no Spanish woman of Izarra's description had checked in over the past few days. Still convinced she was staying somewhere in the area, he decided to return later, but as he turned away from one hostel he caught sight of himself reflected in a shopfront. Unshaven, with wrinkled trousers and wearing the clothes he'd picked up a lifetime ago in Paris, he looked like some kind of unemployed construction worker or poor immigrant. He needed to disguise himself. He glanced up the street; at the end he could see a neon sign advertising an exclusive gentlemen's sauna. There was a ploy he'd used before – unethical but effective. Steeling himself, August began walking.

Apart from August there were two other men in the changing room: a tall well-built businessman who was just pulling off his trousers and a plump Indian who, naked, was rigorously towelling down his rippling back. The whole place smelled of a cheap lemony disinfectant. August glanced surreptitiously around; through a glass door he could see a small plunge pool, around which several naked men lounged on wooden benches; it was obviously a pick-up joint. Opposite the plunge pool door were several doors that looked as if they led to individual steam rooms – this would buy him time. August unbuttoned his shirt and let it fall to the ground. *Look at me, look at me.* He willed the businessman to turn in his direction. *That's it, take the bait.*

The man, in his early forties, glanced appreciatively over at August, who assessed his physical dimensions in seconds. He was roughly the same build as August and the suit, now folded on the bench, looked expensive. August smiled back, a subtle whisper of encouragement. Now wearing only a small towel wrapped around his waist, his excitement evident, the man nodded discreetly in the direction of one of the doors of the steam rooms. August nodded then indicated he would be a few minutes. After giving August another appreciative glance, the businessman stepped into one of the rooms. As he left the Indian went back out to the plunge pool, leaving August alone in the changing room.

Within minutes he had pulled on the business suit, tying the silk tie as he exited.

A block away August ducked into a second-hand shop and purchased an old briefcase and placed all of his belongings into it – the final prop to the disguise.

The United Nations building was vast. It was hard not to be intimidated by the sheer size – built in the style of a Grecian temple, the ionic columns soared up towards an unerringly perfect blue sky. It had been built to impress, to reduce the pedestrian to a mere foot soldier expected to serve greater ideals than his mere mortality. Recalling the ineptitude of the ill-fated League of Nations during the build-up towards the Second World War as a way of stiffening his resolve, August walked briskly up the steep stairs, feigning a familiar casualness. Stepping into the shadow of the columns and through the huge glass doors, he approached the reception desk.

'*Bonjour*, Madame, I am here to see Mr Clarence Winthrop. I believe he is with the US delegation currently in chambers.'

The receptionist, a steely old matron, ran her eye down a list placed before her.

'Mr Winthrop is in the building. Is he expecting you?' Her gaze briefly settled on his jacket. He glanced down and noticed he'd missed a button doing up the jacket.

'Absolutely.' August looked over at the huge clock that hung over the entrance to the inner courtyard. 'About five minutes ago in fact, and Senator Winthrop is a most punctual man.'

The subliminal pressure worked. *Trust the Swiss to care about such matters*, August thought, thankful nevertheless as the receptionist reached for the phone.

'And your name?'

'Monsieur Tubbs,' he told her, with a straight face, knowing his father would recognise the name.

Three minutes later she directed him to the UN offices behind the great assembly hall.

Senator Clarence Winthrop sat behind a vast oak desk, which was more notable for its bare surface than its immensity. A single document sat in the middle and beside that a large glass ashtray in which a cigar – Cuban no doubt –

smouldered. He had his head bent over as he read, his hair, once thick and black, was now thinning and a pure white, August observed with a poignant shock. It was a bleak reminder of how many years had passed since he'd last seen him. The diplomat looked up as August shut the door. Their eyes met and August's stomach clenched despite his resolve. *How could I have been your son, when there is nothing we share except a coldness of heart?*

His father, a large man with an even larger presence, had not lost any of his presidential, patrician air. He stared expressionless at his son, his florid complexion mottled with age. Then without a word he put the cigar to his mouth, sucked, then exhaled, eyes closed, the broad hands August remembered as a child now liver-spotted and latticed with blue veins. So the patriarch *is* mortal, he thought bitterly to himself, *long live the patriarch.* The silence stretched into an unbearable tension. Unsure of his next move, August walked into the middle of the room, noticing a UN pass had been casually left atop a pile of newspapers and magazines on a side table against the wall. His father rubbed his eyes.

'Mr Tubbs? I thought it must be you,' Clarence Winthrop remarked, flatly. 'So all those years of reading *Moby Dick* amounted to something. If only this, the prodigal son returning to haunt his dying father.'

August pulled up a chair opposite the desk. The last time he'd seen his father was in late 1938, just after he'd returned to London from Spain. His father was visiting London to see his good friend Senator Joseph Kennedy, then the US ambassador. Both men were full of admiration for the German chancellor Herr Hitler, an opinion Clarence Winthrop had voiced over an embassy dinner, much to August's horror. Father and son had argued publicly and then privately, August resisting his father's wishes for him to return to Boston and consider a career in either the military or politics – both of which the senator could facilitate. The argument had finished in a violent stalemate and the two men had not spoken since. Now August found himself remembering all those affectations and opinions he'd loathed about his father. Watching him, August noticed with a silent shudder that his father held his cigar in exactly the same manner he himself held cigarettes, same long fingers, same hands. Despite his revulsion, he fought the impulse to light up himself.

'Are you dying?' August asked, trying not to sound hopeful.

'Nope. But you will be soon, if you're not careful. You look like a cheap spiv. I guess this is what you spies call a disguise.' He practically spat the word out, and August guessed he was far better informed than he was revealing.

'Oh, come now, Father, I'm far too candid to be a spy, surely you remember that about me?' It was a calculated risk. Lolling back in the chair, August feigned a blasé amusement, the entitled dilettante. It was the way he imagined his father had always seen his younger self. His father studied him through a cloud of cigar smoke.

'That's right, you're a freelance researcher, writer? Whatever the term is nowadays for agitator. The real question is, August,' he leaned forward, 'why are you visiting me now after fifteen years, here in Geneva at the UN?'

'You know why.'

Clarence flicked his ash into the large ashtray moulded in the shape of an aeroplane, an inscription across the wooden base declaring it to have been a gift from the First Infantry Division 1917–1919. The ash fell in a gentle cascade of grey dust.

'I might and I might not. Maybe I just want to hear you, for once in your life, beg me for something.'

'That's not going to happen.'

'Then I guess I can't help you.'

There was a short pause as the two men stared at each other. Somewhere in an office nearby the telephone rang then stopped.

'How's Mother?'

'You know how she is, son. I know you two write.' Clarence's hand hovered dangerously near the telephone. Any minute August knew he could pick up the receiver and call security.

'Father, I'm here because I know there will be another attempt from the US in the general assembly to have Franco accepted back into the UN and I know that Truman plans to sign a defence pact with the dictator in September.' It was a flat, matter of fact statement, not a plea, not an apology, yet as soon as he said it the old fear of disappointing his father began to churn in his guts. *The bastard still has a hold*. August tried to push down the impulse to leave.

'Jesus, August, when are you going to start surprising me? Don't you know who just died? Stalin! Have you any idea what this could mean in terms of US security? We could be on the brink of a new world war, and we *know* the Soviets have nuclear weapons. Washington could be the next Hiroshima unless we have bases close enough to the Russians to strike first. We need those bases in Spain.'

'Franco is a fascist. Two hundred and twenty-six million dollars will fund him for decades – he has murdered hundreds of thousands of his own people.'

'And the Soviets will murder us given half the chance. I see the bigger picture, August. You were always the blinkered idealist. I suppose you're in cahoots with this crazy Englishman.' He looked down at the dossier in front of him. 'A Jacob Cohen.' He frowned in disgust. 'Probably a Zionist.'

Jacob. August's head whirled with possibilities.

'What about him?'

'He infiltrated the conference and staged a protest yesterday.'

'He's been arrested?'

'He's a British citizen. But the Swiss have detained him. A friend of yours?'

August changed the subject. 'So you won't help me at all?'

'Sure, I'm helping you right now by not picking up that telephone and calling security. Son, you have twelve hours to get out of Geneva before I alert Interpol and the guys over at the Bureau myself. I think that's fair, don't you?'

August got up from the chair.

'I knew it would be a waste of time coming here.'

'And you should know, in case you were thinking of getting materialistic later in life, you are no longer in my will. For me you no longer exist.'

August stared into the face of his father, searching for a flicker of empathy, one tiny window of emotion. There was none. His father's face was as blank as wood, the only betrayal a slight twitch at the corner of his granite jaw.

'Was I really that much of a disappointment?' he asked him, softly.

'I'm just thankful I have two children.' As if that concluded their relationship, Clarence turned his back and stared out the vast glass window beyond which stretched the long perfectly manicured lawn of the Court of Honour. Not daring to dwell on his own emotions, August began walking out, swiping the UN pass from the side table as he went.

'The Swiss have done what?' Malcolm screamed down the telephone to the ambassador's aide. 'Cohen should be under our jurisdiction – he is the subject of an MI5 investigation, and he has nothing to do with the Swiss.'

'He committed a crime on Swiss soil, within the UN itself.'

'How long can they detain him?'

'Another twelve hours.' The attaché sounded young, nervous, straight out of some minor private school west of Kent, Malcolm thought ungenerously. Christ, he hated dealing with amateurs.

'Make sure you thank the Swiss profusely,' he retorted, his voice heavy with irony, then slammed down the phone and directed his attention at the agent lounging on the small couch set against the large Regency window that overlooked Lake Léman.

'Nice suite. Upstairs must like you. Stacked bar fridge?'

'Appearances. I'm a visiting businessman, remember?' Malcolm snapped. He was trying to regain some strategy: the whole situation was getting out of control, and if he didn't get August back now, his job would definitely be on the line. He was certain August was somewhere in Geneva and the last thing he needed to deal with was the distraction of some maverick independent like Jacob Cohen. He turned back to his Swiss counterpart, an ambitious operative they'd originally recruited in Monte Carlo, Roger de Pestre, son of an ex-Belgian diplomat and English mother. De Pestre had welcomed both the intrigue and the financial means to stay on the cocktail circuit. He was already helping himself to some champagne.

'Roger, I want you to go over to the UN building and chat up the secretary of Clarence Winthrop. See if he's had any unusual visitors recently. And if any fit August's description, let me know. After that you're to head over to Le Havre police station on Her Majesty's business. Make Cohen sing. I don't care how and I don't need to know the details. If he doesn't sing, silence him. Make it look self-inflicted.'

De Pestre smiled. Malcolm had always suspected him of

being somewhat of a sadist. 'With pleasure.' De Pestre raised his champagne glass. 'Chin-chin.'

August sat in a small office in Le Havre, the central police station of Geneva, waiting to see Jacob Cohen. At the reception he told them in his best British accent that he was a journalist with *The Times* and unless they allowed Mr Cohen to give his side of the story, August was happy to publish some embarrassing revelations about the lack of press freedom in democratic Switzerland. The ploy worked eventually – after they initially refused he had threatened to phone his old friend the British ambassador, who, August claimed, would be most interested to hear how he was not allowed access to a fellow British subject. In fact August knew the ambassador's aide – they'd been to Oxford together – but he doubted the aide would have remembered him, except for the fact that August had seduced his sister.

They ushered August, clutching his briefcase, into a bare room with a table and a barred window. After a few minutes a guard led Jacob in. He barely bothered to look at August, his demeanour listless and defeated. *Oh God, what have they done to you?* Jacob sat at the table, August opposite him. Sporting a black eye and a bandaged wrist, he showed no signs of recognising the American until the guard had left the room and locked the door behind him.

'So you came after all.' Jacob looked up, struggling to contain his emotions.

August opened the briefcase and pulled out the three photographs of the mazes, and a notepad. He indicated Jacob's wrist.

'Was that the guards?'

'No, they treat me well here. That was UN security. There was a scuffle in the press gallery.'

'I heard you caused quite a disturbance.'

'He was there, August. Tyson. Smug as they come, in person, sitting with the US delegates, like he wasn't a criminal, like he was human. I couldn't help it, I lost control. You've seen your father?'

'It was him who told me you were here. Apart from that it was a total waste of time, except that I now have only', he checked his watch, 'about eleven hours before he gives me up to both the CIA and Interpol.'

'Your own father?'

August didn't need to reply – his face said it all. Jacob leaned forward. 'Tyson is at the Beau Rivage, room thirty-nine,' he said, in an urgent low voice. 'And he isn't the only one. One of the Spanish delegation is there too. A general called Molivio.'

August blanched. 'Cesar Molivio? Are you sure?'

'Positive. You've heard of him?'

The sound of the general's voice came flooding back to August, his calm inflections over August's own screaming: *The trouble with young men like you is idealism. You think your Communist friends will support the people if they get power? My dear young man, you are deluded. They will be worse than Franco. Tell me who they are, save yourself.*

'He tortured me, in Spain. Back then he was only an officer.'

'Sounds like the type that would be a good friend of Tyson's.'

'Where's Izarra? She followed you here about two days ago. Have you seen her?'

'Just before I went into the UN.'

'Is she okay? Where's she staying?'

'Somewhere in Les Pâquis, I don't know where exactly. Listen, you have to get me out of here as soon as possible.

Tyson will have me killed if the English don't claim me, and, frankly, there's little chance of that.'

'I promise we'll get you out of here.'

'Another thing, August, in case something does happen.' He pulled the notebook towards him and scribbled down something. 'This is the number and code of a locker at Cornavin station. Inside is an FBI dossier I stole on Tyson. Everything you need to expose him is inside.'

There was a sharp knock on the door then the guard poked his head around the side. '*Dix minutes!*' he barked, then locked the door again.

'There's one last thing I need from you.' August pointed at the three photographs, laid side by side between them. 'This is the third maze.' He showed Jacob the photograph of the Blankenese maze. 'As you can see, here Tiphareth, the third sephirot from the base, is planted – in this case bay and laurel leaves. Malkuth had lily and vervain while Yesod had anise and mandrake root. Could this somehow make up an anagram?'

Jacob studied the mazes thoughtfully. 'If there was one, it wouldn't lie in the names of the herbs but more the order of the planted sephiroth – "M" for Malkuth, "Y" for Yesod and "T" for Tiphareth. That in itself makes no sense, but if you add a "D" at the end ... ' here he took August's pen and drew a new circle between the top sephirot Kether and Tiphareth in the middle, '... for Da'ath, you get "MYTD". I've seen the Hebrew letters for this before, in a photograph of an old bronze statuette Tyson purchased – one of those mystical icons. I remember it because it was so strange. It was a pair of winged feet. These letters were written across the base. They stand for "The Eyes of God". It was a name taken up by a kabbalistic cult that dated from the late seventeenth century and was adopted by a maverick English black magic cult in the 1920s, headed up by a follower of Aleister Crowley – an Olivia Henries.'

August looked up sharply. Now a logic was beginning to form to the puzzle.

'She was with me at the maze. She died in my arms, trying to protect me.'

'Olivia Henries? Are you sure?'

'I know her, Jacob, from years ago, when I was a student at Oxford. She worked at the museum where I used to study. But how does this "cult" fit in with the disappearance of Baptise?'

'That I can't answer. I am a rationalist – nothing in my life has led me to believe in God or miracles. As far as I'm concerned he's never there when you need him.'

They could hear the guard unlocking the door. Jacob grabbed August's wrist. 'The reason I know all this is that I have information that in the late thirties Tyson attended a few of their meetings before the war. It's all connected,' he finished, urgently, as the guard entered.

'Don't worry, Mr Cohen, I shall endeavour to secure a release for you as soon as possible,' August said, formally as he packed the briefcase. He nodded at the guard and walked out.

August sat back against the chaise longue and stared up at the atrium that loomed over the lobby of the Beau Rivage. The three-storey hotel was famous for the number of celebrities, politicians and aristocrats who had stayed there over the past decades and it amused August that he found himself in such a place under such circumstances. The Beau Rivage had legendary status with his mother, a social climber and Europhile; she had once stayed there as a giddy eighteen-year-old with her mother, on the obligatory trip to

Europe expected of American debutantes. What would she make of her son now? August couldn't help wondering, a fugitive pursuing his nemesis in a stolen suit. Poor Mother, a woman who prided herself on being able to trace her ancestors to the *Mayflower*, she would never forgive him the scandal.

The elegant atrium was built around an enclosed courtyard in which a pink marble fountain tinkled musically through an atmosphere that was equal parts wealth and discretion, in the way only the Swiss could achieve. Rows of pink-marble square columns edged the courtyard, above which open balconies to the upper floors were visible. The private suites were situated on these floors, August noted, as he sat, armed with a cocktail from the hotel bar, under the pretence of meeting a friend. He glanced at the reception desk. The maître d', a professionally handsome man, was busy dealing with an Arab sheikh and his entourage of two wives and assorted nannies and children, all five of whom were clad in neat little black-and-white sailor suits. The commotion had allowed August time to survey both the lobby and the floors open to the atrium: the hotel was extremely exclusive, with only thirty suites, and he knew Tyson's would be located on the first floor. August sipped his gimlet, thankful for the expensive suit he was wearing. Suddenly, he became aware of being watched. He looked to his right and caught the eye of an expensively dressed brunette, somewhere in her forties. She wasn't unattractive and when she smiled coquettishly back, waiting for an invitation to join him, he was actually tempted – an old reflex. After chastising himself he picked up a copy of *Der Spiegel* from a side table and studied it. A few moments later the woman rather pointedly left, leaving a trail of florid perfume behind her as she sauntered past him.

He was distracted by movement on the first floor. A burly, swarthy man had just stepped out from one of the suites and was standing at the rail of the first floor balcony, waiting for whoever was about to walk out of the suite. A second later General Molivio emerged, joining the bodyguard and lighting up a cigarette, his gaze sweeping around the atrium and down towards the lobby where August sat.

August kept his face forward, deeply conscious of the general's presence. The Spaniard seemed suspended before him, now burned into his brain. August would have recognised Molivio anywhere. He looked older but it was unmistakably him; those same deceptively gentle brown eyes, the handsome Spanish face, a little jowly now, but still with the demeanour of intelligence that had so deceived August and many others after him.

August was paralysed, convinced Molivio must have recognised him, but to his amazement the general merely turned away from the courtyard, his back resting on the rail, oblivious to the fact that a man he'd nearly tortured to death was sitting just below him. August shut his eyes, the very sight of the general sweeping his senses back into those four days of terror: the stench of his own urine and vomit, the whirl of a drill under the rhythmic whooshing of a ceiling fan, the terrible humiliation of having to beg, and then the bizarre circumstances of his own rescue, his total disbelief at the sight of Jimmy van Peters standing at his cell door. Forcing himself back into the ambience of the lobby, August looked back up, watching as the general finished his cigarette, then checked his watch, as if waiting for someone.

On the first floor another man stepped out of another hotel room door further down from where Molivio was lounging. As he approached the general his face came into focus. Tyson was taller than he'd looked in the photograph Jacob had shown

August, and broader. Under the dark-blue suit he looked dangerously muscular, groomed for special operations; August recognised the body stance – a kind of prickly alertness that was never turned off. But to August's surprise, Tyson was very different from the man who had shot at him in Hamburg. That man had been taller, heavier– someone working with Tyson, CIA perhaps? Or had that actually been MI6?

Damien Tyson joined General Molivio at the rail and the two men shook hands. August watched, fixated in horror – it was deeply disturbing, this collision of his past with his present, his nemesis with his pursuer. He had the unnerving sensation of having being lured into the moment – as if it had been fate. He could barely breathe. A waiter came over and asked if he'd like another cocktail. August, exhaling, clicked back into his façade and ordered another gimlet as confidently as he could manage. As soon as the waiter was gone he focused on the conversation floating down from above. The two men were speaking in Spanish, Tyson's voice higher, less expressive, broken by Molivio's more guttural tenor. August could hear snippets: something about the night before, Molivio boasting about something, Tyson replying with a joke about good American hospitality. Finally, Tyson asked Molivio a question and they both started towards the elevator. After a minute they emerged from the elevator and walked right past August, who was now concealing his face in his newspaper.

After they passed he watched them leave through the glass rotating doors to be picked up by a limousine with the UN flag attached to its hood. August left a healthy tip for the waiter and followed.

Molivio studied the American sitting in the limousine beside him. Tyson seemed uncharacteristically nervous. He was

jerking his leg up and down impatiently and he kept glancing behind out of the rear windscreen. Misunderstanding
his anxiety, the general leaned forward and tapped him on
the shoulder. Tyson swung around, a little startled.

'My friend, the UN is a mere formality. However they
respond, our governments have agreed, no?'

'Absolutely, the deal is sealed.'

'Then why so agitated? This is not like you, Tyson. Have
you had an unpleasant premonition?' The general sounded
genuinely concerned, but Tyson knew him better than that.
Have we been deceived in some way? he wondered, as an
alarm bell rang somewhere in Tyson's subconscious.
'Someone has marked out my grave,' Tyson answered, in
Spanish, using a proverb he knew Molivio would understand. The general laughed; another man might think he
was ridiculing Tyson.

'Come now, Damien, men like you and I fly in the face of
such trivia. We search out death like others look for sex.'

But Tyson barely heard him. He'd just seen a man exiting
the hotel who looked hauntingly familiar.

The council chamber of the UN building was a square auditorium built to accommodate around five hundred people.
Compared with the giant assembly hall, it was intimate,
and now, filled to capacity, the atmosphere was one of tense
expectation. August found himself a seat in the public
gallery above the auditorium. He'd entered the building
using the pass he'd stolen from his father's office. The
guard at the door had waved him in after examining the
pass and he'd guessed his father hadn't yet noticed its disappearance.

As August made his way into the chamber he glanced
around. The delegates of the UN countries all sat on a large

podium that faced the hall, with microphones for each main member, nametags sitting before them on the curved desk: The Soviet Union, England, China, France, the United States ... Recognising his father, August ducked down behind the person sitting in the row in front of him. Clarence Winthrop was busy talking to another delegate, oblivious to anyone in the public gallery, much to August's relief.

He sat down, making sure he had a clear view. The rest of the hall was filled with delegates from smaller nations and various representatives. Momentarily distracted by the massive murals decorating the three walls, August glanced up at the ceiling and recognised with a shock the great Spanish painter Josep Maria Sert's work. The chamber's interior was decorated with dramatic monochrome murals – five muscular colossuses reached over to clasp hands in the centre of the ceiling, representing the solidity of nations, while opposite the podium a huge battle scene stretched over three panels. The left panel was a marching army – 'The Victors' – of a group of uniformed muscular men, who looked suspiciously fascistic to August's eyes. On the right panel was a raggedy group of soldiers entitled 'The Vanquished', five struggling naked men, who appeared to be fighting over a fallen flagpole, reduced to a grim line of bodies collapsed over battlements, some of them still grasping rifles. August couldn't help noticing that these men were more motley clad, as if they were once an army of peasants, of revolutionary insurgents. It was a militia he knew well and it was obvious where the Spanish painter had got his inspiration; an ironic juxtaposition to the debate that was just about to begin.

Malcolm Hully slipped through the panelled door that led into the auditorium. In front of him stretched the seated rows of spectators and various delegates. Jutting over him was the press balcony. Where was August, if he was here? Malcolm scanned the crowd, looking for a man of appropriately the right height and weight, then he realised there were a number of men who fitted that description. He would just have to be more vigilant, he decided. Gesture would be the give-away – far harder to change the way one moves, especially caught off-guard. Just then Malcolm sighted de Pestre standing at the opposite exit door. He gave a slight nod. Together they began a synchronised walk along the opposing aisles, glancing up and down the rows as they moved towards the podium.

Malcolm looked up at the dramatic mural on the back wall. The muscularity of both armies had a lyrical simplicity – it was definitely Spain. Lorca's lines came back to him:

> Pero tu vendras
> Con la lengua quemada por la lluvia de sal.

> But you will come
> With your tongue burned by the salt rain.

Malcolm paused mid-step, suddenly convinced he knew what Lorca's lines represented – code for a drop point. Somewhere in Spain, some inside information August had for the KGB on the pact – something that could lead to a sabotage. It had to be. Sensing some catastrophe was about to unfurl, Malcolm spun wildly around as he tried to take in the whole auditorium. Several of the audience members indicated that he should sit down, but he ignored them. He moved swiftly towards de Pestre.

Above in the gallery August scrutinised the delegates

below and caught sight of Tyson and Molivio. They were sitting two rows from the front, alongside what looked like two other representatives from Spain. They were less than thirty feet away, well within view, August observed, while also making a note of the proximity of the two exits nearby. In the centre of the podium the chairman leaned forward to make an announcement.

'The next item on the agenda concerns the United States's proposal to broker a pact with General Franco for the right to place military bases on Spanish soil, and what action the UN should make if such a pact were signed, given the trade embargos imposed on Franco's regime. We await a final comment from the US representative Senator Winthrop on the subject.' His amplified voice crackled across the auditorium, echoed by interpreters in French, German and Japanese, like aural ghosts rippling through the hall. August watched with fascinated horror as Tyson and Molivio moved forward in their seats as his father stood to take the microphone.

'Ladies and gentlemen, after much debate, the government of my country has decided that it is vitally important...'

August noticed a blonde wearing glasses and a headscarf in the row in front of him, only a few seats away. She appeared strangely agitated and somehow familiar.

'... that we, the US, prioritise the security of our nation and of Western Europe itself over local politics. We have therefore decided...'

Now the blonde appeared to be looking for something in her handbag. August tensed. Something was wrong, very wrong. His father's voice boomed over his own frenetic thoughts.

'... that the US will be signing a defence pact with General Franco.'

Pandemonium broke out in the hall at the senator's

announcement and the rest of his statement was drowned out by gasps of disapproval, some applause and some catcalls.

Below August, Tyson and Molivio had got to their feet. In the same instant he realised that the woman was Izarra. All sound fell away as he watched her lift her revolver from her handbag and aim it directly at Tyson's head. He leaped forward, throwing himself over the seats in front of him, and tackled her to the aisle floor. Chaos broke out around them.

'Izarra, it's me!' he managed to tell her, holding down her thrashing body. She stopped struggling. 'Say nothing!' Hauling her roughly to her feet, and with one hand clamped around her wrist, he held his security pass high.

'I have her! Security! Let me pass!' Pushing Izarra ahead and behaving as if he were high rank, he manoeuvred them through the security staff who had also wrestled their way over audience members and chairs to reach them. It was an audacious sham, and already August could see the men looking at each other in confusion.

'US security, let us pass!' he added, in French and German, for emphasis, then bundled Izarra towards the nearest exit.

The lobby of the council chamber was empty; everyone was still inside reacting to the defiance of the US. Noticing a door built into the wall, August hurried Izarra towards it then pushed her through. It was a small service office, filled with spare seating and curtains. August pulled off her wig and headscarf.

'Give me your coat,' he ordered.

'I was so close! I was close, why did you stop me!' She fought back. Ignoring her, he yanked the coat from her shoulders.

'Take off your jacket and smooth down your hair.'

'No, I don't care if I'm caught!'

'Just do it!' Sullenly, she smoothed her hair and neatened her skirt. Without the blonde wig and coat, she was unrecognisable. August took off his own glasses.

'Okay, we walk out of here as calmly and casually as possible. If anyone stops us, I do the talking, do you understand?'

'August, I—'

'Do you understand?'

Izarra nodded mutely. August opened the service door by a crack and gazed into the lobby. Four security guards were running through the lobby towards the council chamber itself – leaving the lobby empty.

'Go!' He ushered Izarra out and they both walked quickly out, then sauntered through the lobby of the assembly hall and out into the reception area. Ten minutes later they were out on the avenue de la Paix itself.

August stared out of the barred window at the narrow alley below. It was now late afternoon, but the lane was empty, except for a lone roadsweeper methodically pushing a broom from one end. He pulled down the blind, unwilling to take any risks. He faced Izarra, who was sitting on a high chair, staring out over the cheap coverlet that was flung over the iron single bed. A calendar of skiing resorts – two years out of date – hung on a bare hook on the wall, the only decoration apart from a bible and an old radio on a dresser beside the bed.

'What were you thinking? You would have been killed, shot on the spot, for what?' Furious with her, and the trance-like passivity she had fallen into since they'd returned to her hideout – a cheap migrant hostel in Les Pâquis – August paced the tiny room, the old floorboards creaking beneath him. He stopped then bent down so that she couldn't avoid eye contact.

'Izarra, do you understand me? I could have lost you.' He lowered his voice, trying to reach into those black expressionless eyes.

Abruptly, they flared up and she sprung out of the chair. 'You don't understand! None of this is important! You and I are not important. All that is important is avenging my sister! The betrayal of my *people*.' Her furious words burst out of her, as she reverted to Euskara. She grabbed his shoulder and shook him. 'You destroyed the one chance I had! Maybe the only chance!' Her whole body was shaking with fury.

'Izarra, we get Tyson my way.'

'Your way! Your way is bourgeois, the way of a coward!'

He pushed her away. 'How can you say that? I fought for your independence! I watched my comrades die around me!' His words emerged with far more bitterness than he intended, and Izarra flinched at his anger. But it seemed to jolt her back into some kind of rationality. Reaching out, she rested her hand briefly over his.

'I'm sorry. That was unfair, but you have to understand I would have martyred myself for Andere, we all would have. She was more than just my sister. We were betrayed, profoundly betrayed, and now this ... this deal with the devil. We will never get rid of Franco now.' She finished, broken and near tears.

August struggled to reply; there was too much truth to her statement. She took his silence as acquiescence.

'Do you really think that even if we did have Tyson arrested for war crimes, he would get an unbiased trial? He is government, the US will protect him. How many Germans got away with war crimes? Most of the Nazis were tried by the judges of their own regime!'

'It's different now, in the Hague—'

'Nothing changes, August, you know that. *¡Nada!*' She

collapsed against his body, spent. 'If we don't get Tyson now, my sister will have died in vain.'

'Izarra, I promise you, on my life, we will see Damien Tyson stand as a war criminal.' He looked at her, the exhaustion, shock and anger making her both vulnerable and powerful, her flushed face noble and suddenly beautiful. Without thinking, he pulled her to him, their tongues clashing, probing, finding solace in overwhelming desire, his hands encompassing her as her fingers reached for him and they fell onto the bed, August half-expecting another battle of wills, another struggle for dominance, but instead finding her ready to engulf him, ready for the anger, the sex, the desire and the fear. They made love like soldiers expecting to die in the morning.

Afterwards they lay there in a curling silence that stretched with each tick of the clock in the corner, the afternoon shadows creeping across the floorboards. August, wide awake, stayed wrapped around her, not wanting to break the respite of this anonymity, two lovers luxuriating in the sanctuary of each other's warmth, unencumbered by history or politics or even the sheer weight of experience, the scent of their lovemaking enveloping him in a poignant intimacy. And he found himself wishing they were simple people with simple lives and a simple love, then fell asleep.

An hour later he woke to the sound of a low murmuring. Izarra stood naked by the open window, a breeze wrapping the thin chiffon curtain around her like an undulating cloud. In one hand she held a torn piece of cloth, in the other his lighter, as she chanted in Euskara. He watched, not sure whether he was still asleep or awake. As she chanted she lifted the lighter up and held the cloth in the flame, then, after pulling back the curtain, allowed the wind to carry the flaming ember away.

'May his limbs be carried to the four corners of the world,' she said, August understanding only some of the words.

A distant police siren startled her. She swung around and saw that he was watching her.

'It was a piece of Tyson's jacket. I have carried it with me for all these years. I needed to be in the same city as him – now I have cursed him.'

The belief in her face was absolute; there was nothing he could say. *It is not for me to take this away from her,* he thought, all the Cartesian philosophy he learned at Oxford, all the deconstruction of such ritualistic myth and magic now starkly irrelevant. *She will take power from where she can; let her.* And so he said nothing. Instead he stood and, walking over, the warmth of his body enveloping her cool skin, pulled shut the window.

'You'll catch a cold this way,' he said, pulling her into an embrace.

'I will kill him. I will.' Her muffled voice drummed softly into his shoulder.

Reaching over to the mantelpiece, he switched on the radio. It spluttered into French, a news bulletin: 'We've just received a bulletin that the young Englishman Jacob Cohen, who was arrested earlier this week for a demonstration at the general assembly hall at the Palais des Nations, has been found dead in his cell this afternoon. Authorities have not ruled out foul play and the police are investigating. The British government have demanded an explanation.'

August broke away in shock and turned up the volume on the radio.

'August? Did I understand correctly?' Izarra ventured, her face blanching.

'Jacob's been murdered. He knew they were going to kill him, he tried to tell me.'

'*¡Pobre Jacob, tan joven!*'

'It's got to be Tyson's work. I should have done something. I should have tried to get him out immediately.'

'There wasn't anything you could do, you're wanted yourself.'

August pulled on his trousers.

'Where are you going?'

'If they can murder him just like that, they will murder us. I have to gather evidence.'

'What are you talking about?'

'Jacob had a dossier he stole from the CIA. He told me where it is.'

He put on his shirt and jacket. Izarra hurried out of the bed, the beauty of her nudity still a shock to August.

'I'm coming with you.'

'No, I go alone. There'll be descriptions of you posted everywhere since this morning. It's safer that way.'

'But you can't go like that, you will be recognised. Wait.' She found her handbag, her breasts swaying as she walked, and pulled out a tube of make-up.

'Here, I bought it when I got the wig. It will make you look dark, olive-skinned. If you put it on and those old trousers you wore in Paris, you will look like an immigrant. No one here even sees them as human.'

August smiled. 'You're learning.'

He reached into his kit and pulled out the dark stage make-up, gazing into the cracked mirror over the chipped washstand. He tilted his face in the light to check that he'd plastered Izarra's pancake on evenly, then hollowed out his cheekbones and eye sockets with a touch of the stage make-up. It made him look downtrodden, exhausted, gaunt and unshaven. The challenge was his blue eyes. He looked back into his bag, pulled out a pair of glasses, one arm fixed with wire. They helped conceal the colour of his irises. It was almost impossible to guess that he was Anglo-Saxon.

'How do I look?'

Izarra examined him critically then reached into her own bag and pulled out an old black beret.

'Put this on.'

He pulled it low over his ears.

'Good, now you look like a street worker, you look poor.'

'Stay here. Let no one in. If I'm not back in two hours, take the chronicle and go back to Irumendi.'

'You will come back, I know it.'

In lieu of an answer he kissed her.

The lockers at the Gare de Cornavin were housed in a discreet side room off the main area of the station. The place was still busy and the Swiss gendarme posted to look out for the blond American his superior had supplied the photograph of. The policeman was momentarily distracted by an attractive woman breaking the heel of her shoe right in front of him. As she stumbled, he rushed to help her up, oblivious to the black-haired, dusky man who limped past clutching a battered suitcase, like so many poor day workers that flooded the station each day.

August punched in the code and swung open the locker. Inside, wrapped in a brown paper bag, was the dossier, 'CIA PROPERTY : CLASSIFIED', embossed across the top. August slipped it into his briefcase then walked swiftly to the men's public lavatory. He locked himself into a cubicle and took out the dossier.

Entitled 'Profile on Agent Jester and Operation Lizard, October 31st, 1945', it appeared full of evidence that Tyson had received no orders to execute the Basque soldiers under his command in the village of Irumendi, but had only ever received an order to cease training and withdraw back to Paris, then the US, as soon as possible. The dossier contained sworn statements from four of the officers under Tyson's command that they had carried out his order believing it came directly from headquarters. The dossier also noted that all four officers had died within a year of the event – and not one of their deaths had resulted from any directive from the Agency itself. The report suggested that Tyson himself was implicated in all of their deaths. But the concluding paragraph was the one that caught August's attention:

> Agent Jester is a ruthless, well-trained individual capable of the most demanding tasks that require a certain kind of operative. Jester is such a man. If he has any Achilles heel, it is his investment in the occult, particularly artefacts associated with ritual or occult practices, of which he is a serious collector. The Agency and other organisations have exploited this vulnerability in the past to their advantage, but it should be noted, such a weakness could easily be used by enemies of the state. However, in conclusion, although Agent Jester should be considered a maverick capable of deviating from orders, and has certainly been culpable of serving himself before his nation, he is currently an invaluable asset due to his relationship with the Spanish regime and General Franco himself. This status may change in the future.

*

Izarra clung to his neck, pulling him towards her even before he had a chance to take off his old coat.

'Jacob's information was invaluable.'

She looked up at him, wide-eyed. 'You have something?'

August held out the dossier. 'Everything we need to condemn Tyson is in this – evidence he was behind the massacre, sworn statements, and the beauty of it is that he probably doesn't even know it exists.'

Izarra took the file from him and sat on the bed, then opened it.

'Izarra, before you read it, you need to understand there is a problem.'

She looked up at him questioningly.

'The CIA will not let him go easily.'

'They know who he is and they don't care?' Izarra's voice was full of outrage and despair. August lifted the file from her lap and placed it on the table. 'I promise this will prove to be of immense importance to us. They emphasised his weakness was an obsession with the occult. It's time *we* started moving the chess pieces.'

He pulled the chronicle out of his briefcase, slipped on his reading gloves and opened it.

'Jacob told me that Olivia Henries, the woman in Hamburg, was part of a cult called the Eyes of God and that Tyson had been associated with the cult back in the thirties. What I don't understand is whether Olivia was in partnership with Tyson or they were working against each other in pursuit of the same object. She warned me that he was a great Magus, but what does that mean?'

'It means he is evil.'

'Sorry, but I don't believe in such a concept – the devil doesn't exist for us atheists. There's amorality, sociopaths, but evil? I know Magus means "wise man" or "magician", but unless I hold to the same belief system as Tyson he has absolutely no power over me.'

'He had power. You forget I met him.'

August opened the chronicle. 'And was Shimon Ruiz de Luna also part of this original kabbalist cult that bore the same name? The Eyes of God? Or was the name a metaphor for something more powerful, in a literal way?'

Izarra sat up. 'You say the name translates as "the Eyes of God"?'

'It's what the initials of the four sephiroth mean when joined up.'

Izarra got off the bed and walked over to the desk.

'Can I see?'

He drew the initials out for her. 'The chronicle appears unfinished but there must have been a final clue as to where the treasure, whatever it may be, is hidden – one that signals the location somehow?'

Izarra stared down at the four letters. '*Los ojos de Dios*, the Eyes of God. August! How could I forget! My mother made me promise on her death that I should never forget – *Los ojos de Dios* are in Córdoba! At the time I just thought she was delirious.'

'Córdoba? That makes sense. Córdoba was a big centre for the Jewish kabbalists – they were practising there as early as the twelfth century. I suspect the cult might go as far back as Elazar ibn Yehuda, whose travels Shimon was re-enacting himself, a man who worked for Caliph Al-Walid.'

'Most of the Moors' palaces are in Seville or Alhambra near Granada, not Córdoba.'

'But Shimon was originally from Córdoba.'

He opened the chronicle to the last pages of the unfinished chapter. A simple drawing of a gardenia sat above the title. In silence August began inking the text, then using his small mirror, translated the original reversed words, reading out loud, Shimon's voice echoing through him, as if he were a mere portal into another time.

I write now in the last days of my life; although I am not yet thirty-five years of age, I know I will not see another winter, which might be a blessing in this English prison.

I might be facing Death yet I am no longer dwelling in the time that is of this moment but in the past and the future that stretches out like the burning light of a dying star. I am with Ein Sof and as such I feel no fear.

The last sanctuary I made was in the kingdom of my forefathers, land of the pomegranate and orange, this holds the crucible, the final key to the window of enlightenment, the lightning bolt along which I can now ascend and descend at will. But although my spirit is no longer bound terrestrially, my flesh remains mortal, and I confess I fear the torturer's rack that I know awaits.

But enough of dark meanderings, tomorrow I will be executed, but I still believe King James will visit me and when His Majesty learns of this great treasure I have promised him, one that will put the full weight of responsibility and the shaping of history upon his royal shoulders, I might be pardoned. I hope him worthy, just as I hope myself courageous.

Here the writing broke off and the page was covered with a rusty-looking stain that resembled blood. August gazed at the phrase 'kingdom of my forefathers, land of the pomegranate and orange'. It had to be in the South, in Córdoba.

They left early the next morning. August had decided the safest way to travel would be disguised as a young married couple. He had taken a pillow and created a false pregnancy under Izarra's dress. The disguise was perfect. He adopted the persona of a nervous, solicitous first-time father, while Izarra, rounded and tottering, looked dangerously pregnant. Just before they left, August stole a flower from a vase on the reception desk, then pinned it above the door of their room – a deliberate clue for Tyson to follow.

The petals were a yellow cream, just beginning to curl at the edges, a gardenia. Tyson held it up to the corridor light, an electric bulb in a cheap plastic chintzy lampshade. The flower had a pinkish tinge to its centre that made him think of a heart, of a faint bloodstain threading through its capillaries like memory. It was a calling card, an invitation – the question was to where? Tyson searched his mind – flowers, symbols of sex organs, of lineage, of surrender and conquest; they all had a magical and mystical symbolism, but the gardenia? He looked at the blossom that seemed to be looking back up at him, taunting him, then remembered seeing the flower somewhere else, somewhere meaningful. It came back to him – the flower on the seal of the letter from Alhambra, the one that spoke of the relationship between the Caliph and Elazar ibn Yehuda and the citadel.

Córdoba.

23

August decided he would book a first-class sleeping compartment for them both to go as far as Barcelona, assuming they would be less disturbed travelling that way. It was a two-day journey and he planned to change trains at Valencia and take the minor train onto Alicante, then go inland to Córdoba itself. It would be easier for them to pose as Spaniards on the smaller trains, and the trains themselves would be less policed.

August bustled Izarra through the station at Cornavin, speaking French to her like an authoritative peasant husband to his young, confused wife. At the ticket office he noticed a flyer on the wall with the mugshots of people wanted by Interpol. The image they had of him was at least ten years old and looked like it had been supplied from the old SOE office. *Thank you, MI5*, August thought bitterly to himself, again reflecting on Malcolm Hully's lack of trustworthiness. But the photograph was so out of date they'd unwittingly done him a favour. In the Interpol profile he looked blond and youthful – in his current disguise he was unrecognisable. He saw no photograph of Izarra, but he noticed a separate written description of a potential blonde female 'assassin', who had created the 'disturbance' in the UN building. The ticket officer, a friendly-looking woman in middle age, was just about to check their passports against the Interpol description when August nudged Izarra, who let out a great groan.

'Please,' he asked the inspector. 'My wife!' He indicated Izarra's advanced pregnancy. 'She cannot stand for much longer. Could you possibly hurry the process up?' He flashed one of his famously seductive smiles at the woman, who softened immediately.

'Certainly, Monsieur,' she replied, stamping the tickets, then handing back both tickets and passports. 'I remember what that felt like myself,' she said, smiling. 'Hopefully she won't give birth on the train.'

'Hopefully,' August replied, rather more seriously, then crossed himself piously, as if to make sure.

There were two policemen at the ticket barrier. As they approached August could feel Izarra's hand tightening in his own.

'Say nothing,' he murmured. They arrived at the barrier and August handed over the two passports. The older gendarme inspected them, glancing carefully at August, then the photograph, then at Izarra. He handed them on to his younger colleague.

'Not married?' He glanced at August, evidently surprised at the two different names in the passports.

'She is my sister-in-law.'

The younger one cracked a lewd smile. 'Your sister-in-law? A likely story.'

August, as cool as a cucumber, shrugged, then stepped forward conspiratorially.

'Well, if you really want to know, we plan to get married as soon as we get home to Spain.' He said it in as provincial an accent as he could muster.

The older policeman, now parodying what he perceived as August's simple manner, leaned forward. 'So you must hurry and catch your train, otherwise the child will end up illegitimate.' He handed back the passports with a straight face. As they walked away they could hear the two officers break into laughter.

The Alps gave way to the dramatic coastline of France and the blue of the Mediterranean. Watching the scenery rush by, August wondered how long they would have to keep running before either the authorities or Tyson caught up with them. He glanced at Izarra's aquiline profile as she stared out of the window and he wondered about the morality of involving her. In some ways it had seemed inevitable, their meeting, the way the chronicle had thrown their lives together through a series of connections, Izarra herself a living thread back to Shimon Ruiz de Luna himself. If he wasn't such a sceptic, he might think it destined that she would be one of the final witnesses, the one person apart from himself who would be there when the cipher of the mazes was broken.

August pulled out his research notes and placed them on the small fold-out table, then laid out the bunches of dried herbs he'd found planted at each sephirot. The cuttings placed atop the pages covered with his illegible handwriting looked like the eccentric notes of some mad botanist, and he was glad they had their own compartment.

'The herbs planted in the mazes and the four flowers that appear as headings in the chapters, they all have meaning somehow. They too are clues. The question is, what is their actual symbolism?'

Izarra picked up the first bunch of herbs August had taken from the planted sephirot Malkuth at the maze in Irumendi. A withered lily with strands of vervain wrapped around it. She sniffed it.

'Well, each herb had magical properties – my grandmother used to place vervain at the bottom of our beds to stop demons from taking us when we were sleeping, but she also said it would give us good dreams.' She picked up the next bunch – found in the sephirot Yesod from the maze in Avignon, which was a withered mandrake root and a handful of anise – 'She hung a mandrake root over the back door to protect the house and to bring good luck, and this one, what do you call it?'

'Anise.'

'This one she told us could make you dream your future, but perhaps not recognise it when you do.' Izarra reached for the final bunch of dried herbs, the bay leaves and laurel August had found in the centre sephirot Tiphareth. 'And bay leaves are also considered to give one both psychic powers and prophetic dreams.'

'But what do they mean in the context of the chronicle? How are they linked to Yehuda's great treasure?' he said, thinking out loud. 'If the great treasure of the alchemist is metaphysical, perhaps it's something to do with either psychological or psychic powers? The text of the chronicle could be interpreted that way. In which case what do the flowers over each chapter represent? And why have these been used as calling cards by our pursuers?'

'Because they are linked to the final maze?'

'Where would a red lily, a carnation, a white rose and a gardenia be found together?'

Outside, twilight had descended and already he could see the glittering sea as the train swept down the coastline

towards Spain. They had folded out the seats into narrow
sleeping berths opposite each other, pillow end at the
window of the carriage. August, in his own bed, was lying on
his front staring up at the darkening horizon that was rolling
across the sky in a great wave of purples and blues pushing
out the crimson of the setting sun. Unspeakable beauty of
the eternal and, for a moment, he was out there sailing in the
air with that night wind streaming over his wings and face. If
only. He turned on his side, the dusk rushing by now filling
his whole vision, and thought about Charlie, the three times
he had come to him in the mazes, trying to piece together
those lost moments – *Charlie, did you know I had been ordered
to execute you? Was that what you were trying to tell me in those last
minutes in the forest? Who had actually fired the gun? Myself or you
yourself?* For the first time ever, August wondered if he had
really killed his closest friend.

'Mind if I join you?' Izarra, in just a singlet, swung her long
tanned legs out of her own bed, her breasts swaying under
the white cotton.

In lieu of an answer August threw back the coverlet and
she slipped in beside him. It was a tight squeeze, the length
of her warm and soft pushed up against him. He turned and
faced her, his sex now hard against his belly, her nipples insistent against his chest. They smiled into each other's eyes
and the rest of the world fell away as lightly as pollen lifted by
a breeze. The train bounced over a bump, pushing them
even closer together; it was a cue that made them kiss, his lips
brushing across her full mouth, his tongue finding both
strength and surrender. Izarra rolled on top of him, pinning
down his wrists. They lay like that for a moment, her moist
sex touching the tip of his, their mouths locked, the topogra-
phy of her body undulating like water over his muscularity. It
was a delicious submission and he was ready to let her take

him. The train accelerated and, as if infected by its speed, Izarra hoisted herself up and lowered herself slowly over him, deeply, deliciously; faster and faster she rode him, her head thrown back in undisguised pleasure, the long hair now a wild mane, until he could lay there no longer. As the train entered a tunnel he lifted himself and, wrapping his broad hands around her buttocks, thrust deeper and quicker, her legs now around his hips, the cabin plunged into total darkness, broken only by the staccato of bright electric lights that punctuated the tunnel wall. The two of them wound around each other like there was no tomorrow, the wetness of her pulsating in him and around him, tighter and tighter, her heaving breath beating in his ears, the rhythm of the train becoming their own, faster and faster, until they were the train roaring towards a collision of the senses, a great streaming silver tube of light shooting across the Navarra, until they both came shouting and the train shuddered to a sudden halt.

August opened his eyes, staring into the flushed olive skin of Izarra's shoulder. Then he realised that the train had actually come to a standstill.

'August ... the window.' Izarra sounded pensive.

He turned away from her and found himself looking straight into the shocked faces of a gaggle of young nuns clustered on a small rural railway platform.

'Oops.' He pulled the blind down.

'Now I know I'm going to hell,' Izarra murmured, and they both burst out laughing.

They lay there, in the blissful afterglow, Izarra's head resting against his shoulder as he cradled her, already the outside world crowding back into his consciousness. What would he do if he finally discovered the secret of the chronicle? What was going to happen to Izarra and Gabirel? He couldn't

imagine his life returning to how it was before – too much
had changed. He thought Izarra was sleeping when she
abruptly spoke out loud.

'I think, with you I fall.'

He understood immediately. In lieu of a reply he pulled
her closer as a familiar panic closed around his throat.

Reading his hesitation, she took his hand; he still hadn't
looked down at her.

'Don't worry, this terrifies me as much as you,' she told
him, in Spanish. 'I don't love because, for me, this is loss, and
you and I have both lost enough for ten lifetimes.'

Pushing down his fear, his heart pounding uncomfortably,
he lifted her chin. 'No more loss, I promise,' he finally said,
and kissed her.

The next morning they got ready to change trains at
Barcelona. As they gathered their things, August overheard
some commotion happening further down the first-class carriage. He cautiously opened the door and peered down the
corridor at a man arguing with a couple of officials, his face
flushed in outrage.

'I don't care who you are, I've already had my passport
checked at the border. I refuse to wake my wife over some
ridiculous search.'

August noticed the taller of the officials had that sleek
look that he recognised as Interpol. Before they had a chance
to see him, August had ducked back into their compartment.

'Get rid of the pregnancy.' He threw her the blonde wig.
'Here! Make yourself unrecognisable, they're only a few
compartments away.'

Within seconds Izarra had rid herself of the false pregnancy, donned the blonde wig and sunglasses, while August
pulled a beret low over his hair.

They hoisted their bags over their shoulders and waited until the two officials had entered the next compartment along and the corridor was empty.

'Quick, to the end of the train, but don't run, don't attract attention.' August ushered Izarra out and as fast as they could, without looking as if they were running, they made their way down to the last carriage. It had begun to slow as the front of the train began to pull into the central station of Barcelona.

At the end of the carriage August pushed open the train door – the industrial outskirts of Barcelona streamed by as he helped Izarra down onto the foot rail on the side of the train. He joined her after slamming shut the door. Hanging to handrails set into the side, they both rode the foot rail as the train entered the station, then jumped off as it pulled in, hopping over the railroad tracks to the opposite platform. Within minutes they had been absorbed into the milling crowd of commuters.

They took a local train to Valencia then onto Alicante and Albacete, then a small train inland to Córdoba. As they travelled, August noticed that Izarra had deliberately disguised her Basque accent with a rural Spanish one that sounded as if she might come from near Madrid. He copied her, although he was convinced he sounded hopelessly inauthentic. Finally, on the train to Córdoba he relaxed, convinced they had lost the men tailing them.

They arrived at Córdoba mid-morning the next day. The train station, located at the edge of the old city and built in the thirties, appeared to be the only modern building in the surrounding area. As they disembarked a group of young soldiers, their dark-blue and white uniforms identifying them as Guardia Civil, heads shorn, rifles slung over their shoulders, brazen and olive-skinned, milled around the platform, obviously waiting to climb aboard the next train. Izarra turned to August, a panicked expression on her face.

'I can't,' she whispered.

'Yes, you can. I have your hand, walk with your eyes down and head up. We look like a normal couple to them, but you have to stay calm.'

They began to walk swiftly towards the exit, but Izarra's blonde hair caught the attention of one of the soldiers, who wolf-whistled. '*¡Oye, guapa!*'

Izarra swung around. He looked about seventeen, with pimples. He grinned at her, revealing a missing tooth. August tensed. *Don't panic, don't panic,* he prayed, knowing how terrified Izarra must be. Standing on the other side of the ticket barrier at some distance were several policemen; one of them had turned at the whistle.

'Behave yourself!' she snapped back, in a perfect Madrid accent. 'I'm old enough to be your mother!"

The boy looked sheepish and several of his companions broke up laughing around him. August, keeping his gaze ahead, ushered Izarra through the barrier and in the opposite direction of the policemen, towards an exit marked 'The Old City'. They were only a few feet away when August noticed that the policeman who had noticed Izarra was now looking at him.

'I've been spotted, let's speed it up. But don't run – yet,' he urged. They picked up the pace and headed out the exit. Behind him August could hear the deadly sound of a police whistle. He glanced back; the police were running towards them. Just then a large group of American tourists wandered across the exit. On the other side of the sightseers a tram was pulling up.

'Quick!' August propelled Izarra through the crowd of

tourists, pushing and shoving until they were on the other side, then after leaping onto the footboard of the tram, grabbed Izarra's arm and hauled her inside. Ducking behind one of the windows, they watched as the three policemen emerged from the exit, still pinned by the entrance of the tourists. Helpless, the police scanned the crowd for August and Izarra as the tram trundled away.

They sat back onto one of the tram seats, an old woman opposite, in a headscarf and shawl, a bag of fruit at her feet, watching them with curiosity. She took off her headscarf, then leaned over and put it on Izarra's head, tying it under the chin. 'That's better,' the woman told Izarra in a low voice. 'This way you disappear when you want, much better than to have them disappear you.'

Izarra squeezed her hand. '*Gracias, la madre.*' She then glanced back at August. 'Where to now?'

'La Juderia, the Jewish quarter of the old city, where Shimon Ruiz de Luna grew up, and the centre of medieval kabbalism. There has to be some kind of clue to the last maze there.'

The tram took them to a huge stone entrance to the walled city, at the end of a short street called Puerta Almodova – one of the gates of the old city. As soon as they passed through the old wall, the street transformed into a labyrinth of narrow lanes flanked by high white-painted walls, broken only by the blazing red of a window box full of geraniums beneath a shuttered window. Each building was crammed next to its neighbour; whole villas, temples, community halls hidden behind the high walls. The lanes were packed with sightseers, Americans mainly, some British and a few Italian. August wove a path through the crowd, now swept up by an urgency. He felt intuition propel him forward, guiding his feet, as if he knew where he were going, as if he'd been there before. Noticing how sure-footed he appeared, Izarra followed but asked no questions.

'This is good, we blend in here,' he told her, as they emerged from behind yet another group of tourists led by a guide, and turned into a narrow lane called Almanzor Romero. They passed a small ancient synagogue, the Star of David carved in stone above the tall iron gate studded in decoration. A small girl of about six, her head covered in a headscarf, olive-skinned with huge black eyes, stepped out, revealing for a moment a gravelled interior courtyard planted with orange trees and beyond the courtyard an ornate doorway to the temple itself. *I know I am in the right place, it is almost as if I can see Shimon running as a boy through these lanes, carrying the merchandise of his father. I can feel his exhilaration, his happiness at going home*, August reassured himself. They walked on and an old painted wooden coat of arms hung over an old doorway caught August's eye. It had four flowers clearly embedded in its design. He grabbed Izarra's arm.

'There it is, the magnolia, the carnation, the gardenia and a white rose!'

They both stared up, fascinated – the four flowers had been painted in the centre of a garland of bay and laurel leaves, beneath which appeared a family name.

They stepped into a marbled entrance hall of what must have once been a palatial mansion dating back centuries, but the decor was seventeenth century. A young woman with jet-black hair pulled back severely and the beginnings of a moustache sat behind a desk covered in tourist guides and maps.

'Are you interested in a tour?' she asked, in Spanish. Izarra approached.

'I'm interested in the design of the coat of arms above the entrance. It was of the family that once lived here?'

'*Sí*, this was the shield of the Ruiz de Lunas.'

Izarra paled, and August stepped forward. 'Are you sure?'

The girl smiled patronisingly back. 'Absolutely. This was a local family who for centuries were associated with the Alhambra in Granada before this region was Christian. We suspect, however, the family were *conversos*, originally Jews. They disappeared in the last years of the Inquisition. But the myth is that one of their ancestors was one of the Caliph's favourite women in the harem, and that he bequeathed her this house as a gift on his death. The house was then given as a gift by King Philip to the Marquis of Carmona, a Catholic aristocrat, for his part in the crusades against the Dutch.'

August fought hard to contain his excitement. 'Is there any grounds or gardens in this building?'

'None, except the small interior courtyard you see before you. But there is a country estate that was part of the original Ruiz de Luna estate, also still owned by the Marquis's descendants. It's just outside of Córdoba, south of the city.'

Izarra gripped August's arm and he glanced over at her reassuringly then turned back to the girl.

'Can I have the address?'

The taxi headed past the city walls, out into the low hills and scrubland, the town streets thinning into ramshackle farms – more a group of white mud-brick huts and red-tiled roofs – and brown-green rows of olive groves, the trees themselves only just budding, the branches studded with bright green growth, yawning up from the ploughed earth like thin men with their arms flung high, entreating an invisible sky god. Last time August had seen olive groves like these was in March 1937, marching towards Jarama. Suddenly he found himself scanning the ground for ditches and hollows a man could throw himself into in case a German plane flew over

and strafed the field. It was an impulse that had become forever associated with the terrain. Struggling with the memory,
he looked over at the taxi driver, who had agreed to drive
them for a hefty fare. He appeared a stoically quiet character,
his broad face reddened and creased from hours in the sun,
his black hair streaked with white, and shiny with a fragrant
pomade that smelled like lemons, swept up into a quiff like
a monument to his youth. They'd been on the road for fifteen minutes when he glanced into the rear mirror.

'You have friends?' he asked August, indicating the road
behind. August looked out. He saw nothing until they had
cleared a curve in the road – about a minute later August
could just make out a black car following at some distance.

'We have company,' he said to Izarra, who swung around
to study the car.

'That guy's been following us since town,' the taxi driver
interjected as he watched August through the mirror. 'And
just so you know, if they're the Guarda Militar, they're no
friend of mine.'

'Can you lose them?'

'With pleasure, *camarada*.' As the road turned into a tree-
lined bend the taxi accelerated. Up ahead was a donkey
pulling a cart stacked high with hay, the young farmhand
perched on top, idly swishing at the animal's haunches with
a switch. Just before the high-banked track narrowed the
taxi overtook the cart, then accelerated away. The Mercedes
tried to follow but became trapped behind the cart and
August turned to the driver in relief.

'*Gracias, amigo.*'

'No thanks necessary.'

The estate was only a few miles further, set back from a
lonely road with the hills of the Sierra Nevada behind. It

stood opposite a field of cut wheat. The taxi driver agreed to wait for them, but at August's insistence parked the taxi behind a large haystack near the edge of the track so that it wasn't visible from the road. He settled down behind the wheel with one of August's Lucky Strikes. August and Izarra climbed out and crossed the road, eerily empty of cars. Already the sound of crickets and cicadas could be heard among the olive trees in a field that ran alongside the road and the loud buzzing of bees from over the wall of the hacienda itself. They walked up to the low wall beyond which a paved courtyard planted with orange trees stood in front of the impressive hacienda. There was a massive oak door, locked and barred, a stone arch stretched over it, from which another plaque painted with the family crest hung. Next to the large brass door handle, incongruous in its modernity, was a small electric bell with a single name written on white paper sellotaped under it. Izarra looked up at the plaque.

'Seems like the right place.' She peered over the wall into the courtyard. The orange trees were gnarled and neglected, and rotting fruit lay scattered in the dust beneath each tree. The two-storey hacienda beyond, although once grand, was badly in need of restoration, and there were patches of missing red tile on the sloped roof. Several feral-looking cats lounged in the sun and there was a line of eccentric-looking beehives running along a wall in one corner of the yard, from which came the audible sound of humming.

'It looks deserted,' Izarra observed.

'Except for the beekeeper.' August pressed the bell. Silence. They both peered over the wall, wondering whether it had actually rung out in the mansion beyond. Moments later a tall, thin, white-haired man dressed in a hunting jacket emerged at the entrance of the hacienda.

'*¡Hola!*' he shouted, from the shadow of the doorway.

'*¡Hola!* We're at the front gate,' August shouted back, and the man emerged into the bright light of the courtyard, walking vigorously across, shooing the cats away as he approached them. August could now see he was wearing slippers under a pair of dress trousers.

They moved politely back in front of the door as they heard the shuffle of the old man approaching, and then a small wooden window cut into the door opened. His mottled face peered through.

'What do you want?' he asked, gruffly.

'Good morning, Señor. We have a historical interest in your property.' August deliberately kept his tone friendly and polite.

'Oh, you do, do you? Well, it's not for sale, especially not to foreigners.' He was about to slam shut the little window, when Izarra stepped forward, smiling at him, and almost seeming to curtsey, much to August's amazement.

'Please, Marquis, we are not tourists, and my friend is a very important historian. He is writing an important paper on the ancient estates of southern Spain and he would love to interview both yourself and see your family's illustrious grounds.'

'A thesis, you say?'

'A detailed history that will be available in both English and Spanish.'

'Marvellous!' he barked. Three minutes later the heavy wooden door swung open. 'It's about time we were recognised for all we've done for this country. Come in, come in.'

He ushered them into the courtyard.

'As you can see, the property is not in the best of condition. I refuse to open it to the public, although I might be forced to, for the income, you know, so tiresome. The whole building and the grounds around are virtually untouched since the sixteenth century, although my own family did not come into possession of the estate until 1613.'

'I see you keep bees,' Izarra said, smiling at him, determined to charm.

'My honey is famous around here. It's the flowers and herbs in the area, and it brings in a little money. Besides, my dear, bees are far more industrious than people, as well as trustworthy.'

He was surprisingly energetic for his age and August had to stride to keep up with him. 'I am particularly interested in whether there was an old maze on the estate,' he said to the elderly aristocrat.

'Maze? I'm afraid not, but we do have an old mosaic that is meant to have great historical value. It seems to have sparked a lot of interest all of a sudden – why, only a few weeks ago I had an English visitor asking to look at it, a woman ... not a great beauty like yourself, Señorita,' he told Izarra, with a flirtatious wink. 'But a woman nevertheless.'

'Was she about five-six, with red hair?' asked August.

The old aristocrat grinned. 'The very same. You know her?' Without waiting for a reply he turned to Izarra. 'Seems your friend has been pipped at the post by a competitor!' He swung back to August. 'Perhaps you are too late, my friend!'

'The mosaic?' August prompted him; it was becoming apparent that the man was a little senile.

'That's right, through here, through here!' He propelled them through the entrance hall of the villa. Inside, the marble floor was dusty and cracked. An old family portrait hung on one wall, opposite an array of animal horns – antelope through to stag – hunting trophies. At the other end of the entrance hall stood a glass door that led into another exterior courtyard, also enclosed by yet more floors of the villa. The whole courtyard was covered with a mosaic that looked extremely old, possibly even Roman. August recognised the distinctive motif immediately.

'The Tree of Life,' he murmured, in English.

'What was that, you say?' the old aristocrat barked, in Spanish.

'My friend is overwhelmed by the beauty of the design,' Izarra told him, soothing his suspicions.

August stepped forward eagerly. 'Can I see? The antiquity is extraordinary.' The Marquis, pacified by August's evident awe, pushed open the glass door.

August walked out onto the mosaic. It felt like sacrilege to be standing upon it. The ten sephiroth were all clearly visible, as were the three vertical lines that made up the design of the Tree. Even more incredibly, in the three sephiroth of the three mazes August had already visited were tiny coloured mosaic pieces that clearly represented the designs of the plants he'd found in them. Vervain and lily in Malkuth at the base, then mandrake root and anise in Yesod, and bay and laurel in the centre sephirot Tiphareth. But what immediately struck August as truly extraordinary was the presence of a sephirot that had not appeared in any of the mazes. It hovered just below Kether, the crowning sephirot at the top of the mosaic. *This is it, the key, the first observable trigger to the central mystery.* Izarra, noticing August's excitement, turned to the old man.

'You know I would love to try some of your honey . . .'

The old man looked delighted. 'I can do better than that. I'll have my maid Maria make coffee and we can have it with some of my honeycomb while your friend interviews me. I can tell you, I have stories that will embellish any historical account. I wrote one myself back in the twenties.'

'Really, I'd love to read it some time,' August lied, anticipation now thudding through his chest. *Just go, so I can be alone with the mosaic, with the key. Go now!* The old aristocrat beamed, thrilled to be the centre of his universe once again.

'I'll be back in a moment, my friends,' he announced, then hurried into a doorway, his footsteps fading as he wound his way up a back staircase.

As soon as he was out of sight August ran over to the design and kneeled on the path between Tiphareth and Kether, placing his hands on this new sephirot he'd never seen before. Unlike the other sephiroth, the background within the circle was black, the mosaic fragments glistening darkly, tiny fragments of metallic flake catching the light. It was beautiful and frightening. The imprint of Dominic Baptise's bare footprints came into August's mind. *Had the monk ever seen this? Had he once stood upon the actual portal?*

'Izarra, it's the Da'ath, the hidden sephirot that is so important to the occult. It has to be the final clue, it has to be.'

In the centre of the circle was the mosaic of a single eye – fringed with gilded eyelashes made of tiny gold fragment – underneath, written in tiny pieces of pale blue against the black, was a single Hebrew word.

'There it is, the eye of God, *el ojo de Dios*,' August found himself whispering, as if he were in church. Why did he feel this sudden wave of reverence, as if in the presence of a higher power? Was it the sheer antiquity of the mosaic or the sheer adrenalin of discovery?

'But what does that mean?' Izarra pointed to the Hebrew word.

'*Adonai*, the unnameable name of God.' He leaned across and ran his fingers over the mosaic, over the design of the sephirot. It was flush to the floor. There was nothing different about it from the rest of the mosaic, no secret trapdoors or hidden compartments. 'There has to be a key somewhere,' August murmured.

They heard a sharp crack behind them. Both August and Izarra recognised the sound immediately. Horrified, they looked up. There was a crash, then the sound of running footsteps. They saw the old man tottering for a second at the second-storey window, clutching a tray of coffee cups and honeycomb, his face a blank map of surprise as blood spread through his shirt. Then he toppled over, gone from sight.

In seconds both August and Izarra had bolted for cover behind the pillars that fringed the courtyard, their guns drawn. They waited, breathing hard. A moment later Damien Tyson's face appeared in a ground floor doorway on the opposite side. Izarra crouched and fired at him, the bullet missing by millimetres, ricocheting off the pillar in front of him. Tyson ducked down.

'Why, if it isn't Andere's little sister!' he yelled out. 'I was wondering who your little helper was, August!'

'Surrender! I'll make sure you have a fair trial!' August yelled back, trying to distract him.

A bullet thudded into the pillar behind which August was hiding.

'Surrender? Oh boy, you really are deluded. Interpol is just behind me and MI5 think you're a Soviet spy – you won't make it through to lunchtime and you want me to surrender?' Another bullet clipped the pillar where Izarra had been crouching, but she had already moved to the next, around the corner of the courtyard and closer to Tyson.

'Izarra! You should have seen your sister beg for her life, the great lioness on her knees!' Tyson shouted.

'I will kill him!' Izarra hissed under her breath.

'Izarra!' August whispered, urgently, and signed to her to hold her position and cover him, while he moved in the other direction to pincer Tyson.

'She was a whore with Jimmy, a real whore. You know I

could have had her if I wanted,' Tyson continued to taunt Izarra, who responded by taking another shot at the pillar by the doorway. August took the opportunity to shuffle quickly around the opposite corner of the courtyard to Izarra. A bullet flew behind him as he settled behind the pillar now just a few feet from Tyson. He looked across at Izarra, who signed that she would move forward next. August shook his head furiously, just as Tyson called out once more.

'She offered herself to me then, you know, Izarra, but I told her I'd rather have you. Are you ready for me now?'

Izarra's face had set in grim fury, but she just nodded back at August and stepped out from behind her pillar to run the short distance to the next at the corner nearest Tyson, firing a shot as she went.

August shot twice at Tyson's pillar, to keep him pinned down, but then watched in silent horror as Izarra carried on around the corner, walking between the pillars, now with her arm outstretched, firing three times at Tyson, to whom she presented an open target. Halfway across the yard, August heard the empty click of the chamber as the small clip in her Walther pistol was exhausted, and, praying that one of her bullets had struck its target, he stepped into the open courtyard.

For a second a terrible silence filled the space, then as if time had magnified, August became aware of a single bee dancing across a single shaft of sunlight between Izarra and the column where Tyson remained hidden. The sound of another gunshot ripped through the stillness, Izarra's torso jolting back as she was hit, her body crumpling to the ground with slow fatal grace.

'No!' August ran to her, only to feel the sting of a bullet hit his right arm and the sound of his own gun, flung by the violence of the shot, falling with a clatter onto the mosaic several feet away from him. Before he had a chance to pick it up, Tyson had stepped out from the pillar and trained his gun on August.

'Don't move.' Tyson kicked August's Mauser away.

Ignoring him, August kneeled over Izarra, slipping his good arm under her. Her head fell back, her hair cascading over his arm one last time. Staring down, he couldn't assimilate the reality of the moment; it was as if a parallel life had peeled away when the old man had gone to make coffee and somewhere Izarra was still alive, they were still staring down at the mosaic. *I'm in shock. I have to get back into my skin. I have to survive.*

'Such a shame, she was beautiful. Not quite as beautiful as her sister, but pretty enough. Get up!' Tyson pushed his gun into August's back.

August laid Izarra's body gently down, then stood, his hands up. Close-up, Damien Tyson looked utterly benign, ordinary, his perfectly symmetrical features pleasant yet forgettable. There was nothing definably evil about his persona and yet that in itself was deeply disturbing. *Beware the smiling assassin.* It was something that had once been said to August when training with the SOE, but he'd never imagined it would be in peacetime that he would actually encounter him.

'I've killed but I've never murdered. How does it feel, Tyson?'

'Omnipotent. Such an interesting concept, don't you think? There is an art to murder, just as there is an art to dying. This . . . ' he gestured towards Izarra, '. . . was an expedient necessity. She deserved something a little slower, a littler grander. But you lie, you've murdered – what about Charlie, August?'

Charlie? How do you know about Charlie? Those last seconds in that forest clearing slammed into his mind and body as if

Tyson had already killed him; Charlie turning, something glinting hidden in his hand, Charlie smiling as if he knew. *Did I kill Charlie or did Charlie kill himself?* August stared at Tyson, wondering if he threw himself on the man, how long it would take before Tyson's bullet reached his heart. *Bluff, spin him out, it will give you time. Time for what?*

'That's between me and Charlie and our gods.'

'Whatever gives you moral redemption. Personally, I prefer stark realism. Anyhow, I should thank you personally for doing such a thorough job on translating the alchemist's chronicle. Even if your motivation was naive, you still managed, where many have failed, to follow Shimon Ruiz de Luna's cryptic map. And provide me with the last pieces of the puzzle that had eluded me all those years, you could say, even if you were missing the last pivotal one.'

Tyson pulled out something from inside his jacket. He held it up.

'The last page of the chronicle, August, the last piece of the puzzle Shimon Ruiz de Luna gave his readers, the final letter of his message to the future. But I guess you realised it was missing.'

August stared at the page: it was an illustration of a herb, one he'd never seen before. *Was this, was this what Izarra died for?* The reality of her death had now begun a slow burn up from his heart, clawing his chest and eyes. *Stay focused. You must defeat him, for her, for them all.* Tyson waved the page tantalisingly in front of him then pulled it away before he had a chance to read it.

'Put your hands on your head and turn around!'

Trying to ignore the tickle of blood running from his chipped wrist and gritting his teeth against the pain of the gunshot wound, August obeyed. The next thing he felt was the cold steel of Tyson's gun in the small of his back.

'Start walking.'

'Where?'

'Out, out toward the gate.' Tyson pushed the gun harder into August's back, propelling him towards an iron gate set in the far corner of the courtyard that appeared to lead out to fields behind the property.

'You see, August, you really learned nothing on this journey, did you? Because you were looking for something that was material, something that you thought would be recognisably powerful. The ultimate weapon perhaps, the ultimate treasure?'

Tyson pushed August through the gate. August stumbled on the stony path, his hand throbbing, his mind working desperately to catch Tyson off-guard, but the gun was always there, now held to the back of his head.

'Move!' Tyson commanded, pushing August in the direction of a small field not much bigger than a vegetable patch. 'The reason you saw nothing was because the treasure wasn't gold or some extraordinary weapon but a simple plant ... a very rare herb found only in one particular area of the Iberian Peninsula, originally planted by Elazar ibn Yehuda, the court physician of Caliph Al-Walid centuries ago, then rediscovered by Shimon Ruiz de Luna in the seventeenth century.' They were now nearing the little meadow, an absurdly idyllic patch of almost luminous green, flooded by sunlight. It looked like heaven itself, August thought wildly, aware that his mind had started to free associate wildly due to blood loss. *Don't faint, don't faint, fall down now and you die.* Behind him Tyson's voice continued like a red-hot prod to his back.

'When Shimon rediscovered the plant, he sought ways of cultivating and protecting the secret for it had extraordinary qualities when digested, ones that could be extremely powerful in the right hands.' They stopped in the middle of the little field. Tyson faced August and he held out the page again.

'Look at the page, then around you,' Tyson commanded.

August peered at the page; the distinctive feathering of the leaves, the curious seed pod that looked like a spiky dandelion but heavier, the plant was one he'd never seen anything like before. Then he realised they were standing in a field of the very same plant.

'You mean this was where—'

'Exactly. This was Shimon's gift to the occult world, whether he intended it or not. And it still survives, centuries later. August, this is a living gateway to the eyes of God. Not that you will ever experience it. Kneel!'

August knelt, fully prepared to die. In some strange logic, now that Izarra was gone, it felt almost redemptive, like there was a curious moral symmetry to being murdered in a beautiful field by a man who had perpetuated a massacre, when August himself had once given the command to another unnamed firing squad. He wanted to destroy Tyson, but he'd lost the will to keep living himself. Did he feel fear? With that gun pointing down at his head, he was aware of the terror of the body, the uncontrollable shaking, the loosing of the bowels, the great vertigo of the possibility of life and time falling away. August feared pain, he feared a loss of dignity, but he was ready. He closed his eyes and breathed in the scent of that extraordinary plant, a curious sweet scent – lemony undercut with musk – and waited to die. And suddenly there was Charlie kneeling beside him, the sense of him, his very presence crisp and sharp in its reality.

'It wasn't you,' Charlie whispered, his proximity so tangible that August forgot everything, that he was about to die, that Charlie was dead, Izarra, his past, the war, everything except the fact that he was kneeling beside his friend and they were together, like they used to be, in ageless innocent youth. 'It was never you, August, I killed myself.' And August felt a great weight lift. *Was this death?* he marvelled, waiting.

Instead there was the sound of a single short scream from Tyson and the thudding of a body falling to the ground.

August opened his eyes. Tyson lay writhing in agony on the ground, clutching a wound in his side, blood gushing from it, his gun on the ground inches away. Gabirel crouched nearby, a bloodstained scythe at his feet, his eyes wide with both anger and terror. The youth reached for Tyson's gun and pointed it, hand shaking, at Tyson.

'Gabirel!' Stunned to see the boy, August stood, for a moment in total disbelief, then Tyson's groans bought him sharply back to reality. He took the gun from Gabirel, who, trembling violently, had gone into shock. 'How are you here? How did you know where to find me?' August shook him, trying to make his wide eyes focus.

Before Gabirel had a chance to explain, Tyson, now white-faced, his bloody hand clutching his wound, spoke from where he lay dying. 'He knew where to find you because he has eaten the herb.' Tyson chuckled dryly. 'Tell him, Gabirel, tell him how you've always had second sight!' August looked at Gabirel, who nodded solemnly, his face now a blank mask.

Tyson groaned loudly, struggling to draw breath. 'This was the alchemist's great treasure, *los ojos de Dios*, the gift of prediction – almost faultless. Elazar ibn Yehuda, the Caliph's physician, cultivated the plant to save humanity from continuing to make historical mistakes ...' His voice faded into a whisper.

August kneeled down by Tyson's side to hear what he was saying.

'Historical mistakes?' August queried. Tyson reached out and clutched at August's jacket, pulling him closer.

'Shimon Ruiz de Luna foresaw the Thirty Years' War; he went to England thinking he could prevent it, but was burned as a spy instead. I had other plans. I was going to liberate the natural world from humanity itself. I would have created an elite of soothsayers ... ' His eyes had begun to cloud over, his voice faltering. 'To guide us into the abyss and beyon ... ' The last word hung incomplete as his head rolled to one side and he died, his gaze staring out over the very thing he'd spent his life searching for.

August closed the dead man's eyes and stood; tearing a strip of cloth from his own shirt, he created a tourniquet and wrapped it around his injured arm.

'Izarra is—'

Before he finished his sentence, Gabirel had taken his hand. 'I know,' the boy replied, in English, his voice breaking in grief. With the fury of a madman, he began to pull and trample the plants around him, his arms whirling uncontrollably. August tried to stop him.

'Gabirel, you can't!' They struggled until finally August, his arms wrapped around the shaking youth, managed to contain him.

'You don't understand. I have to destroy it, otherwise it will be abused. I know it, I know it!'

'How do you know?'

'That day in 1945, the day my mother was killed, I was running towards the massacre because I had a prediction of it but I just didn't know exactly when, that's why I arrived too late. The gift is useless. The herb gives you the gift of seeing events but there's no way of telling when they will happen. It is not a gift but a *curse*.'

He was shaking with rage.

August thought about his own life, how if he had known how it would have unravelled, whether he would have had the courage even to have gone to Spain, to have loved and failed, to have fought and lost. He let the youth go.

'I understand.'

Gabirel looked at him disbelievingly, his face streaked in angry tears.

'Do you?'

August picked up the bloodstained scythe and began slicing down the plants around him.

§

Shimon was waiting. Waiting for the sound of the squealing cartwheels outside, the clatter of horses' hooves, the shouting orders and the banging on the door below. A great grief and the certainty of separation had him pinned to the stool in front of the tiny fire that spat out into the dim low-ceilinged room. It was cold, a new chilling damp that was foreign to him that stank of mead, of pipe tobacco and a harsh mercenary expediency that had become their London. For a fleeting second he found himself amused by such a concept, but Uxue's weeping pulled him unwillingly back into the room, the weight of his chronicle, wrapped in silk, pressed against his chest, his arms numb from holding it for so many hours.

'Please, husband, I am begging you to leave, to save yourself, for my sake and our unborn child, please Shimon ... while there's time.'

She was on the floor, her face pressed against his knees. He was only dimly aware of how long she'd been sitting there, her tears already soaking through the cloth of his stockings.

'Uxue, you know it is my fate to be martyred.'

'But why?'

He hated seeing her so undone, his strong woman, she who had always proved to have more courage than him, until now.

'Because I have seen my own death. I now have the eyes of God. I have taken Elazar ibn Yehuda's plant.' Outside, there was the commotion of horsemen turning into the small lane on which the lodging-house was located. Shimon stood and helped Uxue to her feet.

He pressed the chronicle into her hands.

'You must guard this with your life and all the lives that will stretch out into the future we have spawned,' he concluded, smiling, his hand on her womb. She gazed into his eyes, knowing she had lost him. It was too late for anger, too late for more pleading. She knew her man.

'Husband, I promise by the name of Ruiz de Luna, I and my descendants will guard the chronicle.'

Already there was the banging on the door downstairs, the hurried panic of footsteps as the innkeeper went to answer.

'You must go now and hurry – there's a horseman waiting at the back entrance.'

'May God guard your soul,' she whispered, in Euskara, as they embraced for the last time.

Epilogue

The thin piping sound of the txistu, the Basque flute, rang out defiantly across the square, accompanied by the soft patter of rain. A small crowd of mourners was gathered around the fountain.

It was a small stone plaque, a simple design with nine names carved into granite. The phrase 'They died for what they believed in' was etched above, in Euskara. The list began with 'La Leona' Andere Miren Merikaetxebarria, then came the names of the eight men who died with her. The new mayor had just finished a short speech in Spanish – an innocuous soliloquy of the heroism of all those who had died in the Civil War. The mayor's avoidance of mentioning any political specifics was understandable, August observed, glancing over at the motorcycle and its sidecar parked prominently on the other side of the square, two Guardias Civiles, dressed in the black jodhpurs and jacket of the Falangists, leaning up against the motorcycle, watched the proceedings with a threatening air.

A small group had gathered for the unveiling of the monument, in front of the town hall. Gabirel, who was struggling

not to weep, stood next to August. On his other side, standing erect and proud, was Mateo. Apart from the mayor, there
were the priest, the town clerk, the schoolteacher and several
widows and younger women August recognised. At the edge
of the forty-odd people stood a small group of women he'd
never seen before, dressed in brighter-coloured shawls, who
looked as if they had come from outside the village. He
glanced over to Mateo, the café owner, who told him, in an
undertone, that these were the widows and children of the
soldiers who'd died with La Leona, most of whom had come
from beyond Bilbao. They were interrupted by the priest
stepping forward, a silver aspergillum in his hand, ready to
sprinkle holy water over the stone. Murmuring in Latin, he
consecrated the stone, much to the visible disgust of the
watching policemen, one of whom made a dramatic gesture of
spitting in the gutter. Next to him, August could feel Gabirel
stiffen in outrage. Reaching over, he placed a warning hand on
the youth's arm, and the boy began sobbing silently. August
pulled him into an embrace and held him like a child until the
heaving stopped.

The priest finished the blessing and the crowd began to
slip away into the anonymity of the gathering afternoon
shadows. Mateo turned to August.

'Come to the café, there will be talk, drink, reminis-
cences. For once this afternoon we are determined to talk
freely.'

August glanced questioningly over at Gabirel, who, after
wiping his face with his sleeve, had composed himself.

'You go. I'm going back to the house,' he told August. 'I
just want to be alone for a while.' After his aunt's death,
Gabirel seemed to have matured overnight. The stuttering
had ceased and there was a new determination and defiance
in his movement – the hesitancy of youth having vanished

forever. But August worried about him – he knew the men of the village would take the youth under their guidance, but the thought of leaving Gabirel alone in the farmhouse and, more disturbingly, in a regime with few prospects, disturbed him.

'Are you sure?' August tried to read the genuine emotion behind the smile. Gabirel put his arm over August's shoulder.

'I'm sure, but, August, you must go, these people are now your friends. I will come back, maybe in an hour or so.' Then he left them, strolling quickly towards the house and mountain slopes beyond.

Gabirel stumbled through the forest oblivious of everything around him except for a great need that drew him towards the maze. He felt a burning thirst, almost erotic in its intensity, and his whole body ached for something he couldn't intellectually define. It was like a blind knowledge, something that had been forming in him since birth, and now, like a bursting chrysalis, it had broken free and was propelling him forward to a destiny, to a physical place. He couldn't explain it, he couldn't rationalise it and he couldn't fight it. All he knew was that he had to be there. He broke free of the trees and ran, leaping down into the small clearing. Then he was inside, the thirst growing stronger as he moved up the central line of sephiroth, winding his way along the gravel paths sure-footed. Through the circle of Malkuth with its lily and vervain, up through the stone circle of Yesod, up to the centre of the Tree of Life to Tiphareth – the sephirot symbolising Beauty. Here he paused, the sensation was now like a light pulsating within him, overwhelming all thought. He spun around, trying to sense from where he was being called. Finally, he began to walk up the path to the crown – Kether. Halfway along, he paused; on the path before him new grass had sprung up into the shape of a new circle, a sephirot he'd never seen before. He stopped, his whole body feeling as if it were vibrating with a strange profound happiness. He slipped his shoes off, then, stepping into the centre of the circle, lifted up his arms and turned his face to the sky. At last they had come for him.

By the time August realised Gabirel hadn't returned it was near sunset. After thanking Mateo and his friends and apologising for having to leave before a late supper, he made his way up the slope to the farmhouse.

It was just before he reached the door that a great sense of dread filled him.

'Gabirel! Gabirel!' He swung open the oak door, but already he knew the house would be empty. He rushed through the rooms, calling the boy's name, only to have the silence echo back mockingly. Filled with foreboding, he descended into the barn and pulled open the trapdoor leading to the hiding place that had been used in so many wars by Gabirel's ancestors.

The hollowed out stone recess was empty.

Outside, the sun had almost set over the mountains. August pounded his way through the small forest and arrived at the clearing, lungs heaving and covered in sweat. He glanced over the clearing towards the maze. The last rays of sunlight had fallen across the green walls, coming directly down the centre, giving the illusion of a glow arising from the top, near the crowning sephirot. August began running towards it.

Beating his way through the narrow passages of the maze, rosemary scratching at his bare arms, he reached Tiphareth, the central sephirot. Even from here he could see the glimmer of something along the path leading to the crown, to Kether, a great anticipation squeezing at his lungs and heart. He started walking towards it.

A new ring of grass had sprung up in a perfect circle.

Da'ath, higher knowledge, but how?

In the centre he saw a set of footprints – the outline of a boy who had stood there in bare feet. By the side of the circle was a pair of shoes.

August recognised them immediately.

If you want to find out what happens to August next, go to tslearner.com and hit on the link to a free download of an extra chapter and subscribe to T. S. Learner's free quarterly newsletter . . .

Acknowledgements

I am indebted to the following individuals for their invaluable insights and contributions. Firstly, special thanks to Dr Ana Aguirregabiria, whose love of her own culture was my initial inspiration, and a special thank you to another Basque and native of Gernika, Jose Agustin Ozamiz Ibinarriaga, PhD in Sociology, Prof. Deusto University. Thanks also goes to Anton Erkoreka Barrena, Basque Museum of the History of Medicine, MUDr, PhD Dir (UPV/EHU); Juan Manuel Etxebarria Ayesta, PhD in Basque Filology, Prof. Deusto University; Jone Iztiria Murua of the library of San Sebastián (Donostiako Vdala, Ayuntaniento de San Sebastián); Julen and Elisa Calzada; Jose Miguel Aguirre for difficult memories; Juana Aroma and Nicolas Arzubia of Goiuria (Irureta), who were kind enough to let us into their beautiful Basque farmhouse; and the staff and owners of Hotel Ibaigune, Bizkaia, for allowing us to stay there; and the Archives Municipales de Bayonne.

Other acknowledgements go to my good friend Henning Bochert and all those kind enough to share their post-war Hamburg experiences; the staff of the Gedenkstätte Ernst Thälmann Hamburg; Ulrich Kluge and Lore Bunger, Uwe

Eccard, Guenther Claus, Edeltraud Jensen, Peter Petersen and Hans Walther of the Zeitzeugenborse at the Seniorenbüro of Hamburg; and Herr Wolfgang Vacano of des Altonaer Stadtarchivs e.V.

For kabbalistic enlightenments I was lucky enough to speak to Z'ev ben Shimon Halevi, principal tutor of the International Kabbalah society; Judith Hawkins-Tillirson, for her herbal magick. I thank my father-in-law Gerald Asher for his Parisian insights; my UK publisher and editor Dan Mallory of Sphere, Little, Brown, for his boundless support, belief and his superb eclectic literary taste; Iain Banks for his copy-editing; Anna Valdinger of HarperCollins, Australia; Charlie King of the Sphere marketing department; my UK agent Julian Alexander for his ongoing and unflappable insight and support; and finally my other half Jeremy Asher for his intelligence, love and editorial input.

Bibliography

Ardagh, John, *Germany and the Germans, After Unification*

Atxaga, Bernardo, *The Accordionist's Son*

Baroja, Julio Caro, *The World of the Witches*

Carr, Raymond, *Spain: A History*

Carroll, Peter N., *The Odyssey of the Abraham Lincoln Brigade*

Darman, Peter, *Heroic Voices of the Spanish Civil War*

Fisher, Adrian, and Georg Gerster, *The Art of the Maze*

García Lorca, Francisco and Donald M. Allen (eds) *The Selected Poems of Federico García Lorca*

Gill, Anton, *An Honourable Defeat – A History of German Resistance to Hitler*

Hawkins-Tillirson, Judith, *The Weiser Concise Guide to Herbal Magick*

Hennessy, Peter, *Having it So Good: Britain in the Fifties*

Hoffman, Edward, *The Wisdom of Maimonides: The Life and Writings of the Jewish Sage*

Kurlansky, Mark, *The Basque History of the World*

Kynaston, David, *Family Britain: 1951–57*

Lalanne, Guy, and Jacques Ospital, *1936–1945: Ascain, Ciboure, Saint-Jean-de-Luz, Urrugne Temoignages d'une Époque*

Marks, Leo, *Between Silk and Cyanide*

Moynihan, Brian, *Looking Back at Britain 1950s: The Road to Recovery*

Pelaez del Rosal, Jesus (ed.) *The Jews in Cordoba (X–XII Centuries)*

Pialloux, Georges, *Memoire en Images Saint-Jean-de-Luz et Ciboure*

Reed Doob, Penelope, *The Idea of the Labyrinth from Classical Antiquity through the Middle Ages*

Regardie, Israel (ed.) *777 and Other Qabalistic Writings of Aleister Crowley*

Wolff, Milton, *Another Hill*

Woodworth, Paddy, *The Basque Country: A Cultural History*

Wright, Peter, *Spycatcher*

Z'ev ben Shimon Halevi, *Kabbalah and Astrology*

Z'ev ben Shimon Halevi, *Kabbalah: Tradition of Hidden Knowledge*